1,000,000 Books
are available to read at

www.ForgottenBooks.com

Read online
Download PDF
Purchase in print

ISBN 978-1-333-84618-3
PIBN 10606258

This book is a reproduction of an important historical work. Forgotten Books uses state-of-the-art technology to digitally reconstruct the work, preserving the original format whilst repairing imperfections present in the aged copy. In rare cases, an imperfection in the original, such as a blemish or missing page, may be replicated in our edition. We do, however, repair the vast majority of imperfections successfully; any imperfections that remain are intentionally left to preserve the state of such historical works.

Forgotten Books is a registered trademark of FB &c Ltd.
Copyright © 2018 FB &c Ltd.
FB &c Ltd, Dalton House, 60 Windsor Avenue, London, SW19 2RR.
Company number 08720141. Registered in England and Wales.

For support please visit www.forgottenbooks.com

1 MONTH OF FREE READING

at

www.ForgottenBooks.com

By purchasing this book you are eligible for one month membership to ForgottenBooks.com, giving you unlimited access to our entire collection of over 1,000,000 titles via our web site and mobile apps.

To claim your free month visit: www.forgottenbooks.com/free606258

* Offer is valid for 45 days from date of purchase. Terms and conditions apply.

English
Français
Deutsche
Italiano
Español
Português

www.forgottenbooks.com

Mythology Photography **Fiction**
Fishing Christianity **Art** Cooking
Essays Buddhism Freemasonry
Medicine **Biology** Music **Ancient Egypt** Evolution Carpentry Physics
Dance Geology **Mathematics** Fitness
Shakespeare **Folklore** Yoga Marketing
Confidence Immortality Biographies
Poetry **Psychology** Witchcraft
Electronics Chemistry History **Law**
Accounting **Philosophy** Anthropology
Alchemy Drama Quantum Mechanics
Atheism Sexual Health **Ancient History**
Entrepreneurship Languages Sport
Paleontology Needlework Islam
Metaphysics Investment Archaeology
Parenting Statistics Criminology
Motivational

THE TUDOR
TRANSLATIONS
EDITED BY
W. E. HENLEY
XXXVII

THE

TRANSLATED OUT OF THE ORIGINAL
TONGUES BY THE COMMANDMENT OF

KING JAMES THE FIRST

ANNO 1611

ApOCRYpHA

LONDON
Published by DAVID NUTT
At the Sign of the Phœnix
LONG ACRE

Edinburgh: T. and A. CONSTABLE, Printers to His Majesty

CONTENTS

VOLUME V

APOCRYPHA:

	PAGE
I. ESDRAS	3
II. ESDRAS	28
TOBIT	69
JUDETH	85
THE REST OF ESTHER	109
THE WISDOM OF SOLOMON	115
ECCLESIASTICUS	150
BARUCH	240
THE SONG OF THE THREE HOLY CHILDREN	252
THE HISTORY OF SUSANNA	256
BEL AND THE DRAGON	259
THE PRAYER OF MANASSES	262
I. MACCABEES	263
II. MACCABEES	312

APOCRYPHA

I. ESDRAS

CHAPTER I

ND Iosias helde the Feast of the Passeover in Ierusalem unto his Lord, and offered the Passeover the fourteenth day of the first moneth: having set the Priests according to their daily courses, being arayed in long garments, in the Temple of the Lord. And hee spake unto the Levites the holy ministers of Israel, that they should hallow themselves unto the Lord, to set the holy Arke of the Lord, in the house that king Solomon the sonne of David had built: and said, Ye shall no more beare the Arke upon your shoulders: now therefore serve the Lord your God, and minister unto his people Israel, and prepare you after your families and kinreds. According as David the king of Israel prescribed, and according to the magnificence of Solomon his sonne: and standing in the Temple according to the severall dignitie of the families of you the Levites, who minister in the presence of your brethren the children of Israel. Offer the Passeover in order, and make ready the sacrifices for your brethren, and keepe the Passeover according to the commaundement of the Lord, which was given unto Moyses. And unto the people that was found there, Iosias gave thirtie thousand lambes, and kids, and three thousand calves: these things were given of the kings allowance, according as hee promised to the people, to the Priestes, and to the Levites. And Helkias, Zacharias, and Sielus the governours of the Temple, gave to the Priests for the Passeover, two thousand and sixe hundred sheepe, and three hundreth calves. And Iechonias, and Samaias, and Nathanael his brother, and Assabias, and Ochiel, and Ioram captaines over thousands, gave to the Levites for the Passeover five thousand sheepe, and seven hundreth calves. And when these things were done, the Priests and Levites having the unleavened bread, stood in very comely order according to the kinreds, and according to the severall dignities of the fathers,

Iosias his charge to the priests and Levites.

A great Passeover is kept.

I. ESDRAS

CHAPTER I

before the people, to offer to the Lord, as it is written in the booke of Moyses: And thus did they in the morning. And they rosted the Passeover with fire, as appertaineth: as for the sacrifices, they sodde them in brasse pots, and pannes with a good savour. And set them before all the people, and afterward they prepared for themselves, and for the Priests their brethren the sonnes of Aaron. For the Priests offered the fat untill night: and the Levites prepared for themselves, and the Priests their brethren the sonnes of Aaron. The holy Singers also, the sonnes of Asaph, were in their order, according to the appointment of David, to wit, Asaph, Zacharias, and Ieduthun, who was of the kings retinue. Moreover the porters were at every gate: it was not lawfull for any to goe from his ordinary service: for their brethren the Levites prepared for them. Thus were the things that belonged to the sacrifices of the Lord accomplished in that day, that they might hold the Passeover, and offer sacrifices upon the altar of the Lord, according to the commandement of king Iosias. So the children of Israel which were present, held the Passeover at that time, and the feast of sweet bread seven dayes. And such a Passeover was not kept in Israel since the time of the Prophet Samuel. Yea all the kings of Israel held not such a Passeover as Iosias, and the Priests and the Levites, and the Iewes held with all Israel that were found dwelling at Ierusalem. In the eighteenth yeere of the reigne of Iosias was this Passeover kept. And the workes of Iosias were upright before his Lord with an heart full of godlinesse. As for the things that came to passe in his time, they were written in former times, concerning those that sinned, and did wickedly against the Lord above all people and kingdomes, and how they grieved him exceedingly, so that the words of the Lord rose up against Israel. Now after all these acts of Iosias, it came to passe that Pharao the king of Egypt came to raise warre at Carchamis upon Euphrates: and Iosias went out against him. But the king of Egypt sent to him saying, What have I to doe with thee, O king of Iudea? I am not sent out from the Lord God against thee: for my warre is upon Euphrates, and now the Lord is with mee, yea the Lord is with mee hasting me forward: Depart from me and be not against the Lord. Howbeit Iosias did not turne backe his chariot from him, but undertooke to fight with him, not regarding the words of the Prophet Ieremie, spoken by the mouth of the Lord: but ioyned battell with him in the plaine of Magiddo, and the princes came against king Iosias. Then said the king unto his servants, Carry me away out of the battell for I am very weake: and immediately his servants tooke him away out

4

I. ESDRAS

of the battell. Then gate he up upon his second chariot, and being brought backe to Ierusalem, dyed, and was buried in his fathers sepulchre. And in all Iury they mourned for Iosias, yea Ieremie the Prophet lamented for Iosias, and the cheefe men with the women made lamentation for him unto this day: and this was given out for an ordinance to be done continually in all the nation of Israel. These things are written in the booke of the stories of the kings of Iudah, and every one of the acts that Iosias did, and his glory, and his understanding in the law of the Lord, and the things that he had done before, and the things now recited, are reported in the bookes of the Kings of Israel and Iudea. And the people tooke Ioachaz the sonne of Iosias, and made him king in stead of Iosias his father, when hee was twentie and three yeeres old. And he reigned in Iudea and in Ierusalem three moneths: and then the King of Egypt deposed him from reigning in Ierusalem. And he set a taxe upon the land of an hundreth talents of silver, and one talent of gold. The king of Egypt also made king Ioacim his brother king of Iudea and Ierusalem. And hee bound Ioacim and the nobles: but Zaraces his brother he apprehended, and brought him out of Egypt. Five and twentie yeere old was Ioacim when he was made king in the land of Iudea and Ierusalem, and he did evill before the Lord. Wherefore against him Nabuchodonosor the King of Babylon came up, and bound him with a chaine of brasse, and carried him unto Babylon. Nabuchodonosor also tooke of the holy vessels of the Lord, and carried them away, and set them in his owne temple at Babylon. But those things that are recorded of him, and of his uncleannes, and impietie, are written in the Chronicles of the kings. And Ioacim his sonne reigned in his stead: he was made king being eighteene yeeres old, and reigned but three moneths and ten dayes in Ierusalem, and did evill before the Lord. So after a yere Nabuchodonosor sent, and caused him to be brought into Babylon with the holy vessels of the Lord, and made Zedechias king of Iudea and Ierusalem, when he was one and twentie yeeres old, and he reigned eleven yeeres: and he did evill also in the sight of the Lord, and cared not for the words that were spoken unto him, by the Prophet Ieremie from the mouth of the Lord. And after that king Nabuchodonosor had made him to sweare by the Name of the Lord, he forswore himselfe, and rebelled, and hardening his necke, and his heart, hee transgressed the lawes of the Lord God of Israel. The governours also of the people and of the priests did many things against the lawes, and passed al the pollutions of all nations, and defiled the Temple of the Lord which was sanctified in Ierusalem.

CHAPTER I

His death is much lamented:

His Successours.

I. ESDRAS

CHAPTER I

Neverthelesse, the God of their fathers sent by his messenger to call them backe, because he spared them and his tabernacle also: but they had his messengers in derision, and looke when the Lorde spake unto them, they made a sport of his prophets, so farre foorth that he being wroth with his people for their great ungodlinesse, commanded the kings of the Caldees to come up against them.

The Temple, Citie, and people are destroyed.

Who slew their yong men with the sword, yea even within the compasse of their holy Temple, and spared neither yong man nor maid, old man nor child among them, for hee delivered all into their hands. And they tooke all the holy vessels of the Lord, both great and small, with the vessels of the Ark of God, and the kings treasures, and caried them away into Babylon. As for the house of the Lord they burnt it, brake downe the walles of Ierusalem,

The rest are caried unto Babylon.

set fire upon her towres. And as for her glorious things, they never ceased til they had consumed and brought them all to nought, and the people that were not slaine with the sword, he caried unto Babylon: who became servants to him and his children, till the Persians reigned, to fulfill the word of the Lord spoken by the mouth of Ieremie: Untill the land had enioyed her Sabbaths, the whole time of her desolation shal she rest, untill the full terme of seventie yeeres.

CHAPTER II

Cyrus is moved by God to build the Temple,

IN the first yeere of Cyrus king of the Persians, that the worde of the Lorde might bee accomplished, that hee had promised by the mouth of Ieremie: the Lord raised up the spirit of Cyrus the king of the Persians, and he made proclamation thorow al his kingdome, and also by writing, saying, Thus saith Cyrus king of the Persians, The Lord of Israel the most high Lord, hath made me king of the whole world, and commanded me to build him an

And giveth leave to the Iewes to returne and contribute to it.

house at Ierusalem in Iurie. If therefore there bee any of you that are of his people, let the Lord, even his Lord be with him, and let him goe up to Ierusalem that is in Iudea, and build the house of the Lord of Israel: for he is the Lord that dwelleth in Ierusalem. Whosoever then dwell in the places about, let them helpe him, those I say that are his neighbours, with gold and with silver, with gifts, with horses, and with cattell, and other things, which have bene set forth by vowe, for the Temple of the Lord at Ierusalem.

Then the chiefe of the families of Iudea, and of the tribes of Beniamin stood up: the priests also and the Levites, and all they whose minde the Lord had moved to goe up, and to build an house

I. ESDRAS

for the Lord at Ierusalem, and they that dwelt round about them, and helped them in all things with silver and gold, with horses and cattell, and with very free gifts of a great number whose miudes were stirred up thereto. King Cyrus also brought foorth the holy vessels which Nabuchodonosor had caried away from Ierusalem, and had set up in his temple of idoles. Now when Cyrus king of the Persians had brought them foorth, hee delivered them to Mithridates his treasurer: and by him they were delivered to Sanabassar the governour of Iudea. And this was the number of them, a thousand golden cuppes, and a thousand of silver, censers of silver twentie nine, vials of gold thirtie, and of silver two thousand foure hundred and ten, and a thousand other vessels. So all the vessels of gold, and of silver which were caried away, were five thousand, foure hundred, threescore and nine. These were brought back by Sanabassar, together with them of the captivity, from Babylon to Ierusalem. But in the time of Artaxerxes king of the Persians, Belemus, and Mithridates, and Tabellius, and Rathumus, and Beeltethmus, and Semellius the Secretarie, with others that were in commission with them, dwelling in Samaria and other places, wrote unto him against them that dwelt in Iudea and Ierusalem, these letters following. To King Artaxerxes our lord, Thy servants Rathumus the story writer, and Semellius the scribe, and the rest of their counsell, and the Iudges that are in Coelosyria and Phenice. Be it now knowen to the lord the king, that the Iewes that are come up from you to us, being come into Ierusalem (that rebellious and wicked citie,) doe build the market places, and repaire the walles of it, and doe lay the foundation of the Temple. Now if this citie, and the walles thereof be made up againe, they will not onely refuse to give tribute, but also rebell against kings. And forasmuch as the things pertaining to the Temple, are now in hand, we thinke it meete not to neglect such a matter, but to speake unto our lord the king, to the intent that if it be thy pleasure, it may be sought out in the bookes of thy fathers: and thou shalt finde in the Chronicles, what is written concerning these things, and shalt understand that that citie was rebellious, troubling both kings and cities: and that the Iewes were rebellious, and raised alwayes warres therin, for the which cause even this citie was made desolate. Wherefore now wee doe declare unto thee, (O lord the king) that if this citie bee built againe, and the walles thereof set up anew, thou shalt from henceforth have no passage into Coelosyria and Phenice. Then the King wrote backe againe to Rathumus the storie-writer, to Beeltethmus, to Semellius the scribe, and to the rest that were in com-

CHAPTER II

He delivereth againe the vessels which had bin taken thence.

Artaxerxes forbiddeth the Iewes to build any more.

I. ESDRAS

CHAPTER II

mission, and dwellers in Samaria and Syria, and Phenice, after this maner. I have read the Epistle which ye have sent unto mee: therefore I commanded to make diligent search, and it hath bene found, that that city was from the beginning practising against Kings. And the men therein were given to rebellion, and warre, and that mightie Kings and fierce were in Ierusalem, who reigned and exacted tributes in Coelosyria and Phenice. Now therefore I have commanded to hinder those men from building the citie, and heed to be taken that there be no more done in it, and that those wicked workers proceed no further to the annoyance of Kings. Then king Artaxerxes his letters being read, Rathumus and Semellius the scribe, and the rest that were in commission with them, remooving in hast towards Ierusalem with a troupe of horsemen, and a multitude of people in battell aray, began to hinder the builders, and the building of the Temple in Ierusalem ceased untill the second yeere of the reigne of Darius King of the Persians.

CHAPTER III

NOW when Darius reigned, hee made a great feast unto all his Subiects and unto all his houshold, and unto all the princes of Media and Persia, and to all the governours and captaines, and lieutenants that were under him, from India unto Ethiopia, of an hundreth twenty and seven provinces. And when they had eaten and drunken, and being satisfied were gone home, then Darius the king went into his bed-chamber, and slept, and *Three strive to excell each other in wise speaches.* soone after awaked. Then three yong men that were of the guard, that kept the kings body, spake one to another: Let every one of us speake a sentence: hee that shall overcome, and whose sentence shall seeme wiser then the others, unto him shall the king Darius give great gifts, and great things in token of victory: as to be clothed in purple, to drink in golde, and to sleepe upon golde, and a chariot with bridles of golde, and an head-tyre of fine linen, and a chaine about his necke: and hee shall sit next to Darius, because of his wisedome, and shalbe called, Darius his cousin. And then every one wrote his sentence, sealed it, and laide it under king *They referre themselves to the iudgement of the King.* Darius his pillow, and sayd, that when the king is risen, some will give him the writings, and of whose side the king, and the three princes of Persia shall iudge, that his sentence is the wisest, to him shall the victory be given as was appointed. The first wrote: Wine is the strongest. The second wrote: The King is strongest. The third wrote; Women are strongest, but above all things trueth beareth away the victory.

I. ESDRAS

Now when the king was risen up, they tooke their writings, and delivered them unto him, and so hee read them. And sending foorth, hee called all the Princes of Persia and Media, and the governours, and the captaines, and the lieutenants, and the chiefe officers, and sate him downe in the royall seate of Iudgement, and the writings were read before them: and he said, Call the young men, and they shall declare their owne sentences: so they were called, and came in. And hee said unto them, Declare unto us your minde, concerning the writings. Then began the first, who had spoken of the strength of wine; and he said thus: O ye men, how exceeding strong is wine! it causeth all men to erre that drinke it: it maketh the minde of the king, and of the fatherlesse childe to be all one; of the bondman and of the freeman, of the poore man and of the rich: it turneth also every thought into iollitie and mirth, so that a man remembreth neither sorow nor debt: and it maketh every heart rich, so that a man remembreth neither king nor governour; and it maketh to speake all things by talents: and when they are in their cups, they forget their love both to friends and brethren, and a litle after draw out swords: but when they are from the wine, they remember not what they have done. O ye men, is not wine the strongest, that enforceth to doe thus? And when hee had so spoken, hee helde his peace.

CHAPTER III

The first declareth the strength of Wine.

CHAPTER IIII

THEN the second that had spoken of the strength of the King, began to say; O yee men, doe not men excel in strength, that beare rule over Sea and land, and all things in them? But yet the King is more mighty: for hee is lord of all these things, and hath dominion over them, and whatsoever he commandeth them, they doe: if hee bid them make warre the one against the other, they doe it: if hee send them out against the enemies, they goe, and breake downe mountaines, walles and towres. They slay and are slaine, and transgresse not the Kings commandement: if they get the victory, they bring all to the King, as well the spoile as all things else. Likewise for those that are no souldiers, and have not to doe with warres, but use husbandrie; when they have reaped againe, that which they had sowen, they bring it to the King, and compell one another to pay tribute unto the King. And yet he is but one man; if hee commaund to kill, they kill, if he command to spare, they spare. If he command to smite, they smite; if he command to make desolate, they make desolate; if hee command to build, they

The second declareth the power of a King.

I. ESDRAS

CHAPTER IIII

build: if he command to cut downe, they cut downe; if he command to plant, they plant. So all his people and his armies obey him; furthermore he lieth downe, he eateth and drinketh, and taketh his rest. And these keepe (watch) round about him, neither may any one depart, and doe his owne businesse, neither disobey they him in any thing. O yee men, how should not the King be mightiest, when in such sort he is obeyed? and he held his tongue.

The third, the force of women:

Then the third, who had spoken of women, and of the truth (this was Zorobabel) beganne to speake. O yee men, it is not the great King, nor the multitude of men, neither is it wine that excelleth; who is it then that ruleth them, or hath the lordship over them, are they not women? Women have borne the King and all the people, that beare rule by sea and land. Even of them came they: and they nourished them up that planted the vineyards from whence the wine commeth. These also make garments for men; these bring glory unto men, and without women cannot men be. Yea and if men have gathered together gold and silver, or any other goodly thing, doe they not love a woman, which is comely in favour and beautie? And letting all those things goe, doe they not gape, and even with open mouth fixe their eyes fast on her; and have not all men more desire unto her, then unto silver or gold, or any goodly thing whatsoever? A man leaveth his owne father that brought him up, and his owne countrie, and cleaveth unto his wife. He stickes not to spend his life with his wife, and remembreth neither father, nor mother, nor countrey. By this also you must know, that women have dominion over you: doe yee not labour and toyle, and give and bring all to the woman? Yea a man taketh his sword, and goeth his way to rob, and to steale, to saile upon the sea, and upon rivers, and looketh upon a lyon, and goeth in the darknesse, and when he hath stolen, spoiled and robbed, he bringeth it to his love. Wherefore a man loveth his wife better then father and mother. Yea many there be that have run out of their wits for women, and become servants for their sakes: many also have perished, have erred, and sinned for women. And now doe yee not believe me? is not the King great in his power? doe not all regions feare to touch him? Yet did I see him and Apame the Kings concubine, the daughter of the admirable Bartacus, sitting at the right hand of the King, and taking the crowne from the Kings head, and setting it upon her owne head; she also strooke the King with her left hand. And yet for all this, the King gaped and gazed upon her with open mouth: if she laughed upon him, hee laughed also: but if she

I. ESDRAS

CHAPTER IIII and of Trueth.

tooke any displeasure at him, the King was faine to flatter, that she might be reconciled to him againe. O ye men, how can it be but women should be strong, seeing they doe thus? Then the king and the princes looked one upon another: so he began to speake of the trueth. O ye men, are not women strong? great is the earth, high is the heaven, swift is the Sunne in his course, for he compasseth the heavens round about, and fetcheth his course againe to his owne place in one day. Is he not great that maketh these things? therefore great is the truth, and stronger then all things. All the earth calleth upon the truth, and the heaven blesseth it, all works shake and tremble at it, and with it is no unrighteous thing. Wine is wicked, the king is wicked, women are wicked, all the children of men are wicked, and such are all their wicked workes, and there is no trueth in them. In their unrighteousnes also they shall perish. As for the trueth it endureth, and is alwayes strong, it liveth and conquereth for evermore. With her there is no accepting of persons, or rewards, but she doeth the things that are iust, and refraineth from all uniust and wicked things, and all men doe well like of her workes. Neither in her iudgement is any unrighteousnesse, and she is the strength, kingdome, power and maiestie of all ages. Blessed be the God of trueth. And with that he held his peace, and al the people then shouted and said, Great is trueth, and mightie above all things. *The third is iudged to be wisest,* Then saide the king unto him, Aske what thou wilt, more then is appointed in the writing, and we wil give it thee, because thou art found wisest, and thou shalt sit next me, and shalt bee called my cousin. Then said hee unto the king, Remember thy vow which thou hast vowed to build Ierusalem in the day when thou camest to the kingdome, and to send away all the vessels that were taken away out of Ierusalem, which Cyrus set apart, when hee vowed to destroy Babylon, and to send them againe thither. Thou also hast vowed to build up the Temple, which the Edomites burnt when Iudea was made desolate by the Chaldees. And now, O lord the king, this is that which I require, and which I desire of thee, and this is the princely liberalitie proceeding from thy selfe: I desire therefore that thou make good the vow, the performance wherof with thine owne mouth thou hast vowed to the king of heaven. Then Darius the king stood up and kissed him, and wrote letters for him unto all the treasurers and lieutenants, and captaines and governours that they should safely convey on their way, both him, and all those that go up with him to build Ierusalem. Hee wrote letters also unto the lieutenants that were in Coelosyria and Phenice, and unto them *and obtaineth Letters of the King to build Ierusalem.*

11

I. ESDRAS

CHAPTER IIII

He praiseth God, and sheweth his brethren what he had done.

in Libanus, that they should bring Cedar wood from Libanus unto Ierusalem, and that they should build the city with him. Moreover he wrote for all the Iewes that went out of his realme up into Iurie, concerning their freedome, that no officer, no ruler, no lieutenant, nor treasurer, should forcibly enter into their dores, and that all the countrey which they hold, should be free without tribute, and that the Edomites should give over the villages of the Iewes which then they held, yea that there should be yeerely given twentie talents to the building of the Temple, untill the time that it were built, and other tenne talents yeerely, to maintaine the burnt offerings upon the Altar every day (as they had a commandement to offer seventeene). And that all they that went from Babylon to build the citie, should have free liberty as well they as their posteritie, and all the priests that went away. He wrote also concerning the charges, and the priests vestments wherein they minister: and likewise for the charges of the Levites, to be given them, untill the day that the house were finished, and Ierusalem builded up. And he commanded to give to all that kept the city, pensions and wages. He sent away also all the vessels from Babylon that Cyrus had set apart, and all that Cyrus had given in commandement, the same charged hee also to be done, and sent unto Ierusalem. Now when this yong man was gone forth, he lifted up his face to heaven toward Ierusalem, and praised the king of heaven, and said, From thee commeth victory, from thee commeth wisedom, and thine is the glory, and I am thy servant. Blessed art thou who hast given me wisedom: for to thee I give thanks, O Lord of our fathers. And so he tooke the letters, and went out, and came unto Babylon, and told it all his brethren. And they praised the God of their fathers: because he had given them freedome and libertie to goe up, and to build Ierusalem, and the Temple which is called by his Name, and they feasted with instruments of musick, and gladnes seven dayes.

CHAPTER V

AFTER this were the principall men of the families chosen according to their tribes, to go up with their wives, and sonnes, and daughters, with their men-servants and maid-servants, and their cattel. And Darius sent with them a thousand horsmen, til they had brought them backe to Ierusalem safely, and with musicall [instruments,] tabrets and flutes: and all their brethren played, and hee made them goe up together with them. And these are the names of the men which went up, according to

I. ESDRAS

their families, amongst their tribes, after their severall heads. The Priestes the sonnes of Phinees, the sonne of Aaron: Iesus the sonne of Iosedec, the sonne of Saraias, and Ioachim the sonne of Zorobabel, the sonne of Salathiel of the house of David, out of the kindred of Phares, of the tribe of Iuda; who spake wise sentences before Darius the king of Persia, in the second yeere of his reigne, in the moneth Nisan, which is the first moneth. And these are they of Iewrie that came up from the captivitie, where they dwelt as strangers, whom Nabuchodonosor the king of Babylon had carried away unto Babylon: and they returned unto Ierusalem, and to the other parts of Iurie every man to his owne city, who came with Zorobabel, with Iesus, Nehemias, and Zacharias, and Reesaias, Enenius, Mardocheus, Beelsarus, Aspharasus, Reelius, Roimus, and Baana their guides. The number of them of the nation, and their governours: sonnes of Phoros two thousand an hundred seventie and two: the sonnes of Saphat foure hundred seventie and two; the sonnes of Ares seven hundred fiftie and sixe: the sonnes of Phaath Moab, two thousand eight hundred and twelve: the sonnes of Elam, a thousand two hundred fifty and foure: the sonnes of Zathui, nine hundred fourtie and five: the sonnes of Corbe seven hundred and five: the sonnes of Bani, sixe hundred fourtie and eight: the sonnes of Bebai, sixe hundred twentie and three: the sonnes of Sadas, three thousand two hundred twentie and two: the sonnes of Adonican, sixe hundred sixtie and seven: the sonnes of Bagoi, two thousand sixtie and sixe: the sonnes of Adin, foure hundred fiftie and foure: the sonnes of Aterezias, ninetie and two: the sonnes of Ceilan and Azetas, threescore and seven: the sonnes of Azuran, foure hundred thirtie and two. The sonnes of Ananias, an hundred and one: the sonnes of Arom thirtie two, and the sonnes of Bassa, three hundred twentie and three: the sonnes of Azephurith, an hundred and two: the sonnes of Meterus, three thousand and five: the sonnes of Bethlomon, an hundred twentie and three. They of Netophah fiftie and five: they of Anathoth, an hundred fiftie and eight: they of Bethsamos, fourtie and two: they of Kiriathiarius, twentie and five: they of Caphira and Beroth, seven hundred fourtie and three: they of Pyra, seven hundred: they of Chadias and Ammidioi, foure hundred twenty and two: they of Cyrama, and Gabdes, sixe hundred twentie and one: they of Macalon, an hundred twentie and two: they of Betolius fiftie and two: the sonnes of Nephis, an hundred fiftie and sixe. The sonnes of Calamolalus, and Onus, seven hundred twentie and five: the sonnes of Ierechus, two hundred fourtie and five: the sonnes of Annaas, three thousand

CHAPTER V

The names and number of the Iewes that returned home.

13

I. ESDRAS

CHAPTER V

three hundred and thirtie: the Priests, the sonnes of Ieddu, the sonne of Iesus, among the sonnes of Sanasib, nine hundred seventie and two: the sonnes of Meruth, a thousand fiftie and two: the sonnes of Phassaron, a thousand fourtie and seven: the sonnes of Carme a thousand and seventeene. The Levites: the sonnes of Iessue, and Cadmiel, and Banuas, and Sudias, seventie and foure. The holy singers: the sonnes of Asaph an hundred twentie and eight. The porters: the sonnes of Salum, the sonnes of Iatal, the sonnes of Talmon, the sonnes of Dacobi, the sonnes of Teta, the sonnes of Sami, in all an hundred thirty and nine. The servants of the Temple: the sonnes of Esau, the sonnes of Asipha, the sonnes of Tabaoth, the sonnes of Ceras: the sonnes of Sud, the sonnes of Phaleas, the sonnes of Labana, the sonnes of Graba: the sonnes of Acua, the sonnes of Uta, the sonnes of Cetab, the sons of Agaba, the sonnes of Subai, the sonnes of Anan, the sonnes of Cathua, the sonnes of Geddur: the sonnes of Airns, the sonnes of Daisan, the sonnes of Noeba, the sonnes of Chaseba, the sonnes of Gazera, the sonnes of Azia, the sonnes of Phinees, the sonnes of Azara, the sonnes of Bastai, the sonnes of Asana, the sonnes of Meani, the sonnes of Naphisi, the sonnes of Acub, the sons of Asipha, the sonnes of Assur, the sonnes of Pharacim, the sons of Basaloth. The sonnes of Meeda: the sons of Coutha, the sonnes of Charea, the sonnes of Chareus, the sonnes of Aserer, the sonnes of Thomoi, the sonnes of Nasith, the sons of Atipha. The sons of the servants of Solomon: the sonnes of Azaphion, the sonnes of Pharira, the sonnes of Ioeli, the sonnes of Lozon, the sonnes of Isdael, the sonnes of Sapheth: the sonnes of Hagia, the sons of Phacareth, the sonnes of Sabie, the sonnes of Sarothie, the sonnes of Masias, the sonnes of Gar, the sons of Addus, the sonnes of Suba, the sonnes of Apherra, the sonnes of Barodis, the sonnes of Sabat, the sonnes of Allom. All the ministers of the Temple, and the sonnes of the servants of Solomon, were three hundred seventy and two. These came up from Thermeleth, and Thelersas, Charaathalar leading them and Aalar. Neither could they shewe their families, nor their stock, how they were of Israel: the sonnes of Ladan, the sonnes of Ban, the sonnes of Necodan, sixe hundred fiftie and two. And of the Priests that usurped the office of the Priesthood, and were not found, the sonnes of Obdia: the sonnes of Accoz, the sonnes of Addus, who married Augia one of the daughters of Berzelus, and was named after his name. And when the description of the kinred of these men was sought in the Register, and was not found, they were remooved from executing the office of the Priesthood. For unto them said Nehemias,

I. ESDRAS

and Atharias, that they should not be partakers of the holy things, till there arose up an high Priest, clothed with Doctrine and Trueth. So of Israel from them of twelve yeeres olde and upward, they were all in number fourtie thousand, besides men servants and women servants, two thousand three hundred and sixtie. Their men servants and handmaids were seven thousand three hundred fourtie and seven: the singing men and singing women, two hundred fortie and five. Foure hundred thirtie and five camels, seven thousand thirtie and sixe horses, two hundred fourtie and five mules, five thousand five hundred twentie and five beasts used to the yoke. And certaine of the chiefe of their families, when they came to the Temple of God that is in Ierusalem, vowed to set up the house againe in his owne place according to their abilitie: and to give into the holy treasurie of the workes, a thousand pounds of golde, five thousand of silver, and an hundred priestly vestments. And so dwelt the Priests, and the Levites, and the people in Ierusalem, and in the countrey: the Singers also, and the Porters, and all Israel in their villages. But when the seventh moneth was at hand, and when the children of Israel were every man in his owne place, they came all together with one consent into the open place of the first gate, which is towards the East. Then stood up Iesus the sonne of Iosedec, and his brethren the Priests, and Zorobabel the sonne of Salathiel, and his brethren, and made ready the Altar of the God of Israel, to offer burnt sacrifices upon it, according as it is expresly commanded in the booke of Moses the man of God. And there were gathered unto them out of the other nations of the land, and they erected the Altar upon his owne place, because all the nations of the land were at enmitie with them, and oppressed them, and they offered sacrifices according to the time, and burnt offerings to the Lord both morning, and evening. Also they held the feast of Tabernacles, as it is commanded in the law, and offered sacrifices daily as was meet: and after that, the continuall oblations, and the sacrifice of the Sabbaths, and of the new Moones, and of all holy feasts. And all they that had made any vow to God, beganne to offer sacrifices to God from the first day of the seventh moneth, although the Temple of the Lord was not yet built. And they gave unto the Masons and Carpenters, money, meate and drinke with cheerefulnesse. Unto them of Sidon also and Tyre, they gave carres that they should bring Cedar trees from Libanus, which should bee brought by flotes to the haven of Ioppe, according as it was commanded them by Cyrus King of the Persians. And in the second yeere and second moneth, after his comming to the Temple of

CHAPTER V

The Altar is set up in his place.

I. ESDRAS

CHAPTER V

The foundation of the Temple is layd.

God at Ierusalem, beganne Zorobabel the sonne of Salathiel, and Iesus the sonne of Iosedec, and their brethren and the priests, and the Levites, and all they that were come unto Ierusalem out of the captivity: and they layd the foundation of the house of God, in the first day of the second moneth, in the second yeere after they were come to Iury and Ierusalem. And they appointed the Levites from twenty yeeres old, over the workes of the Lord. Then stood up Iesus and his sonnes, and brethren, and Cadmiel his brother, and the sonnes of Madiabun, with the sonnes of Ioda the sonne of Eliadun, with their sonnes and brethren, all Levites, with one accord setters forward of the businesse, labouring to advance the workes in the house of God. So the workmen built the temple of the Lord. And the Priests stood arayed in their vestiments with musicall instruments, and trumpets, and the Levites the sonnes of Asaph had Cymbals, singing songs of thanksgiving, and praising the Lord according as David the king of Israel had ordained. And they sung with loud voices songs to the praise of the Lord: because his mercy and glory is for ever in all Israel. And all the people sounded trumpets, and shouted with a loud voyce, singing songs of thankesgiving unto the Lord for the rearing up of the house of the Lord. Also of the Priests and Levites, and of the chiefe of their families the ancients who had seene the former house, came to the building of this with weeping and great crying. But many with trumpets and ioy shouted with loud voyce. Insomuch that the trumpets might not be heard for the weeping of the people: yet the multitude sounded marveilously, so that it was heard a farre off. Wherefore when the enemies of the Tribe of Iuda and Beniamin heard it, they came to know what that noise of trumpets should meane. And they perceived, that they that were of the captivity did build the temple unto the Lord God of Israel. So they went to Zorobabel and Iesus, and to the chiefe of the families, and said unto them, We will build together with you. For we likewise, as you, doe obey your Lord, and doe sacrifice unto him from the dayes of Asbazareth the king of the Assyrians who brought us hither. Then Zorobabel and Iesus, and the chiefe of the families of Israel said unto them, It is not for us and you to build together an house unto the Lord our God. We our selves alone will build unto the Lord of Israel, according as Cyrus the King of the Persians hath commanded us. But the heathen of the land lying heavy upon the inhabitants of Iudea, and holding them straite, hindred their building: and by their secret plots, and popular perswasions, and commotions, they hindred the finishing of the building, all the

The worke is hindred for a time.

I. ESDRAS

time that king Cyrus lived, so they were hindered from building for the space of two yeeres, untill the reigne of Darius.

CHAPTER V

CHAPTER VI

NOW in the second yeere of the reigne of Darius, Aggeus, and Zacharias the sonne of Addo, the prophets prophesied unto the Iewes, in Iurie and Ierusalem in the Name of the Lord God of Israel which was upon them. Then stood up Zorobabel the sonne of Salathiel, and Iesus the son of Iosedec, and beganne to build the house of the Lord at Ierusalem, the prophets of the Lord being with them, and helping them. At the same time came unto them Sisinnes the governor of Syria, and Phenice, with Sathrabuzanes, and his companions, and said unto them, By whose appointment doe you build this house, and this roofe, and performe all the other things? and who are the workemen that performe these things? Neverthelesse the Elders of the Iewes obtained favour: because the Lord had visited the captivitie. And they were not hindred from building until such time as signification was given unto Darius concerning them, and an answere received. The copie of the letters which Sisinnes governour of Syria, and Phenice, and Sathrabuzanes with their companions rulers in Syria and Phenice, wrote and sent unto Darius, To king Darius, greeting. Let all things bee knowen unto our lord the King, that being come into the countrey of Iudea, and entred into the citie of Ierusalem, we found in the citie of Ierusalem the ancients of the Iewes that were of the captivitie; building an house unto the Lord, great, and newe, of hewen and costly stones, and the timber already laid upon the walles. And those workes are done with great speede, and the worke goeth on prosperously in their bandes, and with all glory and diligence is it made. Then asked wee these Elders, saying, By whose commaundement builde you this house, and lay the foundations of these workes? Therefore to the intent that wee might give knowledge unto thee by writing, we demanded of them who were the chiefe doers, and we required of them the names in writing of their principall men. So they gave us this answere: We are the servants of the Lord which made heaven and earth. And as for this house, it was builded many yeeres agoe, by a king of Israel great and strong, and was finished. But when our fathers provoked God unto wrath, and sinned against the Lord of Israel which is in heaven, hee gave them over into the power of Nabuchodonosor king of Babylon of the Chaldees: who pulled downe the house and burnt it, and caried away the people captives

The Prophets stirre up the people to build the Temple.

Darius is solicited to hinder it.

I. ESDRAS

CHAPTER VI

unto Babylon. But in the first yeere that King Cyrus reigned over the country of Babylon, Cyrus the king wrote to build up this house. And the holy vessels of gold and of silver, that Nabuchodonosor had caried away out of the house at Ierusalem, and had set them in his owne temple, those Cyrus the king brought forth againe out of the temple at Babylon, and they were delivered to Zorobabel and to Sanabassarus the ruler, with commaundement that hee should carrie away the same vessels, and put them in the Temple at Ierusalem, and that the Temple of the Lord should be built in his place. Then the same Sanabassarus being come hither, laid the foundations of the house of the Lord at Ierusalem, and from that time to this, being still a building, it is not yet fully ended. Now therefore if it seeme good unto the king, let search be made among the records of King Cyrus, and if it be found, that the building of the house of the Lord at Ierusalem hath bene done with the consent of King Cyrus, and if our lord the king be so minded, let him signifie unto us thereof. Then commanded king Darius to seeke among the records at Babylon: and so at Ecbatana the palace which is in the countrey of Media, there was found a roule wherein these things were recorded. In the first yeere of the reigne of Cyrus, king Cyrus commaunded that the house of the Lord at Ierusalem should bee built againe where they doe sacrifice with continuall fire. Whose height shalbe sixtie cubits, and the breadth sixtie cubits, with three rowes of hewen stones, and one row of new wood of that countrey, and the expenses thereof to bee given out of the house of king Cyrus. And that the holy vessels of the house of the Lord, both of gold and silver that Nabuchodonosor tooke out of the house at Ierusalem, and brought to Babylon, should be restored to the house at Ierusalem, and bee set in the

But he doth further it by all meanes,

place where they were before. And also he commanded that Sisinnes the governour of Syria and Phenice, and Sathrabuzanes, and their companions, and those which were appointed rulers in Syria, and Phenice should be carefull not to meddle with the place, but suffer Zorobabel the servant of the Lord, and governour of Iudea, and the Elders of the Iewes, to build the house of the Lord in that place. I have commanded also to have it built up whole againe, and that they looke diligently to helpe those that be of the captivitie of the Iewes, till the house of the Lord be finished. And out of the tribute of Coelosyria, and Phenice, a portion carefully to be given these men, for the sacrifices of the Lord that is, to Zorobabel the governour, for bullocks, and rammes, and lambes: and also corne, salt, wine and oile, and that continually every yeere without further question, according as the Priests that be

I. ESDRAS

in Ierusalem shall signifie, to be daily spent: that offrings may be made to the most high God, for the king and for his children, and that they may pray for their lives. And he commanded, that whosoever should transgresse, yea, or make light of any thing afore spoken or written, out of his owne house should a tree be taken, and he thereon be hanged, and all his goods seized for the king. The Lord therfore whose Name is there called upon, utterly destroy every king and nation, that stretcheth out his hand to hinder or endammage that house of the Lord in Ierusalem. I Darius the king have ordeined, that according unto these things it be done with diligence.

CHAPTER VI and threatneth those that shall hinder it.

CHAPTER VII

THEN Sisinnes the governour of Coelosyria, and Phenice, and Sathrabuzanes, with their companions, following the commandements of king Darius, did very carefully oversee the holy workes, assisting the ancients of the Iewes, and governours of the Temple. And so the holy workes prospered, when Aggeus, and Zacharias the Prophets prophecied. And they finished these things, by the commandement of the Lord God of Israel, and with the consent of Cyrus, Darius, and Artaxerxes, kings of Persia. And thus was the holy house finished, in the three and twentieth day of the moneth Adar, in the sixt yeere of Darius king of the Persians. And the children of Israel: the Priests, and the Levites, and other that were of the captivitie, that were added unto them, did according to the things written in the booke of Moses. And to the dedication of the Temple of the Lord, they offered an hundred bullockes, two hundred rammes, foure hundred lambes; and twelve goats for the sinne of all Israel, according to the number of the chiefe of the tribes of Israel. The Priests also and the Levites, stood arayed in their vestments according to their kinreds, in the services of the Lord God of Israel, according to the booke of Moses: and the porters at every gate. And the children of Israel that were of the captivitie, held the Passeover the fourteenth day of the first moneth, after that the Priests and the Levites were sanctified. They that were of the captivitie were not all sanctified together: but the Levites were all sanctified together, and so they offered the Passeover for all them of the captivitie, and for their brethren the Priestes, and for themselves. And the children of Israel that came out of the captivitie, did eate, even all they that had separated themselves from the abominations of the people of the land, and sought the Lord.

Sisinnes and others, helpe forward the building.

The Temple is finished, and dedicated.

The Passeover is kept.

19

I. ESDRAS

CHAPTER VII And they kept the feast of unleauened bread seuen dayes, making merry before the Lord, for that he had turned the counsell of the King of Assyria towards them to strengthen their hands in the workes of the Lord God of Israel.

CHAPTER VIII

Esdras bringeth the Kings Commission to build.

AND after these things, when Artaxerxes the king of the Persians reigned, came Esdras the sonne of Saraias, the sonne of Ezerias, the sonne of Helchiah, the sonne of Salum, the sonne of Sadduc, the sonne of Achitob, the sonne of Amarias, the sonne of Ozias, the sonne of Memeroth, the sonne of Zaraias, the sonne of Sauias, the sonne of Boccas, the sonne of Abisum, the sonne of Phinees, the sonne of Eleasar, the sonne of Aaron the chiefe Priest. This Esdras went up from Babylon, as a Scribe being very ready in the Law of Moyses, that was giuen by the God of Israel, and the king did him honour: for he found grace in his sight in all his requests. There went up with him also certaine of the children of Israel, of the Priests, of the Leuites, of the holy Singers, Porters, and Ministers of the Temple, unto Ierusalem, in the seuenth yere of the reigne of king Artaxerxes, in the fifth moneth, (this was the kings seuenth yeere) for they went from Babylon in the first day of the first moneth, and came to Ierusalem, according to the prosperous iourney which the Lord gaue them. For Esdras had very great skill, so that he omitted nothing of the Law and Commaundements of the Lord, but taught all Israel the

The copy of it. Ordinances and Iudgements. Now the copy of the Commission which was written from Artaxerxes the King, and came to Esdras the priest and reader of the Law of the Lord, is this that followeth. King Artaxerxes unto Esdras the Priest and reader of the Law of the Lord, sendeth greeting. Hauing determined to deale graciously, I haue giuen order, that such of the nation of the Iewes, and of the Priests and Leuites being within our Realme, as are willing and desirous, should goe with thee unto Ierusalem. As many therefore as haue a minde thereunto, let them depart with thee, as it hath seemed good both to me, and my seuen friends the counsellors, that they may looke unto the affaires of Iudea and Ierusalem, agreeably to that which is in the Law of the Lord. And cary the gifts unto the Lord of Israel to Ierusalem, which I and my friends haue vowed, and all the golde and siluer that in the countrey of Babylon can be found, to the Lord in Ierusalem, with that also which is giuen of the people, for the Temple of the Lord their God at Ierusalem: and that siluer and golde may be collected for bullocks,

I. ESDRAS

rammes and lambes, and things thereunto appertaining, to the end that they may offer sacrifices unto the Lord, upon the Altar of the Lord their God, which is in Ierusalem. And whatsoever thou and thy brethren will doe with the silver and golde, that doe according to the will of thy God. And the holy vessels of the Lord which are given thee, for the use of the Temple of thy God which is in Ierusalem, thou shalt set before thy God in Ierusalem. And whatsoever thing else thou shalt remember for the use of the Temple of thy God, thou shalt give it out of the kings treasury. And I, king Artaxerxes, have also commaunded the keepers of the treasures in Syria and Phenice, that whatsoever Esdras the priest, and the reader of the law of the most high God shall send for, they should give it him with speed, to the summe of an hundred talents of silver: likewise also of wheat even to an hundred cores, and an hundred pieces of wine, and other things in abundance. Let all things be performed after the law of God diligently unto the most high God, that wrath come not upon the kingdome of the King and his sonnes. I command you also that yee require no taxe, nor any other imposition of any of the Priests or Levites, or holy singers, or porters, or ministers of the temple, or of any that have doings in this temple, and that no man have authority to impose any thing upon them. And thou, Esdras, according to the wisedome of God, ordaine iudges, and iustices, that they may iudge in all Syria and Phenice, all those that know the law of thy God, and those that know it not thou shalt teach. And whosoever shal transgresse the law of thy God, and of the king, shall be punished diligently, whether it be by death or other punishment, by penalty of money, or by imprisonment.

Then said Esdras the Scribe, Blessed be the onely Lord God of my fathers, who hath put these things into the heart of the king, to glorifie his house that is in Ierusalem; and hath honoured mee in the sight of the king and his counsellers, and all his friends and Nobles. Therefore was I encouraged, by the helpe of the Lord my God, and gathered together men of Israel to goe up with me: and these are the chiefe according to their families and severall dignities, that went up with me from Babylon in the reigne of king Artaxerxes. Of the sonnes of Phinees, Gerson: of the sonnes of Ithamar, Gamael: of the sonnes of David; Lettus the sonne of Sechenias: of the sonnes of Pharez, Zacharias, and with him were counted, an hundred and fifty men: of the sonnes of Pahath, Moab; Eliaonias, the sonne of Zaraias, and with him two hundred men: of the sonnes of Zathoe, Sechenias, the sonne of Iezelus, and with him three hundred men; of the sonnes of Adin, Obeth the sonne

CHAPTER VIII

He declareth the names and number of those that came with him:

21

I. ESDRAS

CHAPTER VIII

of Ionathan, and with him two hundred and fifty men. Of the sonnes of Elam, Iosias sonne of Gotholias, and with him seventy men: of the sonnes of Saphatias, Zaraias sonne of Michael, and with him threescore and ten men: of the sonnes of Ioab, Abadias sonne of Iezelus, and with him two hundred and twelve men: of the sonnes of Banid, Assalimoth sonne of Iosaphias, and with him an hundred and threescore men: of the sonnes of Babi, Zacharias sonne of Bebai, and with him twentie and eight men: of the sonnes of Astath, Iohannes sonne of Acatan, and with him an hundred and ten men: of the sonnes of Adonicam the last, and these are the names of them, Eliphalet, Ieuel, and Samaias, and with them seventy men: of the sonnes of Bago, Uthi, the sonne of Istalcurus, and with him seventy men: and these I gathered together to the river, called Theras, where we pitched our tents three dayes, and then I survayed them. But when I had found there, none of the priests and Levites, then sent I unto Eleazar and Iduel, and Masman, and Alnathan, and Mamaias, and Ioribas, and Nathan, Eunatan, Zacharias, and Mosollamon principal men and learned. And I bad them that they should goe unto Saddeus the captaine, who was in the place of the treasury: and commanded them that they should speake unto Daddeus, and to his brethren, and to the treasurers in that place, to send us such men as might execute the Priests office in the house of the Lord. And by the mighty hand of our Lord they brought unto us skilful men of the sonnes of Moli, the sonne of Levi, the sonne of Israel, Asebebia and his sonnes and his brethren, who were eighteene. And Asebia, and Annuus, and Osaias his brother of the sonnes of Channuneus, and their sonnes were twentie men. And of the servants of the Temple whom David had ordeined, and the principall men, for the service of the Levites (to wit) the servants of the Temple, two hundred and twentie, the catalogue of whose names were shewed. And there I vowed a fast unto the yong men before our Lord, to desire of him a prosperous iourney, both for us, and them that were with us: for our children and for the cattell: for I was ashamed to aske the king footmen, and horsemen, and conduct for safegard against our adversaries: for wee had said unto the king, that the power of the Lord our God, should be with them that seeke him, to support them in all wayes. And againe wee besought our Lord, as touching these things, and found him favourable unto us. Then I separated twelve of the chiefe of the priests, Esebrias, and Assanias, and ten men of their brethren with them. And I weighed them the golde, and the silver, and the holy vessels of the house of our Lord, which the king and his counsell,

I. ESDRAS

and the princes, and all Israel had given. And when I had weighed it, I delivered unto them sixe hundred and fiftie talents of silver, and silver vessels of an hundred talents, and an hundred talents of gold, and twentie golden vessels, and twelve vessels of brasse, even of fine brasse, glittering like gold. And I said unto them, Both you are holy unto the Lord, and the vessels are holy, and the golde, and the silver is a vowe unto the Lord, the Lord of our fathers. Watch ye, and keepe them till yee deliver them to the chiefe of the priestes and Levites, and to the principall men of the families of Israel in Ierusalem into the chambers of the house of our God. So the priests and the Levites who had received the silver and the golde, and the vessels, brought them unto Ierusalem into the Temple of the Lord. And from the river Theras wee departed the twelft day of the first moneth, and came to Ierusalem by the mightie hand of our Lord, which was with us: and from the beginning of our iourney, the Lord delivered us from every enemy, and so wee came to Ierusalem. And when wee had bene there three dayes, the golde and silver that was weighed, was delivered in the house of our Lord on the fourth day unto Marmoth the priest, the sonne of Iri. And with him was Eleazar the sonne of Phinees, and with them were Iosabad the sonne of Iesu, and Moeth the sonne of Sabban, Levites: all was delivered them by number and weight. And all the weight of them was written up the same houre. Moreover they that were come out of the captivitie offered sacrifice unto the Lord God of Israel, even twelve bullocks for all Israel, fourescore and sixteene rammes, threescore and twelve lambes, goates for a peace offering, twelve, all of them a sacrifice to the Lord. And they delivered the kings commandements unto the kings stewards, and to the governours of Coelosyria, and Phenice, and they honoured the people, and the Temple of God. Now when these things were done, the rulers came unto me, and said: The nation of Israel, the princes, the priests, and Levites have not put away from them the strange people of the land: nor the pollutions of the Gentiles, to wit, of the Chanaanites, Hittites, Pheresites, Iebusites, and the Moabites, Egyptians, and Edomites. For both they, and their sonnes, have maried with their daughters, and the holy seed is mixed with the strange people of the land, and from the beginning of this matter, the rulers and the great men have bene partakers of this iniquitie. And assoone as I had heard these things, I rent my clothes, and the holy garment, and pulled off the haire from off my head, and beard, and sate me downe sad, and very heavy. So all they that were then mooved at the word of the Lord God of Israel,

CHAPTER VIII

And his iourney.

Hee lamenteth the sinnes of his people,

I. ESDRAS

CHAPTER VIII

assembled unto me, whilest I mourned for the iniquitie: but I sate still full of heavinesse, untill the evening sacrifice. Then rising up from the fast with my clothes and the holy garment rent, and bowing my knees, and stretching foorth my hands unto the Lord: I said, O Lord, I am confounded, and ashamed before thy face; for our sinnes are multiplied above our heads, and our ignorances have reached up unto heaven. For ever since the time of our fathers wee have bene and are in great sinne, even unto this day: and for our sinnes and our fathers, we with our brethren, and our kings, and our priests, were given up unto the Kings of the earth, to the sword, and to captivitie, and for a pray with shame unto this day. And now in some measure hath mercy bene shewed unto us, from thee, O Lord, that there should be left us a roote, and a name, in the place of thy Sanctuary. And to discover unto us a light in the house of the Lord our God, and to give us foode in the time of our servitude. Yea, when we were in bondage, we were not forsaken of our Lord; but he made us gracious before the Kings of Persia, so that they gave us food; yea, and honoured the Temple of our Lord, and raised up the desolate Sion, that they have given us a sure abiding in Iurie, and Ierusalem. And now, O Lord, what shall wee say having these things? for wee have transgressed thy Commaundements, which thou gavest by the hand of thy servants the Prophets, saying, that the land which ye enter into to possesse as an heritage, is a land polluted with the pollutions of the strangers of the land, and they have filled it with their uncleannesse. Therefore now shal ye not ioyne your daughters unto their sonnes, neither shall ye take their daughters unto your sonnes. Moreover you shall never seeke to have peace with them, that yee may be strong, and eate the good things of the land, and that ye may leave the inheritance of the land unto your children for evermore. And all that is befallen, is done unto us for our wicked workes, and great sinnes: for thou, O Lord, didst make our sinnes light: and didst give unto us such a roote : but we have turned backe againe to transgresse thy Law, and to mingle our selves with the uncleannesse of the nations of the land. Mightest not thou be angry with us to destroy us, till thou hadst left us neither root, seed, nor name? O Lord of Israel, thou art true : for we are left a root this day. Behold, now are we before thee in our iniquities, for wee cannot stand any longer by reason of these things before thee. And as Esdras in his praier made his confession, weeping, and lying flat upon the ground before the Temple, there gathered unto him from Ierusalem, a very great multitude of men, and

I. ESDRAS

women, and children: for there was great weeping among the multitude. Then Iechonias the sonne of Ieelus, one of the sonnes of Israel called out and saide, O Esdras, wee have sinned against the Lord God, wee have maried strange women of the nations of the land, and now is all Israel aloft. Let us make an oath to the Lord, that wee will put away all our wives, which we have taken of the heathen, with their children, like as thou hast decreed, and as many as doe obey the Law of the Lord. Arise, and put in execution: for to thee doeth this matter appertaine, and wee will bee with thee: doe valiantly. So Esdras arose, and tooke an oath of the chiefe of the Priestes, and Levites of all Israel, to do after these things, and so they sware.

CHAPTER VIII

And sweareth the Priestes to put away their strange wives.

CHAPTER IX

THEN Esdras rising from the court of the Temple, went to the chamber of Ioanan the sonne of Eliasib, and remained there, and did eate no meate nor drinke water, mourning for the great iniquities of the multitude. And there was a proclamation in all Iury and Ierusalem, to all them that were of the captivitie, that they should be gathered together at Ierusalem: and that whosoever met not there within two or three dayes according as the Elders that bare rule, appointed, their cattell should be seized to the use of the Temple, and himselfe cast out from them that were of the captivitie. And in three dayes were all they of the tribe of Iuda and Beniamin gathered together at Ierusalem the twentieth day of the ninth moneth. And all the multitude sate trembling in the broad court of the Temple, because of the present foule weather. So Esdras arose up, and said unto them, Ye have transgressed the law in marrying strange wives, thereby to increase the sinnes of Israel. And now by confessing give glory unto the Lord God of our fathers, and doe his will, and separate your selves from the heathen of the land, and from the strange women. Then cryed the whole multitude, and sayd with a loude voice; Like as thou hast spoken, so will we doe. But forasmuch as the people are many, and it is foule weather, so that wee cannot stand without, and this is not a worke of a day or two, seeing our sinne in these things is spread farre: therefore let the rulers of the multitude stay, and let all them of our habitations that have strange wives, come at the time appointed, and with them the Rulers and Iudges of every place, till we turne away the wrath of the Lord from us, for this matter. Then Ionathan the sonne of Azael, and Ezechias the sonne of Theocanus,

Esdras assembleth all the people.

They promise to put away the strange wives.

5 : D

I. ESDRAS

CHAPTER IX

accordingly tooke this matter upon them: and Mosollam, and Levis, and Sabbatheus helped them. And they that were of the captivitie, did according to all these things. And Esdras the Priest chose unto him the principal men of their families, all by name: and in the first day of the tenth moneth, they sate together to examine the matter. So their cause that helde strange wives, was brought to an ende in the first day of the first moneth. And of the Priests that were come together, and had strange wives, there were found: of the sonnes of Iesus the sonne of Iosedec, and his brethren, Matthelas, and Eleazar, and Ioribus, and Ioadanus. And they gave their hands to put away their wives, and to offer rammes, to make reconcilement for their errors. And of the sonnes of Emmer, Ananias, and Zabdeus, and Eanes, and Sameius, and Hierel, and Azarias. And of the sonnes of Phaisur, Ellionas, Massias, Ismael, and Nathanael, and Ocidelus, and Talsas. And of the Levites: Iosabad, and Semis, and Colius who was called Calitas, and Patheus, and Iudas, and Ionas. Of the holy Singers: Eleazurus, Bacchurus. Of the Porters: Sallumus, and Tolbanes. Of them of Israel, of the sonnes of Phoros, Hiermas, and Eddias, and Melchias, and Maelus, and Eleazar, and Asibias, and Baanias. Of the sonnes of Ela, Matthanias, Zacharias, and Hierielus, and Hieremoth, and Aedias. And of the sonnes of Zamoth, Eliadas, Elisimus, Othonias, Iarimoth, and Sabatus, and Sardeus. Of the sonnes of Bebai, Iohannes, and Ananias, and Iosabad, and Amatheis. Of the sonnes of Many, Olamus, Mamuchus, Iedeus, Iasubus, Iasael, and Hieremoth. And of the sonnes of Addi, Naathus, and Moosias, Lacunus, and Naidus, and Mathanias, and Sesthel, Balunus, and Manasseas. And of the sonnes of Annas, Elionas, and Aseas, and Milchias, and Sabbeus, and Simon Chosameus. And of the sonnes of Asom, Altaneus, and Matthias, and Bannaia, Eliphalat, and Manasses, and Semei. And of the sonnes of Maani, Ieremias, Momdis, Omaerus, Iuel, Mabdai, and Pelias, and Anos, Carabasion, and Enasibus, and Mamnitanaimus, Eliasis, Bannus, Eliali, Samis, Selenias, Nathanias: And of the sons of Ozora, Sesis, Esril, Azailus, Samatus, Zambis, Iosiphus, and of the sonnes of Ethma, Mazitias, Zabadaias, Edes, Iuel, Banaias. All these had taken strange wives, and they put them away with their children. And the priests, and Levites, and they that were of Israel dwelt in Ierusalem, and in the countrey, in the first day of the seventh month: so the children of Israel were in their habitations. And the whole multitude came together with one accord, into the broad place of the holy porch toward the East. And they spake unto Esdras the priest and reader, that he would

The names and number of them that did so.

I. ESDRAS

bring the law of Moses, that was given of the Lord God of Israel. So Esdras the chiefe priest, brought the law unto the whole multitude from man to woman, and to all the priests, to heare the law in the first day of the seventh moneth. And hee read in the broad court before the holy porch from morning unto midday, before both men and women; and all the multitude gave heed unto the law. And Esdras the priest, and reader of the law stood up, upon a pulpit of wood which was made for that purpose. And there stood up by him Matathias, Sammus, Ananias, Azarias, Urias, Ezecias, Balasamus, upon the right hand. And upon his left hand stood Phaldaius, Misael, Melchias, Lothasubus and Nabarias. Then tooke Esdras the booke of the law before the multitude: for he sate honourably in the first place in the sight of them all. And when hee opened the law, they stood all streight up. So Esdras blessed the Lord God most high, the God of hostes Almighty. And all the people answered Amen, and lifting up their hands they fell to the ground, and worshipped the Lord. Also Iesus, Anus, Sarabias, Adinus, Iacubus, Sabateus, Auteas, Maianeas, and Calitas, Azarias, and Ioazabdus, and Ananias, Biatas, the Levites taught the law of the Lord, making them withall to understand it. Then spake Attharates unto Esdras the chiefe priest, and reader, and to the Levites that taught the multitude, even to all, saying, This day is holy unto the Lord; for they all wept when they heard the law. Goe then and eate the fat, and drinke the sweet, and send part to them that have nothing. For this day is holy unto the Lord, and be not sorrowfull; for the Lord will bring you to honour. So the Levites published all things to the people, saying: This day is holy to the Lord, be not sorrowfull. Then went they their way, every one to eate and drinke, and make mery, and to give part to them that had nothing, and to make great cheere, because they understood the words wherein they were instructed, and for the which they had bin assembled.

CHAPTER IX

The Law of Moses is read and declared before all the people.

They weepe, and are put in mind of the Feast day.

II. ESDRAS

II. ESDRAS

CHAPTER I

Esdras is commanded to reprove the people.

THE second booke of the Prophet Esdras the sonne of Saraias, the sonne of Azarias, the sonne of Helchias, the sonne of Sadamias, the sonne of Sadoc, the sonne of Achitob, the sonne of Achias, the sonne of Phinees, the sonne of Heli, the sonne of Amarias, the sonne of Aziei, the sonne of Marimoth, the sonne of Arna, the sonne of Ozias, the sonne of Borith, the sonne of Abisei, the sonne of Phinees, the sonne of Eleazar, the sonne of Aaron, of the Tribe of Levi, which was captive in the land of the Medes, in the reigne of Artaxerxes king of the Persians. And the word of the Lord came unto me, saying, Goe thy way, and shew my people their sinfull deeds, and their children their wickednes which they have done against me, that they may tell their childrens children, because the sinnes of their fathers are increased in them: for they have forgotten me, and have offered unto strange gods. Am not I even hee that brought them out of the land of Egypt, from the house of bondage? but they have provoked me unto wrath, and despised my counsels. Pull thou off then the haire of thy head, and cast all evill upon them, for they have not beene obedient unto my law, but it is a rebellious people. How long shall I forbeare them unto whom I have done so much good? Many kings have I destroyed for their sakes, Pharao with his servants, and all his power have I smitten downe. All the nations have I destroyed before them, and in the East I have scattered the people of two provinces, even of Tyrus and Sidon, and have slaine all their enemies. Speake thou therefore unto them saying, Thus saith the Lord, I led you through the Sea, and in the beginning gave you a large and safe passage, I gave you Moyses for a leader, and Aaron for a priest, I gave you light in a pillar of fire, and great wonders have I done among you, yet have

II. ESDRAS

CHAPTER I

you forgotten me, saith the Lord. Thus saith the Almightie Lord, The quailes were as a token for you, I gave you tents for your safegard, neverthelesse you murmured there, and triumphed not in my name for the destruction of your enemies, but ever to this day doe ye yet murmure. Where are the benefits that I have done for you? when you were hungry and thirstie in the wildernesse, did you not crie unto me? saying, Why hast thou brought us into this wildernesse to kill us? It had bin better for us to have served the Egyptians, then to die in this wildernesse. Then had I pity upon your mournings, and gave you Manna to eat, so ye did eate Angels bread. When ye were thirstie, did I not cleave the rocke, and waters flowed out to your fill? for the heate I covered you with the leaves of the trees. I divided amongst you a fruitfull land, I cast out the Canaanites, the Pherezites, and the Philistines before you: what shall I yet doe more for you, saith the Lord? Thus saith the Almighty Lord, When you were in the wildernes in the river of the Amorites, being athirst, and blaspheming my Name, I gave you not fire for your blasphemies, but cast a tree in the water, and made the river sweet. What shall I doe unto thee, O Iacob? thou Iuda wouldest not obey me: I will turne me to other nations, and unto those will I give my Name, that they may keepe my Statutes. Seeing yee have forsaken mee, I will forsake you also: when yee desire me to be gracious unto you, I shall have no mercy upon you. Whensoever you shall call upon me, I will not heare you: for yee have defiled your hands with blood, and your feete are swift to commit manslaughter. Yee have not as it were forsaken me, but your owne selves, saith the Lord. Thus saith the Almighty Lord, Have I not prayed you as a father his sonnes, as a mother her daughters, and a nurse her young babes, that yee would be my people, and I shoud be your God, that ye would be my children, and I should be your father? I gathered you together, as a henne gathereth her chickens under her wings: but now, what shall I doe unto you? I will cast you out from my face. When you offer unto me, I will turne my face from you: for your solemne feast dayes, your newe Moone, and your circumcisions have I forsaken. I sent unto you my servants the Prophets, whom yee have taken and slaine, and torne their bodies in pieces, whose blood I will require of your hands, saith the Lord. Thus saith the Almighty Lord, Your house is desolate, I will cast you out, as the wind doth stubble. And your children shall not bee fruitful: for they have despised my Commandement, and done the thing that is evill before me. Your houses wil I give to a people that shall come, which not having heard of mee, yet shall beleeve mee, to

God threatneth to cast them off,

and to give their houses to a people of more grace then they.

II. ESDRAS

CHAPTER I

whom I have shewed no signes, yet they shall doe that I have commaunded them. They have seene no Prophets, yet they shall call their sinnes to remembrance, and acknowledge them. I take to witnesse the grace of the people to come, whose little ones reioyce in gladnesse: and though they have not seene me with bodily eyes, yet in spirit they beleeve the thing that I say. And now brother, behold what glory: and see the people that commeth from the East. Unto whom I will give for leaders, Abraham, Isaac, and Iacob, Oseas, Amos, and Micheas, Ioel, Abdias, and Ionas, Nahum, and Abacuc, Sophonias, Aggeus, Zacharie, and Malachie, which is called also an Angel of the Lord.

CHAPTER II

God complaineth of his people:

THUS saith the Lord, I brought this people out of bondage, and I gave them my Commaundements by my servants the prophets, whom they would not heare, but despised my counsailes. The mother that bare them, saith unto them, Goe your way ye children, for I am a widow, and forsaken. I brought you up with gladnesse, but with sorrow and heavinesse have I lost you: for yee have sinned before the Lord your God, and done that thing that is evil before him. But what shall I now doe unto you? I am a widow and forsaken: goe your way, O my children, and aske mercy of the Lord. As for mee, O father, I call upon thee for a witnesse over the mother of these children, which would not keepe my Covenant, that thou bring them to confusion, and their mother to a spoile, that there may be no off spring of them. Let them bee scattered abroad among the heathen, let their names bee put out of the earth: for they have despised my Covenant. Woe be unto thee Assur, thou that hidest the unrighteous in thee, O thou wicked people, remember what I did unto Sodome and Gomorrhe. Whose land lieth in clods of pitch and heapes of ashes: even so also wil I doe unto them that heare me not, saith the Almightie Lord. Thus saith the Lord unto Esdras, Tell my people that I will give them the kingdome of Hierusalem, which I would have given unto Israel. Their glory also wil I take unto mee, and give these the everlasting Tabernacles, which I had prepared for them. They shall have the tree of Life for an oyntment of sweet savour, they shall neither labour, nor be weary. Goe and yee shall receive: pray for few dayes unto you, that they may be shortned: the kingdome is already prepared for you: Watch. Take heaven and earth to witnesse; for I have broken the evill in pieces, and created the good; for I live, saith the Lord. Mother,

Yet Esdras is willed to comfort them.

II. ESDRAS

embrace thy children, and bring them up with gladnesse, make their feet as fast as a pillar: for I have chosen thee, saith the Lord. And those that be dead wil I raise up againe from their places, and bring them out of the graves: for I have knowen my Name in Israel. Feare not thou mother of the children: for I have chosen thee, saith the Lord. For thy helpe I will send my servants Esay and Ieremie, after whose counsaile I have sanctified and prepared for thee twelve trees, laden with divers fruits; and as many fountaines flowing with milke and hony: and seven mightie mountaines, whereupon there grow roses and lillies, whereby I will fill thy children with ioy. Doe right to the widow, iudge for the fatherlesse, give to the poore, defend the orphane, clothe the naked, heale the broken and the weake, laugh not a lame man to scorne, defend the maimed, and let the blind man come into the sight of my clearenesse. Keepe the olde and yong within thy walles. Wheresoever thou findest the dead, take them and bury them, and I will give thee the first place in my resurrection. Abide still, O my people, and take thy rest, for thy quietnesse shall come. Nourish thy children, O thou good nource, stablish their feete. As for the servants whom I have given thee, there shall not one of them perish; for I will require them from among thy number. Be not weary, for when the day of trouble and heavinesse commeth, others shal weepe and be sorrowfull, but thou shalt be merry, and have abundance. The heathen shall envie thee, but they shall be able to doe nothing against thee, sayth the Lord. My hands shal cover thee, so that thy children shall not see hell. Be ioyfull, O thou mother, with thy children, for I will deliver thee, sayth the Lord. Remember thy children that sleep, for I shall bring them out of the sides of the earth, and shew mercy unto them: for I am mercifull, sayth the Lord Almightie. Embrace thy children untill I come and shew mercy unto them: for my welles runne over, and my grace shall not faile. I Esdras received a charge of the Lord upon the mount Oreb, that I should goe unto Israel; but when I came unto them, they set me at nought, and despised the commandement of the Lord. And therefore I say unto you, O yee heathen, that heare and understand, Looke for your shepheard, hee shall give you everlasting rest; for he is nigh at hand, that shall come in the end of the world. Be ready to the reward of the kingdome, for the everlasting light shal shine upon you for evermore. Flee the shadow of this world, receive the ioyfulnesse of your glory: I testifie my Saviour openly. O receive the gift that is given you, and be glad, giving thankes unto him that hath called you to the heavenly kingdome.

CHAPTER II

Because they refused, the Gentiles are called.

II. ESDRAS

CHAPTER II

Esdras seeth the Sonne of God, and those that are crowned by him.

Arise up and stand, behold the number of those that be sealed in the feast of the Lord: which are departed from the shadow of the world, and have received glorious garments of the Lord. Take thy number, O Sion, and shut up those of thine that are clothed in white, which have fulfilled the Law of the Lord. The number of thy children whom thou longedst for, is fulfilled: beseech the power of the Lord, that thy people which have been called from the beginning, may be hallowed. I Esdras saw upon the mount Sion a great people, whom I could not number, and they all praised the Lord with songs. And in the middest of them there was a young man of a high stature, taller then all the rest, and upon every one of their heads he set crownes, and was more exalted, which I marveiled at greatly. So I asked the Angel, and said, Sir, what are these? Hee answered, and said unto me, These be they that have put off the mortall clothing, and put on the immortall, and have confessed the Name of God: now are they crowned, and receive palmes. Then sayd I unto the Angel, What yong person is it that crowneth them, and giveth them palmes in their handes? So hee answered, and said unto me, It is the sonne of God, whom they have confessed in the world. Then began I greatly to commend them, that stood so stiffely for the Name of the Lord. Then the Angel sayd unto me, Goe thy way, and tell my people what maner of things, and how great wonders of the Lord thy God thou hast seene.

CHAPTER III

Esdras is troubled,

IN the thirtieth yeere after the ruine of the citie, I was in Babylon, and lay troubled upon my bed, and my thoughts came up over my heart. For I saw the desolation of Sion, and the wealth of them that dwelt at Babylon. And my spirit was sore moved, so that I began to speake words full of feare to the most High, and said, O Lord, who bearest rule, thou spakest at the beginning, when thou didst plant the earth (and that thy selfe alone) and commandedst the people, and gavest a body unto Adam without soule, which was the workemanship of thine handes, and didst breathe into him the breath of life, and he was made living before thee. And thou leddest him into paradise, which thy right hand had planted, before ever the earth came forward. And unto him thou gavest commandement to love thy way, which he transgressed, and immediatly thou appointedst death in him, and in his generations, of whom came nations, tribes, people, and kinreds out of number. And every people walked after their

II. ESDRAS

owne will, and did wonderfull things before thee, and despised thy commandements. And againe in processe of time thou broughtest the flood upon those that dwelt in the world, and destroyedst them. And it came to passe in every of them, that as death was to Adam, so was the flood to these. Neverthelesse one of them thou leftest, namely Noah with his household, of whom came all righteous men. And it happened, that when they that dwelt upon the earth began to multiply, and had gotten them many children, and were a great people, they beganne againe to be more ungodly then the first. Now when they lived so wickedly before thee, thou diddest choose thee a man from among them, whose name was Abraham. Him thou lovedst, and unto him onely thou shewedst thy will: and madest an everlasting covenant with him, promising him that thou wouldest never forsake his seede. And unto him, thou gavest Isahac, and unto Isahac also thou gavest Iacob and Esau. As for Iacob thou didst choose him to thee, and put by Esau: and so Iacob became a great multitude. And it came to passe, that when thou leddest his seede out of Egypt, thou broughtest them up to the mount Sina. And bowing the heavens, thou didest set fast the earth, movedst the whole world, and madest the depth to tremble, and troubledst the men of that age. And thy glory went through foure gates, of fire, and of earthquake, and of wind, and of cold, that thou mightest give the law unto the seed of Iacob, and diligence unto the generation of Israel. And yet tookest thou not away from them a wicked heart, that thy law might bring forth fruite in them. For the first Adam bearing a wicked heart transgressed, and was overcome; and so be all they that are borne of him. Thus infirmity was made permanent; and the law (also) in the heart of the people with the malignity of the roote, so that the good departed away, and the evill abode still. So the times passed away, and the yeeres were brought to an end: then diddest thou raise thee up a servant, called David, whom thou commandedst to build a citie unto thy name, and to offer incense and oblations unto thee therein. When this was done many yeeres, then they that inhabited the citie forsooke thee, and in all things did even as Adam, and all his generations had done, for they also had a wicked heart. And so thou gavest the citie over into the hands of thine enemies. Are their deeds then any better that inhabite Babylon, that they should therefore have the dominion over Sion? For when I came thither, and had seene impieties without number, then my soule saw many evill doers in this thirtieth yeere, so that my heart failed me. For I have seene how thou sufferest them sinning, and hast spared

CHAPTER III

and acknow-
ledgeth the
sinnes of the
people:

yet com-
plaineth that
the heathen
were lords over
them, being
more wicked
then they.

II. ESDRAS

CHAPTER III

wicked doers: and hast destroyed thy people, and hast preserved thine enemies, and hast not signified it. I doe not remember how this way may be left: Are they then of Babylon better then they of Sion? or is there any other people that knoweth thee besides Israel? or what generation hath so beleeved thy Covenants as Iacob? And yet their reward appeareth not, and their labour hath no fruite: for I have gone here and there through the heathen, and I see that they flowe in wealth, and think not upon thy commandements. Weigh thou therfore our wickednesse now in the ballance, and theirs also that dwell in the world: and so shall thy Name no where be found, but in Israel. Or when was it that they which dwell upon the earth, have not sinned in thy sight? or what people hath so kept thy commandements? Thou shalt find that Israel by name hath kept thy precepts: but not the heathen.

CHAPTER IIII

The Angel declareth the ignorance of Esdras in Gods iudgments,

AND the Angel that was sent unto me, whose name was Uriel, gave mee an answere, and said, Thy heart hath gone too farre in this world, and thinkest thou to comprehend the way of the most High? Then said I, Yea my Lord: and he answered me and said, I am sent to shew thee three wayes, and to set forth three similitudes before thee. Whereof if thou canst declare me one, I will shew thee also the way that thou desirest to see, and I shall shew thee from whence the wicked heart commeth. And I said, Tel on my Lord. Then said he unto me, Goe thy way, weigh me the weight of the fire, or measure me the blast of the wind, or call me againe the day that is past. Then answered I and said, What man is able to doe that, that thou shouldest aske such things of mee? And he said unto me, If I should aske thee how great dwellings are in the midst of the sea, or how many springs are in the beginning of the deepe, or how many springs are above the firmament, or which are the outgoings of Paradise: peradventure thou wouldest say unto me, I never went downe into the deepe, nor as yet into hell, neither did I ever climbe up into heaven. Nevertheless, now have I asked thee but onely of the fire and winde, and of the day where through thou hast passed, and of things from which thou canst not be separated, and yet canst thou give me no answeere of them. He said moreover unto me, Thine owne things, and such as are growen up with thee, canst thou not know. How should thy vessel then bee able to comprehend the way of the highest, and the world being now outwardly corrupted, to understand the corruption that is evident in my sight? Then

II. ESDRAS

CHAPTER IIII

and adviseth him not to meddle with things above his reach.

said I unto him, It were better that we were not at all, then that we should live still in wickednesse, and to suffer, and not to know wherefore. He answered me and said, I went into a forest into a plaine, and the trees tooke counsell, and said, Come, let us goe and make warre against the Sea, that it may depart away before us, and that we may make us more woods. The floods of the Sea also in like maner tooke counsell, and said, Come, let us goe up and subdue the woods of the plaine, that there also we may make us another countrey. The thought of the wood was in vaine, for the fire came and consumed it. The thought of the floods of the Sea came likewise to nought, for the sand stood up and stopped them. If thou wert iudge now betwixt these two, whom wouldest thou begin to iustifie, or whom wouldest thou condemne? I answered and said, Verily it is a foolish thought that they both have devised: for the ground is given unto the wood, and the sea also hath his place to beare his floods. Then answered he me and said, Thou hast given a right iudgment, but why iudgest thou not thy selfe also? For like as the ground is given unto the wood, and the sea to his floods: even so they that dwell upon the earth may understand nothing, but that which is upon the earth: and hee that dwelleth above the heavens, may onely understand the things that are above the height of the heavens. Then answered I, and said, I beseech thee, O Lord, let me have understanding. For it was not my minde to be curious of the high things, but of such as passe by us dayly, namely wherefore Israel is given up as a reproch to the heathen, and for what cause the people whom thou hast loved, is given over unto ungodly nations, and why the Lawe of our forefathers is brought to nought, and the written Covenants come to none effect. And wee passe away out of the world as grassehoppers, and our life is astonishment and feare, and we are not worthy to obtaine mercie. What will he then doe unto his Name, whereby we are called? of these things have I asked. Then answered he me, and said, The more thou searchest, the more thou shalt marveile, for the world hasteth fast to passe away, and cannot comprehend the things that are promised to the righteous in time to come: for this world is full of unrighteousnesse and infirmities. But as concerning the things whereof thou askest me, I wil tell thee; for the evil is sowen, but the destruction thereof is not yet come. If therefore that which is sowen, be not turned upside downe; and if the place where the evil is sowen passe not away, then cannot it come that is sowen with good. For the graine of evill seed hath bene sowen in the heart of Adam from the beginning, and how much ungodlinesse hath

Neverthelesse Esdras asketh divers questions, and receiveth answeres to them.

II. ESDRAS

CHAPTER IIII

it brought up unto this time? and how much shall it yet bring foorth untill the time of threshing come. Ponder now by thy selfe, how great fruit of wickednesse the graine of evil seed hath brought forth. And when the eares shall bee cut downe, which are without number, how great a floore shall they fill? Then I answered and said, How and when shall these things come to passe? wherefore are our yeeres few and evill? And he answered me, saying, Do not thou hasten above the most Highest: for thy haste is in vaine to be above him, for thou hast much exceeded. Did not the soules also of the righteous aske question of these things in their chambers, saying, How long shall I hope on this fashion? when commeth the fruit of the floore of our reward? And unto these things Uriel the Archangel gave them answere, and said, Even when the number of seedes is filled in you: for he hath weighed the world in the ballance. By measure hath hee measured the times, and by number hath he numbred the times; and he doeth not moove nor stirre them, untill the said measure be fulfilled. Then answered I, and said, O Lord that bearest rule, even we all are full of impietie. And for our sakes peradventure it is that the floores of the righteous are not filled, because of the sinnes of them that dwell upon the earth. So he answered me, and said, Go thy way to a woman with childe, and aske of her, when she hath fulfilled her nine monethes, if her wombe may keepe the birth any longer within her? Then said I, No Lord, that can she not. And he said unto mee, In the grave, the chambers of soules are like the wombe of a woman: for like as a woman that travaileth, maketh haste to escape the necessitie of the travaile: even so doe these places haste to deliver those things that are committed unto them. From the beginning looke what thou desirest to see, it shalbe shewed thee. Then answered I, and said, If I have found favour in thy sight, and if it be possible, and if I be meet therefore, shew me then whether there be more to come then is past, or more past then is to come. What is past I know; but what is for to come I know not. And he said unto me, Stand up upon the right side, and I shal expound the similitude unto you. So I stood and saw, and behold an hot burning oven passed by before mee: and it happened that when the flame was gone by, I looked, and behold, the smoke remained still. After this there passed by before me a watrie cloude, and sent downe much raine with a storme, and when the stormie raine was past, the drops remained still. Then said he unto me, Consider with thy selfe: as the raine is more then the drops, and as the fire is greater then the smoke: but the drops and the smoke remaine behind: so the quantity

II. ESDRAS

which is past, did more exceede. Then I prayed, and sayd, May I live, thinkest thou, untill that time? or what shall happen in those dayes? He answered me, and sayd, As for the tokens whereof thou askest me, I may tell thee of them in part; but as touching thy life, I am not sent to shew thee, for I doe not know it.

CHAPTER IIII

CHAPTER V

NEVERTHELES as concerning the tokens, beholde, the dayes shall come that they which dwell upon earth, shall bee taken in a great number, and the way of trueth shall be hidden, and the land shall be barren of faith. But iniquitie shalbe increased above that which now thou seest, or that thou hast heard long agoe. And the land that thou seest now to have roote, shalt thou see wasted suddenly. But if the most high graunt thee to live, thou shalt see after the third trumpet, that the Sunne shall suddenly shine againe in the night, and the Moone thrice in the day. And blood shal drop out of wood, and the stone shall give his voice, and the people shalbe troubled. And even he shal rule whom they looke not for that dwel upon the earth, and the foules shall take their flight away together. And the Sodomitish sea shall cast out fish, and make a noyse in the night, which many have not knowen: but they shall all heare the voice thereof. There shall be a confusion also in many places, and the fire shalbe oft sent out againe, and the wilde beasts shall change their places, and menstruous women shall bring foorth monsters. And salt waters shall be found in the sweete, and all friends shall destroy one another: then shall wit hide it selfe, and understanding withdraw it selfe into his secret chamber, and shall be sought of many, and yet not be found: then shall unrighteousnesse and incontinencie be multiplyed upon earth. One land also shall aske another, and say, Is righteousnes that maketh a man righteous, gone through thee? And it shall say, No. At the same time shall men hope, but nothing obtaine: they shall labour, but their wayes shall not prosper. To shew thee such tokens I have leave: and if thou wilt pray againe, and weepe as now, and fast seven dayes, thou shalt heare yet greater things. Then I awaked, and an extreme fearefulnesse went through all my body, and my minde was troubled, so that it fainted. So the Angel that was come to talke with me, helde me, comforted me, and set me up upon my feete. And in the second night it came to passe, that Salathiel the captaine of the people came unto mee, saying, Where hast thou beene? and why is thy countenance so heavie? Knowest thou

The signes of the times to come.

II. ESDRAS

CHAPTER V

He asketh why God choosing but one people, did cast them off.

Hee is taught, that Gods Iudgements are unsearchable:

not that Israel is committed unto thee, in the land of their captivitie? Up then, and cate bread, and forsake us not as the shepheard that leaveth his flocke in the handes of cruell wolves. Then sayd I unto him, Goe thy waies from me, and come not nigh me: And he heard what I said, and went from me. And so I fasted seven dayes, mourning and weeping, like as Uriel the Angel commanded me. And after seven dayes, so it was that the thoughts of my heart were very grievous unto me againe. And my soule recovered the spirit of understanding, and I began to talke with the most high againe, and said, O Lord, that bearest rule of every wood of the earth, and of all the trees thereof, thou hast chosen thee one onely vine. And of all lands of the whole world thou hast chosen thee one pit: and of all the flowers thereof, one Lillie. And of all the depths of the Sea, thou hast filled thee one river: and of all builded cities, thou hast hallowed Sion unto thy selfe. And of all the foules that are created, thou hast named thee one Dove: and of all the cattell that are made, thou hast provided thee one sheepe. And among all the multitudes of peoples, thou hast gotten thee one people: and unto this people whom thou lovedst, thou gavest a law that is approved of all. And now O Lord, why hast thou given this one people over unto many? and upon the one roote hast thou prepared others, and why hast thou scattered thy onely one people among many? And they which did gainesay thy promises, and beleeved not thy covenants, have trodden them downe. If thou didst so much hate thy people, yet shouldest thou punish them with thine owne hands. Now when I had spoken these words, the Angell that came to me the night afore, was sent unto me, and said unto me, Heare me, and I will instruct thee, hearken to the thing that I say, and I shal tell thee more. And I said, Speake on, my Lord: then said he unto me, thou art sore troubled in minde for Israels sake: lovest thou that people better then hee that made them? And I said, No Lord, but of very griefe have I spoken: For my reines paine me every houre, while I labour to comprehend the way of the most High, and to seeke out part of his iudgement. And he said unto me, Thou canst not: and I said, Wherfore Lord? wherunto was I borne then? or why was not my mothers wombe then my grave, that I might not have seene the travell of Iacob, and the wearisome toyle of the stocke of Israel? And he said unto me, Number me the things that are not yet come, gather me together the droppes that are scattered abroad, make mee the flowres greene againe that are withered. Open me the places that are closed, and bring me forth the winds that in them are shut up, shew me the image of a

II. ESDRAS

voyce: and then I will declare to thee the thing that thou labourest to knowe. And I said, O Lord, that bearest rule, who may know these things, but hee that hath not his dwelling with men? As for me, I am unwise: how may I then speake of these things whereof thou askest me? Then said he unto me, Like as thou canst doe none of these things that I have spoken of, even so canst thou not find out my iudgement, or in the end the love that I have promised unto my people. And I said, Behold, O Lord, yet art thou nigh unto them that be reserved till the end; and what shall they doe that have beene before me, or we (that be now) or they that shall come after us? And he said unto me, I wil liken my iudgement unto a ring: like as there is no slacknesse of the last, even so there is no swiftnesse of the first. So I answered and said, Couldst thou not make those that have beene made, and be now, and that are for to come, at once, that thou mightest shewe thy iudgement the sooner? Then answered he me, and said, The creature may not hast above the maker, neither may the world hold them at once that shalbe created therin. And I said, As thou hast said unto thy servant, that thou which givest life to all, hast given life at once to the creature that thou hast created, and the creature bare it: even so it might now also beare them that now be present at once. And he said unto me, Aske the wombe of a woman, and say unto her, If thou bringest forth children, why doest thou it not together, but one after another? pray her therefore to bring forth tenne children at once. And I said, She cannot: but must doe it by distance of time. Then said he unto me, Even so have I given the wombe of the earth to those that be sowen in it, in their times. For like as a young child may not bring forth the things that belong to the aged, even so have I disposed the world which I created. And I asked and said, Seeing thou hast now given me the way, I will proceed to speak before thee: for our mother of whom thou hast told me that she is yong, draweth now nigh unto age. He answered me and said, Aske a woman that beareth children, and shee shall tell thee. Say unto her, Wherefore are not they whome thou hast now brought forth, like those that were before, but lesse of stature? and she shall answere thee, They that be borne in the strength of youth, are of one fashion, and they that are borne in the time of age (when the wombe faileth) are otherwise. Consider thou therfore also, how that yee are lesse of stature then those that were before you. And so are they that come after you lesse then ye, as the creatures which now begin to be old, and have passed over the strength of youth. Then saide I, Lord,

CHAPTER V

and that God doeth not all at once.

II. ESDRAS

CHAPTER V

I beseech thee, if I have found favor in thy sight, shew thy servant by whom thou visitest thy creature.

CHAPTER VI

Gods purpose is eternall.

AND he said unto me, in the beginning when the earth was made, before the borders of the world stood, or ever the windes blew, before it thundred and lightned, or ever the foundations of Paradise were laide, before the faire flowers were seene, or ever the moveable powers were established, before the innumerable multitude of Angels were gathered together, or ever the heights of the aire were lifted up, before the measures of the firmament were named, or ever the chimnies in Sion were hot, and ere the present yeeres were sought out, and or ever the inventions of them that now sinne were turned, before they were sealed that have gathered faith for a treasure: then did I consider these things, and they all were made through mee alone, and through none other: by mee also they shall be ended, and by none other. Then answered I and said, What shall bee the parting asunder of the times? or when shall be the ende of the first, and the beginning of it that followeth? And he said unto me, From Abraham unto Isaac, when Iacob and Esau were borne of him, Iacobs hand held first the heele of Esau. For Esau is the end of the world, and Iacob is the beginning of it that followeth. The hand of man is betwixt the beele and the hand: other question, Esdras, aske thou not.

The next world shall follow this immediatly.

What shall fall out at the last.

I answered then and said, O Lord that bearest rule, if I have found favour in thy sight, I beseech thee, shew thy servant the end of thy tokens, whereof thou shewedst me part the last night. So he answered and said unto me, Stand up upon thy feete, and heare a mightie sounding voyce. And it shall be as it were a great motion, but the place where thou standest, shall not be moved. And therefore when it speaketh be not afraid: for the word is of the end, and the foundation of the earth is understood. And why? because the speech of these things trembleth and is mooved: for it knoweth that the ende of these things must be changed. And it happened that when I had heard it, I stood up upon my feet, and hearkened, and behold, there was a voice that spake, and the sound of it was like the sound of many waters. And it said, Behold, the dayes come, that I will begin to draw nigh, and to visit them that dwell upon the earth, and will begin to make inquisition of them, what they be that have hurt uniustly with their unrighteousnesse, and when the affliction of Sion shalbe

40

II. ESDRAS

fulfilled. And when the world that shal begin to vanish away shall bee finished: then will I shew these tokens, the books shalbe opened before the firmament, and they shall see all together. And the children of a yeere olde shall speake with their voyces, the women with childe shall bring foorth untimely children, of three or foure monethes old: and they shall live, and bee raised up. And suddenly shal the sowen places appeare unsowen, the full storehouses shall suddenly be found empty. And the trumpet shall give a sound, which when every man heareth they shalbe suddenly afraid. At that time shall friendes fight one against another like enemies, and the earth shall stand in feare with those that dwell therein, the springs of the fountaines shall stand still, and in three houres they shall not runne. Whosoever remaineth from all these that I have told thee, shall escape, and see my salvation, and the ende of your world. And the men that are received, shall see it, who have not tasted death from their birth: and the heart of the inhabitants shalbe changed, and turned into another meaning. For evil shalbe put out, and deceit shalbe quenched. As for faith, it shall flourish, corruption shalbe overcome, and the trueth which hath bene so long without fruit, shalbe declared. And when hee talked with mee, behold, I looked by little and little upon him before whom I stood. And these words said he unto me, I am come to shew thee the time of the night to come. If thou wilt pray yet more, and fast seven daies againe, I shal tel thee greater things by day, then I have heard. For thy voice is heard before the most High: for the mighty hath seene thy righteous dealing, he hath seene also thy chastitie, which thou hast had ever since thy youth. And therefore hath he sent mee to shew thee al these things, and to say unto thee, Be of good comfort, and feare not. And hasten not with the times that are past, to thinke vaine things, that thou mayest not hasten from the latter times. And it came to passe after this, that I wept againe, and fasted seven dayes in like maner, that I might fulfill the three weekes which he told me. And in the eight night was my heart vexed within mee againe, and I began to speake before the most High. For my spirit was greatly set on fire, and my soule was in distresse. And I said, O Lord, thou spakest from the beginning of the creation, even the first day, and saidest thus, Let heaven and earth bee made: and thy word was a perfect worke. And then was the spirit, and darkenesse and silence were on every side; the sound of mans voice was not yet formed. Then commandedst thou a faire light to come foorth of thy treasures, that thy worke might appeare. Upon the second day thou madest the spirit of

CHAPTER VI

Hee is promised more knowledge,

and reckoneth up the workes of the creation,

II. ESDRAS

CHAPTER VI

the firmament, and commandedst it to part asunder, and to make a division betwixt the waters, that the one part might goe up, and the other remaine beneath. Upon the thirde day thou didst commaund that the waters should bee gathered in the seventh part of the earth: sixe parts hast thou dried up and kept them, to the intent that of these some being planted of God and tilled, might serve thee. For as soone as thy word went foorth, the worke was made. For immediatly there was great and innumerable fruit, and many and divers pleasures for the taste, and flowers of unchangeable colour, and odours of wonderfull smell: and this was done the third day. Upon the fourth day thou commandedst that the Sunne should shine, and the Moone give her light, and the starres should be in order, and gavest them a charge to do service unto man, that was to be made. Upon the fift day, thou saydst unto the seventh part, where the waters were gathered, that it should bring foorth living creatures, foules and fishes: and so it came to passe. For the dumbe water, and without life, brought foorth living things at the commandement of God, that al people might praise thy wondrous works. Then didst thou ordeine two living creatures, the one thou calledst Enoch, and the other Leviathan, and didst separate the one from the other: for the seventh part (namely where the water was gathered together) might not hold them both. Unto Enoch thou gavest one part which was dried up the third day, that he should dwel in the same part, wherein are a thousand hilles. But unto Leviathan thou gavest the seventh part, namely the moist, and hast kept him to be devoured of whom thou wilt, and when. Upon the sixt day thou gavest commaundement unto the earth, that before thee it should bring foorth beasts, cattell, and creeping things: and after these, Adam also whom thou madest lord of all thy creatures, of him come wee all, and the people also whom thou hast chosen. All this have I spoken before thee, O Lord, because thou madest the world for our sakes. As for the other people which also come of Adam, thou hast said that they are nothing, but be like unto spittle, and hast likened the abundance of them unto a drop that falleth from a vessell. And now, O Lord, behold, these heathen, which have ever been reputed as nothing, have begun to be lordes over us, and to devoure us: but wee thy people (whom thou hast called thy first borne, thy onely begotten, and thy fervent lover) are given into their hands. If the world now be made for our sakes, why doe we not possesse an inheritance with the world? how long shall this endure?

and complaineth that they have no part in the world for whome it was made.

42

II. ESDRAS

CHAPTER VII

AND when I had made an ende of speaking these words, there was sent unto mee the Angel which had beene sent unto mee the nights afore. And he said unto me, Up Esdras, and heare the wordes that I am come to tell thee. And I said, Speake on, my God. Then said he unto me, The Sea is set in a wide place, that it might be deepe and great. But put the case the entrance were narrow, and like a river, who then could goe into the Sea to looke upon it, and to rule it? If hee went not through the narrow, how could he come into the broad? There is also another thing. A city is builded, and set upon a broad field, and is full of all good things. The entrance thereof is narrow, and is set in a dangerous place to fall, like as if there were a fire on the right hand, and on the left a deepe water. And one only path between them both, even betweene the fire and the water, so small that there could but one man goe there at once. If this city now were given unto a man for an inheritance, if he never shall passe the danger set before it, how shall he receive this inheritance? And I said, It is so, Lord. Then said he unto me, Even so also is Israels portion: because for their sakes I made the world: and when Adam transgressed my Statutes, then was decreed that now is done. Then were the entrances of this world made narrow, full of sorrow and travaile: they are but few and evill, full of perils, and very painefull. For the entrances of the elder world were wide and sure, and brought immortall fruit. If then they that live, labour not to enter these strait and vaine things, they can never receive those that are laide up for them. Now therefore why disquietest thou thy selfe, seeing thou art but a corruptible man? and why art thou mooved, whereas thou art but mortall? Why hast thou not considered in thy minde this thing that is to come, rather then that which is present? Then answered I, and sayd, O Lord, that bearest rule, thou hast ordained in thy Law, that the righteous should inherite these things, but that the ungodly should perish: neverthelesse, the righteous shal suffer strait things, and hope for wide: for they that have done wickedly, have suffered the strait things, and yet shall not see the wide. And he said unto me, There is no iudge above God, and none that hath understanding above the highest. For there be many that perish in this life, because they despise the Lawe of God that is set before them. For God hath given strait commandement to such as came, what they should doe to live, even as they came, and what they should observe to avoid

CHAPTER VII

The way is narrow.

When it was made narrow.

43

II. ESDRAS

CHAPTER VII

punishment. Neverthelesse they were not obedient unto him, but spake against him, and imagined vaine things: and deceived themselves by their wicked deeds, and sayd of the most Hie, that he is not, and knew not his waies. But his Law have they despised, and denied his covenants; in his statutes have they not beene faithfull, and have not performed his workes. And therfore Esdras, for the emptie, are emptie things, and for the ful, are the full things. Behold, the time shall come, that these tokens which I have told thee, shall come to passe, and the bride shall appeare, and she comming forth shall be seene, that now is withdrawen from the earth. And whosoever is delivered from the foresaid

All shall die and rise againe. evils, shall see my wonders. For my sonne Iesus shall be revealed with those that be with him, and they that remaine shall reioyce within foure hundred yeeres. After these yeeres shall my sonne Christ die, and all men that have life. And the world shall be turned into the old silence seven dayes, like as in the former iudgements: so that no man shall remaine. And after seven dayes, the world that yet awaketh not shall be raised up, and that shall die, that is corrupt. And the earth shall restore those that are asleepe in her, and so shall the dust those that dwell in silence, and the secret places shall deliver those soules that were com-

Christ shall sit in iudgement. mitted unto them. And the most high shall appeare upon the seate of iudgement, and miserie shall passe away, and the long suffering shall have an end. But iudgement onely shall remaine, trueth shall stand, and faith shall waxe strong. And the worke shall follow, and the reward shall be shewed, and the good deeds shall be of force, and wicked deeds shall beare no rule. Then said I, Abraham prayed first for the Sodomites, and Moses for the fathers that sinned in the wildernesse: and Iesus after him for Israel in the time of Achan, and Samuel; and David for the destruction: and Solomon for them that should come to the sanctuary. And Helias for those that received raine, and for the dead that hee might live. And Ezechias for the people in the time of Sennacherib: and many for many. Even so now seeing corruption is growen up, and wickednesse increased, and the righteous have prayed for the ungodly: wherefore shall it not be so now also? He answered me and said, This present life is not the end where much glory doth abide; therefore have they prayed for the weake. But the day of doome shall be the end of this time, and the beginning of the immortality for to come, wherein corruption is past. Intemperancie is at an end, infidelity is cut off, righteousnesse is growen, and trueth is sprung up. Then shall no man be able to save him that is destroyed, nor to oppresse him that hath

II. ESDRAS

gotten the victory. I answered then and said, This is my first and last saying; that it had beene better not to have given the earth unto Adam: or else when it was given him, to have restrained him from sinning. For what profit is it for men now in this present time to live in heavinesse, and after death to looke for punishment? O thou Adam, what hast thou done? for though it was thou that sinned, thou art not fallen alone, but we all that come of thee. For what profit is it unto us, if there be promised us an immortall time, wheras we have done the works that bring death? And that their is promised us an everlasting hope, whereas our selves being most wicked are made vaine? And that there are layd up for us dwellings of health and safety, whereas we have lived wickedly? And that the glory of the most high is kept to defend them which have led a wary life, whereas we have walked in the most wicked wayes of all? And that there should be shewed a paradise whose fruite endureth for ever, wherein is securitie and medicine, sith we shall not enter into it? For we have walked in unpleasant places. And that the faces of them which have used abstinence, shall shine above the starres, whereas our faces shall bee blacker then darkenesse? For while we lived and committed iniquitie, we considered not that we should begin to suffer for it after death. Then answered he me and saide, This is the condition of the battell, which man that is borne upon the earth shall fight, that if he be overcome, he shall suffer as thou hast said, but if he get the victorie, he shall receive the thing that I say. For this is the life whereof Moses spake unto the people while hee lived, saying, Choose thee life that thou mayest live. Neverthelesse they beleeved not him, nor yet the prophets after him, no nor me which have spoken unto them, that there should not be such heavinesse in their destruction, as shall bee ioy over them that are perswaded to salvation. I answered then and saide, I know, Lord, that the most Hie is called mercifull, in that he hath mercy upon them, which are not yet come into the world, and upon those also that turne to his Law, and that he is patient, and long suffereth those that have sinned, as his creatures, and that he is bountifull, for hee is ready to give where it needeth, and that he is of great mercie, for he multiplieth more and more mercies to them that are present, and that are past, and also to them which are to come. For if he shall not multiplie his mercies, the world would not continue with them that inherit therein. And he pardoneth; for if hee did not so of his goodnesse, that they which have committed iniquities might be eased of them, the ten thousand part of men should not remaine living. And being

CHAPTER VII

God hath not made paradise in vaine,

and is merciful.

II. ESDRAS

CHAPTER VII — Iudge, if he should not forgive them that are cured with his word, and put out the multitude of contentions, there should bee very fewe left peradventure in an innumerable multitude.

CHAPTER VIII

Many created, but few saved.

AND he answered me, saying, The most High hath made this world for many, but the world to come for fewe. I will tell thee a similitude, Esdras, As when thou askest the earth, it shall say unto thee, that it giveth much mold wherof earthen vessels are made, but litle dust that golde commeth of: even so is the course of this present world. There be many created, but few shall be saved. So answered I and said, Swallow then downe O my soule, understanding, and devoure wisedome. For thou hast agreed to give eare, and art willing to prophesie: *Hee asketh why God destroyeth his owne worke,* for thou hast no longer space then onely to live. O Lord, if thou suffer not thy servant that we may pray before thee, and thou give us seed unto our heart, and culture to our understanding, that there may come fruit of it, howe shall each man live that is corrupt, who beareth the place of a man? For thou art alone, and we all one workemanship of thine hands, like as thou hast said. For when the body is fashioned now in the mothers wombe, and thou givest it members, thy creature is preserved in fire and water, and nine months doeth thy workemanship endure thy creature which is created in her. But that which keepeth, and is kept, shall both be preserved: and when the time commeth, the wombe preserved, delivereth up the things that grew in it. For thou hast commanded out of the parts of the body, that is to say, out of the breasts milke to be given, which is the fruit of the breasts, that the thing which is fashioned, may bee nourished for a time, till thou disposest it to thy mercy. Thou broughtest it up with thy righteousnesse, and nourturedst it in thy Law, and reformedst it with thy iudgement. And thou shalt mortifie it as thy creature, and quicken it as thy worke. If therefore thou shalt destroy him which with so great labour was fashioned, it is an easie thing to be ordeined by thy Commaundement, that the thing which was made might be preserved. Now therefore, Lord, I will speake (touching man in generall, thou knowest best) but touching thy people, for whose sake I am sory, and for thine inheritance, for whose cause I mourne, and for Israel, for whom I am heavy, and for Iacob, for whose sake I am troubled: therefore will I begin to pray before thee, for my selfe, and for them: for I see the falles of us that dwell in the land. But I have heard the swiftnesse of

II. ESDRAS

the Iudge which is to come. Therefore heare my voyce, and understand my wordes, and I shall speake before thee: this is the beginning of the words of Esdras, before he was taken up: and I said; O Lord, Thou that dwellest in everlastingnes, which beholdest from above, things in the heaven, and in the aire, whose Throne is inestimable, whose glory may not be comprehended, before whom the hosts of Angels stand with trembling, (whose service is conversant in wind and fire,) whose word is true, and sayings constant, whose Commandement is strong, and ordinance fearefull, whose looke drieth up the depths, and indignation maketh the mountaines to melt away, which the trueth witnesseth: O heare the prayer of thy servant, and give eare to the petition of thy creature. For while I live, I will speake, and so long as I have understanding, I wil answere. O looke not upon the sinnes of thy people: but on them which serve thee in trueth. Regard not the wicked inventions of the heathen: but the desire of those that keepe thy Testimonies in afflictions. Thinke not upon those that have walked fainedly before thee: but remember them, which according to thy will have knowen thy feare. Let it not bee thy will to destroy them, which have lived like beasts: but to looke upon them that have clearely taught thy Law. Take thou no indignation at them which are deemed worse then beasts: but love them that alway put their trust in thy righteousnesse, and glory. For we and our fathers doe languish of such diseases; but because of us sinners, thou shalt be called mercifull. For if thou hast a desire to have mercy upon us, thou shalt bee called mercifull, to us namely, that have no workes of righteousnesse. For the iust which have many good workes layed up with thee, shall out of their owne deedes receive reward. For what is man that thou shouldest take displeasure at him? or what is a corruptible generation, that thou shouldest be so bitter toward it? For in trueth there is no man among them that be borne, but he hath dealt wickedly, and among the faithfull, there is none which hath not done amisse. For in this, O Lord, thy righteousnesse, and thy goodnesse shalbe declared, if thou be mercifull unto them which have not the confidence of good workes. Then answered he mee, and said, Some things hast thou spoken aright, and according unto thy words it shalbe. For indeed I will not thinke on the disposition of them which have sinned before death, before iudgement, before destruction. But I will reioyce over the disposition of the righteous, and I wil remember also their pilgrimage, and the salvation, and the reward that they shall have. Like as I have spoken now, so shall it come to passe. For as the husbandman

CHAPTER VIII

and prayeth God to looke upon the people which onely serve him.

II. ESDRAS

CHAPTER VIII

God answereth that all seed commeth not to God,

soweth much seed upon the ground, and planteth many trees, and yet the thing that is sowen good in his season, commeth not up, neither doeth all that is planted take root: even so is it of them that are sowen in the world, they shall not all be saved. I answered then, and said, If I have found grace, let me speake. Like as the husbandmans seede perisheth, if it come not up, and receive not the raine in due season, or if there come too much raine and corrupt it: even so perisheth man also which is formed with thy hands, and is called thine owne image, because thou art like unto him, for whose sake thou hast made all things, and likened him unto the husbandmans seede. Be not wroth with us, but spare thy people, and have mercy upon thine owne inheritance: for thou art mercifull unto thy creature. Then answered he me, and said, Things present are for the present; and things to come, for such as be to come. For thou commest farre short, that thou shouldest be able to love my creature more then I: but I have oft times drawen nigh unto thee, and unto it, but never to the unrighteous. In this also thou art marveilous before the most high; in that thou hast humbled thy selfe as it becommeth thee, and hast not iudged thy selfe worthy to be much glorified among the righteous. For many great miseries shall be done to them, that in the latter time shal dwell in the world, because they have walked in great pride. But understand thou for thy selfe, and

and that glory is prepared for him and such like.

seeke out the glory for such as be like thee. For unto you is Paradise opened, the tree of life is planted, the time to come is prepared, plenteousnesse is made ready, a citie is builded, and rest is allowed, yea perfect goodnesse and wisedome. The root of evil is sealed up from you, weakenesse and the moth is hidde from you, and corruption is fled into hell to be forgotten. Sorrows are passed, and in the end is shewed the treasure of immortalitie. And therefore aske thou no more questions concerning the multitude of them that perish. For when they had taken liberty, they despised the most High, thought scorne of his Lawe, and forsooke his wayes. Moreover, they have troden downe his righteous, and said in their heart, that there is no God, yea and that knowing they must die. For as the things aforesaid shall receive you, so thirst and paine are prepared for them; for it was not his will that men should come to nought. But they which be created, have defiled the Name of him that made them, and were unthankefull unto him which prepared life for them. And therefore is my iudgement now at hand. These things have I not shewed unto all men, but unto thee, and a fewe like thee. Then answered I, and said, Behold, O Lord, now hast thou shewed me the multitude

II. ESDRAS

of the wonders which thou wilt begin to doe in the last times: but at what time, thou hast not shewed me.

CHAPTER VIII

CHAPTER IX

HEE answered me then, and sayde, Measure thou the time diligently in it selfe: and when thou seest part of the signes past, which I have tolde thee before, then shalt thou understand, that it is the very same time, wherein the highest will begin to visite the world which he made. Therefore when there shall bee seene earthquakes and uprores of the people in the world: then shalt thou wel understand, that the most high spake of those things from the dayes that were before thee, even from the beginning. For like as all that is made in the world hath a beginning, and an ende, and the end is manifest: even so the times also of the highest, have plaine beginnings in wonders and powerfull workes, and endings in effects and signes. And every one that shalbe saved, and shalbe able to escape by his works, and by faith, whereby ye have beleeved, shall be preserved from the sayd perils, and shall see my salvation, in my land, and within my borders: for I have sanctified them for me, from the beginning. Then shall they be in pitifull case which now have abused my wayes: and they that have cast them away despitefully, shall dwell in torments. For such, as in their life have received benefits, and have not knowen me: and they that have loathed my law, while they had yet liberty, and when as yet place of repentance was open unto them, understood not, but despised it: the same must know it after death by paine. And therefore be thou not curious, how the ungodly shalbe punished and when: but enquire how the righteous shall be saved, whose the world is, and for whom the world is created. Then answered I, and said, I have said before, and now doe speake, and will speake it also heereafter: that there be many moe of them which perish, then of them which shall be saved, like as a wave is greater then a droppe. And he answered me, saying: Like as the field is, so is also the seed: as the flowres be, such are the colours also: such as the workeman is, such also is the worke: and as the husbandman is himselfe, so is his husbandry also: for it was the time of the world. And now when I prepared the world, which was not yet made, even for them to dwell in that now live, no man spake against me. For then every one obeyed, but now the maners of them which are created in this world that is made, are corrupted by a perpetuall seed, and by a law which is unsearchable, rid themselves. So I considered the world, and

Who shall be saved, and who not.

All the world is now corrupted:

II. ESDRAS

CHAPTER IX

Yet God doeth save a few.

behold there was perill, because of the devices that were come into it. And I saw and spared it greatly, and have kept me a grape of the cluster, and a plant of a great people. Let the multitude perish then, which was borne in vaine, and let my grape be kept and my plant : for with great labour have I made it perfect. Neverthelesse if thou wilt cease yet seven dayes moe (but thou shalt not fast in them.) But goe into a field of flowres, where no house is builded, and eate only the flowres of the field, Tast no flesh, drinke no wine, but eate flowres onely. And pray unto the Highest continually, then wil I come and talke with thee. So I went my way into the field which is called Ardath, like as he commanded me, and there I sate amongst the flowres, and did eate of the herbes of the field, and the meate of the same satisfied me. After seven dayes I sate upon the grasse, and my heart was vexed within me, like as before. And I opened my mouth, and beganne to talke before the most High and said, O Lord, thou that shewest thy selfe unto us, thou wast shewed unto our fathers in the wildernesse, in a place where no man treadeth, in a barren place when they came out of Egypt. And thou spakest, saying, Heare me, O Israel, and marke my words, thou seed of Iacob. For behold I sow my law in you, and it shall bring fruite in you, and yee shall be honoured in it for ever. But our fathers which received the law, kept it not, and observed not thy ordinances, and though the fruite of thy law did not perish, neither could it, for it was thine :

Hee complaineth that those perish which keepe Gods Law :

yet they that received it, perished, because they kept not the thing that was sowen in them. And loe, it is a custome when the ground hath received seed, or the Sea a ship, or any vessel, meate or drinke, that, that being perished wherein it was sowen, or cast into, that thing also which was sowen or cast therein, or received, doth perish, and remaineth not with us : but with us it hath not happened so. For we that have received the law perish by sinne, and our heart also which received it. Notwithstanding the law

and seeth a woman lamenting in a field.

perisheth not, but remaineth in his force. And when I spake these things in my heart, I looked backe with mine eyes, and upon the right side I saw a woman, and behold, she mourned, and wept with a loud voyce, and was much grieved in heart, and her clothes were rent, and she had ashes upon her head. Then let I my thoughts goe that I was in, and turned me unto her, and said unto her, Wherefore weepest thou ? why art thou so grieved in thy minde ? And she said unto me, Sir, let me alone, that I may bewaile my selfe, and adde unto my sorow, for I am sore vexed in my minde, and brought very low. And I said unto her, What aileth thee ? Tell me. She said unto me, I thy servant have bene barren, and

II. ESDRAS

had no childe, though I had an husband thirty yeres. And those thirtie yeeres I did nothing else day and night, and every houre, but make my prayer to the highest. After thirtie yeeres, God heard me thine handmaid, looked upon my misery, considered my trouble, and gave me a sonne: and I was very glad of him, so was my husband also, and all my neighbours, and we gave great honour unto the Almightie. And I nourished him with great travaile. So when he grew up, and came to the time that he should have a wife, I made a feast.

CHAPTER IX

CHAPTER X

AND it so came to passe, that when my sonne was entred into his wedding chamber, he fell downe and died. Then we all overthrew the lights, and all my neighbours rose up to comfort me, so I tooke my rest unto the second day at night. And it came to passe when they had all left off to comfort me, to the end I might be quiet: then rose I up by night and fled, and came hither into this field, as thou seest. And I doe now purpose not to returne into the citie, but here to stay, and neither to eate nor drinke, but continually to mourne, and to fast until I die. Then left I the meditations wherein I was, and spake to her in anger, saying, Thou foolish woman above all other, seest thou not our mourning, and what happeneth unto us? How that Sion our mother is full of all heavinesse, and much humbled, mourning very sore? And now seeing we all mourne, and are sad, for we are all in heavinesse, art thou grieved for one sonne? For aske the earth, and she shall tell thee, that it is she, which ought to mourne, for the fall of so many that grow upon her. For out of her came all at the first, and out of her shal all others come: and behold they walke almost all into destruction, and a multitude of them is utterly rooted out. Who then should make more mourning, then she that hath lost so great a multitude, and not thou which art sory but for one? But if thou sayest unto me, My lamentation is not like the earths, because I have lost the fruit of my wombe, which I brought foorth with paines, and bare with sorrowes. But the earth not so: for the multitude present in it, according to the course of the earth, is gone, as it came. Then say I unto thee, Like as thou hast brought foorth with labour: even so the earth also hath given her fruit, namely man, ever sithence the beginning, unto him that made her. Now therefore keepe thy sorrow to thy selfe, and beare with a good courage that which hath befallen thee. For if thou shalt acknowledge the determination of God to

Hee comforteth the woman in the field.

II. ESDRAS

CHAPTER X

be iust, thou shalt both receive thy sonne in time, and shalt be commended amongst women. Goe thy way then into the citie, to thine husband. And she said unto me, That will I not doe: I will not goe into the city, but here will I die. So I proceeded to speake further unto her, and said, Doe not so, but bee counselled by me: for how many are the adversities of Sion? Bee comforted in regard of the sorow of Ierusalem. For thou seest that our Sanctuary is laid waste, our Altar broken downe, our Temple destroyed. Our Psaltery is laid on the ground, our song is put to silence, our reioycing is at an end, the light of our candlesticke is put out, the Arke of our Covenant is spoiled, our holy things are defiled, and the Name that is called upon us, is almost prophaned: our children are put to shame, our priests are burnt, our Levites are gone into captivitie, our virgines are defiled, and our wives ravished, our righteous men caried away, our litle ones destroyed, our yong men are brought in bondage, and our strong men are become weake. And which is the greatest of all, the seale of Sion hath now lost her honour: for she is delivered into the hands of them that hate us. And therefore shake off thy great heavinesse, and put away the multitude of sorrowes, that the mighty may be mercifull unto thee againe, and the highest shal give thee rest, and ease from thy labour. And it came to passe while I was talking with her, behold her face upon a sudden shined exceedingly, and her countenance glistered, so that I was afraid of her, and mused what it might be. And behold suddenly, she made a great cry very fearful: so that the earth shooke at the noise of the woman. And I looked, and beholde, the woman appeared unto me no more, but there was a city builded, and a large place shewed it selfe from the foundations: then was I afraid, and cried with a lowd voice, and said, Where is Uriel the Angel, who came unto mee at the first? for hee hath caused me to fall into many traunces, and mine end is turned into corruption, and my prayer to rebuke. And as I was speaking these wordes, behold, he came unto me, and looked upon me. And loe, I lay as one that had bene dead, and mine understanding was taken from me, and he tooke me by the right hand, and comforted mee, and set me upon my feet, and said unto me, What aileth thee? and why art thou so disquieted, and why is thine understanding troubled, and the thoughts of thine heart? And I said, Because thou hast forsaken me, and yet I did according to thy words, and I went into the field, and loe I have seene, and yet see, that I am not able to expresse. And hee said unto me, Stand up manfully, and I wil advise thee. Then said I, Speake on, my lord in me, onely forsake me not, lest I die frustrate of my

She vanisheth away, and a citie appeareth in her place.

II. ESDRAS

hope. For I have seene, that I knew not, and heare that I do not know. Or, is my sense deceived, or my soule in a dreame? Now therfore, I beseech thee, that thou wilt shew thy servant of this vision. He answered me then, and said, Heare me, and I shall enforme thee, and tell thee wherefore thou art afraid: for the highest will reveile many secret things unto thee. Hee hath seene that thy way is right: for that thou sorrowest continually for thy people, and makest great lamentation for Sion. This therefore is the meaning of the vision which thou lately sawest. Thou sawest a woman mourning, and thou beganst to comfort her: but now seest thou the likenesse of the woman no more, but there appeared unto thee a city builded. And whereas she told thee of the death of her sonne, this is the solution. This woman whom thou sawest, is Sion: and whereas she said unto thee (even she whom thou seest as a city builded.) Whereas I say, she said unto thee, that she hath bene thirty yeres barren: those are the thirty yeeres wherein there was no offering made in her. But after thirtie yeeres, Solomon builded the city, and offered offrings: and then bare the barren a sonne. And whereas she told thee that shee nourished him with labour: that was the dwelling in Hierusalem. But whereas she said unto thee, That my sonne comming into his marriage chamber, happened to have a fall, and died, this was the destruction that came to Hierusalem. And behold, thou sawest her likenesse, and because she mourned for her sonne, thou beganst to comfort her, and of these things which have chaunced, these are to be opened unto thee. For now the most High seeth, that thou art grieved unfainedly, and sufferest from thy whole heart for her, so hath he shewed thee the brightnes of her glory, and the comelinesse of her beautie. And therfore I bad thee remaine in the field, where no house was builded. For I knew that the Highest would shew this unto thee. Therefore I commanded thee to goe into the field, where no foundation of any building was. For in the place wherein the Highest beginneth to shew his city, ther can no mans building be able to stand. And therfore feare not, let not thy heart be afrighted, but goe thy way in, and see the beautie and greatnesse of the building, as much as thine eyes be able to see: and then shalt thou heare as much as thine eares may comprehend. For thou art blessed above many other, and art called with the highest, and so are but few. But to morrow at night thou shalt remaine here. And so shall the highest shew thee visions of the high things, which the most high will do unto them, that dwel upon earth in the last dayes. So I slept that night and another, like as he commanded me.

CHAPTER X

The Angel declareth these visions in the field.

II. ESDRAS

CHAPTER XI

CHAPTER XI

Hee seeth in his dreame an Eagle comming out of the Sea:

THEN saw I a dreame, and beholde, there came up from the Sea an Eagle, which had twelve feathered wings, and three heads. And I saw, and behold, she spred her wings over all the earth, and all the windes of the ayre blew on her, and were gathered together. And I beheld, and out of her feathers there grewe other contrary feathers, and they became little feathers, and small. But her heads were at rest: the head in the middest was greater then the other, yet rested it with the residue. Moreover I beheld, and loe, the Eagle flew with her feathers, and reigned upon earth, and over them that dwelt therein. And I saw that all things under heaven were subiect unto her, and no man spake against her, no not one creature upon earth. And I beheld, and loe, the Eagle rose upon her talents, and spake to her feathers, saying, Watch not all at once, sleepe every one in his own place, and watch by course. But let the heads be preserved for the last. And I beheld, and loe, the voice went not out of her heads, but from the middest of her body. And I numbred her contrary feathers, and behold, there were eight of them. And I looked, and behold, on the right side there arose one feather, and reigned over all the earth. And so it was, that when it reigned, the ende of it came, and the place thereof appeared no more: so the next following stood up and reigned, and had a great time. And it happened, that when it reigned, the end of it came also, like as the first, so that it appeared no more. Then came there a voice unto it, and sayd, Heare, thou that hast borne rule over the earth so long: this I say unto thee, before thou beginnest to appeare no more. There shall none after thee attaine unto thy time, neither unto the halfe thereof. Then arose the third, and reigned as the other before: and appeared no more also. So went it with all the residue one after another, as that every one reigned, and then appeared no more. Then I beheld, and loe, in processe of time, the feathers that folowed, stood up upon the right side, that they might rule also, and some of them ruled, but within a while they appeared no more: for some of them were set up, but ruled not. After this I looked, and behold, the twelve feathers appeared no more, nor the two little feathers: and there was no more upon the Eagles body, but three heads that rested, and sixe little wings. Then saw I also that two little feathers divided themselves from the sixe, and remained under the head, that was upon the right side: for the foure continued in their place.

54

II. ESDRAS

CHAPTER XI

And I beheld, and loe, the feathers that were under the wing, thought to set up themselves, and to have the rule. And I beheld, and loe, there was one set up, but shortly it appeared no more. And the second was sooner away then the first. And I beheld, and loe, the two that remained, thought also in themselves to reigne. And when they so thought, behold, there awaked one of the heads that were at rest, namely it that was in the middest, for that was greater then the two other heads. And then I saw, that the two other heads were ioyned with it. And behold, the head was turned with them that were with it, and did eate up the two feathers under the wing that would have reigned. But this head put the whole earth in feare, and bare rule in it over all those that dwelt upon the earth, with much oppression, and it had the governance of the world more then all the wings that had beene. And after this I beheld, and loe the head that was in the midst, suddenly appeared no more, like as the wings. But there remained the two heads, which also in like sort ruled upon the earth, and over those that dwelt therein. And I beheld, and loe, the head upon the right side, devoured it, that was upon the left side. Then I heard a voyce, which said unto me, Looke before thee, and consider the thing that thou seest. And I beheld, and loe, as it were a roaring Lyon, chased out of the wood: and I saw that hee sent out a mans voyce unto the Eagle, and said, Heare thou, I will talke with thee, and the highest shall say unto thee, Art not thou it that remainest of the foure beasts, whom I made to raigne in my world, that the end of their times might come through them? And the fourth came and overcame all the beasts that were past, and had power over the world with great fearefulnesse, and over the whole compasse of the earth with much wicked oppression, and so long time dwelt he upon the earth with deceit. For the earth hast thou not iudged with trueth. For thou hast afflicted the meeke, thou hast hurt the peaceable, thou hast loved lyers, and destroyed the dwellings of them that brought forth fruite, and hast cast downe the walles of such, as did thee no harme. Therefore is thy wrongfull dealing come up unto the Highest, and thy pride unto the Mighty. The Highest also hath looked upon the proud times, and behold, they are ended, and his abominations are fulfilled. And therefore appeare no more thou Eagle, nor thy horrible wings, nor thy wicked feathers, nor thy malitious heads, nor thy hurtfull clawes, nor all thy vaine body: that all the earth may be refreshed, and may returne, being delivered from thy violence, and that she may hope for the iudgement, and mercy of him that made her.

And a Lion out of a wood talking to the Eagle.

II. ESDRAS

CHAPTER XII

CHAPTER XII

The Eagle which hee saw, is destroyed.

AND it came to passe whiles the Lyon spake these words unto the Eagle, I saw: and behold, the head that remained, and the foure wings appeared no more, and the two went unto it, and set themselves up to raigne, and their kingdome was small and full of uprore. And I saw, and behold, they appeared no more, and the whole body of the Eagle was burnt, so that the earth was in great feare: then awaked I out of the trouble and traunce of my minde, and from great feare, and said unto my spirit, Loe, this hast thou done unto me, in that thou searchest out the wayes of the Highest. Loe, yet am I weary in my mind, and very weake in my spirit: and litle strength is there in me; for the great feare, wherewith I was affrighted this night. Therefore wil I now beseech the Highest, that hee will comfort me unto the end. And I said, Lord, that bearest rule, If I have found grace before thy sight, and if I am iustified with thee, before many others, and if my prayer indeed be come up before thy face, comfort me then, and shew me thy servant the interpretation, and plaine difference of this fearefull vision, that thou maist perfectly comfort my soule.

The vision is interpreted.

For thou hast iudged me worthy, to shew me the last times. And he said unto me, This is the interpretation of the vision. The Eagle whom thou sawest come up from the sea, is the kingdome which was seene, in the vision of thy brother Daniel. But it was not expounded unto him, therefore now I declare it unto thee. Behold, the dayes will come, that there shall rise up a kingdome upon earth, and it shall be feared above all the kingdomes that were before it. In the same shall twelve kings reigne, one after another. Whereof the second shall begin to reigne, and shall have more time then any of the twelve. And this doe the twelve wings signifie which thou sawest. As for the voice which thou heardest speake, and that thou sawest not to goe out from the heads, but from the mids of the body thereof, this is the interpretation: That after the time of that kingdome, there shall arise great strivings, and it shall stand in perill of falling: neverthelesse it shall not then fall, but shal be restored againe to his beginning. And whereas thou sawest the eight small under feathers sticking to her wings, this is the interpretation: That in him there shal arise eight kings, whose time shall bee but small, and their yeeres swift. And two of them shall perish: the middle time approching, foure shall bee kept untill their end begin to approch: but two shall be kept unto the end. And whereas thou sawest three heads resting,

56

II. ESDRAS

this is the interpretation: In his last dayes shall the most High raise up three kingdomes, and renew many things therein, and they shal have the dominion of the earth, and of those that dwell therein with much oppression, above all those that were before them: therefore are they called the heads of the Eagle. For these are they that shal accomplish his wickednesse, and that shall finish his last end. And whereas thou sawest that the great head appeared no more, it signifieth that one of them shall die upon his bed, and yet with paine. For the two that remaine, shall be slaine with the sword. For the sword of the one shall devoure the other: but at the last shall he fall through the sword himselfe. And whereas thou sawest two feathers under the wings passing over the head, that is on the right side: it signifieth that these are they whom the Highest hath kept unto their end: this is the small kingdom and full of trouble, as thou sawest. And the Lyon whom thou sawest rising up out of the wood, and roaring, and speaking to the Eagle, and rebuking her for her unrighteousnesse, with all the words which thou hast heard, this is the Anointed which the Highest hath kept for them, and for their wickednesse unto the end: he shall reproove them, and shall upbraid them with their crueltie. For hee shall set them before him alive in iudgement, and shall rebuke them and correct them. For the rest of my people shall he deliver with mercie, those that have bin preserved upon my borders, and he shal make them ioyfull untill the comming of the day of iudgement, whereof I have spoken unto thee from the beginning. This is the dreame that thou sawest, and these are the interpretations. Thou onely hast bene meete to know this secret of the Highest. Therefore write all these things that thou hast seene, in a booke, and hide them. And teach them to the wise of the people, whose hearts thou knowest may comprehend, and keepe these secrets. But wait thou here thy selfe yet seven dayes moe, that it may be shewed thee whatsoever it pleaseth the Highest to declare unto thee: And with that he went his way. And it came to passe when all the people saw that the seven dayes were past, and I not come againe into the citie, they gathered them all together, from the least unto the greatest, and came unto me, and said, What have we offended thee? and what evill have we done against thee, that thou forsakest us, and sittest here in this place? For of all the prophets thou only art left us, as a cluster of the vintage, and as a candle in a darke place, and as a haven or ship preserved from the tempest: are not the evils which are come to us, sufficient? If thou shalt forsake us, how much better had it bene for us, if we also had bene

CHAPTER XII

He is bid to write his visions, and to fast, that he may see more.

II. ESDRAS

CHAPTER XII

He doth comfort those, that were grieved for his absence.

burnt in the midst of Sion. For we are not better then they that died there. And they wept with a loud voice: then answered I them, and said, Be of good comfort, O Israel, and be not heavy thou house of Iacob. For the Highest hath you in remembrance, and the mighty hath not forgotten you in temptation. As for mee, I have not forsaken you, neither am I departed from you: but am come into this place, to pray for the desolation of Sion, and that I might seeke mercy for the low estate of your Sanctuary. And now goe your way home every man, and after these dayes will I come unto you. So the people went their way into the city, like as I commanded them: but I remained still in the field seven dayes, as the Angel commanded me, and did eate onely in those dayes, of the flowers of the fielde, and had my meat of the herbes.

CHAPTER XIII

Hee seeth in his dreame a man comming out of the sea.

AND it came to passe after seven dayes, I dreamed a dreame by night. And loe, there arose a winde from the sea that it mooved all the waves thereof. And I beheld, and loe, that man waxed strong with the thousands of heaven: and when he turned his countenance to looke, all the things trembled that were seene under him. And whensoever the voyce went out of his mouth, all they burnt, that heard his voyce, like as the earth faileth when it feeleth the fire. And after this I beheld, and loe, there was gathered together a multitude of men out of number, from the foure windes of the heaven, to subdue the man that came out of the sea. But I beheld, and loe, hee had graved himselfe a great mountaine, and flew up upon it. But I would have seene the region, or place, whereout the hill was graven, and I could not. And after this I beheld, and loe, all they which were gathered together to subdue him, were sore afraid, and yet durst fight. And loe, as hee saw the violence of the multitude that came, hee neither lift up his hand, nor held sword, nor any instrument of warre. But onely I saw that he sent out of his mouth, as it had bene a blast of fire, and out of his lippes a flaming breath, and out of his tongue he cast out sparkes and tempests, and they were all mixt together; the blast of fire, the flaming breath, and the great tempest, and fel with violence upon the multitude, which was prepared to fight, and burnt them up every one, so that upon a sudden, of an innumerable multitude, nothing was to be perceived, but onely dust and smell of smoke: when I saw this, I was afraid. Afterward saw I the same man come downe from the mountaine, and call unto him an other peaceable multitude. And

II. ESDRAS

there came much people unto him, whereof some were glad, some were sory, some of them were bound, and other some brought of them that were offred: then was I sicke through great feare, and I awaked and said, Thou hast shewed thy servant wonders from the beginning, and hast counted me worthy that thou shouldest receive my prayer: shew mee now yet the interpretation of this dreame. For as I conceive in mine understanding, woe unto them that shall be left in those dayes; and much more woe unto them that are not left behinde. For they that were not left, were in heavinesse. Now understand I the things that are layde up in the latter dayes, which shall happen unto them, and to those that are left behinde. Therefore are they come into great perils, and many necessities, like as these dreames declare. Yet is it easier for him that is in danger, to come into these things, then to passe away as a cloud out of the world, and not to see the things that happen in the last dayes. And he answered unto me, and said, The interpretation of the vision shal I shew thee, and I wil open unto thee, the thing that thou hast required. Wheras thou hast spoken of them that are left behinde, this is the interpretation. He that shall endure the perill in that time, hath kept himselfe: they that be fallen into danger, are such as have workes, and faith towards the Almightie. Know this therefore, that they which be left behinde, are more blessed then they that be dead. This is the meaning of the vision: Whereas thou sawest a man comming up from the middest of the Sea: the same is hee whom God the highest hath kept a great season, which by his owne selfe shall deliver his creature: and hee shall order them that are left behinde. And whereas thou sawest, that out of his mouth there came as a blast of winde, and fire, and storme: and that he helde neither sword, nor any instrument of warre, but that the rushing in of him destroyed the whole multitude that came to subdue him, this is the interpretation. Behold, the dayes come, when the most high wil begin to deliver them that are upon the earth. And he shall come to the astonishment of them that dwell on the earth. And one shall undertake to fight against another, one city against another, one place against another, one people against another, and one realme against another. And the time shalbe, when these things shall come to passe, and the signes shall happen which I shewed thee before, and then shall my sonne be declared, whom thou sawest as a man ascending. And when all the people heare his voice, every man shall in their owne land, leave the battaile they have one against another. And an innumerable multitude shalbe gathered together, as thou sawest them willing to come,

CHAPTER XIII

The declaration of his dreame.

II. ESDRAS

CHAPTER XIII

and to overcome him by fighting. But hee shall stand upon the top of the mount Sion. And Sion shall come and shall be shewed to all men, being prepared and builded, like as thou sawest the hill graven without hands. And this my sonne shall rebuke the wicked inventions of those nations, which for their wicked life are fallen into the tempest, and shall lay before them their evill thoughts, and the torments wherwith they shall begin to be tormented, which are like unto a flame: and hee shall destroy them without labour, by the law which is like unto fire. And whereas thou sawest that hee gathered another peaceable multitude unto him; those are the ten tribes, which were caried away prisoners out of their owne land, in the time of Osea the king, whom Salmanasar the king of Assyria ledde away captive, and hee caried them over the waters, and so came they into another land. But they tooke this counsaile amongst themselves, that they would leave the multitude of the heathen, and goe foorth into a further countrey, where never mankind dwelt, that they might there keepe their statutes, which they never kept in their owne land. And they entred into Euphrates by the narrow passages of the River. For the most high then shewed signes for them, and held still the flood, till they were passed over. For through that countrey there was a great way to goe; namely, of a yeere and a halfe: and the same region is called Arsareth. Then dwelt they there untill the latter time; and now when they shall begin to come, the highest shall stay the springs of the streame againe, that they may go through: therefore sawest thou the multitude with peace. But those that be left behinde of thy people, are they that are found within my borders. Now when hee destroyeth the multitude of the nations that are gathered together, he shal defend his people that remaine. And then shall hee shewe them great wonders. Then said I, O Lord, that bearest rule, shew me this: Wherefore have I seene the man comming up from the midst of the Sea? And he said unto me, Like as thou canst neither seeke out, nor know the things that are in the deepe of the sea: even so can no man upon earth see my sonne, or those that be with him, but in the day time. This is the interpretation of the dreame which thou sawest, and whereby thou onely art here

He is praised, and promised to see more.

lightened. For thou hast forsaken thine owne way, and applied thy diligence unto my law, and sought it. Thy life hast thou ordered in wisdome, and hast called understanding thy mother. And therefore have I shewed thee the treasures of the Highest: After other three dayes, I will speake other things unto thee, and declare unto thee mightie and wonderous things. Then went I forth into the field giving praise and thanks greatly unto the most

II. ESDRAS

High, because of his wonders which he did in time, and because hee governeth the same, and such things as fall in their seasons, and there I sate three dayes.

CHAPTER XIII

CHAPTER XIIII

AND it came to passe, upon the third day I sate under an oke, and behold, there came a voyce out of a bush over against me, and said, Esdras, Esdras. And I said, Here am I Lord, and I stood up upon my feet. Then said he unto me, In the bush I did manifestly reveale my selfe unto Moses, and talked with him, when my people served in Egypt. And I sent him, and led my people out of Egypt, and brought him up to the mount of Sinai, where I held him by me, a long season, and told him many wonderous things, and shewed him the secrets of the times, and the end, and commanded him, saying, These wordes shalt thou declare, and these shalt thou hide. And now I say unto thee, that thou lay up in thy heart the signes that I have shewed, and the dreames that thou hast seene, and the interpretations which thou hast heard: for thou shalt be taken away from all, and from henceforth thou shalt remaine with my sonne, and with such as be like thee, untill the times be ended. For the world hath lost his youth, and the times begin to waxe old. For the world is divided into twelve parts, and the ten parts of it are gone already, and halfe of a tenth part. And there remaineth that which is after the halfe of the tenth part. Now therefore set thine house in order, and reprove thy people, comfort such of them as be in trouble, and now renounce corruption. Let go from thee mortall thoughts, cast away the burdens of man, put off now the weake nature, and set aside the thoughts that are most heavy unto thee, and haste thee to flie from these times. For yet greater evils then those which thou hast seene happen, shall bee done hereafter. For looke how much the world shall be weaker through age: so much the more shall evils increase upon them that dwell therein. For the trueth is fled farre away, and leasing is hard at hand: For now hasteth the vision to come, which thou hast seene. Then answered I before thee, and said, Behold, Lord, I will go as thou hast commanded me, and reprove the people which are present, but they that shall be borne afterward, who shall admonish them? thus the world is set in darkenes, and they that dwell therein, are without light. For thy law is burnt, therefore no man knoweth the things that are done of thee, or the works that shal begin. But if I have found grace before thee, send the

A voice out of a bush calleth Esdras,

and telleth him that the world waxeth old,

He desireth, because the Law was burnt, to write all againe,

II. ESDRAS

CHAPTER XIIII

and is bid to get swift writers.

holy Ghost into me, and I shall write all that hath bene done in the world, since the beginning, which were written in thy Lawe, that men may find thy path, and that they which will live in the latter dayes, may live. And he answered me, saying, Goe thy way, gather the people together, and say unto them, that they seeke thee not for fourtie dayes. But looke thou prepare thee many boxe trees, and take with thee Sarea, Dabria, Selemia, Ecanus and Asiel, these five which are ready to write swiftly. And come hither, and I shall light a candle of understanding in thine heart, which shall not be put out, till the things be performed which thou shalt beginne to write. And when thou hast done, some things shalt thou publish, and some things shalt thou shew secretly to the wise: to morrowe this houre shalt thou beginne to write. Then went I foorth as he commanded, and gathered all the people together, and said, Heare these words, O Israel. Our fathers at the beginning were strangers in Egypt, from whence they were delivered: and received the law of life which they kept not, which ye also have transgressed after them. Then was the land, even the land of Sion, parted among you by lot, but your fathers, and yee your selves have done unrighteousnesse, and have not kept the wayes which the Highest commanded you. And for as much as he is a righteous iudge, hee tooke from you in time, the thing that he had given you. And now are you heere, and your brethren amongst you. Therefore if so be that you will subdue your owne understanding, and reforme your hearts, yee shall be kept alive, and after death yee shall obtaine mercy. For after death, shall the iudgement come, when we shall live againe: and then shall the names of the righteous be manifest, and the workes of the ungodly shall be declared. Let no man therefore come unto me now, nor seeke after me these fourty dayes. So I tooke the five men as hee commanded me, and we went into the field, and remained there. And the next day behold a voyce called mee saying, Esdras, open thy mouth and drinke that I give thee to drinke. Then opened I my mouth, and behold, he reached me a full cup, which was full as it were with water, but the colour of it was like fire. And I tooke it, and dranke: and when I had drunke of it, my heart uttered understanding: and wisedome grew in my breast, for my spirit strengthened my memory. And my mouth was opened and shut no more. The highest gave understanding unto the five men, and they wrote the wonderfull visions of the night, that were told, which they knew not: And they sate fourty dayes, and they wrote in the day, and at night they ate bread. As for me I spake in the

Hee and they are filled with understanding:

II. ESDRAS

day, and held not my tongue by night: in fourty dayes they wrote two hundred and foure bookes. And it came to passe when the fourty dayes were fulfilled, that the Highest spake, saying, The first that thou hast written, publish openly, that the worthy and unworthy may read it. But keepe the seventy last, that thou mayest deliver them onely to such as be wise, among the people. For in them is the spring of understanding, the fountains of wisedome, and the streame of knowledge. And I did so.

CHAPTER XIIII
but hee is charged not to publish all that is written.

CHAPTER XV

BEHOLD, speake thou in the eares of my people the words of prophesie, which I will put in thy mouth, saith the Lord. And cause them to be written in paper: for they are faithfull and true. Feare not the imaginations against thee, let not the incredulity of them trouble thee, that speake against thee. For all the unfaithfull shall die in their unfaithfulnesse. Behold, saith the Lord, I will bring plagues upon the world; the sword, famine, death, and destruction. For wickednesse hath exceedingly polluted the whole earth, and their hurtfull workes are fulfilled. Therefore saith the Lord, I will hold my tongue no more as touching their wickednesse, which they prophanely commit, neither wil I suffer them in those things, in which they wickedly exercise themselves: behold, the innocent and righteous blood cryeth unto me, and the soules of the iust complaine continually. And therefore saith the Lord, I wil surely avenge them, and receive unto me, all the innocent blood from among them. Beholde, my people is ledde as a flocke to the slaughter: I wil not suffer them now to dwel in the land of Egypt. But I will bring them with a mighty hand, and a stretched out arme, and smite Egypt with plagues as before, and wil destroy al the land thereof. Egypt shal mourne, and the foundation of it shall bee smitten with the plague and punishment, that God shall bring upon it. They that till the ground shall mourne: for their seedes shall faile, through the blasting, and haile, and with a fearefull constellation. Woe to the world, and them that dwell therein. For the sword and their destruction draweth nigh, and one people shall stand up to fight against another, and swords in their hands. For there shalbe sedition among men, and invading one another, they shal not regard their kings, nor princes, and the course of their actions shall stand in their power. A man shall desire to goe into a citie, and shall not be able. For because of their pride, the cities shalbe troubled, the houses shalbe destroyed, and men shalbe

This prophecie is certaine.

God will take vengeance upon the wicked,

Upon Egypt,

II. ESDRAS

CHAPTER
XV

afraid. A man shall have no pitie upon his neighbour, but shall destroy their houses with the sword, and spoile their goods, because of the lacke of bread, and for great tribulation. Behold, saith God, I will call together all the Kings of the earth to reverence me, which are from the rising of the Sunne, from the South, from the East, and Libanus: to turne themselves one against another, and repay the things that they have done to them. Like as they doe yet this day unto my chosen, so will I doe also and recompense in their bosome, Thus saith the Lord God; My right hand shall not spare the sinners, and my sword shal not cease over them, that shed innocent blood upon earth. The fire is gone foorth from his wrath, and hath consumed the foundations of the earth, and the sinners like the straw that is kindled. Wo to them that sinne and keepe not my commandements, saith the Lord. I will not spare them: goe your way ye children from the power, defile not my Sanctuary: for the Lord knoweth all them that sinne against him, and therefore delivereth he them unto death and destruction. For now are the plagues come upon the whole earth, and ye shall remaine in them, for God shal not deliver you, because ye have sinned against him. Behold an horrible vision, and the appearance thereof from the East. Where the nations of the dragons of Arabia shall come out with many charets, and the multitude of them shalbe caried as the winde upon earth, that all they which heare them, may feare and tremble. Also the Carmanians raging in wrath, shall go forth as the wilde bores of the wood, and with great power shall they come, and ioyne battell with them, and shall waste a portion of the land of the Assyrians. And then shall the dragons have the upper hand, remembring their nature, and if they shall turne themselves, conspiring together in great power to persecute them, then these shalbe troubled, and keepe silence through their power, and shall flee. And from the land of the Assyrians, shall the enemy besiege them, and consume some of them, and in their host shall be feare, and dread and strife among their kings. Behold clouds from the East, and from the North, unto the South, and they are very horrible to looke upon; full of wrath and storme. They shall smite one upon another, and they shall smite downe a great multitude of starres upon the earth, even their owne starre; and blood shalbe from the sword unto the belly. And doung of men unto the camels hough. And there shalbe great fearefulnesse and trembling upon earth: and they that see the wrath, shall be afraid, and trembling shall come upon them. And then shall there come great stormes, from the South, and from the North, and another part from the West. And strong winds

An horrible
vision.

II. ESDRAS

shal arise from the East, and shall open it, and the cloud which hee raised up in wrath, and the starre stirred to cause feare toward the East and West winde, shalbe destroyed. The great and mightie cloudes shall be lifted up full of wrath, and the starre, that they may make all the earth afraid, and them that dwel therein, and they shall powre out over every high and eminent place, an horrible starre. Fire and haile, and fleeing swords, and many waters, that all fields may be full, and all rivers with the abundance of great waters. And they shal breake downe the cities, and walls, mountaines and hils, trees of the wood, and grasse of the medowes, and their corne. And they shal goe stedfastly unto Babylon, and make her afraid. They shall come to her, and besiege her, the starre and all wrath shall they powre out upon her, then shall the dust and smoke goe up unto the heaven: and all they that be about her, shall bewaile her. And they that remaine under her, shall doe service unto them that have put her in feare. And thou Asia that art partaker of the hope of Babylon, and art the glory of her person: woe be unto thee thou wretch, because thou hast made thy selfe like unto her, and hast deckt thy daughters in whoredome, that they might please and glory in thy lovers, which have alway desired to commit whordome with thee. Thou hast followed her, that is hated in all her works and inventions: therefore sayth God, I will send plagues upon thee: widowhood, povertie, famine, sword, and pestilence, to waste thy houses with destruction and death. And the glory of thy power shall be dried up as floure, when the heate shall arise that is sent over thee. Thou shalt bee weakened as a poore woman with stripes, and as one chastised with woundes, so that the mightie and lovers shall not be able to receive thee. Would I with iealousie have so proceeded against thee, saith the Lord, if thou haddest not alway slaine my chosen, exalting the stroke of thine hands, and saying over their dead, when thou wast drunken, Set foorth the beauty of thy countenance. The reward of thy whoredome shall be in thy bosome, therefore shalt thou receive recompense. Like as thou hast done unto my chosen, sayth the Lord; even so shall God doe unto thee, and shall deliver thee into mischiefe. Thy children shall die of hunger, and thou shalt fall through the sword: thy cities shalbe broken downe, and all thine shall perish with the sword in the field. They that be in the mountaines shall die of hunger, and eate their owne flesh, and drinke their owne blood, for very hunger of bread, and thirst of water. Thou, as unhappy, shalt come through the Sea, and receive plagues againe. And in the passage, they shall rush on the idle citie, and shall destroy some portion of thy land, and consume part of thy

CHAPTER XV

Babylon and Asia are threatned.

II. ESDRAS

CHAPTER XV

glory, and shall returne to Babylon that was destroyed. And thou shalt be cast downe by them, as stubble, and they shall be unto thee as fire, and shall consume thee and thy cities, thy land and thy mountaines, all thy woods and thy fruitfull trees shall they burne up with fire. Thy children shall they cary away captive, and looke what thou hast, they shall spoile it, and marre the beauty of thy face.

CHAPTER XVI

Babylon and other places are threatned with plagues that cannot be avoided:

WOE be unto thee, Babylon and Asia, woe be unto thee Egypt and Syria. Gird up your selves with clothes of sacke and haire, bewaile your children, and be sory, for your destruction is at hand. A sword is sent upon you, and who may turne it backe? A fire is sent among you, and who may quench it? Plagues are sent unto you, and what is he that may drive them away? May any man drive away a hungry Lion in the wood? or may any one quench the fire in stubble, when it hath begun to burne? May one turne againe the arrow that is shot of a strong archer? The mightie Lord sendeth the plagues, and who is hee that can drive them away? A fire shall goe foorth from his wrath: and who is he that may quench it? He shall cast lightnings, and who shall not feare? he shall thunder, and who shall not be afraid? The Lord shall threaten, and who shall not be utterly beaten to powder at his presence? The earth quaketh and the foundations thereof, the sea ariseth up with waves from the deepe, and the waves of it are troubled, and the fishes thereof also before the Lord, and before the glorie of his power. For strong is his right hand that bendeth the bow, his arrowes that hee shooteth are sharpe, and shall not misse when they begin to bee shot into the ends of the world. Behold, the plagues are sent, and shall not returne againe, untill they come upon the earth. The fire is kindled, and shall not be put out, till it consume the foundation of the earth. Like as an arrow which is shot of a mightie archer returneth not backward: even so the plagues that shall be sent upon earth, shall not returne againe. Woe is me, woe is me, who will deliver me in those dayes? The beginning of sorrowes, and great mournings, the beginning of famine, and great death: the beginning of warres, and the powers shall stand in feare, the beginning of evils, what shall I doe when these evils shal come? Behold, famine, and plague, tribulation and anguish, are sent as scourges for amendment. But for all these things they shall not turne from their wickednes, nor be alway mindfull of the scourges. Behold, victuals shall be so good cheape upon earth, that they shal think themselves to be in

II. ESDRAS

good case, and even then shall evils growe upon earth, sword, famine, and great confusion. For many of them that dwell upon earth, shall perish of famine, and the other that escape the hunger, shall the sword destroy. And the dead shall be cast out as doung, and there shalbe no man to comfort them, for the earth shall be wasted, and the cities shall be cast downe. There shall be no man left to till the earth, and to sow it. The trees shall give fruite, and who shall gather them? The grapes shall ripe, and who shall treade them? for all places shall be desolate of men. So that one man shall desire to see another, and to heare his voyce. For of a citie there shalbe ten left, and two of the field which shall hide themselves in the thicke groves, and in the clefts of rockes. As in an orchard of olives, upon every tree there are left three or foure olives: or, when as a vineyard is gathered, there are left some clusters of them that diligently seek through the vineyard: even so in those dayes there shalbe three or foure left by them that search their houses with the sword. And the earth shall be laid waste, and the fields therof shal waxe old, and her wayes and all her paths shall grow full of thornes, because no man shall travaile therethrough. The virgins shall mourne having no bridegromes, the women shal mourne having no husbands, their daughters shall mourne having no helpers. In the warres shall their bridegromes bee destroyed, and their husbands shall perish of famine. Heare now these things, and understand them, ye servants of the Lord. Behold the word of the Lord, receive it, beleeve not the gods of whom the Lord spake. Behold, the plagues draw nigh, and are not slacke. As when a woman with childe in the ninth month bringeth forth her son, within two or three honres of her birth great paines compasse her wombe, which paines, when the child commeth forth, they slacke not a moment, even so shall not the plagues bee slacke to come upon the earth, and the world shall mourne, and sorrowes shal come upon it on every side. O my people, Heare my word: make you ready to the battell, and in those evils, be even as pilgrimes upon the earth. He that selleth let him be as hee that fleeth away: and he that buyeth, as one that will loose. He that occupieth merchandize, as he that had no profit by it: and he that buildeth, as hee that shall not dwell therein. He that soweth, as if he should not reape: so also he that planteth the vineyard, as he that shal not gather the grapes. They that marry, as they that shall get no children: and they that marrie not, as the widowers. And therefore they that labour, labour in vaine. For strangers shall reape their fruits, and spoile their goods, overthrowe their houses; and take their children captives, for in captivity and famine shall they

CHAPTER XVI

and with desolation.

The servants of the Lorde must looke for troubles:

II. ESDRAS

CHAPTER XVI

get children. And they that occupy their merchandize with robbery, the more they decke their citties, their houses, their possessions and their owne persons: the more will I be angry with them for their sinne, saith the Lord. Like as an whore envieth a right honest and vertuous woman: so shall righteousnesse hate iniquity, when she decketh her selfe, and shall accuse her, to her face, when he commeth that shall defend him that diligently searcheth out every sinne upon earth. And therfore be yee not like therunto, nor to the workes thereof. For yet a little iniquitie shall be taken away out of the earth, and righteousnesse shall reigne among you. Let not the sinner say that he hath not sinned: for God shall burne coales of fire upon his head, which saith before the Lord God and his glory, I have not sinned. Behold, the Lord knoweth all the workes of men, their imaginations, their thoughts, and their hearts: which spake but the word, let the earth be made, and it was made: let the heaven be made, and it was created. In his word were the starres made, and he knoweth the number of them. He searcheth the deepe, and the treasures thereof, he hath measured the Sea, and what it containeth. He hath shut the Sea in the midst of the waters, and with his word hath he hanged the earth upon the waters. He spreadeth out the heavens like a vault, upon the waters hath he founded it. In the desart hath hee made springs of water, and pooles upon the tops of the mountaines, that the floods might powre downe from the high rockes to water the earth. He made man, and put his heart in the midst of the body, and gave him breath, life, and understanding. Yea and the spirit of Almighty God, which made all things, and searcheth out all hidden things in the secrets of the earth. Surely he knoweth your inventions, and what you thinke in your hearts, even them that sinne, and would hide their sinne. Therefore hath the Lord exactly searched out all your workes, and he will put you all to shame. And when your sinnes are brought foorth yee shalbe ashamed before men, and your owne sinnes shall be your accusers in that day. What will yee doe? or how will yee hide your sinnes before God and his Angels? Behold, God himselfe is the iudge, feare him: leave off from your sinnes, and forget your iniquities to meddle no more with them for ever, so shall God lead you forth, and deliver you from all trouble. For behold, the burning wrath of a great multitude is kindled over you, and they shall take away certaine of you, and feede you being idle with things offered unto idoles. And they that consent unto them shall be had in derision, and in reproch, and troden under foote. For there shall be in every place, and in the next cities a great insurrection upon those that feare

and not hide their sinnes,

II. ESDRAS

the Lord. They shall be like mad men, sparing none, but still spoiling and destroying those that feare the Lord. For they shal waste and take away their goods, and cast them out of their houses. Then shall they be knowen who are my chosen, and they shall be tried, as the gold in the fire: Heare, O yee my beloved, saith the Lord: behold, the dayes of trouble are at hand, but I will deliver you from the same. Be yee not afraid, neither doubt, for God is your guide, and the guide of them who keepe my commaundements, and precepts, saith the Lord God; Let not your sinnes weigh you downe, and let not your iniquities lift up themselves. Woe bee unto them that are bound with their sinnes, and covered with their iniquities: like as a field is covered over with bushes, and the path thereof covered with thornes, that no man may travell through. It is left undressed, and is cast into the fire, to bee consumed therewith.

CHAPTER XVI

but leave them, and they shall be delivered.

TOBIT

CHAPTER I

THE Booke of the wordes of Tobit, sonne of Tobiel, the son of Ananiel, the sonne of Aduel, the sonne of Gabael, of the seed of Asael, of the Tribe of Nephthali, who in the time of Enemessar king of the Assyrians, was led captive out of Thisbe which is at the right hand of that citie, which is called properly Nephthali in Galile above Aser. I Tobit have walked all the dayes of my life in the way of trueth, and iustice, and I did many almes deeds to my brethren, and my nation, who came with me to Nineve into the land of the Assyrians. And when I was in mine owne countrey, in the land of Israel, being but yong, all the tribe of Nephthali my father, fell from the house of Ierusalem, which was chosen out of all the tribes of Israel, that all the tribes should sacrifice there where the Temple of the habitation of the most High was consecrated, and built for all ages. Now all the tribes which together revolted, and the house of my father Nephthali sacrificed unto the heifer Baal. But I alone went

Tobit his stocke, and devotion in his youth,

TOBIT

CHAPTER I

His marriage, And captivitie,

His preferment,

Almes and charitie in burying the dead,

For which he is accused and flieth,

And after returneth to Ninive.

often to Ierusalem at the Feasts, as it was ordeined unto al the people of Israel by an everlasting decree, having the first fruits, and tenths of encrease, with that which was first shorne, and them gave I at the Altar to the Priestes the children of Aaron. The first tenth part of al increase, I gave to the sonnes of Aaron, who ministred at Ierusalem : another tenth part I sold away, and went, and spent it every yeere at Ierusalem. And the third, I gave unto them to whom it was meet, as Debora my fathers mother had commanded mee, because I was left an orphane by my father. Furthermore when I was come to the age of a man, I married Anna of mine owne kinred, and of her I begate Tobias. And when we were caried away captives to Nineve, all my brethren, and those that were of my kinred, did eate of the bread of the Gentiles. But I kept my selfe from eating ; because I remembred God with all my heart. And the most High gave me grace, and favour before Enemessar, so that I was his purveyour. And I went into Media, and left in trust with Gabael, the brother of Gabrias at Rages a citie of Media, ten talents of silver. Now when Enemessar was dead, Sennacherib his sonne reigned in his stead, whose estate was troubled, that I could not goe into Media. And in the time of Enemessar, I gave many almes to my brethren, and gave my bread to the hungry, and my clothes to the naked : and if I saw any of my nation dead, or cast about the walles of Nineve, I buried him. And if the king Sennacherib had slaine any, when hee was come, and fledde from Iudea, I buried them privily, (for in his wrath hee killed many) but the bodies were not found, when they were sought for of the king. And when one of the Ninevites went, and complained of me to the king that I buried them, and hid my selfe: understanding that I was sought for to be put to death, I withdrew my selfe for feare. Then all my goods were forcibly taken away, neither was there any thing left me, besides my wife Anna, and my sonne Tobias. And there passed not five and fiftie dayes before two of his sonnes killed him, and they fled into the mountaines of Ararath, and Sarchedonus his sonne reigned in his stead, who appointed over his fathers accounts, and over all his affaires, Achiacharus my brother Anaels sonne. And Achiacharus entreating for me, I returned to Nineve : now Achiacharus was Cup-bearer, and keeper of the Signet, and Steward, and overseer of the accounts : and Sarchedonus appointed him next unto him : and hee was my brothers sonne.

TOBIT

CHAPTER II

CHAPTER II

NOW when I was come home againe, and my wife Anna was restored unto me, with my sonne Tobias, in the feast of Pentecost, which is the holy Feast of the seven weekes, there was a good dinner prepared me, in the which I sate down to eate. And when I saw abundance of meate, I sayd to my sonne, Goe and bring what poore man soever thou shalt finde out of our brethren, who is mindfull of the Lord, and loe, I tarie for thee. But he came againe and said, Father, one of our nation is strangled, and is cast out in the market place. Then before I had tasted of any meate, I start up and tooke him up into a roume, untill the going downe of the Sunne. Then I returned and washed my selfe, and ate my meate in heavinesse, remembring that prophesie of Amos, as hee said; *Tobit leaveth his meate to bury the dead,*

Your feasts shall be turned into mourning,
And all your mirth into lamentation.

Therefore I wept: and after the going downe of the Sunne, I went and made a grave, and buried him. But my neighbours mocked me, and said, This man is not yet afraide to be put to death for this matter, who fledde away, and yet loe, he burieth the dead againe. The same night also I returned from the buriall, and slept by the wall of my court yard, being polluted, and my face was uncovered: and I knewe not that there were Sparrowes in the wall, and mine eyes being open, the Sparrowes muted warme doung into mine eyes, and a whitenesse came in mine eyes, and I went to the Physicians, but they helped me not: moreover Achiacharus did nourish mee, untill I went into Elymais. And my wife Anna did take womens workes to doe. And when shee had sent them home to the owners, they payd her wages, and gave her also besides a kid. And when it was in mine house, and beganne to crie, I said unto her, From whence is this kidde? is it not stollen? render it to the owners, for it is not lawfull to eate any thing that is stollen. But shee replyed upon me, It was given for a gift more then the wages: Howbeit I did not beleeve her, but bade her render it to the owners: and I was abashed at her. But she replyed upon me, Where are thine almes, and thy righteous deedes? behold, thou and all thy workes are knowen. *and becommeth blinde.*

His wife taketh in worke to get her living.

Her husband and she fall out about a kidde.

71

TOBIT

CHAPTER III

Tobit grieved with his wives taunts, prayeth.

THEN I being grieved, did weepe, and in my sorrowe prayed, saying, O Lord, thou art iust and all thy workes, and all thy wayes are mercie and trueth, and thou iudgest truely and iustly for ever. Remember me, and looke on me, punish me not for my sinnes and ignorances, and the sinnes of my fathers, who have sinned before thee. For they obeyed not thy commandements, wherefore thou hast delivered us for a spoile, and unto captivitie, and unto death, and for a proverbe of reproch to all the nations among whom we are dispersed. And now thy iudgments are many and true: Deale with me according to my sinnes, and my fathers: because we have not kept thy commandements, neither have walked in trueth before thee. Now therefore deale with me as seemeth best unto thee, and command my spirit to be taken from me, that I may be dissolved, and become earth: for it is profitable for me to die, rather then to live, because I have heard false reproches, and have much sorow: command therfore that I may now be delivered out of this distresse, and goe into the everlasting place: turne not thy face away from me. It came to passe the same day, that in Ecbatane a citie of Media, Sara the daughter of Raguel, was also reproched by her fathers maides, because that she had bin maried to seven husbands, whom Asmodeus the evill spirit had killed, before they had lien with her. Doest thou not knowe, said they, that thou hast strangled thine husbands? thou hast had already seven husbands, neither wast thou named after any of them. Wherefore doest thou beate us for them? If they be dead, goe thy wayes after them, let us never see of thee either sonne or daughter. When she heard these things, she was very sorowful, so that she thought to have strangled her selfe, and she said, I am the onely daughter of my father, and if I doe this, it shall bee a reproch unto him, and I shall bring his old age with

Sara reproched by her fathers maides, prayeth also.

sorow unto the grave. Then she prayed toward the window, and said, Blessed art thou, O Lord my God, and thine holy and glorious Name is blessed, and honourable for ever, let al thy works praise thee for ever. And now, O Lord, I set mine eyes and my face toward thee, and say, Take me out of the earth, that I may heare no more the reproch. Thou knowest, Lord, that I am pure from all sinne with man, and that I never polluted my name, nor the name of my father in the land of my captivitie: I am the onely daughter of my father, neither hath he any child to bee his heire, neither any neere kinseman, nor any sonne of his alive, to whome I may keepe my selfe for a wife: my seven husbands are already

TOBIT

dead, and why should I live? but if it please not thee that I should die, command some regard to be had of me, and pitie taken of me, that I heare no more reproch. So the prayers of them both were heard before the Maiesty of the great God. And Raphael was sent to heale them both, that is, to scale away the whitenesse of Tobits eyes, and to give Sara the daughter of Raguel, for a wife to Tobias the sonne of Tobit, and to bind Asmodeus the evill spirit, because she belongeth to Tobias by right of inheritance. The selfe same time came Tobit home, and entred into his house, and Sara, the daughter of Raguel came downe from her upper chamber.

CHAPTER III

An Angel is sent to helpe them both.

CHAPTER IIII

IN that day Tobit remembred the money, which he had committed to Gabael in Rages of Media, and said with himselfe, I have wished for death, wherefore doe I not call for my sonne Tobias, that I may signifie to him of the money before I die. And when he had called him, he said; My sonne, when I am dead, bury me, and despise not thy mother, but honour her all the dayes of thy life, and doe that which shall please her, and greive her not. Remember, my sonne, that shee saw many dangers for thee, when thou wast in her wombe, and when shee is dead, bury her by me in one grave. My sonne, be mindfull of the Lord our God all thy dayes, and let not thy will be set to sinne, or to transgresse his Commandements: doe uprightly all thy life long, and follow not the wayes of unrighteousnesse. For if thou deale truely, thy doings shall prosperously succeed to thee, and to all them that live iustly. Give almes of thy substance, and when thou givest almes, let not thine eye be envious, neither turne thy face from any poore, and the face of God shall not be turned away from thee. If thou hast abundance, give almes accordingly: if thou have but a litle, be not afraid to give according to that litle. For thou layest up a good treasure for thy selfe against the day of necessitie. Because that almes doth deliver from death, and suffereth not to come into darknesse. For almes is a good gift unto all that give it, in the sight of the most High. Beware of all whoredome, my sonne, and chiefely take a wife of the seed of thy fathers, and take not a strange woman to wife, which is not of thy fathers tribe: for we are the children of the Prophets, Noe, Abraham, Isaak, and Iacob: remember, my sonne, that our fathers from the beginning, even that they all maried wives of their owne kinred, and were blessed in their children, and their seede shall inherite

Tobit giveth instructions to his sonne Tobias,

5 : K

TOBIT

CHAPTER IIII

and telleth him of money left with Gabael in Media.

the land. Now therefore my sonne, love thy brethren, and despise not in thy heart thy brethren, the sonnes and daughters of thy people, in not taking a wife of them: for in pride is destruction and much trouble, and in lewdnesse is decay, and great want: for lewdnesse is the mother of famine. Let not the wages of any man, which hath wrought for thee, tary with thee, but give him it out of hand: for if thou serve God he will also repay thee: be circumspect, my sonne, in all things thou doest, and be wise in all thy conversation. Doe that to no man which thou hatest: drinke not wine to make thee drunken; neither let drunkennesse goe with thee in thy iourney. Give of thy bread to the hungry, and of thy garments to them that are naked, and according to thine abundance give almes, and let not thine eye be envious, when thou givest almes. Powre out thy bread on the buriall of the iust, but give nothing to the wicked. Aske counsell of all that are wise, and despise not any counsell that is profitable. Blesse the Lord thy God alway, and desire of him that thy wayes may be directed, and that all thy pathes, and counsels may prosper: for every nation hath not counsell, but the Lord himselfe giveth all good things, and hee humbleth whom he will, as he will; now therefore my sonne, remember my commandements, neither let them be put out of thy minde. And now I signifie this to thee, that I committed tenne talents to Gabael the sonne of Gabrias at Rages in Media. And feare not my sonne, that we are made poore, for thou hast much wealth, if thou feare God, and depart from all sinne, and doe that which is pleasing in his sight.

CHAPTER V

Yong Tobias seeketh a guide into Media.

The Angel will goe with him,

TOBIAS then answered and said, Father, I will doe all things which thou hast commanded me. But how can I receive the money, seeing I know him not? Then he gave him the handwriting, and said unto him, Seeke thee a man which may goe with thee whiles I yet live, and I will give him wages, and goe, and receive the money. Therefore when he went to seeke a man, he found Raphael that was an Angell. But he knew not; and he said unto him, Canst thou goe with me to Rages? and knowest thou those places well? To whom the Angel said, I will goe with thee, and I know the way well: for I have lodged with our brother Gabael. Then Tobias said unto him, Tary for me till I tell my father. Then he said unto him, Goe and tary not; so he went in, and said to his father; Behold, I have found one, which wil goe with me. Then he said, Call him unto me, that I

TOBIT

may know of what tribe he is, and whether hee be a trustie man to goe with thee. So he called him, and he came in, and they saluted one another. Then Tobit said unto him, Brother, shew me of what tribe and family thou art. To whom hee said, Doest thou seeke for a tribe or family, or an hired man to goe with thy sonne? Then Tobit said unto him, I would know, brother, thy kinred, and name. Then he said, I am Azarias, the sonne of Ananias the great, and of thy brethren. Then Tobit said, Thou art welcome brother, be not now angry with mee, because I have enquired to know thy tribe, and thy family, for thou art my brother, of an honest and good stocke: for I know Ananias, and Ionathas sonnes of that great Samaias: as we went together to Ierusalem to worship, and offered the first borne, and the tenths of the fruits, and they were not seduced with the errour of our brethren: my brother, thou art of a good stocke. But tell me, what wages shall I give thee? wilt thou a drachme a day? and things necessary as to my owne sonne? Yea moreover, if ye returne safe, I will adde some thing to the wages. So they were well pleased. Then said he to Tobias; Prepare thy selfe for the iourney, and God send you a good iourney. And when his sonne had prepared all things for the iourney, his father said; Goe thou with this man, and God which dwelleth in heaven prosper your iourney, and the Angel of God keepe you company. So they went foorth both, and the yong mans dogge with them. But Anna his mother wept, and said to Tobit, Why hast thou sent away our sonne? is hee not the staffe of our hand, in going in and out before us? Be not greedy (to adde) money to money: but let it bee as refuse in respect of our childe. For that which the Lord hath given us to live with, doeth suffice us. Then said Tobit to her, Take no care my sister, he shal returne in safety, and thine eyes shall see him. For the good Angel will keepe him company, and his iourney shall be prosperous, and he shall returne safe. Then she made an end of weeping.

CHAPTER V

and saith he is his kinseman.

Tobias and the Angel depart together.

But his mother is grieved for her sonnes departing.

CHAPTER VI

AND as they went on their iourney, they came in the evening to the river Tigris, and they lodged there. And when the yong man went downe to wash himselfe, a fish leaped out of the river, and would have devoured him. Then the Angel said unto him, Take the fish; and the yong man layd hold of the fish, and drew it to land. To whom the Angel said, Open the fish, and take the heart, and the liver and the gall, and put them up safely. So the yong man did as the Angel commaunded him, and

The Angel biddeth Tobias to take the liver, heart and gall out of a fish,

TOBIT

CHAPTER VI

when they had rosted the fish, they did eate it: then they both went on their way, till they drew neere to Ecbatane. Then the yong man saide to the Angel; Brother Azarias, to what use is the heart, and the liver, and the gall of the fish? And he said unto him, Touching the heart and the liver, if a devil, or an evil spirit trouble any, we must make a smoke thereof before the man or the woman, and the party shalbe no more vexed. As for the gall it is good to anoint a man that hath whitenesse in his eyes, and he shalbe healed. And when they were come neere to Rages; the Angel said to the yong man, Brother, to day wee shall lodge with Raguel, who is thy cousin; hee also hath one onely daughter, named Sara, I wil speake for her, that she may be given thee for a wife. For to thee doth the right of her appertaine, seeing thou onely art of her kinred. And the maide is faire and wise, now therefore heare me, and I wil speake to her father, and when wee returne from Rages, we will celebrate the mariage: for I know that Raguel cannot marry her to another according to the Law of Moses, but he shalbe guiltie of death, because the right of inheritance doeth rather appertaine to thee, then to any other. Then the yong man answered the Angel, I have heard, brother Azarias, that this maide hath beene given to seven men, who all died in the marriage chamber: and now I am the onely sonne of my father, and I am afraid, lest if I goe in unto her, I die, as the other before; for a wicked spirit loveth her, which hurteth no body, but those which come unto her; wherefore I also feare, lest I die, and bring my fathers and my mothers life (because of me) to the grave with sorrow, for they have no other sonne to bury them. Then the Angel said unto him, Doest thou not remember the precepts, which thy father gave thee, that thou shouldest marrie a wife of thine owne kinred? wherefore heare me, O my brother, for she shall be given thee to wife, and make thou no reckoning of the evil spirit, for this same night shall shee be given thee in mariage. And when thou shalt come into the mariage chamber, thou shalt take the ashes of perfume, and shalt lay upon them, some of the heart, and liver of the fish, and shalt make a smoke with it. And the devill shall smell it, and flee away, and never come againe any more: but when thou shalt come to her, rise up both of you, and pray to God, which is mercifull, who will have pity on you, and save you: feare not, for shee is appointed unto thee from the beginning; and thou shalt preserve her, and shee shall goe with thee. Moreover I suppose that shee shall beare thee children. Now when Tobias had heard these things, he loved her, and his heart was effectually ioyned to her.

And to marry Sara the daughter of Raguel;

And teacheth how to drive the wicked spirit away.

TOBIT

CHAPTER VII

AND when they were come to Ecbatane, they came to the house of Raguel; and Sara met them: and after that they had saluted one another, shee brought them into the house. Then sayd Raguel to Edna his wife, How like is this yong man to Tobit my cousin? And Raguel asked them, From whence are you, brethren? To whom they said, We are of the sonnes of Nephthali, which are captives in Nineve. Then hee said to them, Doe yee know Tobit our kinseman? And they said, We know him. Then said hee, Is he in good health? And they said, Hee is both alive, and in good health: And Tobias sayd, He is my father. Then Raguel leaped up, and kissed him, and wept, and blessed him, and said unto him, Thou art the sonne of an honest and good man: but when he had heard that Tobit was blinde, he was sorowfull, and wept. And likewise Edna his wife, and Sara his daughter wept. Moreover, they entertained them cheerefully, and after that they had killed a ramme of the flocke, they set store of meat on the table. Then said Tobias to Raphael, Brother Azarias, speak of those things, of which thou diddest talke in the way, and let this businesse be dispatched. So he communicated the matter with Raguel, and Raguel said to Tobias, Eate and drinke, and make merry: for it is meet that thou shouldest marry my daughter: neverthelesse I will declare unto thee the trueth. I have given my daughter in mariage to seven men, who died that night they came in unto her: neverthelesse for the present be merry: But Tobias said, I will eate nothing here, till we agree and sweare one to another. Raguel said, Then take her from henceforth according to the manner, for thou art her cousin, and she is thine, and the mercifull God give you good successe in all things. Then he called his daughter Sara, and she came to her father, and hee tooke her by the hand, and gave her to be wife to Tobias, saying, Behold, take her after the Law of Moses, and leade her away to thy father: And he blessed them, and called Edna his wife, and tooke paper, and did write an instrument of covenants, and sealed it. Then they began to eate. After Raguel called his wife Edna, and said unto her, Sister, prepare another chamber, and bring her in thither. Which when she had done as hee had bidden her, she brought her thither, and she wept, and she received the teares of her daughter, and said unto her, Be of good comfort, my daughter, the Lord of Heaven and earth give thee ioy for this thy sorow: be of good comfort, my daughter.

TOBIT

CHAPTER VIII

CHAPTER VIII

Tobias driveth the wicked spirit away, as hee was taught.

He and his wife rise up to pray.

Raguel thought he was dead:

But finding him alive, praiseth God,

and maketh a wedding feast.

AND when they had supped, they brought Tobias in unto her. And as he went, he remembred the wordes of Raphael, and tooke the ashes of the perfumes, and put the heart, and the liver of the fish thereupon, and made a smoke therewith. The which smell, when the evill spirit had smelled, hee fled into the outmost parts of Egypt, and the Angel bound him. And after that they were both shut in together, Tobias rose out of the bed and said, Sister, arise, and let us pray, that God would have pitie on us. Then began Tobias to say, Blessed art thou, O God of our fathers, and blessed is thy holy and glorious Name for ever, let the heavens blesse thee, and all thy creatures. Thou madest Adam, and gavest him Eve his wife for an helper and stay: of them came mankind: thou hast said, It is not good that man should bee alone, let us make unto him an aide like to himselfe. And now, O Lord, I take not this my sister for lust, but uprightly: therefore mercifully ordeine, that wee may become aged together. And she said with him, Amen. So they slept both that night, and Raguel arose, and went and made a grave saying, I feare lest he be dead. But when Raguel was come into his house, he said unto his wife Edna, Send one of the maids, and let her see, whether he be alive: if he be not, that we may bury him, and no man know it. So the maid opened the doore and went in, and found them both asleepe, and came forth, and told them, that he was alive. Then Raguel praised God, and said, O God, thou art worthy to be praised with all pure and holy praise: therefore let thy Saints praise thee with all thy creatures, and let all thine Angels and thine elect praise thee for ever. Thou art to be praised, for thou hast made mee ioyfull, and that is not come to me, which I suspected: but thou hast dealt with us according to thy great mercie. Thou art to be praised, because thou hast had mercie of two, that were the onely begotten children of their fathers, grant them mercy, O Lord, and finish their life in health, with ioy and mercie. Then Raguel bade his servants to fill the grave. And hee kept the wedding feast fourteene dayes. For before the dayes of the mariage were finished, Raguel had said unto him by an othe, that he should not depart, till the fourteene dayes of the mariage were expired, and then he should take the halfe of his goods, and goe in safetie to his father, and should have the rest when I and my wife be dead.

TOBIT

CHAPTER IX

THEN Tobias called Raphael, and said unto him, Brother Azarias, Take with thee a servant, and two camels, and go to Rages of Media to Gabael, and bring me the money, and bring him to the wedding. For Raguel hath sworne that I shall not depart. But my father counteth the dayes, and if I tarie long, he will be very sorie. So Raphael went out and lodged with Gabael, and gave him the handwriting, who brought forth bags, which were sealed up, and gave them to him. And earely in the morning they went forth both together, and came to the wedding, and Tobias blessed his wife.

[margin: CHAPTER IX. Tobias sendeth the Angel unto Gabael for the money. The Angel bringeth it, and Gabael to the wedding.]

CHAPTER X

NOWE Tobit his father counted every day, and when the dayes of the iourney were expired, and they came not: then Tobit said, Are they detained? or is Gabael dead? and there is no man to give him the money? Therefore he was very sory. Then his wife said to him, My sonne is dead, seeing hee stayeth long, and she beganne to bewaile him, and said, Now I care for nothing, my sonne, since I have let thee goe, the light of mine eyes. To whom Tobit said, Hold thy peace, take no care; for he is safe. But she said, Hold thy peace, and deceive me not: my sonne is dead, and she went out every day into the way which they went, and did eate no meat on the day time, and ceased not whole nights, to bewaile her sonne Tobias, untill the foureteene dayes of the wedding were expired, which Raguel had sworne, that he should spend there: Then Tobias said to Raguel, Let me goe, for my father, and my mother look no more to see me. But his father in law said unto him, Tary with me, and I will send to thy father, and they shall declare unto him, how things goe with thee. But Tobias said, No: but let me goe to my father. Then Raguel arose and gave him Sara his wife, and halfe his goods, servants, and cattell, and money. And hee blessed them, and sent them away, saying, The God of heaven give you a prosperous iourney, my children. And he said to his daughter, Honour thy father and thy mother in law, which are now thy parents, that I may heare good report of thee: and hee kissed her. Edna also said to Tobias, The Lord of heaven restore thee, my deare brother, and grant that I may see thy children of my daughter Sara before

[margin: Tobit and his wife long for their sonne. She will not be comforted by her husband. Raguel sendeth Tobias and his wife away, with halfe their goods, and blesseth them.]

TOBIT

CHAPTER X — I die, that I may reioyce before the Lord: behold, I commit my daughter unto thee of speciall trust, wherefore doe not entreate her evill.

CHAPTER XI

AFTER these things Tobias went his way, praising God that he had given him a prosperous iourney, and blessed Raguel, and Edna his wife, and went on his way till they drew neere unto Nineve. Then Raphael said to Tobias, Thou knowest brother, how thou didst leave thy father. Let us haste before thy wife, and prepare the house. And take in thine hand the gall of the fish: so they went their way, and the dog went after them.

Tobits mother spieth her sonne comming. Now Anna sate looking about towards the way for her sonne. And when she espied him comming, she said to his father, Behold, thy sonne commeth, and the man that went with him. Then said Raphael, I know, Tobias, that thy father will open his eyes. Therefore annoint thou his eies with the gall, and being pricked therewith he shall rub, and the whitenesse shall fall away, and he shall see thee. Then Anna ran forth, and fell upon the necke of her sonne, and said unto him, Seeing I have seene thee my sonne, from henceforth, I am content to die, and they wept both. Tobit

His father meeteth him at the doore, and recovereth his sight. also went forth toward the doore, and stumbled: but his sonne ran unto him, and tooke hold of his father, and he strake of the gall on his fathers eyes, saying, Be of good hope, my father. And when his eyes beganne to smart, he rubbed them. And the whitenesse pilled away from the corners of his eyes, and when he saw his sonne, he fell upon his necke. And he wept, and said, Blessed

Hee praiseth God, art thou, O God, and blessed is thy Name for ever, and blessed are all thine holy Angels: for thou hast scourged, and hast taken pitie on me: for behold, I see my sonne Tobias. And his sonne went in reioycing, and told his father the great things that had happened to him in Media. Then Tobit went out to meete his daughter in law at the gate of Ninive, reioycing and praysing God: and they which saw him goe, marveiled because he had received

And welcommeth his daughter in Lawe. his sight. But Tobit gave thankes before them: because God had mercy on him. And when hee came neere to Sara his daughter in Law, hee blessed her, saying, Thou art welcome daughter: God be blessed which hath brought thee unto us, and blessed be thy father and thy mother; And there was ioy amongst all his brethren which were at Nineve. And Achiacharus, and Nasbas his brothers sonne came. And Tobias wedding was kept seven dayes with great ioy.

TOBIT

CHAPTER XII

THEN Tobit called his son Tobias, and said unto him, My sonne, see that the man have his wages, which went with thee, and thou must give him more. And Tobias said unto him, O father, it is no harme to me to give him halfe of those things which I have brought. For he hath brought me againe to thee in safety, and made whole my wife, and brought mee the money, and likewise healed thee. Then the old man said: It is due unto him. So he called the Angell, and he said unto him, Take halfe of all that yee have brought, and goe away in safety. Then he tooke them both apart, and sayd unto them, Blesse God, praise him, and magnifie him, and praise him for the things which he hath done unto you in the sight of all that live. It is good to praise God and exalt his name, and honorably to shew forth the works of God, therfore be not slacke to praise him. It is good to keepe close the secret of a King, but it is honorable to reveale the works of God: do that which is good, and no evill shall touch you. Praier is good with fasting, and almes and righteousnesse: a little with righteousnes is better then much with unrighteousnesse: it is better to give almes then to lay up gold. For almes doth deliver from death, and shall purge away all sinne. Those that exercise almes, and righteousnesse, shall be filled with life. But they that sinne are enemies to their owne life. Surely I will keep close nothing from you. For I said, it was good to keepe close the secret of a King, but that it was honorable to reveale the works of God. Now therefore, when thou didst pray, and Sara thy daughter in Law, I did bring the remembrance of your prayers before the holy one, and when thou didst bury the dead, I was with thee likewise. And when thou didst not delay to rise up, and leave thy dinner to go and cover the dead, thy good deede was not hidde from me: but I was with thee. And now God hath sent mee to beale thee, and Sara thy daughter in law. I am Raphael one of the seven holy Angels, which present the prayers of the Saints, and which go in and out before the glory of the Holy one. Then they were both troubled, and fel upon their faces: for they feared. But he said unto them, Fcare not, for it shall go well with you, praise God therefore. For not of any favour of mine, but by the will of our God I came, wherefore praise him for ever. All these daies I did appeare unto you, but I did neither eat nor drinke, but you did see a vision. Now therefore give God thanks: for I go up to him that sent me, but write all things which are done, in a booke. And when they rose, they

Tobit offereth halfe to the Angel for his paines; But he calleth them both aside, and exhorteth them, and telleth them that he was an Angel, and was seene no more.

TOBIT

CHAPTER XII — saw him no more. Then they confessed the great and wonderfull workes of God, and how the Angel of the Lord had appeared unto them.

CHAPTER XIII

THEN Tobit wrote a prayer of reioycing, and said,

The thankesgiving unto God, which Tobit wrote.

BLESSED be God that liveth for ever, and blessed be his kingdome:
For he doeth scourge, and hath mercy:
Hee leadeth downe to hell, and bringeth up againe:
Neither is there any that can avoid his hand.
Confesse him before the Gentiles, ye children of Israel:
For he hath scattered us among them.
There declare his greatnesse,
And extoll him before all the living,
For he is our Lord,
And he is the God our father for ever:
And he wil scourge us for our iniquities,
And will have mercy againe, and will gather us out of all nations,
Among whom he hath scattered us.
If you turne to him with your whole heart, and with your whole minde,
And deale uprightly before him,
Then will hee turne unto you,
And will not hide his face from you:
Therefore see what he will doe with you,
And confesse him with your whole mouth,
And praise the Lord of might,
And extoll the everlasting King:
In the land of my captivitie doe I praise him,
And declare his might and maiesty to a sinnefull nation:
O yee sinners turne, and doe iustice before him:
Who can tell if he will accept you,
And have mercy on you?
I wil extoll my God,
And my soule shal praise the King of heaven,
And shal reioyce in his greatnesse.
Let all men speake, and let all praise him for his righteousnesse.
O Ierusalem the holy Citie,
He will scourge thee for thy childrens workes,
And will have mercy againe on the sonnes of the righteous.

TOBIT

Give praise to the Lord, for hee is good: **CHAPTER**
And praise the everlasting King, **XIII**
That his Tabernacle may bee builded in thee againe with ioy:
And let him make ioyfull there in thee, those that are captives,
And love in thee for ever those that are miserable.
Many nations shall come from farre to the Name of the Lord God,
With gifts in their hands, even giftes to the King of heaven
All generations shall praise thee with great ioy.
Cursed are all they which hate thee,
And blessed shall all be, which love thee for ever.
Reioyce and be glad for the children of the iust:
For they shall be gathered together, and shall blesse the Lord of the iust.
O blessed are they which love thee, for they shall reioyce in thy peace:
Blessed are they which have been sorowfull for all thy scourges,
For they shal reioyce for thee, when they have seene all thy glory,
And shalbe glad for ever.
Let my soule blesse God the great King.
For Ierusalem shall be built up with Saphires, and Emerauds, and precious stone:
Thy walles and towres, and battlements with pure golde.
And the streets of Ierusalem shal be paved with Berill, and Carbuncle, and stones of Ophir.
And all her streets shall say, Halleluiah,
And they shall praise him, saying, Blessed be God
Which hath extolled it for ever.

CHAPTER XIIII

SO Tobit made an ende of praising God. And he was eight and fifty yeeres olde when hee lost his sight, which was restored to him after eight yeeres, and he gave almes, and he increased in the feare of the Lord God, and praised him. And when he was very aged, hee called his sonne, and the sixe sons of his sonne, and said to him, My sonne, take thy children; for behold, I am aged, and am ready to depart out of this life. Goe into Media, my sonne, for I surely beleeve those things which Ionas the Prophet spake of Nineve, that it shall be overthrowen, Tobit giveth instructions to his sonne,

TOBIT

CHAPTER XIIII

and that for a time peace shal rather be in Media, and that our brethren shall lie scattered in the earth from that good land, and Ierusalem shall be desolate, and the house of God in it shalbe burned, and shall be desolate for a time: and that againe God will have mercie on them, and bring them againe into the land where they shall build a Temple, but not like to the first, untill the time of that age be fulfilled, and afterward they shall returne from all places of their captivitie, and build up Ierusalem gloriously, and the house of God shall be built in it for ever, with a glorious building, as the prophets have spoken thereof. And all nations shall turne, and feare the Lord God truely, and shall burie their idoles. So shall all nations praise the Lord, and his people shal confesse God, and the Lord shall exalt his people, and all those which love the Lord God in trueth and iustice, shall reioyce, *Specially to leave Nineve.* shewing mercie to our brethren. And now, my sonne, depart out of Nineve, because that those things which the Prophet Ionas spake, shall surely come to passe. But keepe thou the Law and the Commandements, and shew thy selfe mercifull and iust, that it may goe well with thee. And burie me decently, and thy mother with me, but tarie no longer at Nineve. Remember, my sonne, how Aman handled Achiacharus that brought him up, how out of light he brought him into darkenes, and how he rewarded him againe: yet Achiacharus was saved, but the other had his reward, for hee went downe into darkenesse. Manasses gave almes, and escaped the snares of death which they had set for *Hee and his wife die, and are buried.* him: but Aman fell into the snare and perished. Wherefore now, my sonne, consider what almes doeth, and how righteousnesse doth deliver. When he had said these things, he gave up the ghost in the bed, being an hundred, and eight and fiftie yeeres *Tobias removeth to Ecbatane,* old, and he buried him honourably. And when Anna his mother was dead, he buried her with his father: but Tobias departed with his wife and children to Ecbatane, to Raguel his father in law: where hee became old with honour, and hee buried his father and mother in lawe honourably, and hee inherited their substance, *and there died, after hee had heard of the destruction of Nineve.* and his father Tobits. And he died at Ecbatane in Media, being an hundred and seven and twentie yeeres old. But before he died, he heard of the destruction of Nineve, which was taken by Nabuchodonosor and Assuerus: and before his death hee reioyced over Nineve.

IUDETH

IUDETH

CHAPTER I

IN the twelfth yeere of the reigne of Nabuchodo-nosor, who reigned in Nineve the great citie, (in the dayes of Arphaxad, which reigned over the Medes in Ecbatane, and built in Ecbatane walles round about of stones hewen, three cubites broad, and sixe cubites long, and made the height of the wall seventy cubites, and the breadth thereof fiftie cubites: and set the towers thereof upon the gates of it, an hundred cubites high, and the breadth thereof in the foundation threescore cubites. And he made the gates thereof, even gates that were raised to the height of seventie cubites, and the breadth of them was fourtie cubites, for the going foorth of his mightie armies, and for the setting in aray of his footmen.) Even in those dayes, king Nabuchodonosor made warre with king Arphaxad in the great plaine, which is the plaine in the borders of Ragau. And there came unto him, all they that dwelt in the hill countrey, and all that dwelt by Euphrates, and Tigris, and Hydaspes, and the plaine of Arioch the king of the Elimeans, and very many nations of the sonnes of Chelod, assembled themselves to the battell. Then Nabuchodonosor king of the Assyrians, sent unto all that dwelt in Persia, and to all that dwelt Westward, and to those that dwelt in Cilicia, and Damascus and Libanus, and Antilibanus, and to all that dwelt upon the Sea coast, and to those amongst the nations that were of Carmel, and Galaad, and the higher Galile, and the great plaine of Esdrelon, and to all that were in Samaria, and the cities thereof: and beyond Iordan unto Ierusalem, and Betane, and Chellus, and Kades, and the river of Egypt, and Taphnes, and Ramesse, and all the land of Gesem, untill you come beyond Tanis, and Memphis, and to all the inhabitants of Egypt, untill you come to the borders of Ethiopia. But all the inhabitants of the land made light of the commandement of Nabuchodonosor king of the

Arphaxad doeth fortifie Ecbatane.

Nabuchodonosor maketh warre against him,

and craveth aide.

85

IUDETH

CHAPTER I

Hee threatneth those that would not aide him,

Assyrians, neither went they with him to the battell: for they were not afraid of him: yea he was before them as one man, and they sent away his Ambassadours from them without effect, and with disgrace. Therefore Nabuchodonosor was very angry with all this countrey, and sware by his throne and kingdome, that hee would surely be avenged upon all those coasts of Cilicia, and Damascus, and Syria, and that he would slay with the sword all the inhabitants of the land of Moab, and the children of Ammon, and all Iudea, and all that were in Egypt, till you come to the borders of the two Seas. Then he marched in battell aray with his power against king Arphaxad in the seventeenth yeere, and he prevailed in his battell: for he overthrew all the power of Arphaxad, and all his horsemen and all his chariots, and became Lord of his cities, and came unto Ecbatane, and tooke the towers, and spoiled the streetes thereof, and turned the beauty thereof into shame.

and killeth Arphaxad,

Hee tooke also Arphaxad in the mountaines of Ragau, and smote him through with his dartes, and destroyed him utterly that day.

and returneth to Nineve.

So he returned afterward to Nineve, both he and all his company of sundry nations: being a very great multitude of men of warre, and there he tooke his ease and banketted, both he and his armie an hundred and twenty dayes.

CHAPTER II

AND in the eighteenth yeere, the two and twentieth day of the first month, there was talke in the house of Nabuchodonosor king of the Assyrians, that he should as he said avenge himselfe on all the earth. So he called unto him all his officers, and all his nobles, and communicated with them his secret counsell, and concluded the afflicting of the whole earth out of his owne mouth. Then they decreed to destroy all flesh that did not obey the commaundement of his mouth. And when he had ended his counsell, Nabuchodonosor king of the Assyrians called Olofernes the chiefe captaine of his army, which was next unto him, and said unto him, Thus saith the great king, the Lord of the whole earth: Behold, thou shalt goe forth from my presence, and take with thee men that trust in their owne strength, of footemen an hundred and twenty thousand, and the number of horses with their riders twelve thousand. And thou shalt goe against all the West countrey, because they disobeyed my commandement. And thou shalt declare unto them that they prepare for me earth and water: for I will goe forth in my wrath against them, and will cover the whole face of the earth with the feete of mine armie,

Olofernes is appointed generall,

IUDETH

and I will give them for a spoile unto them. So that their slaine shall fill their vallies, and brookes, and the river shall be filled with their dead, til it overflow. And I will lead them captives to the utmost parts of all the earth. Thou therefore shalt goe foorth, and take before hand for me all their coasts, and if they will yeeld themselves unto thee, thou shalt reserve them for me till the day of their punishment. But concerning them that rebell, let not thine eye spare them: but put them to the slaughter, and spoile them wheresoever thou goest. For as I live, and by the power of my kingdome, whatsoever I have spoken, that will I doe by mine hand. And take thou heede that thou transgresse none of the Commaundements of thy Lord, but accomplish them fully, as I have commaunded thee, and deferre not to doe them. Then Olofernes went foorth from the presence of his Lord, and called all the governours and Captaines, and the officers of the army of Assur. And he mustered the chosen men for the battell, as his Lord had commaunded him, unto an hundred and twenty thousand, and twelve thousand archers on Horsebacke. And he ranged them as a great army is ordered for the warre. And he tooke Camels, and Asses for their cariages a very great number, and sheepe, and Oxen, and Goates without number, for their provision, and plenty of vittaile for every man of the army, and very much gold, and silver, out of the Kings house. Then he went foorth and all his power to go before King Nabuchodonosor in the voyage, and to cover al the face of the earth Westward with their charets, and horsemen, and their chosen footmen. A great multitude also of sundry countries came with them, like locusts, and like the sand of the earth: for the multitude was without number. And they went foorth of Nineve, three dayes iourney toward the plaine of Bectileth, and pitched from Bectileth neere the mountaine, which is at the left hand of the upper Cilicia. Then he tooke all his armie, his footmen, and horsemen and chariots, and went from thence into the hill countrey, and destroyed Phud, and Lud: and spoiled all the children of Rasses, and the children of Ismael, which were toward the wildernesse at the South of the land of the Chellians. Then he went over Euphrates, and went through Mesopotamia, and destroyed all the high cities that were upon the river Arbonai, till you come to the sea. And hee tooke the borders of Cilicia, and killed all that resisted him, and came to the borders of Iapheth, which were toward the South, over against Arabia. He compassed also all the children of Madian, and burnt up their tabernacles, and spoiled their sheepcoats. Then hee went downe into the plaine of Damascus in the time of

CHAPTER II

and charged to spare none, that will not yeeld.

His armie and provision,

the places which he wonne and wasted, as he went.

IUDETH

CHAPTER II

wheat-harvest, and burnt up all their fieldes, and destroyed their flockes, and heards, also he spoiled their cities, and utterly wasted their countreys, and smote all their yong men with the edge of the sword. Therefore the feare and dread of him, fell upon all the inhabitants of the sea coastes, which were in Sidon and Tyrus, and them that dwelt in Sur, and Ocina, and all that dwelt in Iemnaan, and they that dwelt in Azotus, and Aschalon feared him greatly.

CHAPTER III

They of the Sea-coasts entreat for peace.

SO they sent Embassadours unto him, to treat of peace, saying, Behold, we the servants of Nabuchodonosor the great king lie before thee; use us as shall be good in thy sight. Behold, our houses, and all our places, and all our fieldes of wheat, and flockes, and heards, and all the lodges of our tents, lie before thy face: use them as it pleaseth thee. Behold, even our cities and the inhabitants thereof are thy servants, come and deale with them, as seemeth good unto thee. So the men came to Holofernes, and declared unto him after this maner. Then came hee downe toward the Sea coast, both hee and his armie, and set garisons in the high cities, and tooke out of them chosen men for *Olofernes is received there:* aide. So they and all the countrey round about, received them with garlands, with dances, and with timbrels. Yet hee did *Yet he destroyeth* cast downe their frontiers, and cut downe their groves: for hee *their gods, that* had decreed to destroy all the gods of the land, that all nations *they might* should worship Nabuchodonosor onely, and that all tongues and *worship onely Nabuchodonosor.* tribes should call upon him as God. Also he came over against Esdraelon neere unto Iudea, over against the great strait of Iudea. *He commeth neere to Iudea.* And hee pitched betweene Geba, and Scythopolis, and there hee taried a whole moneth, that he might gather together all the cariages of his armie.

CHAPTER IIII

NOW the children of Israel that dwelt in Iudea, heard all that Holofernes the chiefe captaine of Nabuchodonosor king of the Assyrians had done to the nations, and after what manner hee had spoiled all their Temples, and brought them to nought. Therefore they were exceedingly afraid of him, and were troubled for Ierusalem, and for the Temple of the Lord their God. For they were newly returned from the captivitie, and all the people of Iudea were lately gathered together: and the vessels, and the Altar, and the house, were sanctified after the profanation. There-

IUDETH

fore they sent into all the coasts of Samaria, and the villages, and to Bethoron, and Belmen, and Iericho, and to Choba, and Esora, and to the valley of Salem, and possessed themselves beforehand of all the tops of the high mountaines, and fortified the villages that were in them, and laid up victuals for the provision of warre: for their fieldes were of late reaped. Also Ioacim the hie Priest which was in those daies in Ierusalem, wrote to them that dwelt in Bethulia, and Betomestham which is over against Esdraelon toward the open countrey neere to Dothaim, charging them to keepe the passages of the hill countrey: for by them there was an entrance into Iudea, and it was easie to stoppe them that would come up, because the passage was strait for two men at the most. And the children of Israel did as Ioacim the hie Priest had commanded them, with the ancients of all the people of Israel, which dwelt at Ierusalem. Then every man of Israel cryed to God with great fervencie, and with great vehemency did they humble their soules: both they and their wives, and their children, and their cattell, and every stranger and hireling, and their servants bought with money, put sackecloth upon their loynes. Thus every man and woman, and the little children, and the inhabitants of Ierusalem fell before the temple, and cast ashes upon their heads, and spread out their sackcloth before the face of the Lord: also they put sackecloth about the Altar, and cryed to the God of Israel all with one consent earnestly, that hee would not give their children for a pray, and their wives for a spoile, and the cities of their inheritance to destruction, and the Sanctuary to profanation and reproch, and for the nations to reioyce at. So God heard their prayers, and looked upon their afflictions: for the people fasted many dayes in all Iudea, and Ierusalem, before the Sanctuary of the Lord Almighty. And Ioacim the high Priest, and all the Priestes that stood before the Lord, and they which ministred unto the Lord, had their loines girt with sackecloth, and offered the daily burnt offerings, with the vowes and free gifts of the people, and had ashes on their miters, and cried unto the Lord with all their power, that he would looke upon all the house of Israel graciously.

CHAPTER IIII

The Iewes are afraid of Holofernes, and fortifie the hilles.
They of Bethulia take charge of the passages.

All Israel fall to fasting and prayer.

CHAPTER V

THEN was it declared to Holofernes the chief captaine of the armie of Assur that the children of Israel had prepared for warre, and had shut up the passages of the hill countrey, and had fortified all the tops of the high hilles, and had laide impediments in the champion countreys. Wherewith he was very

IUDETH

CHAPTER V

Achior telleth Holofernes what the Iewes are,

and what their God had done for them:

angry, and called all the princes of Moab, and the captaines of Ammon, and all the governours of the Sea coast. And he said unto them, Tell mee now, ye sonnes of Canaan, who this people is that dwelleth in the hill countrey? and what are the cities that they inhabite? and what is the multitude of their armie? and wherein is their power and strength, and what king is set over them, or captaine of their armie? and why have they determined not to come and meet me, more then all the inhabitants of the West? Then said Achior, the captaine of all the sonnes of Ammon: Let my lord now heare a word from the mouth of thy servant, and I will declare unto thee the trueth, concerning this people which dwelleth neere thee, and inhabiteth the hill countreys: and there shall no lie come out of the mouth of thy servant. This people are descended of the Caldeans, and they soiourned heretofore in Mesopotamia, because they would not follow the gods of their fathers, which were in the land of Caldea. For they left the way of their ancestours, and worshipped the God of heaven, the God whom they knew: so they cast them out from the face of their gods, and they fled into Mesopotamia, and soiourned there many dayes. Then their God commaunded them to depart from the place where they soiourned, and to goe into the land of Chanaan, where they dwelt, and were increased with gold and silver, and with very much cattell. But when a famine covered all the land of Chanaan, they went downe into Egypt, and soiourned there, while they were nourished, and became there a great multitude, so that one could not number their nation. Therefore the king of Egypt rose up against them, and dealt subtilly with them, and brought them low, with labouring in bricke, and made them slaves. Then they cried unto their God, and he smote all the land of Egypt with incurable plagues, so the Egyptians cast them out of their sight. And God dried the red Sea before them: and brought them to mount Sina, and Cades Barne, and cast forth all that dwelt in the wildernesse. So they dwelt in the land of the Amorites, and they destroyed by their strength all them of Esebon, and passing over Iordan they possessed all the hill countrey. And they cast forth before them, the Chanaanite, the Pheresite, the Iebusite, and the Sychemite, and all the Gergesites, and they dwelt in that countrey many dayes. And whilest they sinned not before their God, they prospered, because the God that hateth iniquitie, was with them. But when they departed from the way which he appointed them, they were destroyed in many battels very sore, and were led captives into a land that was not theirs, and the Temple of their God was cast to the ground, and their cities

IUDETH

were taken by the enemies. But nowe are they returned to their God, and are come up from the places, where they were scattered, and have possessed Ierusalem, where their Sanctuary is, and are seated in the hill countrey, for it was desolate. Now therefore, my lord and governour, if there be any errour in this people, and they sinne against their God, let us consider that this shal be their ruine, and let us goe up, and we shal overcome them. But if there be no iniquitie in their nation, let my lord now passe by, lest their Lord defend them, and their God be for them, and wee become a reproch before all the world. And when Achior had finished these sayings, all the people standing round about the tent, murmured, and the chiefe men of Holofernes, and all that dwelt by the Sea side, and in Moab, spake that he should kill him. For, say they, we will not be afraid of the face of the children of Israel, for loe, it is a people that have no strength, nor power for a strong battell. Now therefore, Lord Holofernes, we will goe up, and they shall be a pray, to be devoured of all thine armie.

CHAPTER V

and adviseth not to meddle with them.

All that heard him, were offended at him.

CHAPTER VI

AND when the tumult of men that were about the councell was ceased, Holofernes the chiefe captaine of the armie of Assur, said unto Achior and all the Moabites, before all the company of other nations, And who art thou Achior and the hirelings of Ephraim, that thou hast prophesied amongst us as to day, and hast said, that we should not make warre with the people of Israel, because their God will defend them? and who is God but Nabuchodonosor? He will send his power, and will destroy them from the face of the earth, and their God shall not deliver them: but we his servants will destroy them as one man, for they are not able to sustaine the power of our horses. For with them we will tread them under foote, and their mountains shall be drunken with their blood, and their fields shall be filled with their dead bodies, and their footesteps shall not be able to stand before us, for they shal utterly perish, saith king Nabuchodonosor Lord of all the earth; for hee said, None of my words shall be in vaine. And thou Achior, an hireling of Ammon, which hast spoken these words in the day of thine iniquity, shalt see my face no more, from this day untill I take vengeance of this nation that came out of Egypt. And then shall the sword of mine armie, and the multitude of them that serve me, passe through thy sides, and thou shalt fal among their slaine, when I returne. Now therefore my servants shall bring thee backe into the hill countrey, and

Holofernes despiseth God.

He threatneth Achior and sendeth him away.

IUDETH

CHAPTER VI

shall set thee in one of the cities of the passages. And thou shalt not perish till thou be destroyed with them. And if thou perswade thy selfe in thy minde, that they shall not be taken, let not thy countenance fall: I have spoken it, and none of my words shall be in vaine. Then Holofernes commanded his servants that waited in his tent, to take Achior and bring him to Bethulia, and deliver him into the hands of the children of Israel. So his servants tooke him, and brought him out of the campe into the plaine, and they went from the midst of the plaine into the hill countrey, and came unto the fountaines that were under Bethulia. And when the men of the citie saw them, they tooke up their weapons, and went out of the citie to the toppe of the hill, and every man that used a sling kept them from comming up by casting of stones against them. Neverthelesse having gotten privily under the hill, they bound Achior and cast him downe, and left him at the foote of the hill, and returned to their Lord. But the Israelites descended from their citie, and came unto him, and loosed him, and brought him into Bethulia, and presented him to the governours of the citie, which were in those dayes Ozias the sonne of Micha of the tribe of Simeon, and Chabris the sonne of Gothoniel, and Charmis the sonne of Melchiel. And they called together all the ancients of the citie, and all their youth ranne together, and their women to the assembly, and they set Achior in the midst of all their people. Then Ozias asked him of that which was done. And he answered and declared unto them the words of the counsell of Holofernes, and all the words that he had spoken in the midst of the princes of Assur, and whatsoever Holofernes had spoken proudly against the house of Israel. Then the people fell downe, and worshipped God, and cryed unto God, saying, O Lord God of heaven, behold their pride, and pity the low estate of our nation, and looke upon the face of those that are sanctified unto thee this day. Then they comforted Achior and praised him greatly. And Ozias tooke him out of the assembly unto his house, and made a feast to the Elders, and they called on the God of Israel all that night for helpe.

The Bethulians receive and heare him.

They fall to prayer, and comfort Achior.

CHAPTER VII

Holofernes besiegeth Bethulia,

THE next day Holofernes commanded all his army, and all his people which were come to take his part, that they should remoove their campe against Bethulia, to take aforehand the ascents of the hill countrey, and to make warre against the children of Israel. Then their strong men removed their campes in that day, and the armie of the men of warre was, an

IUDETH

hundred and seventy thousand footmen, and twelve thousand horsemen, beside the baggage, and other men that were afoot amongst them, a very great multitude. And they camped in the valley neere unto Bethulia, by the fountaine, and they spred themselves in breadth over Dothaim, even to Belmaim, and in length from Bethulia unto Cyamon which is over against Esdraelon. Now the children of Israel, when they saw the multitude of them, were greatly troubled, and said every one to his neighbour: Now will these men licke up the face of the earth; for neither the high mountaines, nor the valleys, nor the hils, are able to beare their waight. Then every man tooke up his weapons of warre, and when they had kindled fires upon their towers, they remained and watched all that night. But in the second day Holofernes brought foorth all his horsemen, in the sight of the children of Israel which were in Bethulia, and viewed the passages up to the city, and came to the fountaine of their waters, and tooke them, and set garrisons of men of warre over them, and he himselfe remooved towards his people. Then came unto him all the chiefe of the children of Esau, and al the governours of the people of Moab, and the captaines of the sea coast, and said, Let our lord now heare a word, that there be not an overthrow in thine armie. For this people of the children of Israel do not trust in their speares, but in the height of the mountaines wherein they dwell, because it is not easie to come up to the tops of their mountains. Now therefore my lord, fight not against them in battell aray, and there shall not so much as one man of thy people perish. Remaine in thy campe, and keepe all the men of thine army, and let thy servants get into their hands the fountaine of water which issueth foorth of the foot of the mountaine. For all the inhabitants of Bethulia have their water thence: so shall thirst kil them, and they shall give up their citie, and we and our people shal goe up to the tops of the mountaines that are neere, and will campe upon them, to watch that none goe out of the city. So they and their wives, and their children shalbe consumed with famine, and before the sword come against them, they shall be overthrowen in the streets where they dwel. Thus shalt thou render them an evil reward: because they rebelled and met not thy person peaceably. And these words pleased Holofernes, and al his servants, and he appointed to doe as they had spoken. So the campe of the children of Ammon departed, and with them five thousand of the Assyrians, and they pitched in the valley, and tooke the waters, and the fountaines of the waters of the children of Israel. Then the children of Esau went up, with the children of Ammon, and camped in the hil

CHAPTER VII

and stoppeth the water from them.

IUDETH

CHAPTER VII

They faint and murmure against the governours,

Who promise to yeeld within five dayes.

countrey over against Dotha-em: and they sent some of them toward the South, and toward the East over against Ekrebel, which is neere unto Chusi, that is upon the brooke Mochmur, and the rest of the army of the Assyrians camped in the plaine, and covered the face of the whole land, and their tents and cariages were pitched to a very great multitude. Then the children of Israel cried unto the Lord their God, because their heart failed, for all their enemies had compassed them round about, and there was no way to escape out from among them. Thus all the company of Assur remained about them, both their footmen, charets and horsemen, foure and thirtie dayes, so that all their vessels of water failed all the inhabitants of Bethulia. And the cisternes were emptied, and they had not water to drinke their fill, for one day; for they gave them drinke by measure. Therefore their young children were out of heart, and their women and yong men fainted for thirst, and fell downe in the streetes of the city, and by the passages of the gates, and there was no longer any strength in them. Then all the people assembled to Ozias, and to the chiefe of the city, both young men, and women, and children, and cryed with a loude voice, and saide before all the Elders; God be Iudge betweene us and you: for you have done us great iniury in that you have not required peace of the children of Assur. For now we have no helper: but God hath sold us into their hands, that wee should be throwen downe before them with thirst, and great destruction.' Now therefore call them unto you, and deliver the whole citie for a spoile to the people of Olofernes, and to all his armie. For it is better for us to be made a spoile unto them, then to die for thirst: for wee will be his servants, that our soules may live, and not see the death of our infants before our eyes, nor our wives nor our children to die. We take to witnesse against you, the heaven and the earth, and our God, and Lord of our fathers, which punisheth us according to our sinnes, and the sinnes of our fathers, that hee doe not according as we have said this day. Then there was great weeping with one consent in the middest of the assembly, and they cryed unto the Lord God with a loude voice. Then said Ozias to them, Brethren, be of good courage, let us yet endure five dayes, in the which space the Lord our God may turne his mercy toward us, for he will not forsake us utterly. And if these dayes passe, and there come no helpe unto us, I wil doe according to your word. And he dispersed the people every one to their owne charge, and they went unto the walles and towres of their citie, and sent the women and children into their houses, and they were very low brought in the city.

IUDETH

CHAPTER VIII

N OW at that time Iudeth heard thereof, which was the daughter of Merari the sonne of Ox, the sonne of Ioseph, the sonne of Oziel, the sonne of Eleia, the son of Ananias, the son of Gedeon, the sonne of Raphaim, the son of Acitho, the sonne of Eliu, the sonne of Eliab, the sonne of Nathanael, the sonne of Samael, the sonne of Salasadai, the son of Israel. And Manasses was her husband of her tribe and kinred, who died in the barley harvest. For as hee stood overseeing them that bound sheaves in the field, the heat came upon his head, and hee fell on his bed, and died in the city of Bethulia, and they buried him with his fathers, in the field betweene Dothaim and Balamo. So Iudeth was a widow in her house three yeeres, and foure moneths. And she made her a tent upon the top of her house, and put on sackecloth on her loynes, and ware her widowes apparell. And she fasted all the dayes of her widowhood, save the eves of the Sabbath, and the Sabbaths, and the eves of the newe Moones, and the newe Moones, and the Feasts, and solemne dayes of the house of Israel. Shee was also of a goodly countenance, and very beautifull to behold: and her husband Manasses had left her golde and silver, and men servants and maide servants, and cattell, and lands, and she remained upon them. And there was none that gave her an ill worde; for shee feared God greatly. Now when shee heard the evill wordes of the people against the governor that they fainted for lacke of water (for Iudeth had heard all the wordes that Ozias had spoken unto them, and that he had sworne to deliver the citie unto the Assyrians after five dayes) Then shee sent her waiting woman that had the government of all things that she had, to call Ozias, and Chabris, and Charmis, the ancients of the citie. And they came unto her, and she said unto them, Heare me now, O yee governours of the inhabitants of Bethulia: for your wordes that you have spoken before the people this day are not right, touching this othe which ye made, and pronounced betweene God and you, and have promised to deliver the citie to our enemies, unlesse within these daies the Lord turne to helpe you. And now who are you, that have tempted God this day, and stand in stead of God amongst the children of men? And now trie the Lord Almighty, but you shall never know any thing. For you cannot find the depth of the heart of man, neither can ye perceive the things that he thinketh: then how can you search out God, that hath made all these things, and knowe his minde, or comprehend his purpose? Nay my brethren, provoke not the

CHAPTER VIII

The state and behaviour of Iudeth a widow.

She blameth the governors for their promise to yeeld:

IUDETH

CHAPTER VIII

and adviseth them to trust in God.

Lord our God to anger. For if he will not helpe us within these few dayes, he hath power to defend us when he will, even every day, or to destroy us before our enemies. Doe not binde the counsels of the Lord our God, for God is not as man, that he may be threatned, neither is he as the sonne of man that he should bee wavering. Therefore let us waite for salvation of him, and call upon him to helpe us, and he will heare our voyce if it please him. For there arose none in our age, neither is there any now in these daies, neither tribe, nor familie, nor people, nor city among us, which worship gods made with hands, as hath bene aforetime. For the which cause our fathers were given to the sword, and for a spoile, and had a great fall before our enemies. But we know none other god: therefore we trust that he will not despise us, nor any of our nation. For if we be taken so, all Iudea shall lie waste, and our Sanctuarie shal be spoiled, and he will require the prophanation thereof, at our mouth. And the slaughter of our brethren, and the captivitie of the countrey, and the desolation of our inheritance, will he turne upon our heads among the Gentiles, wheresoever we shall bee in bondage, and we shall be an offence and a reproch to all them that possesse us. For our servitude shall not be directed to favour: but the Lord our God shall turne it to dishonour. Now therefore, O brethren, let us shew an example to our brethren, because their hearts depend upon us, and the Sanctuary, and the house, and the Altar rest upon us. Moreover, let us give thankes to the Lord our God, which trieth us, even as he did our fathers. Remember what things he did to Abraham, and how he tried Isaac, and what happened to Iacob in Mesopotamia of Syria, when he kept the sheepe of Laban his mothers brother. For, hee hath not tried us in the fire as he did them, for the examination of their hearts, neither hath hee taken vengeance on us: but the Lord doeth scourge them that come neere unto him to admonish them.

They excuse their promise.

Then said Ozias to her, all that thou hast spoken, hast thou spoken with a good heart, and there is none that may gainesay thy words. For this is not the first day wherin thy wisedome is manifested, but from the beginning of thy dayes all thy people have knowen thy understanding, because the disposition of thine heart is good. But the people were very thirsty, and compelled us to doe unto them as we have spoken, and to bring an othe upon our selves, which wee will not breake. Therefore now pray thou for us, because thou art a godly woman, and the Lord will send us raine to fill our cisternes, and we shall faint no more. Then said Iudeth unto them, Heare me, and I wil doe a thing,

96

IUDETH

which shall goe throughout all generations, to the children of our nation. You shall stand this night in the gate, and I will goe foorth with my waiting woman: and within the dayes that you have promised to deliver the citie to our enemies, the Lord will visit Israel by mine hand. But inquire not you of mine act: for I will not declare it unto you, til the things be finished that I doe. Then said Ozias and the princes unto her, Goe in peace, and the Lord God be before thee, to take vengeance on our enemies. So they returned from the tent, and went to their wards.

CHAPTER VIII

She promiseth to doe something for them.

CHAPTER IX

THEN Iudeth fell upon her face, and put ashes upon her head, and uncovered the sackcloth wherewith she was clothed, and about the time, that the incense of that evening was offered in Ierusalem, in the house of the Lord, Iudeth cryed with a loud voyce, and said, O Lord God of my father Simeon, to whom thou gavest a sword to take vengeance of the strangers, who loosened the girdle of a maide to defile her, and discovered the thigh to her shame, and polluted her virginity to her reproch, (for thou saidst it shall not be so, and yet they did so.) Wherefore thou gavest their rulers to be slaine, so that they died their bed in blood, being deceived, and smotest the servants with their Lords, and the Lords upon their thrones: and hast given their wives for a pray, and their daughters to bee captives, and all their spoiles to be divided amongst thy deere children: which were mooved with thy zeale, and abhorred the pollution of their blood, and called upon thee for aide: O God, O my God, heare me also a widow. For thou hast wrought not onely those things, but also the things which fell out before, and which ensewed after, thou hast thought upon the things which are now, and which are to come. Yea what things thou didst determine were redy at hand, and said, Loe we are heere; for all thy wayes are prepared, and thy iudgements are in thy foreknowledge. For behold, the Assyrians are multiplyed in their power: they are exalted with horse and man: they glory in the strength of their footemen: they trust in shield and speare, and bow, and sling, and know not that thou art the Lord that breakest the battels: the Lord is thy name. Throw downe their strength in thy power, and bring downe their force in thy wrath; for they have purposed to defile thy Sanctuary, and to pollute the Tabernacle, where thy glorious name resteth, and to cast downe with sword the horne of thy altar. Behold their pride, and send thy wrath

Iudeth humbleth herselfe, and prayeth God to prosper her purpose against the enemies of his sanctuarie.

IUDETH

CHAPTER IX

upon their heads: give into mine hand which am a widow, the power that I have conceived. Smite by the deceit of my lips the servant with the prince, and the prince with the servant: breake downe their statelinesse by the hand of a woman. For thy power standeth not in multitude, nor thy might in strong men, for thou art a God of the afflicted, an helper of the oppressed, an upholder of the weake, a protector of the forelorne, a saviour of them that are without hope. I pray thee, I pray thee, O God of my father, and God of the inheritance of Israel, Lord of the heavens, and earth, creator of the waters, king of every creature: heare thou my prayer: and make my speech and deceit to be their wound and stripe, who have purposed cruell things against thy covenant, and thy hallowed house, and against the top of Sion, and against the house of the possession of thy children. And make every nation and tribe to acknowledge that thou art the God of all power and might, and that there is none other that protecteth the people of Israel but thou.

CHAPTER X

Iudeth doth set forth herselfe.

NOW after that she had ceased to cry unto the God of Israel, and had made an end of all these words, she rose where she had fallen downe, and called her maide, and went downe into the house, in the which she abode in the Sabbath dayes and in her feast dayes, and pulled off the sackcloth which she had on, and put off the garments of her widowhood, and washed her body all over with water, and annointed herselfe with precious ointment, and braided the haire of her head, and put on a tire upon it, and put on her garments of gladnesse, wherewith she was clad during the life of Manasses her husband. And she tooke sandals upon her feete, and put about her, her bracelets and her chaines, and her rings, and her earerings, and all her ornaments, and decked her selfe bravely to allure the eyes of all men that should see her. Then she gave her mayd a bottle of wine, and a cruse of oyle, and filled a bagge with parched corne, and lumpes of figs, and with fine bread, so she folded all these things together, and layd them upon her. Thus they went forth to the gate of the citie of Bethulia, and found standing there Ozias, and the ancients of the city Chabris, and Charmis. And when they saw her, that her countenance was altered, and her apparel was changed, they wondered at her beautie very greatly, and said unto her, The God, the God of our fathers give thee favour, and accomplish thine enterprises to the glory of the children of Israel, and to the

IUDETH

exaltation of Ierusalem: then they worshipped God. And she said unto them, Command the gates of the city to be opened unto me, that I may goe forth to accomplish the things, whereof you have spoken with me; so they commanded the yong men to open unto her, as shee had spoken. And when they had done so, Iudeth went out, she and her mayd with her, and the men of the citie looked after her, untill shee was gone downe the mountaine, and till she had passed the valley, and could see her no more. Thus they went straight foorth in the valley: and the first watch of the Assyrians met her; and tooke her, and asked her, Of what people art thou? and whence commest thou? and whither goest thou? And she said, I am a woman of the Hebrewes, and am fled from them: for they shalbe given you to be consumed: and I am comming before Olofernes the chiefe captaine of your army, to declare words of trueth, and I will shew him a way, whereby he shall goe, and winne all the hil countrey, without loosing the body or life of any one of his men. Now when the men heard her wordes, and beheld her countenance, they wondered greatly at her beautie, and said unto her; Thou hast saved thy life, in that thou hast hasted to come downe to the presence of our lord: now therfore come to his tent, and some of us shall conduct thee, untill they have delivered thee to his hands. And when thou standest before him, bee not afraid in thine heart: but shew unto him according to thy word, and he will intreat thee well. Then they chose out of them an hundred men, to accompany her and her mayd, and they brought her to the tent of Olofernes. Then was there a concourse throughout all the campe: for her comming was noised among the tents, and they came about her, as she stood without the tent of Olofernes, till they told him of her. And they wondered at her beautie, and admired the children of Israel because of her, and every one said to his neighbour; Who would despise this people, that have among them such women, surely it is not good that one man of them be left, who being let goe, might deceive the whole earth. And they that lay neere Olofernes, went out, and all his servants, and they brought her into the tent. Now Olofernes rested upon his bed under a canopie which was woven with purple, and gold, and emeraudes, and precious stones. So they shewed him of her, and he came out before his tent, with silver lampes going before him. And when Iudeth was come before him and his servants, they all marveiled at the beautie of her countenance; and she fel downe upon her face, and did reverence unto him; and his servants tooke her up.

CHAPTER X

She and her maide goe forth into the campe.

The watch take and conduct her to Olofernes.

IUDETH

CHAPTER XI

Olofernes asketh Iudeth the cause of her comming.

She telleth him how, and when hee may prevaile.

THEN said Olofernes unto her, Woman, bee of good comfort, feare not in thine heart: for I never hurt any, that was willing to serve Nabuchodonosor the king of all the earth. Now therefore if thy people that dwelleth in the mountaines, had not set light by me, I would not have lifted up my speare against them: but they have done these things to themselves. But now tell me wherefore thou art fled from them, and art come unto us: for thou art come for safeguard, be of good comfort, thou shalt live this night, and hereafter. For none shall hurt thee, but intreat thee well, as they doe the servants of king Nabuchodonosor my lord. Then Iudeth said unto him, Receive the words of thy servant, and suffer thine handmaid to speake in thy presence, and I will declare no lie to my lord this night. And if thou wilt follow the words of thine handmaid, God will bring the thing perfectly to passe by thee, and my lord shall not faile of his purposes, as Nabuchodonosor king of all the earth liveth, and as his power liveth, who hath sent thee for the upholding of every living thing: for not only men shall serve him by thee, but also the beasts of the field, and the cattell, and the foules of the aire shall live by thy power, under Nabuchodonosor and all his house. For wee have heard of thy wisedome, and thy policies, and it is reported in all the earth, that thou onely art excellent in all the kingdome, and mightie in knowledge, and wonderfull in feates of warre. Now as concerning the matter which Achior did speake in thy counsell, we have heard his words; for the men of Bethulia saved him, and hee declared unto them all that hee had spoken unto thee. Therefore, O lord and governor, reiect not his word, but lay it up in thine heart, for it is true, for our nation shall not be punished, neither can the sword prevaile against them, except they sinne against their God. And now, that my lord be not defeated, and frustrate of his purpose, even death is now fallen upon them, and their sinne hath overtaken them, wherewith they will provoke their God to anger, whensoever they shall doe that which is not fit to be done. For their victuals faile them, and all their water is scant, and they have determined to lay hands upon their cattell, and purposed to consume all those things, that God hath forbidden them to eate by his Lawes, and are resolved to spend the first fruits of the corne, and the tenths of wine and oyle, which they had sanctified, and reserved for the Priests that serve in Ierusalem, before the face of our God, the which things it is not lawfull for any of the people so much as to touch with their

IUDETH

hands. For they have sent some to Ierusalem, because they also that dwel there have done the like, to bring them a license from the Senate. Now when they shall bring them word, they will forthwith doe it, and they shall be given thee to be destroyed the same day. Wherefore I thine handmaide knowing all this, am fledde from their presence, and God hath sent me to worke things with thee, whereat all the earth shalbe astonished, and whosoever shall heare it. For thy servant is religious, and serveth the God of heaven day and night: now therefore, my lord, I will remaine with thee, and thy servant will goe out by night into the valley, and I will pray unto God, and he wil tel me when they have committed their sinnes. And I will come, and shew it unto thee: then thou shalt goe forth with all thine army, and there shall be none of them that shall resist thee. And I will leade thee through the midst of Iudea, untill thou come before Ierusalem, and I will set thy throne in the midst thereof, and thou shalt drive them as sheep that have no shepheard, and a dogge shall not so much as open his mouth at thee: for these things were tolde mee, according to my foreknowledge, and they were declared unto me, and I am sent to tell thee. Then her wordes pleased Olofernes, and all his servants, and they marveiled at her wisedome, and said, There is not such a woman from one end of the earth to the other, both for beautie of face, and wisedome of wordes. Likewise Olofernes said unto her, God hath done well to send thee before the people, that strength might be in our hands, and destruction upon them that lightly regard my lord: and now thou art both beautifull in thy countenance, and wittie in thy wordes; surely if thou doe as thou hast spoken, thy God shall be my God, and thou shalt dwel in the house of king Nabuchodonosor, and shalt be renowmed through the whole earth.

CHAPTER XI

Hee is much pleased with her wisedome and beautie.

CHAPTER XII

THEN hee commaunded to bring her in, where his plate was set, and bad that they should prepare for her of his owne meats, and that she should drinke of his owne wine. And Iudeth said, I will not eat thereof, lest there bee an offence: but provision shall be made for mee of the things that I have brought. Then Olofernes said unto her, If thy provision should faile, howe should we give thee the like? for there be none with us of thy nation. Then said Iudeth unto him, As thy soule liveth, my lord, thine handmaid shall not spend those things that I have, before the Lord worke by mine hand, the things that he hath determined.

Iudeth will not eate of Olofernes meate.

IUDETH

CHAPTER XII

She taried three dayes in the cam'pe, and everie night went forth to pray.

Then the servants of Olofernes brought her into the tent, and shee slept til midnight, and she arose when it was towards the morning watch, and sent to Olofernes, saying, Let my lord now command, that thine handmaid may goe forth unto prayer. Then Olofernes commaunded his guard that they should not stay her: thus she abode in the camp three dayes, and went out in the night into the valley of Bethulia, and washed her selfe in a fountaine of water by the campe. And when she came out, shee besought the Lord God of Israel to direct her way, to the raising up of the children of her people. So she came in cleane, and remained in the tent, untill shee did eate her meat at evening. And in the fourth day Olofernes made a feast to his owne servants only, and called none of the officers to the banquet. Then said he to Bagoas the Eunuch, who had charge over all that he had: Goe now, and perswade this Ebrewe woman which is with thee, that she come unto us, and eate and drinke with us. For loe, it will be a shame for our person, if we shall let such a woman go, not having had her company: for if we draw her not unto us, she will laugh us to scorne.

Bagoas doth move her to be merry with Olofernes,

Then went Bagoas from the presence of Olofernes, and came to her, and he said, Let not this faire damosell feare to come to my lord, and to bee honoured in his presence, and drink wine, and be merry with us, and be made this day as one of the daughters of the Assyrians, which serve in the house of Nabuchodonosor. Then said Iudeth unto him, Who am I now, that I should gainesay my lord? surely whatsoever pleaseth him, I will doe speedily, and it shall bee my ioy unto the day of my death. So she arose, and decked her selfe with her apparell, and all her womans attire, and her maid went and laid soft skinnes on the ground for her, over against Olofernes, which she had received of Bagoas for her daily use, that she might sit, and eate upon them. Now when Iudeth came in, and sate downe, Olofernes his heart was ravished with her, and his minde was moved, and he desired greatly her company, for hee waited a time to deceive her, from the day that he had seene her. Then said Olofernes unto her, Drinke now, and be merry with us. So Iudeth saide, I will drinke now my lord, because my life is magnified in me this day, more then all the dayes since I was borne. Then she tooke and ate

who for ioy of her companie drunke much.

and dranke before him what her maide had prepared. And Olofernes tooke great delight in her, and dranke much more wine, then he had drunke at any time in one day, since he was borne.

102

IUDETH

CHAPTER XIII

NOW when the evening was come, his servants made haste to depart, and Bagoas shut his tent without, and dismissed the waiters from the presence of his lord, and they went to their beds: for they were all weary, because the feast had bene long. And Iudeth was left alone in the tent, and Olofernes lying along upon his bed, for hee was filled with wine. Now Iudeth had commanded her maide to stand without her bedchamber, and to waite for her comming forth as she did daily: for she said, she would goe forth to her prayers, and she spake to Bagoas, according to the same purpose. So all went forth, and none was left in the bedchamber, neither little, nor great. Then Iudeth standing by his bed, said in her heart: O Lord God of all power, looke at this present upon the workes of mine hands for the exaltation of Ierusalem. For now is the time to helpe thine inheritance, and to execute mine enterprises, to the destruction of the enemies, which are risen against us. Then she came to the pillar of the bed, which was at Olofernes head, and tooke downe his fauchin from thence, and approched to his bed, and tooke hold of the haire of his head, and said, Strengthen mee, O Lord God of Israel, this day. And she smote twise upon his necke with all her might, and she tooke away his head from him, and tumbled his body downe from the bed, and pulled downe the canopy from the pillars, and anon after she went forth, and gave Olofernes his head to her maide. And she put it in her bag of meate, so they twaine went together according to their custome unto prayer, and when they passed the campe, they compassed the valley, and went up the mountaine of Bethulia, and came to the gates thereof. Then said Iudeth a farre off to the watchmen at the gate, Open, open now the gate: God, even our God is with us, to shew his power yet in Ierusalem, and his forces against the enemie, as he hath even done this day. Now when the men of her citie heard her voyce, they made haste to goe downe to the gate of their citie, and they called the Elders of the citie. And then they ranne altogether both small and great, for it was strange unto them that she was come: so they opened the gate, and received them, and made a fire for a light, and stood round about them. Then she said to them with a loud voyce, Praise, praise God, praise God, (I say) for hee hath not taken away his mercy from the house of Israel, but hath destroyed our enemies by mine hands this night. So she tooke the head out of the bag, and shewed it, and said unto them, Behold the head of Olofernes the chiefe captaine of

CHAPTER XIII

Iudeth is left alone with Olofernes in his tent.

She prayeth God to give her strength.

She cut off his head while hee slept:

And returned with it to Bethulia:

103

IUDETH

CHAPTER XIII

They saw it, and commend her.

the armie of Assur, and behold the canopy wherein he did lie in his drunkennesse, and the Lord hath smitten him by the hand of a woman. As the Lord liveth, who hath kept me in my way that I went, my countenance hath deceived him to his destruction, and yet hath hee not committed sinne with mee, to defile and shame mee. Then all the people were wonderfully astonished, and bowed themselves, and worshipped God, and said with one accord: Blessed be thou, O our God, which hast this day brought to nought the enemies of thy people. Then said Ozias unto her, O daughter, blessed art thou of the most high God, above all the women upon the earth, and blessed be the Lord God, which hath created the heavens, and the earth, which hath directed thee to the cutting off of the head of the chiefe of our enemies. For this thy confidence shall not depart from the heart of men, which remember the power of God for ever. And God turne these things to thee for a perpetuall praise, to visite thee in good things, because thou hast not spared thy life for the affliction of our nation, but hast revenged our ruine, walking a straight way before our God: and all the people said, So be it, so be it.

CHAPTER XIIII

THEN saide Iudeth unto them, Heare me now, my brethren, and take this head, and hang it upon the highest place of your walles. And so soone as the morning shall appeare, and the Sunne shal come forth upon the earth, take you every one his weapons, and goe forth every valiant man out of the city, and set you a captaine over them, as though you would goe downe into the field toward the watch of the Assyrians, but goe not downe. Then they shal take their armour, and shal goe into their campe, and raise up the captaines of the army of Assur, and they shall runne to the tent of Olofernes, but shall not finde him, then feare shall fall upon them, and they shall flee before your face. So you, and all that inhabite the coast of Israel, shall pursue them, and overthrow them as they goe. But before you doe these things, call me Achior the Ammonite, that hee may see and know him that despised the house of Israel, and that sent him to us as it were to his death. Then they called Achior out of the house of Ozias, and when hee was come, and saw the head of Olofernes in a mans hand, in the assembly of the people, he fell downe on his face, and his spirit failed. But when they had recovered him, hee fell at Iudeths feete, and reverenced her, and said: Blessed art thou in all the tabernacle of Iuda, and in all

IUDETH

nations, which hearing thy name shall be astonished. Now therefore tell mee all the things that thou hast done in these dayes: Then Iudeth declared unto him in the midst of the people, all that shee had done from the day that shee went foorth, untill that houre she spake unto them. And when shee had left off speaking, the people shouted with a lowd voice, and made a ioyful noise in their citie. And when Achior had seene all that the God of Israel had done, hee beleeved in God greatly, and circumcised the foreskinne of his flesh, and was ioyned unto the house of Israel unto this day. And assoone as the morning arose, they hanged the head of Olofernes upon the wall, and every man took his weapons, and they went foorth by bandes unto the straits of the mountaine. But when the Assyrians sawe them, they sent to their leaders, which came to their Captaines, and tribunes, and to every one of their rulers. So they came to Olofernes tent, and said to him that had the charge of all his things, Waken now our lord: for the slaves have beene bold to come downe against us to battell, that they may be utterly destroyed. Then went in Bagoas, and knocked at the doore of the tent: for he thought that he had slept with Iudeth. But because none answered, he opened it, and went into the bedchamber, and found him cast upon the floore dead, and his head was taken from him. Therefore he cried with a lowd voice, with weeping, and sighing, and a mighty cry, and rent his garments. After, hee went into the tent, where Iudeth lodged, and when hee found her not, he leaped out to the people, and cried; These slaves have dealt treacherously, one woman of the Hebrewes hath brought shame upon the house of king Nabuchodonosor: for behold, Olofernes lieth upon the ground without a head. When the captaines of the Assyrians armie heard these words, they rent their coats, and their minds were wonderfully troubled, and there was a cry, and a very great noise throughout the campe.

CHAPTER XIIII

Achior heareth Iudeth shewe what she had done, and is circumcised.

the head of Olofernes is hanged up,

hee is found dead, and much lamented.

CHAPTER XV

AND when they that were in the tents heard, they were astonished at the thing that was done. And feare and trembling fell upon them, so that there was no man that durst abide in the sight of his neighbour, but rushing out altogether, they fled into every way of the plaine, and of the hill countrey. They also that had camped in the mountaines, round about Bethulia, fled away. Then the children of Israel every one that was a warriour among them, rushed out upon them. Then

The Assyrians are chased and slaine.

IUDETH

CHAPTER XV

The high Priest commeth to see Iudeth.

The stuffe of Olofernes is given to Iudeth.

The women crowne her with a garland.

sent Ozias to Bethomasthem, and to Bebai, and Chobai, and Cola, and to all the coasts of Israel, such as should tell the things that were done, and that all should rush forth upon their enemies to destroy them. Now when the children of Israel heard it, they all fell upon them with one consent, and slewe them unto Choba likewise also they that came from Ierusalem, and from all the hill country, for men had told them what things were done in the campe of their enemies, and they that were in Galaad and in Galile chased them with a great slaughter, untill they were past Damascus, and the borders thereof. And the residue that dwelt at Bethulia, fell upon the campe of Assur, and spoiled them, and were greatly enriched. And the children of Israel that returned from the slaughter, had that which remained, and the villages, and the cities that were in the mountaines, and in the plaine, gate many spoiles: for the multitude was very great. Then Ioacim the high Priest, and the Ancients of the children of Israel that dwelt in Ierusalem, came to behold the good things that God had shewed to Israel, and to see Iudeth, and to salute her. And when they came unto her, they blessed her with one accord, and said unto her, Thou art the exaltation of Ierusalem: thou art the great glory of Israel: thou art the great reioycing of our nation. Thou hast done all these things by thine hand: thou hast done much good to Israel, and God is pleased therewith: blessed bee thou of the Almightie Lord for evermore: and all the people said, So be it. And the people spoiled the campe, the space of thirty dayes, and they gave unto Iudeth Olofernes his tent, and all his plate, and beds, and vessels, and all his stuffe: and she tooke it, and laide it on her mule, and made ready her carts, and laid them thereon. Then all the women of Israel ran together to see her, and blessed her, and made a dance among them for her: and shee tooke branches in her hand, and gave also to the women that were with her. And they put a garland of olive upon her, and her maid that was with her, and shee went before the people in the dance, leading all the women: and all the men of Israel followed in their armor with garlands, and with songs in their mouthes.

CHAPTER XVI

The song of Iudeth.

THEN Iudeth began to sing this thanksgiving in all Israel, and all the people sang after her this song of praise. And Iudeth said.

BEGIN unto my God with timbrels,
Sing unto my Lord with cymbals:
Tune unto him a newe Psalme:

IUDETH

Exalt him, and cal upon his name.
For God breaketh the battels:
For amongst the campes in the midst of the people
Hee hath delivered me out of the hands of them that persecuted me.
Assur came out of the mountains from the North,
He came with ten thousands of his army,
The multitude wherof stopped the torrents,
And their horsemen have covered the hilles.
He bragged that he would burne up my borders,
And kill my young men with the sword,
And dash the sucking children against the ground,
And make mine infants as a pray,
And my virgins as a spoile.
But the Almighty Lord hath disappointed them by the hand of a woman.
For the mighty one did not fall by the yong men,
Neither did the sonnes of the Titans smite him,
Nor high gyants set upon him:
But Iudeth the daughter of Merari weakned him with the beautie of her countenance.
For she put off the garment of her widowhood, for the exaltation of those that were oppressed in Israel,
And anointed her face with oyntment,
And bound her haire in a tyre,
And tooke a linnen garment to deceive him.
Her sandals ravished his eyes,
Her beautie tooke his minde prisoner,
And the fauchin passed through his necke.
The Persians quaked at her boldnesse,
And the Medes were daunted at her hardinesse.
Then my afflicted shouted for ioy,
And my weake ones cryed aloude; but they were astonished
These lifted up their voices, but they were overthrowen.
The sonnes of the damosels have pierced them through,
And wounded them as fugitives children:
They perished by the battell of the Lord.
I will sing unto the Lord a new song,
O Lord thou art great and glorious,
Wonderful in strength and invincible.
Let all creatures serve thee:
For thou spakest, and they were made,
Thou didst send forth thy spirit, and it created them,

CHAPTER XVI

IUDETH

CHAPTER XVI

And there is none that can resist thy voyce.
For the mountaines shall be mooved from their foundations
　　with the waters,
The rockes shall melt as waxe at thy presence:
Yet thou art mercifull to them that feare thee.
For all sacrifice is too little for a sweete savour unto thee,
And all the fat is not sufficient, for thy burnt offering:
But he that feareth the Lord is great at all times.
Woe to the nations that rise up against my kinred:
The Lord almighty will take vengeance of them in the day
　　of iudgement
In putting fire and wormes in their flesh,
And they shall feele them and weepe for ever.

Now assoone as they entred into Ierusalem, they worshipped the Lord, and assoone as the people were purified, they offered their *She dedicateth the stuffe of Olofernes.* burnt offerings, and their free offerings, and their gifts. Iudeth also dedicated all the stuffe of Olofernes, which the people had given her, and gave the canopy which she had taken out of his bed chamber, for a gift unto the Lord. So the people continued feasting in Ierusalem before the Sanctuarie, for the space of three moneths, and Iudeth remained with them. After this time, every one returned to his owne inheritance, and Iudeth went to Bethulia, and remained in her owne possession, and was in her time honourable in all the countrey. And many desired her, but none knew her all the dayes of her life, after that Manasses her husband was *Shee died at Bethulia a widow of great honour.* dead, and was gathered to his people. But she encreased more and more in honour, and waxed olde in her husbands house, being an hundred and five yeeres olde, and made her maide free, so shee died in Bethulia: and they buried her in the cave *All Israel did lament her death.* of her husband Manasses. And the house of Israel lamented her seaven dayes, and before shee dyed, she did distribute her goods to all them that are neerest of kinred to Manasses her husband: and to them that were the neerest of her kinred.

And there was none that made the children of Israel
　　any more afraide, in the dayes of Iudeth, nor a
　　　　long time after her death.

ESTHER

The rest of the Chapters of
THE BOOKE OF ESTHER,
which are found neither in the Hebrewe
nor in the Calde.

Part of the tenth Chapter after the Greeke.

THEN Mardocheus saide, God hath done these things. For I remember a dreame, which I sawe concerning these matters, and nothing thereof hath failed. A little fountaine became a river, and there was light, and the Sunne, and much water: this river is Esther, whom the King married and made Queene. And the two Dragons are I, and Aman. And the nations were those that were assembled, to destroy the name of the Iewes. And my nation is this Israel, which cryed to God and were saved: for the Lord hath saved his people, and the Lord hath delivered us from all those evils, and God hath wrought signes, and great wonders, which have not bin done among the Gentiles. Therefore hath hee made two lots, one for the people of God, and another for all the Gentiles. And these two lots came at the houre, and time, and day of iudgement before God amongst all nations. So God remembred his people, and iustified his inheritance. Therefore those dayes shall be unto them in the moneth Adar, the foureteenth and fifteenth day of the same moneth, with an assembly, and ioy, and with gladnesse, before God, according to the generations for ever among his people.

Mardocheus remembreth and expoundeth his dreame, of the river and the two dragons.

CHAPTER XI

IN the fourth yeere of the raigne of Ptolomeus, and Cleopatra, Dositheus, who said hee was a priest and Levite, and Ptolomeus his sonne brought this Epistle of Phurim, which they said was the same, and that Lysimachus the sonne of Ptolomeus,

ESTHER

CHAPTER XI

The stocke and qualitie of Mardocheus.

that was in Ierusalem, had interpreted it. In the second yeere of the raigne of Artaxerxes the great: in the first day of the moneth Nisan, Mardocheus the sonne of Iairus, the sonne of Semei, the sonne of Cisai of the tribe of Beniamin, had a dreame. Who was a Iew and dwelt in the citie of Susa, a great man, being a servitour in the kings court. He was also one of the captives, which Nabuchodonosor the king of Babylon caried from Ierusalem, with Iechonias king of Iudea ; and this was his dreame. Behold a noise of a tumult with thunder, and earthquakes, and uproare in the

He dreameth of two dragons comming forth to fight,

land. And behold, two great dragons came forth ready to fight, and their crie was great. And at their cry all nations were prepared to battel, that they might fight against the righteous people. And loe a day of darknesse and obscurity: tribulation, and anguish, affliction, and great uproare upon the earth. And the whole righteous nation was troubled, fearing their owne evils, and were

and of a little fountaine, which became a great water.

ready to perish. Then they cryed unto God, and upon their cry, as it were from a little fountaine, was made a great flood, even much water. The light and the Sunne rose up, and the lowly were exalted, and devoured the glorious. Now when Mardocheus, who had seene this dreame, and what God had determined to doe, was awake: he bare this dreame in minde, and untill night by all meanes was desirous to know it.

CHAPTER XII

AND Mardocheus tooke his rest in the court with Gabatha, and Tharra, the two Eunuches of the king, and keepers of

The conspiracie of the two Eunuchs is discovered by Mardocheus,

the palace. And he heard their devices, and searched out their purposes, and learned that they were about to lay hands upon Artaxerxes the king, and so he certified the king of them. Then the king examined the two Eunuches, and after that they had confessed it, they were strangled. And the king made a

for which he is entertained by the king and rewarded.

record of these things, and Mardocheus also wrote thereof. So the king commaunded Mardocheus to serve in the court, and for this he rewarded him. Howbeit Aman the sonne of Amadathus the Agagite, who was in great honour with the king, sought to molest Mardocheus and his people, because of the two Eunuches of the king.

CHAPTER XIII

The copie of the kings letters to destroy the Iewes.

THE copy of the letters was this. The great king Artaxerxes, writeth these things to the princes, and governours that are under him from India unto Ethiopia, in an hundred and seven and twentie provinces. After that I became Lord over

ESTHER

many nations, and had dominion over the whole world, not lifted up with presumption of my authoritie, but carying my selfe alway with equitie and mildenesse, I purposed to settle my subiects continually in a quiet life, and making my kingdome peaceable, and open for passage to the utmost coasts, to renne peace which is desired of all men. Now when I asked my counsellers how this might bee brought to passe, Aman that excelled in wisedome among us, and was approved for his constant good will, and stedfast fidelitie, and had the honour of the second place in the kingdome, declared unto us, that in all nations throughout the world, there was scattered a certaine malitious people, that had Lawes contrary to all nations, and continually despised the commandements of Kings, so as the uniting of our kingdomes honourably intended by us, cannot goe forward. Seeing then we understand that this people alone is continually in opposition unto all men, differing in the strange maner of their Lawes, and evill affected to our state, working all the mischiefe they can, that our kingdome may not be firmely stablished: therefore have we commanded that al they that are signified in writing unto you by Aman (who is ordained over the affaires, and is next unto us) shall all with their wives and children bee utterly destroyed, by the sword of their enemies, without all mercie and pitie, the fourteenth day of the twelfth moneth Adar of this present yeere: that they, who of old, and now also are malitious, may in one day with violence goe into the grave, and so ever hereafter, cause our affaires to be well settled, and without trouble. Then Mardocheus thought upon all the works of the Lord, and made his prayer unto him, saying, O Lord, Lord, the king Almightie: for the whole world is in thy power; and if thou hast appointed to save Israel, there is no man that can gainesay thee. For thou hast made heaven and earth, and all the wonderous things under the heaven. Thou art Lord of all things, and there is no man that can resist thee, which art the Lord. Thou knowest all things, and thou knowest Lord, that it was neither in contempt nor pride, nor for any desire of glory, that I did not bow downe to proud Aman. For I could have bene content with good will for the salvation of Israel, to kisse the soles of his feet. But I did this, that I might not preferre the glory of man above the glory of God: neither will I worship any but thee, O God, neither wil I doe it in pride. And now, O Lord God, and King, spare thy people: for their eyes are upon us, to bring us to nought, yea they desire to destroy the inheritance that hath beene thine from the beginning. Despise not the portion which thou hast delivered out of Egypt for thine owne selfe: heare my

CHAPTER XIII

The prayer of Mardocheus for them.

ESTHER

CHAPTER XIII

prayer, and be mercifull unto thine inheritance: turne our sorrow into ioy, that wee may live, O Lord, and praise thy Name: and destroy not the mouthes of them that praise thee, O Lord. All Israel in like maner cried most earnestly unto the Lord, because their death was before their eyes.

CHAPTER XIIII

The prayer of Queene Esther, for herselfe, and her people.

QUEENE ESTHER also being in feare of death, resorted unto the Lord, and layd away her glorious apparel, and put on the garments of anguish, and mourning: and in stead of pretious oyntments, she covered her head with ashes, and doung, and she humbled her body greatly, and all the places of her ioy she filled with her torne haire. And shee prayed unto the Lord God of Israel, saying, O my Lord, thou onely art our king: helpe me desolate woman, which have no helper but thee: for my danger is in mine hand. From my youth up I have heard in the tribe of my family, that thou, O Lord, tookest Israel from among all people, and our fathers from all their predecessours, for a perpetuall inheritance, and thou hast performed whatsoever thou didst promise them. And now we have sinned before thee: therefore hast thou given us into the hands of our enemies, because wee worshipped their gods: O Lord, thou art righteous. Neverthelesse it satisfieth them not, that we are in bitter captivitie, but they have striken hands with their idols, that they will abolish the thing, that thou with thy mouth hast ordained, and destroy thine inheritance, and stop the mouth of them that praise thee, and quench the glory of thy house, and of thine Altar, and open the mouthes of the heathen to set foorth the praises of the Idoles, and to magnifie a fleshly king for ever. O Lord, give not thy scepter unto them that be nothing, and let them not laugh at our fall, but turne their device upon themselves, and make him an example that hath begunne this against us. Remember, O Lord, make thy selfe knowen in time of our affliction, and give mee boldnesse, O King of the nations, and Lord of all power. Give me eloquent speech in my mouth before the lyon: turne his heart to hate him that fighteth against us, that there may be an end of him, and of all that are like minded to him: but deliver us with thine hand, and helpe me that am desolate, and which have no other helper but thee. Thou knowest all things, O Lord, thou knowest that I hate the glory of the unrighteous, and abhorre the bed of the uncircumcised, and of all the heathen. Thou knowest my necessitie: for I abhorre the signe of my high estate, which is upon mine head, in the dayes wherein

ESTHER

I shewe my selfe, and that I abhorre it as a menstruous ragge, and that I weare it not when I am private by my selfe. And that thine handmaid hath not eaten at Amans table, and that I have not greatly esteemed the Kings feast, nor drunke the wine of the drinke offerings: neither had thine handmaid any ioy, since the day that I was brought hither to this present, but in thee, O Lord God of Abraham. O thou mightie God above all, heare the voice of the forlorne, and deliver us out of the handes of the mischievous, and deliver me out of my feare.

CHAPTER XIIII

CHAPTER XV

AND upon the third day when shee had ended her prayer, she laide away her mourning garments, and put on her glorious apparell. And being gloriously adorned, after she had called upon God, who is the beholder, and Saviour of all things, she tooke two maids with her. And upon the one shee leaned as carying her selfe daintily. And the other followed bearing up her traine. And she was ruddy through the perfection of her beautie, and her countenance was cheerefull, and very amiable: but her heart was in anguish for feare. Then having passed through all the doores, shee stood before the King, who sate upon his royall throne, and was clothed with all his robes of maiestie, all glittering with golde and precious stones, and he was very dreadfull. Then lifting up his countenance that shone with maiestie, he looked very fiercely upon her: and the Queene fell downe and was pale, and fainted, and bowed her selfe upon the head of the maide that went before her. Then God changed the spirit of the king into mildnesse, who in a feare leaped from his throne, and tooke her in his armes till she came to her selfe againe, and comforted her with loving words, and sayd unto her: Esther, what is the matter? I am thy brother, be of good cheere. Thou shalt not die, though our commandement be generall: come neere. And so he held up his golden scepter, and laid it upon her necke, and embraced her, and said, Speake unto me. Then said shee unto him, I saw thee, my lord, as an Angel of God, and my heart was troubled for feare of thy maiestie. For wonderfull art thou, lord, and thy countenance is full of grace. And as she was speaking, she fell downe for faintnesse. Then the king was troubled, and all his servants comforted her.

Esther commeth into the Kings presence.

Hee looketh angerly, and she fainteth.

The king doth take her up, and comfort her.

ESTHER

CHAPTER XVI

The Letter of Artaxerxes,

THE great king Artaxerxes unto the princes and governours of an hundreth and seven and twenty provinces, from India unto Ethiopia, and unto all our faithfull Subiects, greeting. Many, the more often they are honoured with the great bountie of their gracious princes, the more proud they are waxen, and endeavour to hurt not our Subiects onely, but not being able to beare abundance, doe take in hand to practise also against those that doe them good: and take not only thankfulnesse away from among men, but also lifted up with the glorious words of lewde persons that were never good, they thinke to escape the iustice of God, that seeth all things, and hateth evill. Often times also faire speech of those that are put in trust to manage their friends affaires, hath caused many that are in authority to be partakers of innocent blood, and hath enwrapped them in remedilesse calamities: beguiling with the falshood and deceit of their lewd disposition, the innocencie and goodnesse of princes. Now yee may see this as we have declared, not so much by ancient histories, as yee may, if ye search what hath beene wickedly done of late through the pestilent behaviour of them that are unworthily placed in authoritie. And we must take care for the time to come, that our kingdome may bee quiet and peaceable for all men, both by changing our purposes, and alwayes iudging things that are evident, *wherein hee taxeth Aman,* with more equall proceeding. For Aman a Macedonian the son of Amadatha, being indeed a stranger from the Persian blood, and far distant from our goodnesse, and as a stranger received of us: had so farre forth obtained the favour that wee shew toward every nation, as that he was called our father, and was continually honoured of all men, as the next person unto the king. But he not bearing his great dignitie, went about to deprive us of our kingdome and life: having by manifold and cunning deceits sought of us the destruction as well of Mardocheus, who saved our life, and continually procured our good, as also of blamelesse Esther partaker of our kingdome, with their whole nation. For by these meanes he thought, finding us destitute of friends, to have translated the kingdome of the Persians to the Macedonians. But wee finde that the Iewes, whom this wicked wretch hath delivered to utter destruction, are no evill doers, but live by most iust lawes: and that they be children of the most high and most mighty living God, who hath ordered the kingdome both unto us, and to our progenitors in the most excellent maner. Wherefore ye shall doe well not to put in execution the Letters sent unto you by Aman

ESTHER

the sonne of Amadatha. For hee that was the worker of these things, is hanged at the gates of Susa with all his family: God, who ruleth all things, speedily rendring vengeance to him according to his deserts. Therefore ye shall publish the copy of this Letter in all places, that the Iewes may freely live after their owne lawes. And ye shall aide them, that even the same day, being the thirteenth day of the twelfth moneth Adar, they may be avenged on them, who in the time of their affliction shall set upon them. For Almightie God hath turned to ioy unto them the day, wherein the chosen people should have perished. You shall therefore among your solemne feasts keepe it an high day with all feasting, that both now and hereafter there may be safetie to us, and the well affected Persians: but to those which doe conspire against us, a memoriall of destruction. Therefore every citie and countrey whatsoever, which shall not doe according to these things, shall bee destroyed without mercy,
with fire and sword, and shall be made not onely unpassable for men, but also most hatefull to wilde
beasts and foules for ever.

<small>CHAPTER XVI
and revoketh the decree procured by Aman to destroy the Iewes, and commandeth the day of their deliverance to be kept holy.</small>

THE WISEDOME OF SOLOMON

CHAPTER I

LOVE righteousnesse, yee that be iudges of the earth:
Thinke of the Lord with a good (heart)
And in simplicitie of heart seeke him.
For hee will bee found of them that tempt him not:
And sheweth himselfe unto such as doe not distrust him.
For froward thoughts separate from God:
And his power when it is tryed, reprooveth the unwise.
For into a malitious soule wisedome shall not enter:
Nor dwell in the body that is subiect unto sinne.
For the holy spirit of discipline will flie deceit,
And remove from thoughts that are without understanding:
And will not abide when unrighteousnesse commeth in.

<small>To whom God sheweth himselfe,

and Wisedome herselfe.</small>

WISEDOME OF SOLOMON

CHAPTER I

An evill speaker can not lie hid.

For wisedome is a loving spirit:
And will not acquite a blasphemour of his words:
For God is witnesse of his reines,
And a true beholder of his heart,
And a hearer of his tongue.
For the spirit of the Lord filleth the world:
And that which containeth all things hath knowledge of the voice.
Therefore he that speaketh unrighteous things, cannot be hid:
Neither shal vengeance, when it punisheth, passe by him.
For inquisition shall be made into the counsels of the ungodly:
And the sound of his words, shall come unto the Lord,
For the manifestation of his wicked deedes.
For the eare of iealousie heareth al things:
And the noise of murmurings is not hid.
Therefore beware of murmuring, which is unprofitable,
And refraine your tongue from backbiting:
For there is no word so secret that shall goe for nought:
And the mouth that belieth, slayeth the soule.

We procure our owne destruction:

Seeke not death in the errour of your life:
And pull not upon your selves destruction, with the workes of your hands.

for God created not death.

For God made not death:
Neither hath he pleasure in the destruction of the living.
For he created all things, that they might have their being:
And the generations of the world were healthfull:
And there is no poyson of destruction in them:
Nor the kingdome of death upon the earth.
For righteousnesse is immortall.
But ungodly men with their workes, and words called it to them:
For when they thought to have it their friend, they consumed to nought,
And made a covenant with it,
Because they are worthy to take part with it.

CHAPTER II

The wicked thinke this life short,

FOR the ungodly said, reasoning with themselves, but not aright:
Our life is short and tedious,
And in the death of a man there is no remedie:

WISEDOME OF SOLOMON

Neither was there any man knowen to have returned from the grave.   **CHAPTER II**
For wee are borne at all adventure:
And we shalbe heereafter as though we had never bene:
For the breath in our nostrils is as smoke,
And a litle sparke in the moving of our heart.
Which being extinguished, our body shall be turned into ashes,
And our spirit shall vanish as the soft aire:
And our name shalbe forgotten in time,
And no man shall have our works in remembrance,
And our life shall passe away as the trace of a cloud:
And shall be dispersed as a mist
That is driven away with the beames of the Sunne,
And overcome with the heat thereof.
For our time is a very shadow that passeth away: *and of no other after this.*
And after our end there is no returning:
For it is fast sealed, so that no man commeth againe.
Come on therefore, let us enioy the good things that are present: *Therefore they will take their pleasure in this,*
And let us speedily use the creatures like as in youth.
Let us fill our selves with costly wine, and ointments
And let no flower of the Spring passe by us.
Let us crowne our selves with Rose buds, before they be withered.
Let none of us goe without his part of our voluptuousnesse:
Let us leave tokens of our ioyfulnesse in every place:
For this is our portion, and our lot is this.
Let us oppresse the poore righteous man,   *and conspire against the iust.*
Let us not spare the widow,
Nor reverence the ancient gray haires of the aged.
Let our strength bee the Lawe of justice:
For that which is feeble is found to be nothing worth.
Therefore let us lye in wait for the righteous:
Because he is not for our turne,
And he is cleane contrary to our doings:
He upbraideth us with our offending the Law,
And obiecteth to our infamy the transgressings of our education.
Hee professeth to have the knowledge of God:
And hee calleth himselfe the childe of the Lord.
Hee was made to reproove our thoughts.
Hee is grievous unto us even to beholde:

WISEDOME OF SOLOMON

<small>CHAPTER II</small>

For his life is not like other mens,
His waies are of another fashion.
We are esteemed of him as counterfeits:
He abstaineth from our wayes as from filthinesse:
He pronounceth the end of the iust to be blessed,
And maketh his boast that God is his father.
Let us see if his wordes be true:
And let us prove what shall happen in the end of him.
For if the iust man be the sonne of God, he will helpe him,
And deliver him from the hand of his enemies.
Let us examine him with despitefulnesse and torrture,
That we may know his meekenesse,
And proove his patience.
Let us condemne him with a shamefull death:
For by his owne saying, he shall be respected.

<small>What that is which doth blind them.</small>

Such things they did imagine, and were deceived:
For their owne wickednesse hath blinded them.
As for the mysteries of God, they knew them not:
Neither hoped they for the wages of righteousnesse:
Nor discerned a reward for blamelesse soules.
For God created man to bee immortall,
And made him to be an image of his owne eternitie.
Neverthelesse through envie of the devill came death into the world:
And they that doe holde of his side doe finde it.

CHAPTER III

<small>The godly are happie in their death,</small>

BUT the soules of the righteous are in the hand of God,
And there shall no torment touch them.
In the sight of the unwise they seemed to die:
And their departure is taken for misery,
And their going from us to be utter destruction:
But they are in peace.
For though they bee punished in the sight of men:
Yet is their hope full of immortalitie.

<small>and in their troubles;</small>

And having bene a little chastised, they shalbe greatly rewarded:
For God proved them, and found them worthy for himselfe.
As gold in the furnace hath hee tried them,
And received them as a burnt offering.
And in the time of their visitation, they shall shine and runne to and fro,

WISEDOME OF SOLOMON

Like sparkes among the stubble.
They shall iudge the nations, and have dominion over the people,   CHAPTER III
And their Lord shall raigne for ever.
They that put their trust in him, shall understand the trueth:
And such as be faithfull in love, shall abide with him:
For grace and mercy is to his saints,
And he hath care for his elect.
But the ungodly shalbe punished according to their owne imaginations,   *The wicked are not, nor their children:*
Which have neglected the righteous, and forsaken the Lord.
For who so despiseth wisedome, and nurture, he is miserable,
And their hope is vaine, their labours unfruitfull,
And their workes unprofitable.
Their wives are foolish,
And their children wicked.
Their of-spring is cursed:
Wherefore blessed is the barren that is undefiled,
Which hath not knowen the sinfull bed   *But they that are pure, are happie, though they have no children:*
She shall have fruit in the visitation of soules.
And blessed is the Eunuch which with his hands hath wrought no iniquitie:
Nor imagined wicked things against God:
For unto him shall be given the speciall gift of faith,
And an inheritance in the Temple of the Lord more acceptable to his minde.
For glorious is the fruit of good labours:
And the root of wisedom shall never fall away.
As for the children of adulterers, they shall not come to their perfection,   *For the adulterer and his seed shall perish.*
And the seed of an unrighteous bed shal be rooted out.
For though they live long, yet shall they bee nothing regarded:
And their last age shall be without honour.
Or if they die quickly, they have no hope,
Neither comfort in the day of triall.
For horrible is the end of the unrighteous generation.

WISEDOME OF SOLOMON

CHAPTER IIII

CHAPTER IIII
The chaste man shall be crowned.

BETTER it is to have no children, and to have vertue:
For the memoriall thereof is immortal:
Because it is knowen with God and with men.
When it is present, men take example at it,
And when it is gone they desire it:
It weareth a crown, and triumpheth for ever,
Having gotten the victorie, striving for undefiled rewards.

Bastard slips shall not thrive.

But the multiplying brood of the ungodly shall not thrive,
Nor take deepe rooting from bastard slips,
Nor lay any fast foundation.
For though they flourish in branches for a time:
Yet standing not fast, they shall be shaken with the winde:
And through the force of windes they shall be rooted out.
The unperfect branches shall bee broken off,
Their fruit unprofitable,
Not ripe to eate: yea meet for nothing.

They shall witnesse against their parents.

For children begotten of unlawfull beds, are witnesses of wickednes
Against their parents in their triall.

The iust die yong, and are happie.

But though the righteous be prevented with death: yet shal he be in rest.
For honourable age is not that which standeth in length of time,
Nor that is measured by number of yeeres.
But wisedome is the gray haire unto men,
And an unspotted life is old age.
He pleased God, and was beloved of him:
So that living amongst sinners, he was translated.
Yea, speedily was he taken away, lest that wickednes should alter his understanding,
Or deceit beguile his soule.
For the bewitching of naughtines doth obscure things that are honest:
And the wandring of concupiscence, doth undermine the simple mind.
He being made perfect in a short time,
Fulfilled a long time.
For his soule pleased the Lord:
Therefore hasted he to take him away, from among the wicked.
This the people saw, and understood it not:

WISEDOME OF SOLOMON

Neither laid they up this in their mindes,   CHAPTER
That his grace and mercie is with his Saints,   IIII
And that he hath respect unto his chosen.
Thus the righteous that is dead, shall condemne the ungodly, which are living,
And youth that is soone perfected, the many yeeres and old age of the unrighteous.
For they shall see the end of the wise,
And shall not understand what God in his counsell hath decreed of him,
And to what end the Lord hath set him in safetie.
They shal see him and despise him,
But God shall laugh them to scorne,
And they shal hereafter be a vile carkeis,
And a reproch among the dead for evermore.
For he shall rend them, and cast them downe headlong, that they shalbe speechles: *The miserable ende of the wicked.*
And he shal shake them from the foundation:
And they shall bee utterly laid waste, and be in sorow:
And their memoriall shall perish.
And when they cast up the accounts of their sinnes, they shall come with feare:
And their owne iniquities shall convince them to their face.

CHAPTER V

THEN shal the righteous man stand in great boldnesse, *The wicked shal wonder at the godly,*
   Before the face of such as have afflicted him,
   And made no account of his labours.
When they see it, they shalbe troubled with terrible feare,
And shall be amazed at the strangenesse of his salvation, so farre beyond all that they looked for.
And they repenting, and groning for anguish of spirit, shall say within themselves,
This was he whom wee had sometimes in derision, and a proverbe of reproch.
We fooles accounted his life madnes,   *and confesse*
And his end to be without honour.   *their errour,*
How is hee numbred among the children of God,   *and the vanitie*
And his lot is among the Saints?   *of their lives.*
Therefore have wee erred from the way of trueth,
And the light of righteousnesse hath not shined unto us,
And the Sunne of righteousnesse rose not upon us.

WISEDOME OF SOLOMON

CHAPTER V

We wearied our selves in the way of wickednesse, and destruction:
Yea, we have gone through deserts, where there lay no way:
But as for the way of the Lord, we have not knowen it.
What hath pride profited us?
Or what good hath riches with our vaunting brought us?
All those things are passed away like a shadow,
And as a Poste that hasted by.
And as a ship that passeth over the waves of the water,
Which when it is gone by, the trace thereof cannot bee found:
Neither the path way of the keele in the waves.
Or as when a bird hath flowen thorow the aire,
There is no token of her way to be found,
But the light aire being beaten with the stroke of her wings,
And parted with the violent noise and motion of them, is passed thorow,
And therin afterwards no signe where she went, is to be found.
Or like as when an arrow is shot at a marke,
It parteth the aire, which immediatly commeth together againe:
So that a man cannot know where it went thorow:
Even so we in like maner, assoone as we were borne, began to draw to our end,
And had no signe of vertue to shew:
But were consumed in our owne wickednesse.
For the hope of the ungodly is like dust that is blowen away with the wind,
Like a thinne froth that is driven away with the storme:
Like as the smoke which is dispersed here and there with a tempest,
And passeth away as the remembrance of a guest that tarieth but a day.

God will reward the Iust,
But the righteous live for evermore,
Their reward also is with the Lord,
And the care of them is with the most High.
Therfore shall they receive a glorious kingdome,
And a beautiful crowne from the Lords hande:
For with his right hand shall he cover them,
And with his arme shall he protect them.

and warre against the wicked.
He shall take to him his ielousie for complete armour,
And make the creature his weapon for the revenge of his enemies.

WISEDOME OF SOLOMON

He shal put on righteousnesse as a brestplate,   CHAPTER
And true iudgement in stead of an helmet.   V
He shall take holinesse for an invincible shield.
His severe wrath shall he sharpen for a sword,
And the world shall fight with him against the unwise.
Then shal the right-aiming thunder bolts goe abroad,
And from the cloudes, as from a well-drawen bow, shall they
    flie to the marke.
And hailestones full of wrath shal be cast as out of a
    stonebow,
And the water of the Sea shall rage against them,
And the floods shall cruelly drowne them.
Yea a mightie wind shall stand up against them,
And like a storme shall blow them away:
Thus iniquity shal lay wast the whole earth,
And ill dealing shall overthrow the thrones of the mightie.

CHAPTER VI

HEARE therefore, O yee kings, and understand,   Kings must
    Learne yee that be iudges of the ends of the earth.   give eare.
Give eare you that rule the people,
And glory in the multitude of nations.
For power is given you of the Lord,   They have
And soveraigntie from the Highest,   their power
Who shall try your workes,   from God,
And search out your counsels.
Because being Ministers of his kingdome, you have not
    iudged aright,
Nor kept the law, nor walked after the counsell of God,
Horribly and speedily shall he come upon you: Who will not
For a sharpe iudgement shall be to them that be in high   spare them.
    places.
For mercy will soone pardon the meanest:
But mighty men shall be mightily tormented.
For he which is Lord over all, shall feare no mans person:
Neither shall he stand in awe of any mans greatnesse:
For he hath made the small and great,
And careth for all alike.
But a sore triall shall come upon the mighty.
Unto you therefore, O kings, doe I speake,
That yee may learne wisedome, and not fall away.
For they that keepe holinesse holily, shall be iudged holy:

WISEDOME OF SOLOMON

CHAPTER VI

And they that have learned such things, shall find what to answere.
Wherefore set your affection upon my words,
Desire them, and yee shall be instructed.

Wisedome is soone found.

Wisedome is glorious and never fadeth away:
Yea she is easily seene of them that love her,
And found of such as seeke her.
She preventeth them that desire her, in making herselfe first knowen unto them.
Whoso seeketh her earely, shall have no great travaile:
For he shall find her sitting at his doores.
To thinke therefore upon her is perfection of wisedome:
And who so watcheth for her, shall quickly be without care.
For she goeth about seeking such as are worthy of her,
Sheweth herselfe favourably unto them in the wayes,
And meeteth them in every thought.
For the very true beginning of her, is the desire of discipline,
And the care of discipline is love:
And love is the keeping of her lawes;
And the giving heed unto her lawes, is the assurance of incorruption.
And incorruption maketh us neere unto God.
Therefore the desire of wisedome bringeth to a kingdome.

princes must seeke for it:

If your delight be then in thrones and scepters, O ye kings of the people,
Honour wisedome that yee may raigne for evermore.
As for wisedome what she is, and how she came up, I will tell you,
And will not hide mysteries from you:
But will seeke her out from the beginning of her nativity,
And bring the knowledge of her into light,
And will not passe over the trueth.
Neither will I goe with consuming envy:
For such a man shall have no fellowship with wisedome.

For a wise Prince is the stay of his people.

But the multitude of the wise is the welfare of the world:
And a wise king is the upholding of the people.
Receive therefore instruction thorough my words,
And it shall doe you good.

WISEDOME OF SOLOMON

CHAPTER VII

I MY selfe also am a mortall man, like to all, *All men have their beginning and end alike.*
And the ofspring of him that was first made of the earth,
And in my mothers wombe was fashioned to be flesh in the time of tenne monethes
Being compacted in blood, of the seed of man, and the pleasure that came with sleepe.
And when I was borne, I drew in the common aire,
And fell upon the earth which is of like nature,
And the first voice which I uttered, was crying as all others doe.
I was nursed in swadling clothes, and that with cares.
For there is no king that had any other beginning of birth.
For all men have one entrance unto life, and the like going out. *He preferred wisedome before all things else.*
Wherefore I prayed, and understanding was given mee:
I called upon God, and the spirit of wisedome came to me.
I preferred her before scepters, and thrones, *God gave him all the knowledge, which he had.*
And esteemed riches nothing in comparison of her.
Neither compared I unto her any precious stone,
Because all gold in respect of her is as a little sand,
And silver shalbe counted as clay before her.
I loved her above health and beautie,
And chose to have her in stead of light:
For the light that commeth from her never goeth out.
All good things together came to me with her,
And innumerable riches in her hands.
And I reioyced in them all, because wisedome goeth before them:
And I knew not that shee was the mother of them.
I learned diligently, and doe communicate her liberally:
I doe not hide her riches.
For shee is a treasure unto men that never faileth:
Which they that use, become the friends of God:
Being commended for the gifts that come from learning.
God hath granted me to speake as I would,
And to conceive as is meet for the things that are given mee:
Because it is hee that leadeth unto wisedome, and directeth the wise.
For in his hand are both we and our wordes:
All wisedome also and knowledge of workemanship.

125

WISEDOME OF SOLOMON

CHAPTER VII

For hee hath given mee certaine knowledge of the things that are,
Namely to know how the world was made, and the operation of the elements:
The beginning, ending, and midst of the times:
The alterations of the turning of the Sunne, and the change of seasons:
The circuits of yeres, and the positions of starres:
The natures of living creatures, and the furies of wilde beasts:
The violence of windes, and the reasonings of men:
The diversities of plants, and the vertues of rootes:
And all such things as are either secret or manifest: them I know.

The praise of wisedome.

For wisedome which is the worker of all things, taught mee:
For in her is an understanding spirit, holy,
One onely, manifold,
Subtile, lively,
Cleare, undefiled,
Plaine, not subiect to hurt,
Loving the thing that is good, quicke, which cannot be letted,
Ready to do good:
Kinde to man, stedfast, sure, free from care,
Having all power, overseeing all things,
And going through all understanding, pure, and most subtile spirits.
For wisedome is more mooving then any motion:
She passeth and goeth through all things by reason of her purenesse.
For she is the breath of the power of God,
And a pure influence flowing from the glory of the Almighty:
Therefore can no undefiled thing fall into her.
For shee is the brightnesse of the everlasting light:
The unspotted mirrour of the power of God,
And the Image of his goodnesse.
And being but one she can doe all things:
And remayning in her selfe, she maketh all things new:
And in all ages entring into holy soules,
She maketh them friends of God, and Prophets.
For God loveth none but him, that dwelleth with wisedome.
For she is more beautiful then the Sunne,
And above all the order of starres,
Being compared with the light, she is found before it.

WISEDOME OF SOLOMON

For after this commeth night: CHAPTER
But vice shall not prevaile against wisdome.   VII

CHAPTER VIII

WISDOME reacheth from one ende to another mightily:
And sweetly doeth she order all things.
I loved her and sought her out,   *He is in love*
From my youth I desired to make her my spouse,   *with wisedome:*
And I was a lover of her beautie.
In that she is conversant with God, she magnifieth her nobilitie:
Yea, the Lord of all things himselfe loved her.
For she is privy to the mysteries of the knowledge of God,   *For he that*
And a lover of his workes.   *hath it, hath*
If riches be a possession to be desired in this life   *every good*
What is richer then wisedome that worketh all things?   *thing.*
And if prudence worke;
Who of all that are, is a more cunning workeman then she?
And if a man love righteousnesse,
Her labours are vertues:
For she teacheth temperance and prudence: iustice and fortitude,
Which are such things as men can have nothing more profitable in their life.
If a man desire much experience:
She knoweth things of old, and coniectureth aright what is to come
Shee knoweth the subtilties of speaches, and can expound darke sentences:
She foreseeth signes and wonders, and the events of seasons and times.
Therefore I purposed to take her to me to live with mee,
Knowing that shee would be a counsellour of good things,
And a comfort in cares and griefe.
For her sake I shall have estimation among the multitude,
And honour with the Elders, though I be yong.
I shall be found of a quicke conceit in iudgement,
And shall be admired in the sight of great men.
When I hold my tongue they shal bide my leisure,
And when I speake they shall give good care unto me:
If I talke much, they shall lay their bandes upon their mouth.

WISEDOME OF SOLOMON

CHAPTER VIII

Moreover, by the meanes of her, I shall obtaine immortalitie,
And leave behind me an everlasting memoriall to them that come after me.
I shall set the people in order,
And the nations shalbe subiect unto me.
Horrible tyrants shall be afraide when they doe but heare of me,
I shall be found good among the multitude, and valiant in warre.
After I am come into mine house, I will repose my selfe with her:
For her conversation hath no bitternes,
And to live with her, hath no sorrow, but mirth and ioy.
Now when I considered these things in my selfe,
And pondered them in mine heart, how that to be allyed unto wisedome, is immortalitie,
And great pleasure it is to have her friendship,
And in the workes of her hands are infinite riches,
And in the exercise of conference with her, prudence:
And in talking with her a good report:
I went about seeking how to take her to me.
For I was a wittie child, and had a good spirit.
Yea rather being good, I came into a body undefiled.

It cannot be had, but from God.

Nevertheless when I perceived that I could not otherwise obtaine her, except God gave her me
(And that was a point of wisdome also to know whose gift she was)
I prayed unto the Lord, and besought him,
And with my whole heart I said:

CHAPTER IX

A prayer unto God for his wisdome,

O GOD of my fathers, and Lord of mercy,
Who hast made all things with thy word,
And ordained man through thy wisedome,
That he should have dominion over the creatures, which thou hast made,
And order the world according to equitie and righteousnesse,
And execute iudgement with an upright heart:
Give me wisedome that sitteth by thy Throne,
And reiect me not from among thy children:
For I thy servant and sonne of thine handmaide,
Am a feeble person, and of a short time,

WISEDOME OF SOLOMON

And too young for the understanding of iudgement and lawes.
For though a man be never so perfect among the children of men,
Yet if thy wisedome be not with him, hee shall be nothing regarded.

<small>CHAPTER IX</small>

<small>without which the best man is nothing worth,</small>

Thou hast chosen me to be a king of thy people,
And a Iudge of thy sons and daughters:
Thou hast commaunded me to build a Temple upon thy holy mount,
And an Altar in the city wherein thou dwellest,
A resemblance of the holy Tabernacle which thou hast prepared from the beginning:
And wisedome was with thee: which knoweth thy workes,
And was present when thou madest the world,
And knew what was acceptable in thy sight,
And right in thy Commaundements.
O send her out of thy holy heavens,
And from the Throne of thy glory,
That being present shee may labour with mee,
That I may know what is pleasing unto thee.
For she knoweth and understandeth all things,
And shee shall leade me soberly in my doings,
And preserve me in her power.
So shall my workes be acceptable,
And then shall I iudge thy people righteously,
And be worthy to sit in my fathers seate.
For what man is hee that can know the counsell of God?
Or who can thinke what the will of the Lord is?
For the thoughts of mortall men are miserable,
And our devices are but uncertaine.

<small>neither can he tell how to please God.</small>

For the corruptible body presseth downe the soule,
And the earthy tabernacle weigheth downe the minde that museth upon many things.
And hardly doe we gesse aright at things that are upon earth,
And with labour doe wee find the things that are before us:
But the things that are in heaven, who hath searched out?
And thy counsell who hath knowen, except thou give wisedome,
And send thy holy spirit from above?
For so the wayes of them which lived on the earth were reformed,
And men were taught the things that are pleasing unto thee,
And were saved through wisedome.

WISEDOME OF SOLOMON

CHAPTER X

What wisedome did for Adam,

SHE preserved the first formed father of the world that was created alone,
And brought him out of his fall,
And gave him power to rule all things.
But when the unrighteous went away from her in his anger,
He perished also in the fury wherwith he murdered his brother.

Noe,

For whose cause the earth being drowned with the flood,
Wisedome againe preserved it,
And directed the course of the righteous, in a piece of wood, of small value.

Abraham,

Moreover, the nations in their wicked conspiracie being confounded,
She found out the righteous, and preserved him blamelesse unto God,
And kept him strong against his tender compassion towards his sonne.

Lot, and against the five cities,

When the ungodly perished, shee delivered the righteous man,
Who fled from the fire which fell downe upon the five cities.
Of whose wickednesse even to this day the waste land that smoketh, is a testimonie,
And plants bearing fruite that never come to ripenesse:
And a standing pillar of salt is a monument of an unbeleeving soule.
For regarding not wisedome,
They gate not only this hurt, that they knew not the things which were good:
But also left behind them to the world a memoriall of their foolishnes:
So that in the things wherein they offended, they could not so much as be hid.
But Wisedome delivered from paine those that attended upon her.

for Iacob,

When the righteous fled from his brothers wrath, she guided him in right paths:
Shewed him the kingdome of God: and gave him knowledge of holy things,
Made him rich in his travailes, and multiplied the fruit of his labours.
In the covetousnesse of such as oppressed him,

WISEDOME OF SOLOMON

She stood by him, and made him rich. CHAPTER X
She defended him from his enemies,
And kept him safe from those that lay in wait,
And in a sore conflict she gave him the victory,
That he might knowe that godlinesse is stronger then all.
When the righteous was solde, she forsooke him not, *Ioseph,*
But delivered him from sinne:
She went downe with him into the pit,
And left him not in bonds
Till she brought him the scepter of the kingdom
And power against those that oppressed him:
As for them that had accused him, she shewed them to be liers,
And gave him perpetuall glory.
She delivered the righteous people, and blamelesse seed from the nation that oppressed them.
She entred into the soule of the servant of the Lord, *Moses,*
And withstood dreadfull kings in wonders and signes,
Rendred to the righteous a reward of their labours, *and the*
Guided them in a marveilous way, *Israelites.*
And was unto them for a cover by day,
And a light of starres in the night season:
Brought them through the red sea,
And led them thorow much water.
But she drowned their enemies,
And cast them up out of the bottome of the deepe.
Therefore the righteous spoiled the ungodly,
And praised thy holy Name, O Lord,
And magnified with one accord thine hand that fought for them.
For wisedome opened the mouth of the dumbe,
And made the tongues of them that cannot speake, eloquent.

CHAPTER XI

SHE prospered their works in the hand of the holy Prophet.
They went thorough the wildernesse that was not inhabited,
And pitched tents in places where there lay no way.
They stood against their enemies, and were avenged of their adversaries.

WISEDOME OF SOLOMON

CHAPTER XI

The Egyptians were punished, and the Israelites reserved in the same thing.

When they were thirsty they called upon thee,
And water was given them out of the flinty rocke,
And their thirst was quenched out of the hard stone.
For by what things their enemies were punished,
By the same they in their neede were benefited.
For in stead of a fountaine of a perpetuall running river, troubled with foule blood,
For a manifest reproofe of that commandement, whereby the infants were slaine,
Thou gavest unto them abundance of water by a meanes which they hoped not for,
Declaring by that thirst then, how thou hadst punished their adversaries.
For when they were tryed, albeit but in mercy chastised,
They knew how the ungodly were iudged in wrath and tormented thirsting in another maner then the Iust.
For these thou didst admonish, and trie as a father:
But the other as a severe king thou didst condemne and punish.
Whether they were absent, or present, they were vexed alike.
For a double griefe came upon them,
And a groaning for the remembrance of things past.
For when they heard by their owne punishments the other to be benefited,
They had some feeling of the Lord.
For whom they reiected with scorne when hee was long before throwen out at the casting forth of the infants,
Him in the end, when they saw what came to passe, they admired,

They were plagued by the same things, wherein they sinned.

But for the foolish devises of their wickednesse,
Wherewith being deceived, they worshipped serpents voyd of reason, and vile beasts:
Thou didst send a multitude of unreasonable beasts upon them for vengeance,
That they might knowe that wherewithall a man sinneth, by the same also shall he be punished.
For thy Almighty hand
That made the world of matter without forme,
Wanted not meanes to send among them a multitude of Beares, or fierce Lyons,
Or unknowen wild beasts full of rage newly created,
Breathing out either a fiery vapour,

WISEDOME OF SOLOMON

Or filthy sents of scattered smoake,   CHAPTER XI
Or shooting horrible sparkles out of their eyes:
Whereof not onely the harme might dispatch them at once:
But also the terrible sight utterly destroy them.
Yea and without these might they have fallen downe with one blast, *God could have destroyed them otherwise,*
Being persecuted of vengeance, and scattered abroad thorough the breath of thy power,
But thou hast ordered all things in measure, and number, and weight.
For thou canst shew thy great strength at all times when thou wilt,
And who may withstand the power of thine arme?
For the whole world before thee is as a litle graine of the ballance,
Yea as a drop of the morning dew that falleth downe upon the earth.
But thou hast mercy upon all: for thou canst doe all things, *but he is merci-*
And winkest at the sinnes of men: because they should *full to all.* amend.
For thou lovest all the things that are,
And abhorrest nothing which thou hast made:
For never wouldest thou have made any thing, if thou hadst hated it.
And how could any thing have endured if it had not beene thy will?
Or beene preserved, if not called by thee?
But thou sparest all:
For they are thine, O Lord, thou lover of soules.

CHAPTER XII

FOR thine uncorruptible spirit is in all things.
Therefore chastnest thou them by little, and little, that offend, *God did not destroy those of Canaan all at once.*
And warnest them by putting them in remembrance, wherin they have offended,
That leaving their wickednesse they may beleeve on thee O Lord.
For it was thy will to destroy by the handes of our fathers,
Both those old inhabitants of thy holy land,
Whom thou hatedst for doing most odious workes of witchcrafts, and wicked sacrifices;

WISEDOME OF SOLOMON

CHAPTER XII

And also those mercilesse murderers of children,
And devourers of mans flesh, and the feasts of blood;
With their Priests out of the midst of their idolatrous crew,
And the parents that killed with their owne hands, soules destitute of helpe:
That the land which thou esteemedst above all other,
Might receive a worthy colonie of Gods children.
Nevertheless, even those thou sparedst as men,
And didst send waspes forerunners of thine hoste,
To destroy them by little and little.
Not that thou wast unable to bring the ungodly under the hand of the righteous in battell,
Or to destroy them at once with cruel beastes, or with one rough word:
But executing thy iudgements upon them by little and little, thou gavest them place of repentance,
Not being ignorant that they were a naughtie generation, and that their malice, was bred in them,
And that their cogitation would never be changed.
For it was a cursed seed, from the beginning,
Neither didst thou for feare of any man give them pardon for those things wherein they sinned.

If he had done so, who could controll him?

For who shall say, What hast thou done?
Or who shall withstand thy iudgement,
Or who shall accuse thee for the nations that perish whom thou hast made?
Or who shall come to stand against thee, to be revenged for the unrighteous men?
For neither is there any God but thou, that careth for all,
To whom thou mightest shew that thy iudgement is not unright.
Neither shall king or tyrant bee able to set his face against thee, for any whom thou hast punished.
For so much then as thou art righteous thy selfe, thou orderest all things righteously:
Thinking it not agreeable with thy power to condemne him that hath not deserved to be punished.
For thy power is the beginning of righteousnesse,
And because thou art the Lord of all, it maketh thee to be gracious unto all.
For when men will not beleeve, that thou art of a full power, thou shewest thy strength,

WISEDOME OF SOLOMON

And among them that know it, thou makest their boldnesse manifest.
But thou, mastering thy power, iudgest with equitie,
And orderest us with great favour:
For thou mayest use power when thou wilt.
But by such workes hast thou taught thy people,
That the inst man should be mercifull,
And hast made thy children to be of a good hope,
That thou givest repentance for sinnes.
For if thou didst punish the enemies of thy children,
And the condemned to death with such deliberation,
Giving them time and place, wherby they might be delivered from their malice.
With how great circumspection diddest thou iudge thine owne sonnes,
Unto whose fathers thou hast sworne, and made covenants of good promises?
Therefore whereas thou doest chasten us, thou scourgest our enemies a thousand times more,
To the intent that when wee iudge, wee should carefully thinke of thy goodnesse,
And when we our selves are iudged, wee should looke for mercy.
Wherefore, whereas men have lived dissolutely and unrighteously,
Thou hast tormented them with their owne abominations.
For they went astray very farre in the wayes of errour,
And held them for gods (which even amongst the beasts of their enemies were despised)
Being deceived as children of no understanding.
Therefore unto them, as to children without the use of reason, thou didst send a iudgement to mocke them.
But they that would not be refourmed by that correction wherein he dallied with them,
Shall feele a iudgement worthy of God.
For looke, for what things they grudged when they were punished,
(That is) for them whom they thought to be gods, [now] being punished in them;
When they saw it, they acknowledged him to be the true God, whome before they denyed to know:
And therefore came extreme damnation upon them.

CHAPTER XII

but by sparing them hee taught us,

they were punished with their Gods.

135

WISEDOME OF SOLOMON

CHAPTER XIII

CHAPTER XIII

They were not excused that worshipped any of Gods workes:

SURELY vaine are all men by nature, who are ignorant of God,
And could not out of the good things that are seene, know him that is:
Neither by considering the workes, did they acknowledge the worke-master;
But deemed either fire, or wind, or the swift aire,
Or the circle of the stars, or the violent water, or the lights of heaven
To be the gods which governe the world:
With whose beautie, if they being delighted, tooke them to be gods:
Let them know how much better the Lord of them is;
For the first Author of beautie hath created them.
But if they were astonished at their power and vertue,
Let them understand by them, how much mightier he is that made them.
For by the greatnesse and beautie of the creatures,
Proportionably the Maker of them is seene.
But yet for this they are the lesse to bee blamed:
For they peradventure erre
Seeking God, and desirous to finde him.
For being conversant in his workes, they search him diligently,
And beleeve their sight: because the things are beautifull that are seene.
Howbeit, neither are they to bee pardoned.
For if they were able to know so much,
That they could aime at the world;
How did they not sooner finde out the Lord thereof?

But most wretched are they that worship the works of mens hands.

But miserable are they, and in dead things is their hope,
Who called them gods which are the workes of mens hands,
Golde and silver, to shewe arte in, and resemblances of beasts,
Or a stone good for nothing, the worke of an ancient hand.
Now a carpenter that felleth timber, after hee hath sawen downe a tree meet for the purpose,
And taken off all the barke skilfully round about,
And hath wrought it handsomely,
And made a vessell thereof fit for the service of mans life:

WISEDOME OF SOLOMON

And after spending the refuse of his worke to dresse his meat, hath filled himselfe: CHAPTER XIII
And taking the very refuse among those which served to no use
(Being a crooked piece of wood, and ful of knots)
Hath carved it diligently when hee had nothing else to doe,
And formed it by the skill of his understanding,
And fashioned it to the image of a man:
Or made it like some vile beast, laying it over with vermilion,
And with paint, colouring it red,
And covering every spot therein:
And when he had made a convenient roume for it,
Set it in a wall, and made it fast with yron:
For he provided for it, that it might not fall:
Knowing that it was unable to helpe it selfe,
(For it is an image and hath neede of helpe:)
Then maketh hee prayer for his goods,
For his wife and children,
And is not ashamed to speake to that which hath no life.
For health, hee calleth upon that which is weake:
For life, prayeth to that which is dead:
For aide, humbly beseecheth that which hath least meanes to helpe:
And for a good iourney, hee asketh of that which cannot set a foot forward:
And for gaining and getting, and for good successe of his hands,
Asketh abilitie to doe, of him that is most unable to doe any thing.

CHAPTER XIIII

AGAINE, one preparing himselfe to saile, and about to passe through the raging waves,   Though men doe not pray to their shippes,
Calleth upon a piece of wood more rotten then the vessell that carieth him.
For verely desire of gaine devised that,
And the workeman built it by his skill:
But thy providence, O Father, governeth it:
For thou hast made a way in the Sea,
And a safe path in the waves:
Shewing that thou canst save from all danger:
Yea though a man went to Sea without arte.

WISEDOME OF SOLOMON

CHAPTER XIIII

Yet are they saved rather by them then by their Idoles.

Neverthelesse thou wouldest not that the works of thy wisedome should be idle,
And therefore doe men commit their lives to a small piece of wood,
And passing the rough sea in a weake vessell, are saved.
For in the old time also when the proud gyants perished,
The hope of the world governed by thy hand, escaped in a weake vessell,
And left to all ages a seed of generation.
For blessed is the wood, whereby righteousnesse commeth.

Idoles are accursed, and so are the makers of them.

But that which is made with hands, is cursed, aswell it, as hee that made it:
He, because he made it, and it, because being corruptible it was called God.
For the ungodly and his ungodlines are both alike hatefull unto God.
For that which is made, shall bee punished together with him that made it.
Therfore even upon the idoles of the Gentiles shall there be a visitation:
Because in the creature of God they are become an abomination
And stumbling blocks to the soules of men,
And a snare to the feet of the unwise.
For the devising of idoles was the beginning of spiritual fornication,
And the invention of them the corruption of life.
For neither were they from the beginning, neither shall they be for ever.

The beginning of Idolatrie,

For by the vaine glory of men they entred into the world,
And therefore shall they come shortly to an end.
For a father afflicted with untimely mourning,
When he hath made an image of his childe soone taken away,
Now honoured him as a god, which was then a dead man,
And delivered to those that were under him, ceremonies and sacrifices.
Thus in process of time an ungodly custome growen strong, was kept as a law,
And graven images were worshipped by the commandements of kings,
Whom men could not honour in presence, because they dwelt farre off,

WISEDOME OF SOLOMON

They tooke the counterfeit of his visage from farre,   CHAPTER
And made an expresse image of a king whom they honoured,   XIIII
To the end that by this their forwardnes, they might flatter him that was absent, as if he were present.
Also the singular diligence of the artificer did helpe
To set forward the ignorant to more superstition.
For he peradventure willing to please one in authoritie,
Forced all his skill to make the resemblance of the best fashion.
And so the multitude allured by the grace of the worke,
Tooke him now for a god, which a litle before was but honoured as a man.
And this was an occasion to deceive the world:
For men serving either calamitie or tyrannie,
Did ascribe unto stones, and stockes, the incommunicable Name.
Moreover this was not enough for them, that they erred in the knowledge of God,
But whereas they lived in the great warre of ignorance,
Those so great plagues called they peace.
For whilest they slew their children in sacrifices, or used secret ceremonies,   And the effects thereof.
Or made revellings of strange rites,
They kept neither lives nor mariages any longer undefiled:
But either one slew another traiterously, or grieved him by adulterie:
So that there reigned in all men without exception, blood, manslaughter, theft, and dissimulation,
Corruption, unfaithfulnesse, tumults, periurie,
Disquieting of good men,
Forgetfulnesse of good turnes,
Defiling of soules, changing of kinde,
Disorder in mariages, adulterie, and shameles uncleannesse.
For the worshipping of idoles not to be named,
Is the beginning, the cause, and the end of all evill.
For either they are mad when they be merry, or prophesie lies,
Or live uniustly, or else lightly forsweare themselves.
For insomuch as their trust is in idoles which have no life,
Though they sweare falsly, yet they looke not to bee hurt.   God wil punish them that
Howbeit for both causes shal they be iustly punished   :   sweare falsely
Both because they thought not well of God, giving heed by their Idoles.
   unto idols,

WISEDOME OF SOLOMON

CHAPTER XIIII

And also uniustly swore in deceit, despising holinesse.
For it is not the power of them by whom they sweare:
But it is the iust vengeance of sinners,
That punisheth alwayes the offence of the ungodly.

CHAPTER XV

We doe acknowledge the true God.

BUT thou O God, art gracious and true:
Long suffering, and in mercy ordering all things.
For if we sinne we are thine, knowing thy power:
But we will not sinne, knowing that we are counted thine.
For to know thee is perfect righteousnesse:
Yea to know thy power is the roote of immortality.
For neither did the mischievous invention of men deceive us:
Nor an image spotted with divers colours,
The painters fruitlesse labour.
The sight wherof entiseth fooles to lust after it,
And so they desire the forme of a dead image that hath no breath.
Both they that make them, they that desire them, and they that worship them, are lovers of evill things,
And are worthy to have such things to trust upon.

The follie of Idole-makers,

For the potter tempering soft earth,
Fashioneth every vessell with much labour for our service:
Yea of the same clay
Hee maketh both the vessels that serve for cleane uses:
And likewise also all such as serve to the contrary:
But what is the use of either sort,
The potter himselfe is the iudge.
And employing his labours lewdly, he maketh a vaine God of the same clay,
Even he which a little before was made of earth himselfe,
And within a little while after returneth to the same out of the which he was taken:
When his life which was lent him shall be demanded.
Notwithstanding his care is,
Not that hee shall have much labour,
Nor that his life is short:
But striveth to excel goldsmiths, and silversmiths,
And endevoureth to doe like the workers in brasse,
And counteth it his glory to make counterfeit things.
His heart is ashes,
His hope is more vile then earth,

WISEDOME OF SOLOMON

And his life of lesse value then clay: CHAPTER
Forasmuch as hee knew not his maker, XV
And him that inspired into him an active soule,
And breathed in a living spirit.
But they counted our life a pastime,
And our time here a market for gaine:
For, say they, we must be getting every way, though it be by evil meanes.
For this man that of earthly matter maketh brickle vessels, and graven images,
Knoweth himselfe to offend above all others.
And all the enemies of thy people, that hold them in and of the
 subiection enemies of Gods
Are most foolish and are more miserable then very babes. people:
For they counted all the idoles of the heathen to be gods: because besides
Which neither have the use of eyes to see, the idoles of the
Nor noses to draw breath, Gentiles,
Nor eares to heare,
Nor fingers of hands to handle,
And as for their feete they are slow to goe.
For man made them,
And he that borrowed his owne spirit fashioned them,
But no man can make a god like unto himselfe.
For being mortall he worketh a dead thing with wicked hands:
For hee himselfe is better then the things which he worshippeth:
Whereas he lived once, but they never.
Yea they worshipped those beasts also that are most hatefull: they wor-
For being compared together, some are worse then others. shipped vile
Neither are they beautifull, so much, as to bee desired in beasts.
 respect of beasts,
But they went without the praise of God and his blessing.

CHAPTER XVI

THEREFORE by the like were they punished worthily, God gave
 And by the multitude of beasts tormented. strange meate
 In stead of which punishment, dealing graciously to his people, to
  with thine owne people stirre up their
Thou preparedst for them meate of a strange taste: appetite, and
Even quailes to stirre up their appetite: vile beasts to
To the end that they desiring food their enemies
 to take it from
 them.

141

WISEDOME OF SOLOMON

Might for the ougly sight of the beasts sent among them,
Loath even that which they must needs desire:
But these suffering penury for a short space,
Might be made partakers of a strange taste.
For it was requisite, that upon them excercising tyranny should come penury which they could not avoyde:
But to these it should onely be shewed how their enemies were tormented.
For when the horrible fiercenesse of beasts came upon these,
And they perished with the stings of crooked serpents,
Thy wrath endured not for ever.
But they were troubled for a smal season that they might be admonished,
Having a signe of salvation,
To put them in remembrance of the commandement of thy Law.
For hee that turned himselfe towards it, was not saved by the thing that he saw:
But by thee that art the saviour of all.
And in this thou madest thine enemies confesse,
That it is thou who deliverest from all evill:
For them the bitings of grasshoppers and flies killed,
Neither was there found any remedy for their life:
For they were worthy to bee punished by such.
But thy sonnes, not the very teeth of venemous dragons overcame:
For thy mercy was ever by them, and healed them.
·y **were** pricked, that they should remember thy ·ds,
·ere quickly saved, that not falling into deep ·rgetfulnesse,
· might be **continually** mindefull of thy goodnesse.
· **it was** neither herbe, nor mollifying plaister that **restored them to** health:
But thy word, O Lord, which healeth all things.
For thou hast **power of** life and death:
Thou leadest to the gates of hell, and bringest up againe.
A man indeed **killeth** through his malice:
And the spirit when it is gone foorth returneth not;
Neither the **soule** received up, commeth againe.
But it is not **possible** to escape thine hand.
For the ungodly that denied to know thee, were scourged by the **strength** of thine arme:

WISEDOME OF SOLOMON

With strange raines, hailes, and shower were they persecuted, that they could not avoyd,
And through fire were they consumed.
For, which is most to be wondered at,
The fire had more force in the water that quencheth all things:
For the world fighteth for the righteous.
For sometimes the flame was mitigated,
That it might not burne up the beast that were sent against the ungodly:
But themselves might see and perceive that they were persecuted with the iudgement of God.
And at another time it burneth even in the midst of water, above the power of fire,
That it might destroy the fruits of an uniust land.
In stead whereof thou feddest thine owne people, with Angels food,
And didst send them from heaven bread repared without their labour,
Able to content every mans delight, and ⟨a⟩greeing to every taste.
For thy sustenance declared thy sweetnesse unto thy children,
And serving to the appetite of the eater
Tempered it selfe to every mans liking.
But snow and yce endured the fire and meltd not,
That they might know that fire burning i the haile, and sparkling in the raine,
Did destroy the fruits of the enemies.
But this againe did even forget his owne strngth,
That the righteous might be nourished.
For the creature that serveth thee who art ⟨t⟩e maker,
Encreaseth his strength against the unrigteous for their punishment,
And abateth his strength for the benefit of such as put their trust in thee.
Therefore even then was it altered into all fshions,
And was obedient to thy grace that nourishdh all things,
According to the desire of them that had ned
That thy children, O Lord, whom thou loves, might know
That it is not the growing of fruits that nousheth man:
But that it is thy word which preserveth hem that put their trust in thee.

CHAPTER XVI

The creatures altred their nature to pleasure Gods people, and to offend their enemies.

143

WISEDOME OF SOLOMON

CHAPTER XVI

Might for the ougly sight of the beasts sent among them,
Loath even that which they must needs desire:
But these suffering penury for a short space,
Might be made partakers of a strange taste.
For it was requisite, that upon them excercising tyranny should come penury which they could not avoyde:
But to these it should onely be shewed how their enemies were tormented.

Hee stung with his serpents,

For when the horrible fiercenesse of beasts came upon these,
And they perished with the stings of crooked serpents,
Thy wrath endured not for ever.
But they were troubled for a smal season that they might be admonished,
Having a signe of salvation,
To put them in remembrance of the commandement of thy Law.
For hee that turned himselfe towards it, was not saved by the thing that he saw:
But by thee that art the saviour of all.
And in this thou madest thine enemies confesse,
That it is thou who deliverest from all evill:
For them the bitings of grassehoppers and flies killed,
Neither was there found any remedy for their life:
For they were worthy to bee punished by such.
But thy sonnes, not the very teeth of venemous dragons overcame:
For thy mercy was ever by them, and healed them.
For they were pricked, that they should remember thy words,
And were quickly saved, that not falling into deep forgetfulnesse,
They might be continually mindefull of thy goodnesse.

but soone healed them by his word onely.

For it was neither herbe, nor mollifying plaister that restored them to health:
But thy word, O Lord, which healeth all things.
For thou hast power of life and death:
Thou leadest to the gates of hell, and bringest up againe.
A man indeed killeth through his malice:
And the spirit when it is gone foorth returneth not;
Neither the soule received up, commeth againe.
But it is not possible to escape thine hand.
For the ungodly that denied to know thee, were scourged by the strength of thine arme:

142

WISEDOME OF SOLOMON

With strange raines, hailes, and showers were they persecuted, that they could not avoyd,
And through fire were they consumed.
For, which is most to be wondered at,
The fire had more force in the water that quencheth all things:
For the world fighteth for the righteous.
For sometimes the flame was mitigated,
That it might not burne up the beasts that were sent against the ungodly:
But themselves might see and perceive that they were persecuted with the iudgement of God.
And at another time it burneth even in the midst of water, above the power of fire,
That it might destroy the fruits of an uniust land.
In stead whereof thou feddest thine owne people, with Angels food,
And didst send them from heaven bread prepared without their labour,
Able to content every mans delight, and agreeing to every taste.
For thy sustenance declared thy sweetnesse unto thy children,
And serving to the appetite of the eater
Tempered it selfe to every mans liking.
But snow and yce endured the fire and melted not,
That they might know that fire burning in the haile, and sparkling in the raine,
Did destroy the fruits of the enemies.
But this againe did even forget his owne strength,
That the righteous might be nourished.
For the creature that serveth thee who art the maker,
Encreaseth his strength against the unrighteous for their punishment,
And abateth his strength for the benefit of such as put their trust in thee.
Therefore even then was it altered into all fashions,
And was obedient to thy grace that nourisheth all things,
According to the desire of them that had need:
That thy children, O Lord, whom thou lovest, might know
That it is not the growing of fruits that nourisheth man:
But that it is thy word which preserveth them that put their trust in thee.

CHAPTER XVI

The creatures altred their nature to pleasure Gods people, and to offend their enemies

WISEDOME OF SOLOMON

CHAPTER XVI

For that which was not destroied of the fire,
Being warmed with a litle Sunne beame, soone melted away,
That it might bee knowen, that wee must prevent the Sunne, to give thee thanks,
And at the day-spring pray unto thee.
For the hope of the unfaithfull, shal melt away as the Winters hoare-frost,
And shall runne away as unprofitable water.

CHAPTER XVII

Why the Egyptians were punished with darkenesse,

FOR great are thy Iudgements, and cannot be expressed: Therefore unnourtured soules have erred.
For when unrighteous men thought to oppresse the holy nation:
They being shut up in their houses, the prisoners of darkenesse, and fettered with the bondes of a long night,
Lay [there] exiled from the eternall providence.
For while they supposed to lie hid in their secret sinnes,
They were scattered under a darke vaile of forgetfulnesse,
Being horribly astonished, and troubled with (strange) apparitions.

The terrours of that darknes.

For neither might the corner that helde them keepe them from feare:
But noises (as of waters) falling downe, sounded about them,
And sadde visions appeared unto them with heavie countenances.
No power of the fire might give them light:
Neither could the bright flames of the starres endure to lighten that horrible night.
Onely there appeared unto them a fire kindled of it selfe, very dreadfull:
For being much terrified, they thought the things which they saw
To be worse then the sight they saw not.
As for the illusions of arte Magicke, they were put downe,
And their vaunting in wisedome was reproved with disgrace.
For they that promised to drive away terrours, and troubles from a sicke soule,
Were sicke themselves of feare worthy to be laughed at.
For though no terrible thing did feare them:
Yet being skared with beasts that passed by, and hissing of serpents, they died for feare,

144

WISEDOME OF SOLOMON

Denying that they saw the ayre, which could of no side be avoided. CHAPTER XVII

For wickednesse condemned by her owne witnesse, is very timorous,

And being pressed with conscience, alwayes forecasteth grievous things.

For feare is nothing else, but a betraying of the succours which reason offereth.   The terrours of an ill conscience.

And the expectation from within being lesse,

Counteth the ignorance more then the cause which bringeth the torment.

But they sleeping the same sleepe that night which was indeed intolerable,

And which came upon them out of the bottomes of inevitable hell:

Were partly vexed with monstrous apparitions,

And partly fainted, their heart failing them:

For a suddaine feare and not looked for, came upon them.

So then, whosoever there fell downe, was straitly kept,

Shut up in a prison without yron barres.

For whether hee were husbandman, or shepheard,

Or a labourer in the field,

He was overtaken, and endured that necessitie, which could not be avoided:

For they were all bound with one chaine of darkenesse.

Whether it were a whistling winde,

Or a melodious noise of birdes among the spreading branches,

Or a pleasing fall of water running violently:

Or a terrible sound of stones cast downe,

Or a running that could not be seene of skipping beasts,

Or a roaring voice of most savage wilde beasts,

Or a rebounding Eccho from the hollow mountaines:

These things made them to swoone for feare.

For the whole world shined with cleare light,

And none were hindered in their labour.

Over them onely was spread an heavie night,

An image of that darkenesse which should afterwards receive them:

But yet were they unto themselves more grievous then the darkenesse.

5 : T

WISEDOME OF SOLOMON

CHAPTER XVIII

NEVERTHELESSE, thy Saints had a very great light,
  Whose voice they hearing and not seeing their shape,
Because they also had not suffered the same things, they counted them happy.
But for that they did not hurt them now, of whom they had beene wronged before, they thanked them,
And besought them pardon, for that they had beene enemies.
In stead whereof thou gavest them a burning pillar of fire,
Both to be a guide of the unknowen iourney,
And an harmelesse Sunne to entertaine them honourably.

Why Egypt was punished with darkenesse,

For they were worthy to be deprived of light, and imprisoned in darknesse,
Who had kept thy sonnes shut up,
By whom the uncorrupt light of the law was to be given unto the world.

and with the death of their children,

And when they had determined to slay the babes of the Saints,
One child being cast forth, and saved: to reprove them,
Thou tookest away the multitude of their children,
And destroyedst them altogether in a mightie water.
Of that night were our fathers certified afore,
That assuredly knowing unto what oathes they had given credence, they might afterwards bee of good cheere.
So of thy people was accepted both the salvation of the righteous, and destruction of the enemies.
For wherewith thou didst punish our adversaries,
By the same thou didst glorifie us whom thou hadst called.
For the righteous children of good men did sacrifice secretly,
And with one consent made a holy lawe,
That the Saints should bee alike partakers of the same good and evill,
The fathers now singing out the songs of praise.
But on the other side there sounded an ill-according crie of the enemies,
And a lamentable noise was caried abroad for children that were bewailed.
The master and the servaunt were punished after one maner,
And like as the king, so suffered the common person.

WISEDOME OF SOLOMON

So they altogether had innumerable dead with one kind of death,   CHAPTER XVIII
Neither were the living sufficient to burie them:
For in one moment the noblest ofspring of them was destroyed.
For whereas they would not beleeve any thing by reason of the enchantments,
Upon the destruction of the first borne, they acknowledged this people to be the sonnes of God.
For while all things were in quiet silence,
And that night was in the midst of her swift course,
Thine almighty word leapt downe from heaven, out of thy royall throne,
As a fierce man of warre into the midst of a land of destruction,
And brought thine unfained commandement as a sharpe sword,
And standing up filled all things with death,
And it touched the heaven, but it stood upon the earth.
Then suddenly visions of horrible dreames troubled them sore,
And terrours came upon them unlooked for.
And one throwen here, another there halfe dead.   They themselves saw the cause thereof.
Shewed the cause of his death.
For the dreames that troubled them, did foreshew this,
Lest they should perish, and not know why they were afflicted.
Yea, the tasting of death touched the righteous also,   God also plagued his owne people.
And there was a destruction of the multitude in the wildernes:
But the wrath endured not long.
For then the blamelesse man made haste, and stood foorth to defend them,   By what meanes that plague was stayed.
And bringing the shield of his proper ministerie,
Even prayer and the propitiation of incense,
Set himselfe against the wrath, and so brought the calamity to an end,
Declaring that hee was thy servant.
So hee overcame the destroyer,
Not with strength of body, nor force of armes,
But with a word subdued he him that punished,
Alleaging the oathes and covenants made with the fathers.
For when the dead were now fallen downe by heaps one upon another,

WISEDOME OF SOLOMON

CHAPTER XVIII

Standing betweene, he staied the wrath,
And parted the way to the living.
For in the long garment was the whole world,
And in the foure rowes of the stones was the glory of the fathers graven,
And thy maiestie upon the diademe of his head.
Unto these the destroyer gave place, and was afraid of them:
For it was enough that they onely tasted of the wrath.

CHAPTER XIX

Why God shewed no mercie to the Egyptians.

AS for the ungodly, wrath came upon them without mercie unto the end:
For he knew before what they would doe;
Howe that having given them leave to depart,
And sent them hastily away,
They would repent and pursue them.
For whilest they were yet mourning,
And making lamentation at the graves of the dead,
They added another foolish device,
And pursued them as fugitives, whom they had entreated to be gone.
For the destiny, whereof they were worthy, drew them unto this end,
And made them forget the things that had already happened,
That they might fulfill the punishment which was wanting to their torments,

And how wonderfully hee dealt with his people.

And that thy people might passe a wonderfull way:
But they might find a strange death.
For the whole creature in his proper kind was fashioned againe anew,
Serving the peculiar commandements that were given unto them,
That thy children might be kept without hurt.
As namely, a cloud shadowing the campe,
And where water stood before drie land appeared,
And out of the red Sea a way without impediment,
And out of the violent streame a greene field:
Where-thorough all the people went that were defended with thy hand,
Seeing thy marveilous strange wonders.
For they went at large like horses,

WISEDOME OF SOLOMON

And leaped like lambes,
Praising thee O Lord, who hadst delivered them.
For they were yet mindefull of the things that were done while they soiourned in the strange land,
How the ground brought forth flies in stead of cattell,
And how the river cast up a multitude of frogs in stead of fishes.
But afterwards they saw a new generation of foules,
When being led with their appetite they asked delicate meates.
For quailes came up unto them from the Sea, for their contentment.
And punishments came upon the sinners
Not without former signes by the force of thunders:
For they suffered iustly, according to their owne wickednesse,
Insomuch as they used a more hard and hatefull behaviour towards strangers:
For the Sodomits did not receive those whom they knew not when they came:
But these brought friends into bondage, that had well deserved of them.
And not onely so: but peradventure some respect shall be had of those,
Because they used strangers not friendly.
But these very grievously afflicted them,
Whom they had received with feastings,
And were already made partakers of the same lawes with them.
Therefore even with blindnesse were these stricken,
As those were at the doores of the righteous man:
When being compassed about with horrible great darknesse,
Every one sought the passage of his owne doores.
For the elements were changed in themselves by a kind of harmonie,
Like as in a Psaltery notes change the name of the tune,
And yet are alwayes sounds, which may well be perceived by the sight of the things that have beene done.
For earthly things were turned into watry,
And the things that before swamme in the water, now went upon the ground.
The fire had power in the water, forgetting his owne vertue:
And the water forgat his owne quenching nature.

CHAPTER XIX

The Egyptians were worse then the Sodomites.

The wonderfull agreement of the creatures to serve Gods people.

WISEDOME OF SOLOMON

CHAPTER XIX

On the other side, the flames wasted not the flesh of the corruptible living things, though they walked therin,
Neither melted they the ycie kind of heavenly meate, that was of nature apt to melt.
For in all things, O Lord, thou didst magnifie thy people,
And glorifie them, neither didst thou lightly regard them:
But didst assist them in every time and place.

The Wisdome of IESUS the Sonne of Sirach,

OR

ECCLESIASTICUS

A Prologue made by an uncertaine Authour.

THIS Iesus was the sonne of Sirach, and grand-childe to Iesus of the same name with him; This man therefore lived in the latter times, after the people had bene led away captive, and called home againe, and almost after all the Prophets. Now his grandfather Iesus (as he himselfe witnesseth) was a man of great diligence and wisedome among the Hebrewes, who did not onely gather the grave and short Sentences of wise men, that had bene before him, but himselfe also uttered some of his owne, full of much understanding and wisedome. When as therefore the first Iesus died, leaving this booke almost perfected, Sirach his sonne receiving it after him, left it to his owne sonne Iesus, who having gotten it into his hands, compiled it all orderly into one Volume, and called it Wisdome, Intituling it, both by his owne name, his fathers name, and his grandfathers, alluring the hearer by the very name of Wisedome, to have a greater love to the studie of this Booke. It conteineth therefore wise Sayings, darke Sentences, and Parables, and certaine particular ancient godly stories of men that pleased God. Also his Prayer and Song. Moreover, what benefits God had vouchsafed his people, and what plagues he had heaped upon their enemies. This Iesus did imitate Solomon, and was no lesse famous for Wisedome, and learning, both being indeed a man of great learning, and so reputed also.

ECCLESIASTICUS

The Prologue of the Wisdome of Jesus the sonne of Sirach.

WHEREAS many and great things have bene delivered unto us by the Law and the Prophets, and by others that have followed their steps, for the which things Israel ought to be commended for learning and Wisedome, and whereof not onely the Readers must needs become skilful themselves, but also they that desire to learne, be able to profit them which are without, both by speaking and writing: My grandfather Iesus, when he had much given himselfe to the reading of the Law, and the Prophets, and other Bookes of our fathers, and had gotten therein good iudgement, was drawen on also himselfe, to write something pertayning to learning and Wisedome, to the intent that those which are desirous to learne, and are addicted to these things, might profit much more in living according to the Law. Wherefore, let me intreat you to reade it with favour and attention, and to pardon Us, wherein wee may seeme to come short of some words which we have laboured to interprete. For the same things uttered in Hebrew, and translated into an other tongue, have not the same force in them: and not onely these things, but the Law it selfe, and the Prophets, and the rest of the Bookes, have no small difference, when they are spoken in their owne language. For in the eight and thirtieth yeere comming into Egypt, when Euergetes was King, and continuing there some time, I found a Booke of no small learning, therefore I thought it most necessary for mee, to bestow some diligence and travaile to interprete it: Using great watchfulnesse, and skill in that space, to bring the Booke to an end, and set it foorth for them also, which in a strange countrey are willing to learne, being prepared before in maners to live after the Law.

CHAPTER I

ALL wisedome commeth from the Lord,
And is with him for ever.
Who can number the sand of the sea,
And the drops of raine,
And the dayes of eternity?
Who can find out the height of heaven,

All wisedome is from God.

ECCLESIASTICUS

CHAPTER I

And the breadth of the earth, and the decpe, and wisedome?
Wisedome hath beene created before all things,
And the understanding of prudence from everlasting.
¶ The word of God most high, is the fountaine of wisdome,
And her wayes are everlasting commandements.
To whom hath the root of wisdome beene revealed?
Or who hath knowen her wise counsels?
[Unto whom hath the knowledge of wisedome beene made manifest?
And who hath understood her great experience?]
There is one wise and greatly to bee feared;
The Lord sitting upon his Throne.
He created her, and saw her, and numbred her,
And powred her out upon all his workes.

He giveth it to them that love him.
Shee [is] with all flesh according to his gift,
And hee hath given her to them that love him.
The feare of the Lord is honour, and glory,
And gladnesse, and a crowne of reioycing.

The feare of God is full of many blessings.
The feare of the Lord maketh a merrie heart,
And giveth ioy and gladnesse, and a long life.
Who so feareth the Lord, it shall goe well with him at the last,
And he shall finde favour in the day of his death.
To feare the Lord, is the beginning of wisedome:
And it was created with the faithfull in the wombe.
Shee hath built an everlasting foundation with men,
And she shal continue with their seede.
To feare the Lord, is fulnesse of wisedome,
And filleth men with her fruits.
Shee filleth all their house with things desireable,
And the garners with her increase.
The feare of the Lord is a crowne of wisedome,
Making peace and perfect health to flourish, both which are the gifts of God:
And it enlargeth their reioycing that love him.
Wisedome raineth downe skill and knowledge of understanding,
And exalteth them to honour that holde her fast.
The root of wisedome is to feare the Lord,
And the branches thereof are long life.
The feare of the Lord driveth away sinnes:
And where it is present, it turneth away wrath.
A furious man cannot be iustified,

ECCLESIASTICUS

CHAPTER I

For the sway of his fury shalbe his destruction.
A patient man will beare for a time,
And afterward ioy shall spring up unto him.
He wil hide his words for a time,
And the lippes of many shall declare his wisedome.
The parables of knowledge are in the treasures of wisedome:
But godlines is an abomination to a sinner.
If thou desire wisedome, keepe the commaundements,
And the Lord shall give her unto thee.
For the feare of the Lord is wisdome, and instruction:
And faith and meekenesse are his delight.
Distrust not the feare of the Lord when thou art poore: *To feare God without hypocrisie.*
And come not unto him with a double heart.
Be not an hypocrite in the sight of men,
And take good heede what thou speakest.
Exalt not thy selfe, lest thou fall,
And bring dishonour upon thy soule,
And so God discover thy secrets,
And cast thee downe in the midst of the congregation,
Because thou camest not in truth, to the feare of the Lord:
But thy heart is full of deceit.

CHAPTER II

MY sonne, if thou come to serve the Lorde, *Gods servants must looke for trouble,*
Prepare thy soule for temptation.
Set thy heart aright, and constantly endure,
And make not haste in time of trouble.
Cleave unto him, and depart not away,
That thou mayest be increased at thy last end.
Whatsoever is brought upon thee, take cheerefully,
And bee patient when thou art changed to a lowe estate.
For gold is tried in the fire,
And acceptable men in the furnace of adversitie.
Beleeve in him, and he will helpe thee,
Order thy way aright, and trust in him.
Ye that feare the Lord, waite for his mercie, *and be patient, and trust in him.*
And goe not aside, lest ye fall.
Yee that feare the Lord, beleeve him,
And your reward shall not faile.
Ye that feare the Lord, hope for good,

ECCLESIASTICUS

<small>CHAPTER II</small>

And for everlasting ioy and mercy.
Looke at the generations of old, and see,
Did ever any trust in the Lord, and was confounded?
Or did any abide in his feare, and was forsaken?
Or whom did hee ever despise, that called upon him?
For the Lord is full of compassion, and mercie, long suffering, and very pitifull,
And forgiveth sinnes, and saveth in time of affliction.

<small>For woe to them that doe not so.</small>

Woe be to fearefull hearts, and faint hands,
And the sinner that goeth two wayes.
Woe unto him that is faint hearted, for he beleeveth not,
Therefore shall he not be defended.
Woe unto you that have lost patience:
And what will ye doe when the Lord shall visite you?

<small>But they that feare the Lord, will doe so.</small>

They that feare the Lord, will not disobey his word,
And they that love him, will keepe his wayes.
They that feare the Lord, will seeke that which is well pleasing unto him,
And they that love him, shall bee filled with the Law.
They that feare the Lord, will prepare their hearts,
And humble their soules in his sight:
Saying, We wil fal into the hands of the Lord, and not into the hands of men:
For as his maiestie is, so is his mercie.

CHAPTER III

HEARE mee your father, O children,
And doe thereafter, that ye may be safe.
For the Lord hath given the father honour over the children,
And hath confirmed the authoritie of the mother over the sonnes.

<small>Children must honour, and helpe both their parents.</small>

Who so honoureth his father, maketh an atonement for his sinnes.
And he that honoureth his mother, is as one that layeth up treasure.
Who so honoureth his father, shal have ioy of his owne children,
And when he maketh his prayer, hee shall bee heard.
He that honoureth his father, shal have a long life,

ECCLESIASTICUS

CHAPTER III

And he that is obedient unto the Lord, shall bee a comfort to his mother.
He that feareth the Lord, will honour his father,
And will doe service unto his parents, as to his masters.
Honour thy father and mother, both in word and deed,
That a blessing may come upon thee from them.
For the blessing of the father establisheth the houses of children,
But the curse of the mother rooteth out foundations.
Glory not in the dishonour of thy father,
For thy fathers dishonour is no glory unto thee.
For the glory of a man, is from the honour of his father,
And a mother in dishonour, is a reproch to the children.
My sonne, helpe thy father in his age,
And grieve him not as long as hee liveth.
And if his understanding faile, have patience with him,
And despise him not, when thou art in thy ful strength.
For the relieving of thy father shall not be forgotten:
And in stead of sinnes it shall be added to build thee up.
In the day of thine affliction it shall be remembred,
Thy sinnes also shal melt away, as the yce in the faire warme weather.
He that forsaketh his father, is as a blasphemer,
And he that angreth his mother, is cursed of God.
My sonne, goe on with thy businesse in meekenesse,
So shalt thou be beloved of him that is approved.
The greater thou art, the more humble thy selfe,
And thou shalt find favour before the Lord.
Many are in high place and of renowne:
But mysteries are reveiled unto the meeke.
For the power of the Lord is great,
And hee is honoured of the lowly.
Seeke not out the things that are too hard for thee, *We may not desire to knowe all things.*
Neither search the things that are above thy strength.
But what is commaunded thee, thinke thereupon with reverence,
For it is not needfull for thee, to see with thine eyes, the things that are in secret.
Be not curious in unnecessarie matters:
For moe things are shewed unto thee, then men understand.
For many are deceived by their owne vaine opinion,
And an evill suspition hath overthrowen their iudgement.

ECCLESIASTICUS

<small>CHAPTER III
The incorrigible must needes perish.</small>

Without eyes thou shalt want light: professe not the knowledge therfore that thou hast not.
A stubborne heart shall fare evill at the last,
And he that loveth danger shall perish therein.
An obstinate heart shall be laden with sorrowes,
And the wicked man shall heape sinne upon sinne.
In the punishment of the proud there is no remedie:
For the plant of wickednesse hath taken roote in him.
The heart of the prudent will understand a parable,
And an attentive eare is the desire of a wise man.

<small>Almes are rewarded.</small>

Water will quench a flaming fire,
And almes maketh an attonement for sinnes.
And hee that requiteth good turnes, is mindfull of that which may come heereafter:
And when he falleth he shall find a stay.

CHAPTER IIII

<small>We may not despise the poore or fatherlesse,</small>

MY sonne, defraude not the poore of his living,
And make not the needy eies to waite long.
Make not an hungry soule sorrowfull,
Neither provoke a man in his distresse.
Adde not more trouble to an heart that is vexed,
And deferre not to give to him that is in neede.
Reiect not the supplication of the afflicted,
Neither turne away thy face from a poore man.
Turne not away thine eye from the needy,
And give him none occasion to curse thee:
For if he curse thee in the bitternesse of his soule,
His prayer shall be heard of him that made him.
Get thy selfe the love of the congregation,
And bow thy head to a great man.
Let it not grieve thee to bowe downe thine eare to the poor,
And give him a friendly answere with meekenesse.
Deliver him that suffreth wrong, from the hand of the oppressour,
And be not faint hearted when thou sittest in iudgement.
Be as a father unto the fatherlesse,
And in stead of a husband unto their mother,
So shalt thou be as the sonne of the most high,
And he shall love thee more then thy mother doeth.

<small>but seeke for Wisedome,</small>

Wisedome exalteth her children,
And layeth hold of them that seeke her.

ECCLESIASTICUS

He that loveth her, loveth life,   CHAPTER
And they that seeke to her earely, shall be filled with   IIII
   ioy.
He that holdeth her fast shall inherit glory,
And wheresoever she entreth, the Lord will blesse.
They that serve her shall minister to the Holy one,
And them that love her, the Lord doth love.
Who so giveth eare unto her, shall iudge the nations,
And he that attendeth unto her, shall dwell securely.
If a man commit himselfe unto her, he shall inherite her,
And his generation shall hold her in possession.
For at the first she will walke with him by crooked wayes,
And bring feare and dread upon him,
And torment him with her discipline,
Untill she may trust his soule,
And try him by her Lawes.
Then wil she returne the straight way unto him,
And comfort him, and shew him her secrets.
But if he goe wrong, she will forsake him,
And give him over to his owne ruine.
Observe the opportunitie, and beware of evill,   *and not be*
And be not ashamed when it concerneth thy soule.   *ashamed of*
For there is a shame that bringeth sinne,   *some things,*
And there is a shame which is glorie and grace.   *nor gainsay*
Accept no person against thy soule,   *the trueth,*
And let not the reverence of any man cause thee to fall:
And refraine not to speake, when there is occasion to doe
   good,
And hide not thy wisedome in her beautie.
For by speach wisedome shall be knowen,
And learning by the word of the tongue.
In no wise speake against the trueth,
But be abashed of the errour of thine ignorance.
Bee not ashamed to confesse thy sinnes,
And force not the course of the river.
Make not thy selfe an underling to a foolish man,
Neither accept the person of the mighty.
Strive for the trueth unto death, and the Lord shall fight
   for thee.
Be not hastie in thy tongue,
And in thy deeds slacke and remisse.
Bee not as a Lion in thy house,   *nor be as lyons*
Nor franticke among thy servants.   *in our houses.*

ECCLESIASTICUS

<small>CHAPTER IIII</small>

Let not thine hand bee stretched out to receive,
And shut when thou shouldest repay.

CHAPTER V

<small>Wee must not presume of our wealth and strength,</small>

SET not thy heart upon thy goods,
And say not, I have ynough for my life.
Folow not thine owne minde,
And thy strength, to walke in the wayes of thy heart:
And say not, Who shall controll mee for my workes?
For the Lord will surely revenge thy pride.
Say not, I have sinned, and what harme hath happened unto mee?
For the Lord is long-suffering, he wil in no wise let thee goe.
Concerning propitiation, bee not without feare
To adde sinne unto sinne.

<small>Nor of the mercie of God to sinne.</small>

And say not, His mercy is great,
Hee will be pacified for the multitude of my sinnes:
For mercy and wrath come from him,
And his indignation resteth upon sinners.
Make no tarying to turne to the Lord,
And put not off from day to day:
For suddenly shal the wrath of the Lord come foorth,
And in thy securitie thou shalt be destroyed,
And perish in the day of vengeance.
Set not thy heart upon goods uniustly gotten:
For they shall not profit thee in the day of calamitie.

<small>We must not be double tongued,</small>

Winnow not with every winde,
And goe not into every way:
For so doth the sinner that hath a double tongue.
Be stedfast in thy understanding,
And let thy word be the same.
Be swift to heare, and let thy life be sincere,
And with patience give answere.

<small>Nor answere without knowledge.</small>

If thou hast understanding, answer thy neighbour,
If not, lay thy hand upon thy mouth.
Honour and shame is in talke;
And the tongue of man is his fall.
Be not called a whisperer,
And lye not in wait with thy tongue:
For a foule shame is upon the thiefe,
And an evill condemnation upon the double tongue.
Be not ignorant of any thing, in a great matter or a small.

ECCLESIASTICUS

CHAPTER VI

IN stead of a friend, become not an enemie;
   For [thereby] thou shalt inherite an ill name, shame,
     and reproch:
Even so shall a sinner that hath a double tongue.
Extoll not thy selfe in the counsell of thine owne heart,   *Doe not extoll*
That thy soule bee not torne in pieces as a bull [straying alone.] *thy owne conceit,*
Thou shalt eat up thy leaves, and loose thy fruit,
And leave thy selfe as a dry tree.
A wicked soule shall destroy him that hath it,
And shall make him to be laughed to scorne of his enemies.
Sweet language will multiply friends:
And a faire speaking tongue will increase kinde greetings.
Be in peace with many:
Neverthelesse have but one counseller of a thousand.
If thou wouldst get a friend, prove him first,   *But make*
And be not hasty to credit him.   *choise of a friend.*
For some man is a friend for his owne occasion,
And will not abide in the day of thy trouble.
And there is a friend, who being turned to enmitie, and
   strife,
Will discover thy reproch.
Againe some friend is a companion at the table,
And will not continue in the day of thy affliction.
But in thy prosperitie hee will be as thy selfe,
And will be bould over thy servants.
If thou be brought low, he will be against thee,
And will hide himselfe from thy face.
Separate thy selfe from thine enemies,
And take heed of thy friends.
A faithfull friend is a strong defence:
And hee that hath found such an one, hath found a treasure.
Nothing doeth countervaile a faithful friend,
And his excellencie is unvaluable.
A faithfull friend is the medicine of life,
And they that feare the Lord shal finde him.
Who so feareth the Lord shall direct his friendship aright,
For as he is, so shall his neighbour be also.
My sonne, gather instruction from thy youth up: *Seeke wisedome*
So shalt thou finde wisedome till thine old age.   *betimes:*
Come unto her as one that ploweth, and soweth,
And wait for her good fruits,

ECCLESIASTICUS

<small>CHAPTER VI
It is grievous to some,</small>

For thou shalt not toile much in labouring about her,
But thou shalt eat of her fruits right soone.
She is very unpleasant to the unlearned:
He that is without understanding, will not remaine with her.
She wil lye upon him as a mightie stone of triall,
And hee will cast her from him ere it be long.
For wisedome is according to her name,
And she is not manifest unto many.
Give eare, my sonne, receive my advice,
And refuse not my counsell,
And put thy feet into her fetters,
And thy necke into her chaine.
Bow downe thy shoulder, and beare her,
And be not grieved with her bonds.
Come unto her with thy whole heart,
And keepe her wayes with all thy power.
Search and seeke, and shee shall bee made knowen unto thee,
And when thou hast got hold of her, let her not goe.

<small>yet the fruits thereof are pleasant.</small>

For at the last thou shalt finde her rest,
And that shalbe turned to thy ioy.
Then shall her fetters be a strong defence for thee,
And her chaines a robe of glory.
For there is a golden ornament upon her,
And her bandes are purple lace.
Thou shalt put her on as a robe of honour:
And shalt put her about thee as a crowne of ioy.
My sonne, if thou wilt, thou shalt bee taught:
And if thou wilt apply thy minde, thou shalt be prudent.
If thou love to heare, thou shalt receive understanding:
And if thou bow thine eare, thou shalt be wise.
Stand in the multitude of the elders,
And cleave unto him that is wise.

<small>Be ready to heare wise men.</small>

Be willing to heare every godly discourse,
And let not the parables of understanding escape thee.
And if thou seest a man of understanding, get thee betimes unto him,
And let thy foote weare the steps of his doore.
Let thy minde be upon the ordinances of the Lord,
And meditate continually in his commandements:
He shal establish thine heart,
And give thee wisedome at thine owne desire.

ECCLESIASTICUS

CHAPTER VII

Doe no evill, so shall no harme come unto thee. *Wee are exhorted from sinne,*
Depart from the uniust, and iniquitie shall turne away from thee.
My sonne, sow not upon the furrowes of unrighteousnesse,
And thou shalt not reape them seven folde.
Seeke not of the Lord preheminence, *from ambition,*
Neither of the King the seate of honour.
Iustifie not thy selfe before the Lord,
And boast not of thy wisedome before the king.
Seeke not to be iudge,
Being not able to take away iniquitie,
Lest at any time thou feare the person of the mightie,
And lay a stumbling blocke in the way of thy uprightnesse.
Offend not against the multitude of a city,
And then thou shalt not cast thy selfe downe among the people.
Bind not one sinne upon another, *presumption,*
For in one thou shalt not be unpunished.
Say not, God wil looke upon the multitude of my oblations,
And when I offer to the most High God, he will accept it.
Be not faint hearted when thou makest thy prayer, *and fainting in prayer:*
And neglect not to give almes.
Laugh no man to scorne in the bitternesse of his soule:
For there is one which humbleth and exalteth.
Devise not a lie against thy brother: *from lying and backebiting,*
Neither doe the like to thy friend.
Use not to make any maner of lie:
For the custome thereof is not good.
Use not many words in a multitude of Elders,
And make not much babling when thou prayest.
Hate not laborious worke,
Neither husbandrie, which the most High hath ordeined.
Number not thy selfe among the multitude of sinners,
But remember that wrath will not tary long.
Humble thy soule greatly
For the vengeance of the ungodly is fire and wormes.
Change not a friend for any good by no meanes: *and how to esteeme a friend:*
Neither a faithfull brother for the gold of Ophir.
Forgoe not a wise and good woman: *A good wife:*
For her grace is above gold.
Whereas thy servant worketh truely, entreate him not evill, *a servant:*

ECCLESIASTICUS

CHAPTER VII

Nor the hireling that bestoweth himselfe wholly for thee.
Let thy soule love a good servant,
And defraud him not of liberty.

our cattell:
Hast thou cattell? have an eye to them,
And if they be for thy profit, keepe them with thee.

our children and parents:
Hast thou children? instruct them,
And bow downe their necke from their youth.
Hast thou daughters? have care of their body,
And shewe not thy selfe cheerefull toward them.
Marrie thy daughter, and so shalt thou have performed a weightie matter:
But give her to a man of understanding.
Hast thou a wife after thy minde? forsake her not,
But give not thy selfe over to a light woman.
Honour thy father with thy whole heart,
And forget not the sorrowes of thy mother.
Remember that thou wast begot of them,
And how canst thou recompense them the things that they have done for thee?
Feare the Lord with all thy soule,
And reverence his priests.
Love him that made thee with all thy strength,
And forsake not his ministers.

the Lord and his priests:
Feare the Lord, and honour the priest:
And give him his portion, as it is commanded thee,
The first fruits, and the trespasse offering,
And the gift of the shoulders,
And the sacrifice of sanctification, and the first fruits of the holy things.

the poore and those that mourne.
And stretch thine hand unto the poore,
That thy blessing may be perfected.
A gift hath grace in the sight of every man living,
And for the dead deteine it not.
Faile not to bee with them that weepe,
And mourne with them that mourne.
Be not slow to visit the sicke:
For that shall make thee to be beloved.
Whatsoever thou takest in hand, remember the end,
And thou shalt never doe amisse.

ECCLESIASTICUS

CHAPTER VIII

STRIVE not with a mighty man,
Lest thou fall into his hands.
Bee not at variance with a rich man,
Lest he overweigh thee:
For gold hath destroyed many,
And perverted the hearts of kings.
Strive not with a man that is full of tongue,
And heape not wood upon his fire.
Iest not with a rude man,
Lest thy ancestours be disgraced.
Reproch not a man that turneth from sinne,
But remember that we are all worthy of punishment.
Dishonour not a man in his old age:
For even some of us waxe old.
Reioice not over thy greatest enemie being dead,
But remember that we die all.
Despise not the discourse of the wise,
But acquaint thy selfe with their proverbs;
For of them thou shalt learne instruction,
And how to serve great men with ease.
Misse not the discourse of the Elders:
For they also learned of their fathers,
And of them thou shalt learne understanding,
And to give answere as need requireth.
Kindle not the coales of a sinner,
Lest thou be burnt with the flame of his fire.
Rise not up (in anger) at the presence of an iniurious person,
Least he lie in waite to entrap thee in thy words.
Lend not unto him that is mightier then thy selfe;
For if thou lendest him, count it but lost.
Be not surety above thy power:
For if thou be surety, take care to pay it.
Goe not to law with a iudge,
For they will iudge for him according to his honour.
Travaile not by the way with a bold fellow,
Least he become grievous unto thee:
For he will doe according to his owne will,
And thou shalt perish with him through his folly.
Strive not with an angry man,
And goe not with him into a solitary place:
For blood is as nothing in his sight,

CHAPTER VIII
Whom we may not strive with,

nor despise,

nor provoke,

nor have to doe with.

ECCLESIASTICUS

CHAPTER VIII

And where there is no helpe, he will overthrow thee.
Consult not with a foole;
For he cannot keepe counsell.
Doe no secret thing before a stranger,
For thou knowest not what he will bring forth.
Open not thine heart to every man,
Least he requite thee with a shrewd turne.

CHAPTER IX

We are advised how to use our wives.

BE not iealous over the wife of thy bosome,
And teach her not an evil lesson against thy selfe.
Give not thy soule unto a woman,
To set her foot upon thy substance.

What women to avoide.

Meete not with an harlot,
Least thou fall into her snares.
Use not much the companie of a woman that is a singer,
Least thou be taken with her attempts.
Gaze not on a maide,
That thou fall not by those things, that are pretious in her.
Give not thy soule unto harlots,
That thou loose not thine inheritance.
Looke not round about thee, in the streets of the citie,
Neither wander thou in the solitary places thereof.
Turne away thine eye from a beautifull woman,
And looke not upon anothers beautie:
For many have beene deceived by the beautie of a woman,
For heerewith love is kindled as a fire.
Sit not at all with another mans wife,
Nor sit downe with her in thine armes,
And spend not thy money with her at the wine,
Least thine heart incline unto her,
And so thorough thy desire thou fall into destruction.

And not to change an old friend.

Forsake not an old friend,
For the new is not comparable to him:
A new friend is as new wine:
When it is old, thou shalt drinke it with pleasure.
Envy not the glory of a sinner:
For thou knowest not what shall be his end.
Delight not in the thing that the ungodly have pleasure in,
But remember they shall not goe unpunished unto their grave.

ECCLESIASTICUS

Keepe thee farre from the man that hath power to kill,   CHAPTER IX
So shalt thou not doubt the feare of death:
And if thou come unto him, make no fault,   Not to be familiar with men in authority,
Least he take away thy life presently:
Remember that thou goest in the midst of snares,
And that thou walkest upon the battlements of the citie.
As neere as thou canst, ghesse at thy neighbour,   But to knowe our neighbours,
And consult with the wise.
Let thy talke be with the wise,   And to converse with wise men.
And all thy communication in the law of the most High.
And let iust men eate and drinke with thee,
And let thy glorying be in the feare of the Lord.
For the hand of the artificer, the worke shall be commended:
And the wise ruler of the people, for his speech.
A man of an ill tongue is dangerous in his citie,
And he that is rash in his talke shall be hated.

CHAPTER X

A WISE iudge will instruct his people,   The commodities of a wise ruler.
    And the governement of a prudent man is well ordered.
As the iudge of the people is himselfe, so are his officers,
And what maner of man the ruler of the citie is, such are all they that dwell therein.
An unwise king destroyeth his people,
But through the prudence of them which are in authoritie, the citie shalbe inhabited.
The power of the earth is in the hand of the Lord,   God setteth him up.
And in due time hee will set over it one that is profitable.
In the hand of God is the prosperitie of man:
And upon the person of the scribe shall he lay his honour.
Beare not hatred to thy neighbour for every wrong,
And do nothing at all by iniurious practises.
Pride is hatefull before God, and man: The inconveniences of pride, iniustice, and covetousnesse.
And by both doeth one commit iniquitie.
Because of unrighteous dealings, iniuries, and riches got by deceit,
The kingdome is translated from one people to another.
Why is earth and ashes proude?
There is not a more wicked thing, then a covetous man:
For such an one setteth his owne soule to sale,

165

ECCLESIASTICUS

<small>CHAPTER X</small>

Because while he liveth, he casteth away his bowels.
The Phisition cutteth off a long disease,
And he that is to day a King, to morrow shall die.
For when a man is dead,
Hee shall inherite creeping things, beastes and wormes.
The beginning of pride is, when one departeth from God,
And his heart is turned away from his maker.
For pride is the beginning of sinne,
And hee that hath it, shall powre out abomination:
And therefore the Lord brought upon them strange calamities,
And overthrew them utterly.

<small>What God hath done to the proud.</small>

The Lord hath cast downe the thrones of proud Princes,
And set up the meeke in their stead.
The Lord hath plucked up the rootes of the proud nations:
And planted the lowly in their place.
The Lord overthrew countreys of the heathen:
And destroyed them to the foundations of the earth.
He tooke some of them away, and destroyed them,
And hath made their memoriall to cease from the earth.
Pride was not made for men,
Nor furious anger for them that are borne of a woman.

<small>Who shall be honored,</small>

They that feare the Lord are a sure seed,
And they that love him, an honourable plant:
They that regard not the Law, are a dishonourable seed,
They that transgresse the commandements, are a deceivable seed.
Among brethren he that is chiefe is honourable,
So are they that feare the Lord in his eyes.
The feare of the Lord goeth before the obtayning of authoritie:
But roughnesse and pride, is the loosing thereof.
Whether hee bee rich, noble, or poore,
Their glorie is the feare of the Lord.
It is not meet to despise the poore man that hath understanding,
Neither is it convenient to magnifie a sinnefull man.
Great men, and Iudges, and Potentates shall bee honoured,
Yet is there none of them greater than he that feareth the Lord.
Unto the servant that is wise, shall they that are free doe service:

ECCLESIASTICUS

And hee that hath knowledge, will not grudge when he is reformed.   CHAPTER X
Be not overwise in doing thy busines,
And boast not thy selfe in the time of thy distresse.
Better is he that laboureth and aboundeth in all things,
Then hee that boasteth himselfe, and wanteth bread.
My sonne, glorifie thy soule in meekenesse,
And give it honour according to the dignitie thereof.
Who wil iustifie him that sinneth against his owne soule?   And who not.
And who will honour him that dishonoureth his owne life?
The poore man is honoured for his skill,
And the rich man is honoured for his riches.
Hee that is honoured in povertie, how much more in riches?
And he that is dishonourable in riches, how much more in povertie?

CHAPTER XI

WISEDOME lifteth up the head of him that is of low degree,
    And maketh him to sit among great men.
Commend not a man for his beautie,
Neither abhorre a man for his outward appearance.
The Bee is little among such as flie,
But her fruite is the chiefe of sweete things.
Boast not of thy cloathing and raiment,   Wee may not
And exalt not thy selfe in the day of honour: vaunt or set
For the workes of the Lord are wonderfull,   foorth our
And his workes among men are hidden.   selves,
Many kings have sit downe upon the ground,
And one that was never thought of, hath worne the crowne.
Many mightie men have beene greatly disgraced:
And the honourable delivered into other mens hands.
Blame not before thou hast examined the trueth:
Understand first, and then rebuke.
Answere not, before thou hast heard the cause: Nor answere
Neither interrupt men in the midst of their talke.   rashly,
Strive not in a matter that concerneth thee not:
And sit not in iudgement with sinners.
My sonne, meddle not with many matters: Nor meddle
For if thou meddle much, thou shalt not be innocent: with many
And if thou follow after, thou shalt not obtaine,   matters.

ECCLESIASTICUS

<small>CHAPTER XI</small>

Neither shalt thou escape by flying.
There is one that laboureth and taketh paines, and maketh haste,
And is so much the more behinde.
Againe, there is another that is slow, and hath neede of helpe,
Wanting abilitie, and full of povertie,
Yet the eye of the Lord looked upon him for good,
And set him up from his low estate,
And lifted up his head from miserie,
So that many that saw it, marveiled at him.

<small>Wealth and all things else, are from God.</small>

Prosperitie and adversitie, life and death,
Poverty and riches, come of the Lord.
Wisedome, knowledge, and understanding of the Lawe, are of the Lord:
Love, and the way of good workes, are from him.
Errour and darkenesse had their beginning together with sinners:
And evill shall waxe old with them that glory therein.
The gift of the Lord remaineth with the godly,
And his favour bringeth prosperitie for ever.
There is that waxeth rich by his warinesse, and pinching,
And this is the portion of his reward:
Whereas he sayth, I have found rest,
And now will eate continually of my goods,
And yet hee knoweth not what time shall come upon him,
And that hee must leave those things to others, and die.
Be stedfast in thy covenant, and be conversant therein,
And waxe olde in thy worke.
Marveile not at the workes of sinners,
But trust in the Lord, and abide in thy labour:
For it is an easie thing in the sight of the Lord, on the sudden to make a poore man rich.
The blessing of the Lord is in the reward of the godly,
And suddenly he maketh his blessing to flourish.
Say not, What profit is there of my service?
And what good things shal I have hereafter?

<small>Bragge not of thy wealth,</small>

Againe, say not, I have enough, and possesse many things;
And what evill can come to me hereafter?
In the day of prosperitie, there is a forgetfulnesse of affliction:
And in the day of affliction, there is no remembrance of prosperitie.

ECCLESIASTICUS

For it is an easie thing unto the Lord in the day of death, CHAPTER XI
To reward a man according to his wayes.
The affliction of an houre, maketh a man forget pleasure:
And in his end, his deeds shalbe discovered.
Iudge none blessed before his death:
For a man shall bee knowen in his children.
Bring not every man into thine house, Nor bring every man into thy house.
For the deceitfull man hath many traines.
Like as a Partrich taken [and kept] in a cage, so is the heart of the proud;
And like as a spie, watcheth hee for thy fall.
For hee lieth in wait, and turneth good into evill,
And in things worthy praise, will lay blame upon thee.
Of a sparke of fire, a heape of coales is kindled:
And a sinnefull man layeth waite for blood.
Take heed of a mischievous man, (for hee worketh wickednesse)
Lest hee bring upon thee a perpetuall blot.
Receive a stranger into thine house, and hee will disturbe thee,
And turne thee out of thine owne.

CHAPTER XII

WHEN thou wilt doe good, know to whom thou doest it,
So shalt thou be thanked for thy benefites.
Do good to the godly man, and thou shalt find a recompence, Be not liberall to the ungodly.
And if not from him, yet from the most High.
There can no good come to him that is alwayes occupied in evill:
Nor to him that giveth no almes.
Give to the godly man,
And helpe not a sinner.
Doe well unto him that is lowly,
But give not to the ungodly:
Hold backe thy bread, and give it not unto him,
Lest he overmaster thee thereby.
For [else] thou shalt receive twice as much evill,
For all the good thou shalt have done unto him.
For the most High hateth sinners,
And will repay vengeance unto the ungodly,

ECCLESIASTICUS

CHAPTER XII

And keepeth them against the mightie day of their punishment.
Give unto the good,
And helpe not the sinner.
A friend cannot be knowen in prosperitie,
And an enemy cannot be hidden in adversitie.
In the prosperitie of a man, enemies will be grieved,
But in his adversitie, even a friend will depart.

Trust not thine enemie, nor the wicked.

Never trust thine enemie:
For like as yron rusteth, so is his wickednesse.
Though he humble himselfe, and goe crouching,
Yet take good heed, and beware of him,
And thou shalt bee unto him, as if thou hadst wiped a looking glasse,
And thou shalt knowe that his rust hath not beene altogether wiped away.
Set him not by thee,
Lest when he hath overthrowen thee, he stand up in thy place,
Neither let him sit at thy right hand,
Lest he seeke to take thy seat,
And thou at the last remember my wordes,
And be pricked therewith.
Who will pitie a charmer that is bitten with a serpent,
Or any such as come nigh wilde beasts?
So one that goeth to a sinner, and is defiled with him in his sinnes, who will pitie?
For a while hee will abide with thee,
But if thou begin to fall, he wil not tarie.
An enemie speaketh sweetly with his lippes,
But in his heart he imagineth how to throw thee into a pit:
Hee will weepe with his eyes,
But if he find opportunitie, hee will not be satisfied with blood.
If adversitie come upon thee, thou shalt find him there first,
And though he pretend to helpe thee, yet shal he undermine thee.
He will shake his head and clap his handes,
And whisper much, and change his countenance.

ECCLESIASTICUS

CHAPTER XIII

HE that toucheth pitch, shal be defiled therewith,
    And hee that hath fellowship with a proude man,
        shall be like unto him.
Burthen not thy selfe above thy power, while thou livest,
And have no fellowship with one that is mightier, and richer
    then thy selfe.
For how agree the kettle and the earthen pot together?
For if the one be smitten against the other, it shall be broken.
The rich man hath done wrong,
And yet he threatneth withall:
The poore is wronged, and he must intreat also.
If thou be for his profit, he will use thee:
But if thou have nothing, he will forsake thee.
If thou have any thing, he will live with thee,
Yea he will make thee bare, and will not be sorie for it.
If he have need of thee, hee will deceive thee,
And smile upon thee, and put thee in hope,
He will speake thee faire, and say, What wantest thou?
And hee will shame thee by his meates,
Untill he have drawen thee drie twice or thrice,
And at the last hee will laugh thee to scorne:
Afterward when he seeth thee, he will forsake thee,
And shake his head at thee.
Beware that thou bee not deceived, and brought downe in
    thy iolitie.
If thou be invited of a mighty man, withdraw thy selfe,
And so much the more will he invite thee.
Presse thou not upon him, lest thou be put backe,
Stand not farre off, lest thou be forgotten.
Affect not to be made equall unto him in talke,
And beleeve not his many words:
For with much communication will he tempt thee,
And smiling upon thee will get out thy secrets.
But cruelly he will lay up thy words,
And will not spare to doe thee hurt, and to put thee in
    prison.
Observe and take good heed,
For thou walkest in peril of thy overthrowing:
When thou hearest these things, awake in thy sleepe.
Love the Lord all thy life,
And call upon him for thy salvation.

Sidenote: CHAPTER XIII. Keepe not companie with the proude, or a mightier then thy selfe.

ECCLESIASTICUS

CHAPTER XIII

Like will to like.

Every beast loveth his like,
And every man loveth his neighbour.
All flesh consorteth according to kind,
And a man will cleave to his like:
What fellowship hath the wolfe with the lambe?
So the sinner with the godly.
What agreement is there betweene the Hyena and a dogge?
And what peace betweene the rich and the poore?
As the wilde asse is the lyons pray in the wildernesse:
So the rich eate up the poore.
As the proud hate humilitie:
So doth the rich abhorre the poore.

The difference betweene the rich and the poore.

A rich man beginning to fall, is held up of his friends:
But a poore man being downe, is thrust also away by his friends.
When a rich man is fallen, he hath many helpers:
He speaketh things not to be spoken, and yet men iustifie him:
The poore man slipt, and yet they rebuked him too:
He spake wisely, and could have no place.
When a rich man speaketh, every man holdeth his tongue,
And looke what hee sayeth, they extoll it to the clouds:
But if the poore man speake, they say, What fellow is this?
And if he stumble, they will helpe to overthrowe him.
Riches are good unto him that hath no sinne,
And poverty is evill in the mouth of the ungodly.

A mans heart will change his countenance.

The heart of a man changeth his countenance,
Whether it be for good or evill:
And a merry heart maketh a cheerefull countenance.
A cheerefull countenance is a token of a heart that is in prosperity,
And the finding out of parables, is a wearisome labour of the minde.

CHAPTER XIIII

A good conscience maketh men happie.

BLESSED is the man that hath not slipt with his mouth,
And is not pricked with the multitude of sinnes.
Blessed is hee whose conscience hath not condemned him,
And who is not fallen from his hope in the Lord.
Riches are not comely for a niggard:

ECCLESIASTICUS

And what should an envious man doe with money?   CHAPTER
He that gathereth by defrauding his owne soule,   XIIII
Gathereth for others, that shall spend his goods riotously.
Hee that is evill to himselfe, to whom will he be good?   The niggard
He shall not take pleasure in his goods.   doth good to
There is none worse then he that envieth himselfe;   none.
And this is a recompence of his wickednesse.
And if he doth good, he doth it unwillingly,
And at the last he will declare his wickednesse.
The envious man hath a wicked eye,
He turneth away his face and despiseth men.
A covetous mans eye is not satisfied with his portion,
And the iniquity of the wicked dryeth up his soule.
A wicked eye envieth [his] bread,
And he is a niggard at his table.
My sonne, according to thy habilitie doe good to thy selfe,
And give the Lord his due offering.
Remember that death will not be long in comming,
And that the covenant of the grave is not shewed unto thee.
Doe good unto thy friend before thou die,   But doe thou
And according to thy abilitie, stretch out thy hand and give   good.
      to him.
Defraud not thy selfe of the good day,
And let not the part of a good desire overpasse thee.
Shalt thou not leave thy travailes unto another?
And thy labours to be divided by lot?
Give, and take, and sanctifie thy soule,
For there is no seeking of dainties in the grave.
All flesh waxeth old as a garment:
For the covenant from the beginning is; thou shalt die the
      death.
As of the greene leaves on a thicke tree,
Some fall, and some grow;
So is the generation of flesh and blood,
One commeth to an end, and another is borne.
Every worke rotteth and consumeth away,
And the worker therof shal goe withall.
Blessed is the man that doeth meditate good things in   Men are happy
      wisdome,   that draw neere
And that reasoneth of holy things by his understanding.   to wisedome.
He that considereth her wayes in his heart,
Shall also have understanding in her secrets.
Goe after her as one that traceth,

173

ECCLESIASTICUS

<small>CHAPTER XIIII</small>

And lie in wait in her wayes.
Hee that prieth in at her windowes,
Shal also hearken at her doores.
Hee that doeth lodge neere her house,
Shall also fasten a pin in her walles.
He shall pitch his tent nigh unto her,
And shall lodge in a lodging where good things are.
He shal set his children under her shelter,
And shall lodge under her branches.
By her he shall be covered from heat,
And in her glory shall he dwell.

CHAPTER XV

HE that feareth the Lord will doe good,
And he that hath the knowledge of the Law shal obtaine her.

<small>Wisedome embraceth those that feare God.</small>

And as a mother shall she meet him,
And receive him as a wife maried of a virgin.
With the bread of understanding shall she feed him,
And give him the water of wisedome to drinke.
Hee shall be stayed upon her, and shall not be moved,
And shall rely upon her, and shall not be confounded.
Shee shall exalt him above his neighbours,
And in the midst of the congregation shall she open his mouth.
He shall finde ioy, and a crowne of gladnesse,
And she shall cause him to inherit an everlasting name.

<small>The wicked shall not get her.</small>

But foolish men shall not attaine unto her,
And sinners shall not see her.
For she is farre from pride,
And men that are liers cannot remember her.
Praise is not seemly in the mouth of a sinner,
For it was not sent him of the Lord:
For praise shalbe uttered in wisdome,
And the Lord wil prosper it.

<small>We may not charge God with our faults:</small>

Say not thou, It is through the Lord, that I fell away,
For thou oughtest not to doe the things that he hateth.
Say not thou, He hath caused mee to erre,
For hee hath no need of the sinfull man.
The Lord hateth all abomination,
And they that feare God love it not.
Hee himselfe made man from the beginning,

ECCLESIASTICUS

And left him in the hand of his counsell,
If thou wilt, to keepe the Commandements,
And to performe acceptable faithfulnesse.
He hath set fire and water before thee:
Stretch forth thy hand unto whether thou wilt.
Before man is life and death,
And whether him liketh shalbe given him.
For the wisedome of the Lord is great,
And he is mighty in power, and beholdeth all things,
And his eyes are upon them that feare him,
And hee knoweth every worke of man.
Hee hath commanded no man to do wickedly,
Neither hath he given any man license to sinne.

CHAPTER XV

For he made, and left us to our selves.

CHAPTER XVI

DESIRE not a multitude of unprofitable children,
    Neither delight in ungodly sonnes.
    Though they multiply, reioyce not in them,
Except the feare of the Lord be with them.
Trust not thou in their life,
Neither respect their multitude:
For one that is iust, is better then a thousand,
And better it is to die without children, then to have them
    that are ungodly.
For by one that hath understanding, shall the city be replenished,
But the kindred of the wicked, shall speedily become desolate.
Many such things have I seene with mine eyes,
And mine eare hath heard greater things then these.
In the congregation of the ungodly, shall a fire be kindled,
And in a rebellious nation, wrath is set on fire.
Hee was not pacified towards the olde giants,
Who fell away in the strength of their foolishnesse.
Neither spared he the place where Lot soiourned,
But abhorred them for their pride.
Hee pitied not the people of perdition,
Who were taken away in their sinnes.
Nor the sixe hundreth thousand footmen,
Who were gathered together in the hardnesse of their
    hearts.
And if there be one stiffe-necked among the people,
It is marveile, if he escape unpunished;

It is better to have none then many lewd children.

The wicked are not spared for their number.

ECCLESIASTICUS

CHAPTER XVI

Both the wrath and the mercy of the Lord are great.

For mercy and wrath are with him,
Hee is mighty to forgive, and to powre out displeasure.
As his mercy is great, so is his correction also:
He iudgeth a man according to his workes.
The sinner shall not escape with his spoiles,
And the patience of the godly shall not be frustrate.
Make way for every worke of mercy:
For every man shall finde according to his workes.
The Lord hardened Pharaoh, that hee should not know him,
That his powerfull workes might be knowen to the world.
His mercy is manifest to every creature,
And hee hath separated his light from the darkenesse with an Adamant.

The wicked cannot be hid.

Say not thou, I will hide my selfe from the Lord:
Shall any remember me from above?
I shall not be remembred among so many people:
For what is my soule among such an infinite number of creatures?
Behold, the heaven, and the heaven of heavens,
The deepe and the earth, and all that therein is, shall be mooved when he shall visit.
The mountaines also, and foundations of the earth
Shall bee shaken with trembling, when the Lord looketh upon them.

Gods workes are unsearchable.

No heart can thinke upon these things worthily:
And who is able to conceive his wayes?
It is a tempest, which no man can see:
For the most part of his workes are hidde.
Who can declare the workes of his iustice?
Or who can endure them?
For his Covenant is afarre off,
And the triall of all things is in the ende.
He that wanteth understanding, will thinke upon vaine things:
And a foolish man erring, imagineth follies.
My sonne, hearken unto mee, and learne knowledge,
And marke my words with thy heart.
I will shewe foorth doctrine in weight,
And declare his knowledge exactly.
The works of the Lord are done in iudgement from the beginning:
And from the time he made them, hee disposed the parts thereof.

ECCLESIASTICUS

Hee garnished his workes for ever,
And in his hand are the chiefe of them unto all generations:
They neither labour, nor are weary,
Nor cease from their workes.
None of them hindreth another,
And they shall never disobey his word.
After this, the Lord looked upon the earth,
And filled it with his blessings.
With all maner of living things hath hee covered the face thereof,
And they shall returne into it againe.

CHAPTER XVII

THE Lord created man of the earth,
And turned him into it againe.
He gave them few dayes, and a short time,
And power also over the things therein.
He endued them with strength by themselves,
And made them according to his image,
And put the feare of man upon all flesh,
And gave him dominion over beasts and foules.
[They received the use of the five operations of the Lord,
And in the sixt place he imparted them understanding,
And in the seventh, speech, an interpreter of the cogitations thereof.]
Counsell, and a tongue, and eyes,
Eares, and a heart, gave he them to understand.
Withall, hee filled them with the knowledge of understanding,
And shewed them good and evill.
Hee set his eye upon their hearts,
That he might shew them the greatnesse of his workes.
He gave them to glory in his marveilous actes for ever,
That they might declare his works with understanding.
And the elect shall praise his holy Name.
Beside this he gave them knowledge,
And the law of life for an heritage.
He made an everlasting covenant with them,
And shewed them his iudgements.
Their eyes saw the maiestie of his glory,
And their eares heard his glorious voyce.
And he said unto them, Beware of all unrighteousnes,

ECCLESIASTICUS

CHAPTER XVII

And he gave every man commandement concerning his neighbour,
Their wayes are ever before him,
And shall not be hid from his eyes.
Every man from his youth is given to evill,
Neither could they make to themselves fleshie hearts for stonie.
For in the division of the nations of the whole earth, he set a ruler over every people,
But Israel is the Lords portion.
Whom being his first borne, hee nourisheth with discipline,
And giving him the light of his love, doth not forsake him.

For God seeth all things.

Therefore all their workes are as the Sunne before him,
And his eyes are continually upon their wayes.
None of their unrighteous deeds are hid from him,
But all their sinnes are before the Lord:
But the Lord being gracious, and knowing his workemanship,
Neither left nor forsooke them, but spared them.
The almes of a man is as a signet with him,
And he will keep the good deedes of man, as the apple of the eye,
And give repentance to his sonnes and daughters.
Afterward he will rise up and reward them,
And render their recompense upon their heads.
But unto them that repent, he granted them returne,
And comforted those that faile in patience.

Turne to him while thou livest.

Returne unto the Lord, and forsake thy sinnes,
Make thy prayer before his face, and offend lesse.
Turne againe to the most High, and turne away from iniquitie:
For he will leade thee out of darkenesse into the light of health,
And hate thou abomination vehemently.
Who shall praise the most High in the grave,
In stead of them which live and give thanks?
Thankesgiving perisheth from the dead, as from one that is not:
The living and sound in heart, shall praise the Lord.
How great is the loving kindnes of the Lord our God,
And his compassion unto such as turne unto him in holinesse?
For all things cannot bee in men,
Because the sonne of man is not immortal.
What is brighter then the Sun? yet the light thereof faileth:

178

ECCLESIASTICUS

And flesh and blood will imagine evill.   CHAPTER
Hee vieweth the power of the height of heaven,   XVII
And all men are but earth and ashes.

CHAPTER XVIII

HEE that liveth for ever, created all things in generall.
    The Lord onely is righteous,
    And there is none other but he.
Who governeth the world with the palme of his hand, and all things obey his will,
For he is the king of all,
By his power dividing holy things among them from prophane.
To whom hath he given power to declare his works?   *Gods workes*
And who shall finde out his noble actes?   *are to be*
Who shall number the strength of his maiestie?   *wondred at.*
And who shall also tel out his mercies?
As for the wonderous workes of the Lord, there may nothing bee taken from them, neither may any thing bee put unto them,
Neither can the ground of them be found out.
When a man hath done, then he beginneth,
And when hee leaveth off, then he shall be doubtfull.
What is man, and whereto serveth he?
What is his good, and what is his evil?
The number of a mans dayes at the most are an hundred   *Mans life*
    yeeres.   *is short.*
As a drop of water unto the Sea, and a gravell stone in comparison of the sand,
So are a thousand yeeres to the dayes of eternitie.
Therfore is God patient with them,   *God is*
And powreth forth his mercy upon them.   *mercifull.*
He saw and perceived their end to be evill,
Therefore he multiplied his compassion.
The mercy of man is toward his neighbour,
But the mercy of the Lord is upon all flesh:
He reprooveth and nurtureth, and teacheth,
And bringeth againe as a shepheard his flocke.
He hath mercy on them that receive discipline,
And that diligently seeke after his iudgements.   *Doe not*
My sonne, blemish not thy good deeds,   *blemish thy*
    good deeds
Neither use uncomfortable words when thou givest any thing. *with ill wordes.*

ECCLESIASTICUS

<small>CHAPTER
XVIII</small>

Shall not the deaw asswage the heate?
So is a word better then a gift.
Loe is not a word better then a gift?
But both are with a gracious man.
A foole will upbraide churlishly,
And a gift of the envious consumeth the eyes.
Learne before thou speake,
And use phisicke, or ever thou be sicke.
Before iudgement examine thy selfe,
And in the day of visitation thou shalt find mercy.
Humble thy selfe before thou be sicke,
And in the time of sinnes shew repentance.

<small>Deferre not to
bee iustified.</small>

Let nothing hinder thee to pay thy vowe in due time,
And deferre not untill death to be iustified.
Before thou prayest, prepare thy selfe,
And be not as one that tempteth the Lord.
Thinke upon the wrath that shall be at the end;
And the time of vengeance when he shall turne away his face.
When thou hast enough remember the time of hunger,
And when thou art rich thinke upon poverty and need.
From the morning untill the evening the time is changed,
And all things are soone done before the Lord.
A wise man will feare in every thing,
And in the day of sinning he will beware of offence:
But a foole will not observe time.
Every man of understanding knoweth wisedome,
And wil give praise unto him that found her.
They that were of understanding in sayings, became also wise themselves,
And powred forth exquisite parables.

<small>Followe not
thy lustes.</small>

Goe not after thy lustes,
But refraine thy selfe from thine appetites.
If thou givest thy soule the desires that please her,
She will make thee a laughing stocke to thine enemies, that maligne thee.
Take not pleasure in much good cheere,
Neither be tyed to the expence thereof.
Be not made a begger by banquetting upon borrowing,
When thou hast nothing in thy purse,
For thou shalt lie in waite for thy owne life:
And be talked on.

ECCLESIASTICUS

CHAPTER XIX

A LABOURING man that is given to drunkennesse shal not be rich,
    And hee that contemneth small things shall fall by little and little.
Wine and women will make men of understanding to fall away, *Wine and women seduce wise men.*
And he that cleaveth to harlots will become impudent.
Mothes and wormes shall have him to heritage,
And a bold man shall be taken away.
He that is hasty to give credit is light minded,
And he that sinneth shall offend against his owne soule.
Who so taketh pleasure in wickednesse shall be condemned,
But he that resisteth pleasures, crowneth his life.
He that can rule his tongue shall live without strife,
And he that hateth babbling, shall have lesse evill.
Rehearse not unto another that which is told unto thee, *Say not all thou bearest.*
And thou shalt fare never the worse.
Whether it be to friend or foe, talk not of other mens lives,
And if thou canst without offence reveale them not.
For he heard and observed thee,
And when time commeth he will hate thee.
If thou hast heard a word, let it die with thee,
And be bold it will not burst thee.
A foole travaileth with a word,
As a woman in labour of a child.
As an arrowe that sticketh in a mans thigh,
So is a word within a fooles belly.
Admonish a friend, it may be he hath not done it,
And if he have [done it] that he doe it no more.
Admonish thy friend, it may be he hath not said it,
And if he have, that he speake it not againe.
Admonish a friend : for many times it is a slander,
And beleeve not every tale.
There is one that slippeth in his speach, but not from his heart,
And who is he that hath not offended with his tongue ?
Admonish thy neighbour before thou threaten him, *Reprove thy friend without anger.*
And not being angry give place to the Law of the most high.
The feare of the Lord is the first step to be accepted [of him,]
And wisedome obtaineth his love.

ECCLESIASTICUS

CHAPTER XIX

The knowledge of the Commandments of the Lord, is the doctrine of life,
And they that do things that please him, shall receive the fruit of the tree of immortalitie.
The feare of the Lord is all wisedome,
And in all wisedome is the performance of the Law, and the knowledge of his omnipotencie.
If a servant say to his master, I will not doe as it pleaseth thee,
Though afterward hee doe it, hee angereth him that nourisheth him.

There is no wisedome in wickednesse.

The knowledge of wickednes is not wisedome,
Neither at any time the counsell of sinners, prudence.
There is a wickednesse, and the same an abomination,
And there is a foole wanting in wisedome.
He that hath smal understanding and feareth God,
Is better then one that hath much wisedome, and transgresseth the Law of the most High.
There is an exquisite subtilty, and the same is uniust,
And there is one that turneth aside to make iudgement appeare:
And there is a wise man that iustifieth in iudgement.
There is a wicked man that hangeth downe his head sadly;
But inwardly he is full of deceit,
Casting downe his countenance, and making as if he heard not:
Where he is not knowen, he will do thee a mischiefe before thou be aware.
And if for want of power hee be hindered from sinning,
Yet when he findeth opportunitie he wil doe evil.
A man may bee knowen by his looke,
And one that hath understanding, by his countenance, when thou meetest him.
A mans attire, and excessive laughter,
And gate, shew what he is.

CHAPTER XX

Of silence and speaking.

THERE is a reproofe that is not comely:
Againe some man holdeth his tongue, and he is wise.
It is much better to reproove, then to be angry secretly,
And he that confesseth his fault, shall be preserved from hurt.
How good is it when thou art reproved, to shew repentance?

ECCLESIASTICUS

For so shalt thou escape wilfull sinne.
As is the lust of an Eunuch to defloure a virgine;
So is he that executeth iudgement with violence.
There is one that keepeth silence and is found wise:
And another by much babling becommeth hatefull.
Some man holdeth his tongue, because hee hath not to answere,
And some keepeth silence, knowing his time.
A wise man wil hold his tongue till he see opportunitie:
But a babler and a foole will regard no time.
He that useth many words shalbe abhorred;
And hee that taketh to himselfe authoritie therein, shalbe hated.
There is a sinner that hath good successe in evill things;
And there is a gaine that turneth to losse.
There is a gift that shall not profit thee;
And there is a gift whose recompence is double.
There is an abasement because of glory;
And there is that lifteth up his head from a low estate.
There is that buyeth much for a little,
And repayeth it seven fold.
A wise man by his words maketh himselfe beloved:
But the graces of fooles shalbe powred out.
The gift of a foole shall doe thee no good when thou hast it;
Neither yet of the envious for his necessitie:
For hee looketh to receive many things for one.
Hee giveth little and upbraideth much;
He openeth his mouth like a crier;
To day he lendeth, and to morrow will he aske it againe:
Such an one is to be hated of God and man.
The foole saith, I have no friends,
I have no thanke for all my good deeds:
And they that eate my bread speake evill of me.
How oft, and of how many shall he be laughed to scorne?
For hee knoweth not aright what it is to have;
And it is all one unto him, as if he had it not.
To slip upon a pavement, is better then to slip with the tongue:
So, the fall of the wicked shall come speedily.
An unseasonable tale will alwayes be in the mouth of the unwise.
A wise sentence shall be reiected when it commeth out of a fools mouth:

CHAPTER XX

Of gifts, and gaine.

Of slipping by the tongue.

ECCLESIASTICUS

CHAPTER XX

For he will not speake it in due season.
There is that is hindred from sinning through want:
And when hee taketh rest, he shall not be troubled.
There is that destroyeth his owne soule through bashfulnesse,
And by accepting of persons overthroweth himselfe.
There is that for bashfulnes promiseth to his friend,
And maketh him his enemy for nothing.

Of lying.

A lie is a foule blot in a man,
Yet it is continually in the mouth of the untaught.
A thiefe is better then a man that is accustomed to lie:
But they both shall have destruction to heritage.
The disposition of a liar is dishonourable,
And his shame is ever with him.

Of divers advertisements.

A wise man shall promote himselfe to honour with his words:
And hee that hath understanding, will please great men.
He that tilleth his land, shall increase his heape:
And he that pleaseth great men, shal get pardon for iniquity.
Presents and gifts blind the eyes of the wise,
And stoppe up his mouth that he cannot reproove.
Wisedome that is hidde, and treasure that is hoarded up,
What profit is in them both?
Better is he that hideth his folly,
Then a man that hideth his wisedome.
Necessary patience in seeking the Lord,
Is better then he that leadeth his life without a guide.

CHAPTER XXI

MY sonne, hast thou sinned? doe so no more,
But aske pardon for thy former sinnes.

Flee from sinne as from a serpent.

Flee from sinne as from the face of a Serpent:
For if thou commest too neere it, it will bite thee:
The teeth thereof, are as the teeth of a lyon,
Slaying the soules of men.
All iniquitie is as a two edged sword,
The wounds whereof cannot be healed.

His oppression will undoe the rich.

To terrifie and doe wrong, will waste riches:
Thus the house of proude men shalbe made desolate.
A prayer out of a poore mans mouth reacheth to the **eares** of God,
And his iudgement commeth speedily.
He that hateth to be reprooved, is in the way of sinners:

ECCLESIASTICUS

But hee that feareth the Lord, will repent from his heart.   CHAPTER
An eloquent man is knowen farre and neere,   XXI
But a man of understanding knoweth when he slippeth.
He that buildeth his house with other mens money,
Is like one that gathereth himselfe stones for the tombe of
    his buriall,
The congregation of the wicked is like tow wrapped together: *The ende of the*
And the end of them is a flame of fire to destroy them.   *uniust shall be*
The way of sinners is made plaine with stones,   *naught.*
But at the end thereof is the pit of hell.
Hee that keepeth the Law of the Lord, getteth the under-
    standing thereof:
And the perfection of the feare of the Lord, is wisedome.
He that is not wise, will not be taught: *The differences*
But there is a wisedome which multiplieth bitternesse.   *betweene the*
The knowledge of a wise man shall abound like a flood: *foole and the*
And his counsell is like a pure fountaine of life.   *wise.*
The inner parts of a foole, are like a broken vessell,
And he will holde no knowledge as long as he liveth.
If a skilfull man heare a wise word,
Hee will commend it, and adde unto it:
But assoone as one of no understanding heareth it, it dis-
    pleaseth him,
And he casteth it behinde his backe.
The talking of a foole is like a burden in the way:
But grace shall be found in the lips of the wise.
They inquire at the mouth of the wise man in the congrega-
    tion,
And they shall ponder his words in their heart.
As is a house that is destroyed, so is wisedome to a foole:
And the knowledge of the unwise, is as talke without sense.
Doctrine unto fooles, is as fetters on the feete,
And like manacles on the right hand.
A foole lifteth up his voyce with laughter,
But a wise man doeth scarce smile a litle.
Learning is unto a wise man, as an ornament of gold,
And like a bracelet upon his right arme.
A foolish mans foote is soone in his [neighbours] house:
But a man of experience is ashamed of him.
A foole will peepe in at the doore into the house,
But he that is well nurtured, will stand without.
It is the rudenesse of a man to hearken at the doore
But a wise man will be grieved with the disgrace.

ECCLESIASTICUS

CHAPTER XXI

The lips of talkers will bee telling such things as pertaine not unto them:
But the words of such as have understanding, are weighed in the ballance.
The heart of fooles is in their mouth,
But the mouth of the wise is in their heart.
When the ungodly curseth Satan,
He curseth his owne soule.
A whisperer defileth his owne soule,
And is hated wheresoever hee dwelleth.

CHAPTER XXII

Of the slouthfull man,

A SLOUTHFUL man is compared to a filthy stone,
And every one will hisse him out to his disgrace.
A slouthfull man is compared to the filth of a dunghill:
Every man that takes it up, will shake his hand.

and a foolish daughter.

An evill nurtured sonne is the dishonour of his father that begate him:
And a [foolish] daughter is borne to his losse.
A wise daughter shall bring an inheritance to her husband:
But shee that liveth dishonestly, is her fathers heavinesse.
Shee that is bold, dishonoureth both her father and her husband,
But they both shall despise her.
A tale out of season [is as] musick in mourning:
But stripes and correction of wisedome are never out of time.
Who so teacheth a foole, is as one that gleweth a potsheard together,
And as hee that waketh one from a sound sleepe.
Hee that telleth a tale to a foole, speaketh to one in a slumber:
When hee hath told his tale, he will say, What is the matter?
If children live honestly, and have wherwithall,
They shall cover the basenesse of their parents.
But children being haughtie through disdaine, and want of nurture,
Doe staine the nobilitie of their kinred.

Weepe rather for fooles, then for the dead.

Weepe for the dead, for hee hath lost the light:
And weepe for the foole, for he wanteth understanding:
Make litle weeping for the dead, for hee is at rest:
But the life of the foole is worse then death.
Seven dayes doe men mourne for him that is dead;

ECCLESIASTICUS

But for a foole, and an ungodly man, all the dayes of his life.   CHAPTER
Talke not much with a foole,   XXII
And goe not to him that hath no understanding,   Meddle not
Beware of him lest thou have trouble,   with them.
And thou shalt never be defiled with his fooleries:
Depart from him, and thou shalt find rest,
And never bee disquieted with madnesse.
What is heavier then lead?
And what is the name thereof, but a foole?
Sand, and salt, and a masse of yron is easier to beare
Then a man without understanding.
As timber girt and bound together in a building, cannot be   The wise mans
    loosed with shaking: heart will not
So the heart that is stablished by advised counsel, shal feare   shrinke.
    at no time.
A heart setled upon a thought of understanding,
Is as a faire plaistering on the wall of a gallerie.
Pales set on an high place will never stand against the wind:
So a fearefull heart in the imagination of a foole, can not
    stand against any feare.
He that pricketh the eye, wil make teares to fall:
And he that pricketh the heart, maketh it to shewe her
    knowledge.
Who so casteth a stone at the birds, frayeth them away,   What will lose
And he that upbraideth his friend, breaketh friendship.   a friend.
Though thou drewest a sword at thy friend, yet despaire not,
For there may be a returning (to favour.)
If thou hast opened thy mouth against thy friend, feare not,
For there may be a reconciliation:
Except for upbraiding, or pride, or disclosing of secrets, or
    a treacherous wound,
For, for these things every friend will depart.
Be faithfull to thy neighbour in his povertie,
That thou mayest reioyce in his prosperitie:
Abide stedfast unto him in the time of his trouble,
That thou mayest bee heire with him in his heritage:
For a meane estate is not alwayes to be contemned,
Nor the rich that is foolish, to be had in admiration.
As the vapour and smoke of a furnace goeth before the fire:
So reviling before blood.
I will not be ashamed to defend a friend:
Neither will I hide my selfe from him.
And if any evill happen unto me by him,

ECCLESIASTICUS

<small>CHAPTER XXII</small>

Every one that heareth it will beware of him.
Who shall set a watch before my mouth,
And a seale of wisedome upon my lippes,
That I fall not suddenly by them, and that my tongue destroy me not?

CHAPTER XXIII

<small>A prayer for grace to flee sinne.</small>

O LORD, father and governour of all my whole life,
Leave me not to their counsels,
And let me not fall by them.
Who will set scourges over my thoughts,
And the discipline of wisedome over mine heart?
That they spare me not for mine ignorances
And it passe not by my sinnes:
Least mine ignorances increase,
And my sinnes abound to my destruction,
And I fall before mine adversaries,
And mine enemie reioyce over mee,
Whose hope is farre from thy mercy.
O Lord, father and God of my life,
Give me not a proud looke,
But turne away from thy servants alwaies a haughty minde:
Turne away from mee vaine hopes, and concupiscence,
And thou shalt hold him up that is desirous alwaies to serve thee.
Let not the greedinesse of the belly, nor lust of the flesh take hold of me,
And give not over me thy servant into an impudent minde.
Heare, O yee children, the discipline of the mouth:
He that keepeth it, shall never be taken in his lippes.
The sinner shall be left in his foolishnesse:
Both the evill speaker and the proud shall fall thereby.

<small>We may not use swearing:</small>

Accustome not thy mouth to swearing:
Neither use thy selfe to the naming of the holy one.
For as a servant that is continually beaten, shall not be without a blew marke:
So hee that sweareth and nameth God continually, shal not be faultlesse.
A man that useth much swearing shall be filled with iniquity,
And the plague shall never depart from his house:
If he shall offend, his sinne shall be upon him:

ECCLESIASTICUS

And if he acknowledge not his sinne, hee maketh a double offence,   CHAPTER XXIII
And if he sweare in vaine, he shall not be innocent,
But his house shall be full of calamities.
There is a word that is clothed about with death:
God graunt that it be not found in the heritage of Iacob,
For all such things shall be farre from the godly,
And they shall not wallow in their sinnes.
Use not thy mouth to untemperate swearing,
For therein is the word of sinne.
Remember thy father and thy mother,   *But remember*
When thou sittest among great men.   *our parents.*
Be not forgetfull before them,
And so thou by thy custome become a foole,
And wish that thou hadst not beene borne,
And curse the day of thy nativitie.
The man that is accustomed to opprobrious words,
Will never be reformed all the daies of his life.
Two sorts of men multiply sinne,   *Of three sorts*
And the third will bring wrath: *of sinne.*
A hot minde is as a burning fire, it will never be quenched till it be consumed:
A fornicatour in the body of his flesh, will never cease till he hath kindled a fire.
All bread is sweete to a whoremonger,
He will not leave off till he die.
A man that breaketh wedlocke,
Saying thus in his heart, Who seeth me?
I am compassed about with darknesse: the walles cover me;
And no body seeth me, what neede I to feare?
The most high wil not remember my sinnes:
Such a man only feareth the eies of men,
And knoweth not that the eies of the Lord are tenne thousand times brighter then the Sunne,
Beholding all the waies of men,
And considering the most secret parts.
He knew all things ere ever they were created,
So also after they were perfited, he looked upon them all:
This man shall bee punished in the streets of the citie,
And where he suspecteth not, he shall be taken.
Thus shall it goe also with the wife, that leaveth her husband,
And bringeth in an heire by another:
For first she hath disobeyed the Law of the most High:

189

ECCLESIASTICUS

<small>CHAPTER XXIII
The adultresse wife sinneth many waies.</small>

And secondly, she hath trespassed against her owne husband,
And thirdly, she hath played the whore in adultery,
And brought children by another man.
Shee shall be brought out into the congregation,
And inquisition shalbe made of her children.
Her children shall not take root,
And her branches shall bring foorth no fruit.
She shall leave her memorie to be cursed,
And her reproch shall not be blotted out.
And they that remaine, shall know that there is nothing better then the feare of the Lord,
And that there is nothing sweeter then to take heed unto the Commandement of the Lord.
It is great glory to follow the Lord,
And to be received of him is long life.

CHAPTER XXIIII

<small>Wisdome doeth praise herselfe, shew her beginning,</small>

WISEDOME shall praise her selfe,
And shall glory in the midst of her people.
In the Congregation of the most high, shall she open her mouth,
And triumph before his power.
I came out of the mouth of the most High,
And covered the earth as a cloud.

<small>Her dwelling,</small>

I dwelt in high places,
And my throne is in a cloudy pillar.
I alone compassed the circuit of heaven,
And walked in the bottome of the deepe.
In the waves of the sea, and in all the earth,
And in every people, and nation, I got a possession.
With all these I sought rest:
And in whose inheritance shall I abide?
So the creatour of all things gave mee a commandement,
And hee that made me, caused my tabernacle to rest:
And said, Let thy dwelling be in Iacob,
And thine inheritance in Israel.
Hee created mee from the beginning before the world,
And I shall never faile.
In the holy Tabernacle I served before him:
And so was I established in Sion.
Likewise in the beloved citie he gave mee rest,
And in Ierusalem was my power.

ECCLESIASTICUS

And I tooke roote in an honourable people, — CHAPTER XXIIII
Even in the portion of the Lords inheritance.
I was exalted like a Cedar in Libanus, — Her glory,
And as a Cypresse tree upon the mountaines of Hermon.
I was exalted like a palme tree in Engaddi,
And as a rose-plant in Iericho,
As a faire olive tree in a pleasant fielde,
And grew up as a planetree by the water.
I gave a sweete smell like cinamon, and aspalathus,
And I yeelded a pleasant odour like the best mirrhe,
As Galbanum and Onix, and sweet Storax,
And as the fume of franckincense in the Tabernacle.
As the Turpentine tree, I stretched out my branches,
And my branches are the branches of honour and grace.
As the Vine brought I foorth pleasant savour, — Her fruit,
And my flowers are the fruit of honour and riches.
I am the mother of faire love, and feare, and knowledge, and holy hope,
I therefore being eternall, am given to all my children which are named of him.
Come unto me all ye that be desirous of mee,
And fill your selves with my fruits.
For my memorial is sweeter then hony,
And mine inheritance then the hony combe.
They that eate mee shall yet be hungry,
And they that drinke me shall yet be thirstie.
He that obeyeth me, shall never be confounded,
And they that worke by me, shall not doe amisse.
All these things are the booke of the Covenant of the most high God,
Even the Law which Moses commanded for an heritage unto the Congregations of Iacob.
Faint not to bee strong in the Lord;
That he may confirme you, cleave unto him:
For the Lord Almightie is God alone,
And besides him there is no other Saviour.
He filleth all things with his wisdome, as Physon,
And as Tigris in the time of the new fruits.
He maketh the understanding to abound like Euphrates, — Her increase, and perfection.
And as Iorden in the time of the harvest.
He maketh the doctrine of knowledge appeare as the light,
And as Geon in the time of vintage.
The first man knew her not perfectly:

ECCLESIASTICUS

<small>CHAPTER XXIIII</small>

No more shall the last finde her out.
For her thoughts are more then the Sea,
And her counsels profounder then the great decpe.
I also came out as a brooke from a river,
And as a conduit into a garden.
I said, I will water my best garden,
And will water abundantly my garden bedde:
And loe, my brooke became a river,
And my river became a sea.
I will yet make doctrine to shine as the morning,
And will send forth her light afarre off.
I will yet powre out doctrine as prophecie,
And leave it to all ages for ever.
Behold that I have not laboured for my selfe onely,
But for all them that seeke wisedome.

CHAPTER XXV

<small>What things are beautifull, and what hatefull.</small>

IN three things I was beautified,
   And stoode up beautiful, both before God and men
   The unitie of brethren, the love of neighbours,
A man and a wife that agree together.
Three sorts of men my soule hateth,
And I am greatly offended at their life:
A poore man that is proud, a rich man that is a lyar,
And an olde adulterer that doteth.
If thou hast gathered nothing in thy youth,
How canst thou finde any thing in thine age?
Oh how comely a thing is iudgement for gray haires,
And for ancient men to know counsell?
Oh how comely is the wisedome of olde men,
And understanding and counsell to men of honour?

<small>What is the crowne of age.</small>

Much experience is the crowne of olde men,
And the feare of God is their glory.

<small>What things make men happy.</small>

There be nine things which I have iudged in mine heart to be happy,
And the tenth I will utter with my tongue:
A man that hath ioy of his children,
And he that liveth to see the fall of his enemie.
Well is him that dwelleth with a wife of understanding,
And that hath not slipped with his tongue,
And that hath not served a man more unworthy then himselfe.

ECCLESIASTICUS

Well is him that hath found prudence,   CHAPTER
And he that speaketh in the cares of him that will heare.   XXV
Oh how great is he that findeth wisedome !
Yet is there none above him that feareth the Lord.
But the love of the Lord passeth all things for illumination :
He that holdeth it, whereto shall he be likened ?
The feare of the Lord is the beginning of his love :
And faith is the beginning of cleaving unto him.
[Give mee] any plague, but the plague of the heart :   Nothing worse
And any wickednesse, but the wickednesse of a woman.   then a wicked
And any affliction, but the affliction from them that hate me : woman.
And any revenge, but the revenge of enemies.
There is no head above the head of a serpent,
And there is no wrath above the wrath of an enemie.
I had rather dwell with a lyon and a dragon,
Then to keepe house with a wicked woman.
The wickednesse of a woman changeth her face,
And darkeneth her countenance like sackecloth.
Her husband shall sit among his neighbours :
And when hee heareth it, shall sigh bitterly.
All wickednesse is but little to the wickednesse of a woman :
Let the portion of a sinner fall upon her.
As the climbing up a sandie way is to the feete of the aged,
So is a wife full of words to a quiet man.
Stumble not at the beautie of a woman,
And desire her not for pleasure.
A woman, if shee maintaine her husband,
Is full of anger, impudencie, and much reproch.
A wicked woman abateth the courage,
Maketh a heavie countenance, and a wounded heart :
A woman that will not comfort her husband in distresse,
Maketh weake hands, and feeble knees.
Of the woman came the beginning of sinne,
And through her wee all die.
Give the water no passage :
Neither a wicked woman libertie to gad abroad.
If she goe not as thou wouldest have her,
Cut her off from thy flesh,
And give her a bill of divorce, and let her goe.

ECCLESIASTICUS

CHAPTER XXVI

A good wife,

BLESSED is the man that hath a vertuous wife,
For the number of his dayes shall be double.
A vertuous woman reioyceth her husband,
And he shall fulfill the yeeres of his life in peace.
A good wife is a good portion,
Which shall be given in the portion of them that feare the Lord.

and a good conscience doe glad men.

Whether a man be rich or poore,
If he have a good heart towards the Lord, he shall at all times reioyce with a cheerefull countenance.
There bee three things that mine heart feareth:
And for the fourth I was sore afraid:
The slander of a citie, the gathering together of an unruly multitude, and a false accusation:
All these are worse then death.

A wicked wife is a feareful thing.

But a griefe of heart and sorrow, is a woman that is ielous over another woman,
And a scourge of the tongue which communicateth withall.
An evil wife is a yoke shaken to and fro:
He that hath hold of her, is as though he held a scorpion.
A drunken woman and a gadder abroad, causeth great anger,
And shee will not cover her owne shame.
The whordome of a woman may be knowen in her haughty lookes,
And eye lids.
If thy daughter be shamelesse, keepe her in straitly:
Lest she abuse her selfe through overmuch libertie.
Watch over an impudent eye:
And marveile not, if shee trespasse against thee.
Shee will open her mouth as a thirstie traveiler, when he hath found a fountaine:
And drinke of every water neere her:
By every hedge will she sit downe,
And open her quiver against every arrow.

Of good and bad wives.

The grace of a wife delighteth her husband,
And her discretion will fat his bones.
A silent and loving woman is a gift of the Lord,
And there is nothing so much worth, as a mind well instructed.
A shamefast and faithfull woman is a double grace,
And her continent mind cannot be valued.

ECCLESIASTICUS

As the Sunne when it ariseth in the high heaven: CHAPTER
So is the beautie of a good wife in the ordering of her house. XXVI
As the cleare light is upon the holy candlesticke:
So is the beautie of the face in ripe age.
As the golden pillars are upon the sockets of silver:
So are the faire feete with a constant heart.
My sonne, keepe the flowre of thine age sound:
And give not thy strength to strangers.
When thou hast gotten a fruitfull possession through all the field:
Sowe it with thine owne seede, trusting in the goodnesse of thy stocke.
So thy race which thou leavest shalbe magnified,
Having the confidence of their good descent.
An harlot shall bee accounted as spittle:
But a maried woman is a towre against death to her husband.
A wicked woman is given as a portion to a wicked man:
But a godly woman is given to him that feareth the Lord.
A dishonest woman contemneth shame,
But an honest woman will reverence her husband.
A shamelesse woman shalbe counted as a dog:
But she that is shamefast will feare the Lord.
A woman that honoureth her husband, shall bee iudged wise of all:
But she that dishonoureth him in her pride, shall be counted ungodly of all.
A loude crying woman, and a scolde,
Shall be sought out to drive away the enemies.
There be two things that grieve my heart: Of three
And the third maketh me angry: things that
A man of warre that suffereth poverty, are grievous.
And men of understanding that are not set by:
And one that returneth from righteousnesse to sinne:
The Lord prepareth such a one for the sword.
A merchant shall hardly keepe himselfe from doing wrong: Merchants and
And an huckster shall not be freed from sinne. hucksters are
not without
sinne.

CHAPTER XXVII

MANY have sinned for a smal matter: Of sinnes in
And he that seeketh for abundance will turne his selling and
eies away. buying.
As a naile sticketh fast betweene the ioynings of the stones:

ECCLESIASTICUS

<small>CHAPTER XXVII</small>

So doth sinne sticke close betweene buying and selling.
Unlesse a man hold himselfe diligently in the feare of the Lord,
His house shall soone be overthrowen.
As when one sifteth with a sieve, the refuse remaineth,
So the filth of man in his talke.
The furnace prooveth the potters vessell:
So the triall of man is in his reasoning.
The fruite declareth if the tree have beene dressed:
So is the utterance of a conceit in the heart of man.

<small>Our speach will tell what is in us.</small>

Praise no man before thou hearest him speake,
For this is the triall of men.
If thou followest righteousnesse, thou shalt obtaine her,
And put her on, as a glorious long robe.
The birds will resort unto their like,
So will truth returne unto them that practise in her.
As the Lyon lieth in waite for the pray:
So sinne for them that worke iniquity.
The discourse of a godly man is alwaies with wisedome:
But a foole changeth as the Moone.
If thou be among the undiscreet, observe the time:
But be continually among men of understanding.
The discourse of fooles is irksome,
And their sport is in the wantonnesse of sinne.
The talke of him that sweareth much, maketh the haire stand upright:
And their braules make one stop his eares.
The strife of the proud is blood-shedding,
And their revilings are grievous to the eare.

<small>A friend is lost by discovering his secrets.</small>

Who so discovereth secrets, looseth his credit:
And shall never find friend to his minde.
Love thy friend, and be faithfull unto him:
But if thou bewrayest his secrets, follow no more after him.
For as a man hath destroyed his enemie:
So hast thou lost the love of thy neighbour.
As one that letteth a bird goe out of his hand,
So hast thou let thy neighbour goe, and shalt not get him againe.
Follow after him no more, for he is too far off,
He is as a roe escaped out of the snare.
As for a wound it may be bound up, and after reviling there may be reconcilement
But he that bewrayeth secrets is without hope.

ECCLESIASTICUS

He that winketh with the eies worketh evil,   CHAPTER
And he that knoweth him will depart from him.   XXVII
When thou art present he will speake sweetly,
And will admire thy words:
But at the last he will writhe his mouth,
And slander thy sayings.
I have hated many things, but nothing like him,
For the Lord will hate him.
Who so casteth a stone on high, casteth it on his owne head,   Hee that
And a deceitfull stroke shall make wounds.   diggeth a pit
Who so diggeth a pit shall fall therein: shall fall into it.
And he that setteth a trap shall be taken therein.
He that worketh mischiefe, it shall fall upon him,
And he shall not know whence it commeth.
Mockery and reproach are from the proud:
But vengeance as a Lyon shall lie in waite for them.
They that reioyce at the fall of the righteous shalbe taken in
    the snare,
And anguish shall consume them before they die.
Malice and wrath, even these are abhominations,
And the sinfull man shall have them both.

CHAPTER XXVIII

HE that revengeth shall find vengeance from the Lord,   Against
   And he will surely keepe his sinnes (in remembrance.)   revenge,
   Forgive thy neighbour the hurt that he hath done
       unto thee,
So shall thy sinnes also be forgiven when thou prayest.
One man beareth hatred against another,
And doeth he seeke pardon from the Lord?
Hee sheweth no mercy to a man, which is like himselfe:
And doeth hee aske forgivenesse of his owne sinnes?
If he that is but flesh nourish hatred,
Who will intreat for pardon of his sinnes?
Remember thy end, and let enimitie cease,
[Remember] corruption and death, and abide in the Com-
    mandements.
Remember the Commaundements, and beare no malice to
    thy neighbour:
[Remember] the Covenant of the highest, and winke at
    ignorance.
Abstaine from strife, and thou shalt diminish thy sinnes: Quarrelling,

ECCLESIASTICUS

CHAPTER XXVIII

Anger,

For a furious man will kindle strife.
A sinfull man disquieteth friends,
And maketh debate among them that be at peace.
As the matter of the fire is, so it burneth:
And as a mans strength is, so is his wrath,
And according to his riches his anger riseth,
And the stronger they are which contend, the more they will be inflamed.
An hastie contention kindleth a fire,
And an hasty fighting sheddeth blood.
If thou blow the sparke, it shall burne:
If thou spit upon it, it shall be quenched,
And both these come out of thy mouth.
Curse the whisperer, and double tongued:
For such have destroyed many that were at peace.
A backbiting tongue hath disquieted many,
And driven them from nation to nation,
Strong cities hath it pulled down,
And overthrowen the houses of great men,

And backbiting.

A backbiting tongue hath cast out vertuous women,
And deprived them of their labours.
Who so hearkeneth unto it, shall never finde rest,
And never dwel quietly.
The stroke of the whip maketh markes in the flesh,
But the stroke of the tongue breaketh the bones.
Many have fallen by the edge of the sword:
But not so many as have fallen by the tongue.
Well is hee that is defended from it,
And hath not passed through the venime thereof:
Who hath not drawen the yoke thereof,
Nor hath bene bound in her bands.
For the yoke thereof is a yoke of yron,
And the bands thereof are bandes of brasse.
The death therof is an evil death,
The grave were better then it.
It shall not have rule over them that feare God,
Neither shall they be burnt with the flame thereof.
Such as forsake the Lord shall fall into it,
And it shall burne in them, and not be quenched,
It shalbe sent upon them as a Lion,
And devoure them as a Leopard.
Looke that thou hedge thy possession about with thornes,
And binde up thy silver and gold:

ECCLESIASTICUS

And weigh thy words in a ballance,
And make a doore and barre for thy mouth.
Beware thou slide not by it,
Lest thou fall before him that lieth in wait.

CHAPTER XXVIII

CHAPTER XXIX

HEE that is mercifull, will lende unto his neighbour,
And hee that strengthneth his hande, keepeth the Commandements.
Lend to thy neighbour in time of his need,
And pay thou thy neighbour againe in due season.
Keepe thy word and deale faithfully with him,
And thou shalt alwaies finde the thing that is necessary for thee.

Wee must shew mercy and lend:

Many when a thing was lent them, reckoned it to be found,
And put them to trouble that helped them.
Till he hath received, he will kisse a mans hand:
And for his neighbours money he will speake submissely:
But when he should repay, he will prolong the time,
And returne words of griefe, and complaine of the time.
If he prevaile, he shall hardly receive the halfe,
And he will count as if he had found it:
If not; he hath deprived him of his money,
And he hath gotten him an enemy without cause:
He payeth him with cursings, and raylings:
And for honour he will pay him disgrace.
Many therefore have refused to lend for other mens ill dealing,
Fearing to be defrauded.

but the borower must not defraud the lender.

Yet have thou patience with a man in poore estate,
And delay not to shew him mercy.
Helpe the poore for the commandements sake,
And turne him not away because of his povertie.
Lose thy money for thy brother and thy friend,
And let it not rust under a stone to be lost.
Lay up thy treasure according to the commandements of the most high,
And it shall bring thee more profite then golde.
Shut up almes in thy storehouses:
And it shall deliver thee from all affliction.
It shal fight for thee against thine enemies,
Better then a mightie shield and strong speare.

Give almes.

ECCLESIASTICUS

CHAPTER XXIX
A good man will not undoe his suretie.

An honest man is suretie for his neighbour :
But hee that is impudent, will forsake him.
Forget not the friendship of thy suretie :
For hee hath given his life for thee.
A sinner will overthrow the good estate of his suretie :
And he that is of an unthankfull minde,
Will leave him in [danger] that delivered him.

To be suretie and undertake for others is dangerous.

Suretiship hath undone many of good estate,
And shaked them as a wave of the Sea :
Mightie men hath it driven from their houses,
So that they wandred among strange nations.
A wicked man transgressing the commandements of the Lord, shall fall into suretiship :
And hee that undertaketh and followeth other mens businesse for gaine, shall fall into suits.
Helpe thy neighbour according to thy power,
And beware that thou thy selfe fall not into the same.
The chiefe thing for life is water and bread,
And clothing, and an house to cover shame.

It is better to live at home, then to soiourne.

Better is the life of a poore man in a meane cottage,
Then delicate fare in another mans house.
Be it little or much, holde thee contented,
That thou heare not the reproch of thy house.
For it is a miserable life to goe from house to house :
For where thou art a stranger, thou darest not open thy mouth.
Thou shalt entertaine and feast, and have no thankes :
Moreover, thou shalt heare bitter words.
Come thou stranger, and furnish a table,
And feede me of that thou hast ready.
Give place thou stranger to an honourable man,
My brother commeth to be lodged, and I have neede of mine house.
These things are grievous to a man of understanding :
The upbraiding of house-roome, and reproching of the lender.

CHAPTER XXX

It is good to correct our children,

HEE that loveth his sonne, causeth him oft to feele the rodde,
That hee may have ioy of him in the end.
He that chastiseth his sonne, shall have ioy in him,
And shall reioyce of him among his acquaintance.
He that teacheth his sonne, grieveth the enemie :

ECCLESIASTICUS

And before his friends he shall reioyce of him.
Though his father die, yet he is as though hee were not dead:
For hee hath left one behinde him that is like himselfe.
While he lived, he saw and reioyced in him:
And when he died hee was not sorrowfull.
He left behinde him an avenger against his enemies,
And one that shall requite kindnesse to his friends.
He that maketh too much of his sonne, shall binde up his wounds,   and not to cocker them.
And his bowels wil be troubled at every cry.
An horse not broken becommeth headstrong:
And a childe left to himselfe will be wilfull.
Cocker thy childe, and hee shall make thee afraid:
Play with him, and he will bring thee to heavinesse.
Laugh not with him, lest thou have sorrow with him,
And lest thou gnash thy teeth in the end.
Give him no liberty in his youth,
And winke not at his follies.
Bow downe his necke while hee is young,
And beate him on the sides while he is a childe,
Lest hee waxe stubborne, and be disobedient unto thee,
And so bring sorrow to thine heart.
Chastise thy sonne, and hold him to labour,
Lest his lewd behaviour be an offence unto thee.
Better is the poore being sound and strong of constitution,   Health is better then wealth.
Then a rich man that is afflicted in his body.
Health and good state of body are above all gold,
And a strong body above infinite wealth.
There is no riches above a sound body,
And no ioy above the ioy of the heart.
Death is better then a bitter life, or continuall sickenesse.
Delicates powred upon a mouth shut up,
Are as messes of meat set upon a grave.
What good doth the offering unto an idole?
For neither can it eat nor smell.
So is he that is persecuted of the Lord.
Hee seeth with his eyes and groneth,
As an Eunuch that embraceth a virgine, and sigheth.
Give not over thy mind to heavinesse,
And afflict not thy selfe in thine owne counsell.
The gladnesse of the heart is the life of man,   Health and life are shortened by griefe.
And the ioyfulnes of a man prolongeth his dayes.
Love thine owne soule, and comfort thy heart,

CHAPTER XXX

ECCLESIASTICUS

CHAPTER XXX

Remove sorrow far from thee:
For sorrow hath killed many,
And there is no profit therein.
Envie and wrath shorten the life,
And carefulnesse bringeth age before the time.
A cherefull and good heart
Will have a care of his meat and diet.

CHAPTER XXXI

Of the desire of riches.

WATCHING for riches, consumeth the flesh,
And the care therof driveth away sleepe.
Watching care will not let a man slumber,
As a sore disease breaketh sleepe.
The rich hath great labour in gathering riches together,
And when he resteth, he is filled with his delicates.
The poore laboureth in his poore estate,
And when he leaveth off, hee is still needie.
He that loveth gold shall not bee iustified,
And he that followeth corruption, shall have enough thereof.
Gold hath bin the ruine of many,
And their destruction was present.
It is a stumbling block unto them that sacrifice unto it,
And every foole shall be taken therewith.
Blessed is the rich that is found without blemish,
And hath not gone after gold:
Who is he? and we will call him blessed:
For wonderfull things hath hee done among his people.
Who hath bene tried thereby, and found perfit?
Then let him glory.
Who might offend and hath not offended,
Or done evill, and hath not done it?
His goods shall be established,
And the congregation shall declare his almes.

Of moderation and excesse in eating, or drinking wine.

If thou sit at a bountifull table, bee not greedy upon it,
And say not, There is much meate on it.
Remember that a wicked eye is an evill thing:
And what is created more wicked then an eye?
Therefore it weepeth upon every occasion.
Stretch not thine hand whithersoever it looketh,
And thrust it not with him into the dish.
Iudge of thy neighbour by thy selfe:
And be discreet in every point.

ECCLESIASTICUS

CHAPTER XXXI

Eate as it becommeth a man those things which are set before thee:
And devoure not, lest thou be hated.
Leave off first for maners sake,
And be not unsatiable, lest thou offend.
When thou sittest among many,
Reach not thine hand out first of all.
A very litle is sufficient for a man well nurtured,
And he fetcheth not his wind short upon his bed.
Sound sleepe commeth of moderate eating
He riseth early, and his wits are with him,
But the paine of watching and choller,
And pangs of the bellie are with an unsatiable man.
And if thou hast bin forced to eate,
Arise, goe forth, vomit, and thou shalt have rest.
My sonne, heare me, and despise me not,
And at the last thou shalt finde as I told thee:
In all thy workes bee quicke,
So shall there no sickenesse come unto thee.
Who so is liberall of his meat, men shall speake well of him,
And the report of his good housekeeping will be beleeved.
But against him that is a niggard of his meate, the whole citie shall murmure;
And the testimonies of his niggardnesse shall not be doubted of.
Shew not thy valiantnesse in wine,
For wine hath destroyed many.
The furnace prooveth the edge by dipping:
So doth wine the hearts of the proud by drunkennesse.
Wine is as good as life to a man if it be drunke moderatly:
What life is then to a man that is without wine?
For it was made to make men glad.
Wine measurably drunke, and in season,
Bringeth gladnesse of the heart and cheerefulnesse of the minde.
But wine drunken with excesse, maketh bitternesse of the minde,
With brawling and quarreling.
Drunkennesse increaseth the rage of a foole till he offend,
It diminisheth strength, and maketh wounds.
Rebuke not thy neighbour at the wine,
And despise him not in his mirth:

ECCLESIASTICUS

<small>CHAPTER XXXI</small>

Give him no despitefull words,
And presse not upon him with urging him (to drinke.)

CHAPTER XXXII

<small>Of his duty that is cheefe or master in a feast.</small>

IF thou be made the master (of the feast)
Lift not thy selfe up,
But bee among them as one of the rest,
Take diligent care for them, and so sit downe.
And when thou hast done all thy office, take thy place
That thou mayest be merry with them,
And receive a crowne for thy well ordering of the feast.
Speake thou that art the elder, for it becometh thee, but with sound iudgement,
And hinder not musicke.
Powre not out words where there is a musitian,
And shew not forth wisedome out of time.
A consort of musicke in a banket of wine,
Is as a signet of Carbuncle set in gold.
As a signet of an Emeraud set in a worke of gold,
So is the melodie of musicke with pleasant wine.
Speake yong man, if there be need of thee:
And yet scarsely when thou art twise asked:
Let thy speach be short, comprehending much in few words,
Be as one that knoweth, and yet holdeth his tongue.
If thou be among great men, make not thy selfe equall with them,
And when ancient men are in place, use not many words.
Before the thunder goeth lightening:
And before a shamefast man shall goe favour.
Rise up betimes, and be not the last:
But get thee home without delay.
There take thy pastime, and do what thou wilt:
But sinne not by proud speach.
And for these things blesse him that made thee,
And hath replenished thee with his good things.

<small>Of the feare of God,</small>

Who so feareth the Lord, will receive his discipline,
And they that seeke him early, shall find favour.
He that seeketh the law, shall be filled therewith:
But the hypocrite will be offended thereat.
They that feare the Lord shall find iudgement,
And shall kindle iustice as a light.
A sinfull man will not be reproved,

ECCLESIASTICUS

But findeth an excuse according to his will.
A man of counsell will be considerate,
But a strange and proud man is not daunted with feare,
Even when of himselfe he hath done without counsell.
Doe nothing without advice,
And when thou hast once done, repent not.
Goe not in a way wherein thou maiest fall,
And stumble not among the stones.
Be not confident in a plaine way.
And beware of thine owne children.
In every good worke trust thy owne soule:
For this is the keeping of the commandements.
He that beleeveth in the Lord, taketh heed to the commandement,
And he that trusted in him, shall fare never the worse.

CHAPTER XXXII
Of counsell.

Of a ragged and a smooth way.

Trust not to any but to thy selfe and to God.

CHAPTER XXXIII

THERE shall no evill happen unto him that feareth the Lord,
But in temptation even againe he wil deliver him.
A wise man hateth not the Law,
But he that is an hypocrite therein, is as a ship in a storme.
A man of understanding trusteth in the Law,
And the Law is faithfull unto him, as an oracle.
Prepare what to say, and so thou shalt be heard,
And binde up instruction, and then make answere.
The heart of the foolish is like a cartwheele:
And his thoughts are like a rolling axeltree.
A stallion horse is as a mocking friend,
Hee neigheth under every one that sitteth upon him.
Why doth one day excell another?
When as all the light of every day in the yeere is of the Sunne.
By the knowledge of the Lord they were distinguished:
And he altered seasons and feasts.
Some of them hath hee made high dayes, and hallowed them,
And some of them hath hee made ordinary dayes.
And all men are from the ground,
And Adam was created of earth.
In much knowledge the Lord hath divided them,
And made their wayes divers.

The safety of him that feareth the Lord.

The wise and the foolish.

Times and seasons are of God.

Men are in his hands, as clay in the hands of the potter.

ECCLESIASTICUS

CHAPTER XXXIII

Some of them hath hee blessed, and exalted,
And some of them hath hee sanctified, and set neere himselfe:
But some of them hath hee cursed, and brought low,
And turned out of their places.
As the clay is in the potters hand to fashion it at his pleasure:
So man is in the hand of him that made him,
To render to them as liketh him best.
Good is set against evill,
And life against death:
So is the godly against the sinner,
And the sinner against the godly.
So looke upon all the workes of the most High,
And there are two and two, one against another.
I awaked up last of all,
As one that gathereth after the grape-gatherers:
By the blessing of the Lord I profited,
And filled my wine-presse, like a gatherer of grapes.
Consider that I laboured not for my selfe onely,
But for all them that seeke learning;

Cheefely regard thy selfe.

Heare me, O ye great men of the people,
And hearken with your eares ye rulers of the Congregation:
Give not thy sonne, and wife, thy brother and friend
Power over thee while thou livest,
And give not thy goods to another,
Lest it repent thee: and thou intreat for the same againe.
As long as thou livest and hast breath in thee,
Give not thy selfe over to any.
For better it is that thy children should seeke to thee,
Then that thou shouldst stand to their courtesie.
In all thy workes keepe to thy selfe the preheminence,
Leave not a staine in thine honour.
At the time when thou shalt end thy dayes,
And finish thy life, distribute thine inheritance.

Of servants.

Fodder, a wand, and burdens, are for the asse:
And bread, correction, and worke for a servant.
If thou set thy servant to labour, thou shalt finde rest:
But if thou let him goe idle, he shall seeke libertie.
A yoke and a collar doe bow the necke:
So are tortures and torments for an evill servant.
Sende him to labour that hee be not idle:
For idlenesse teacheth much evill.
Set him to worke, as is fit for him;
If he be not obedient, put on more heavy fetters.

ECCLESIASTICUS

But be not excessive toward any,   CHAPTER
And without discretion doe nothing.   XXXIII
If thou have a servant, let him bee unto thee as thy selfe,
Because thou hast bought him with a price.
If thou have a servant, intreate him as a brother:
For thou hast neede of him, as of thine owne soule:
If thou intreate him evill, and he runne from thee,
Which way wilt thou goe to seeke him?

CHAPTER XXXIIII

THE hopes of a man voyd of understanding are vaine, *Of dreames,*
    and-false:
    And dreames lift up fooles.
Who so regardeth dreames,
Is like him that catcheth at a shadow, and followeth after
    the winde.
The vision of dreames is the resemblance of one thing to
    another,
Even as the likenesse of a face to a face.
Of an uncleane thing, what can be cleansed?
And from that thing which is false, what trueth can come?
Divinations, and soothsayings, and dreames are vaine:
And the heart fancieth as a womans heart in travell.
If they be not sent from the most high in thy visitation,
Set not thy heart upon them.
For dreames have deceived many,
And they have failed that put their trust in them.
The Law shall be found perfect without lies:
And wisedome is perfection to a faithfull mouth.
A man that hath travailed knoweth many things:
And hee that hath much experience, wil declare wisedome.
He that hath no experience, knoweth little:
But he that hath travailed, is full of prudence.
When I travailed, I saw many things:
And I understand more, then I can expresse.
I was oft times in danger of death,
Yet I was delivered because of these things.
The spirit of those that feare the Lord shall live,   *The praise and*
For their hope is in him that saveth them.   *blessing of*
Who so feareth the Lord, shall not feare nor be afraid, *them that feare*
For hee is his hope.   *the Lord.*
Blessed is the soule of him that feareth the Lord:

ECCLESIASTICUS

CHAPTER XXXIIII

To whom doeth hee looke? and who is his strength?
For the eyes of the Lord are upon them that love him,
He is their mightie protection, and strong stay,
A defence from heat, and a cover from the Sunne at noone,
A preservation from stumbling, and a helpe from falling.
He raiseth up the soule, and lighteneth the eyes:
Hee giveth health, life, and blessing.

The offering of the ancient, and praier of the poore innocent.

Hee that sacrificeth of a thing wrongfully gotten, his offering is ridiculous,
And the giftes of uniust men are not accepted.
The most high is not pleased with the offerings of the wicked,
Neither is he pacified for sinne by the multitude of sacrifices.
Who so bringeth an offering of the goods of the poore,
Doeth as one that killeth the sonne before his fathers eyes.
The bread of the needie, is their life:
He that defraudeth him thereof, is a man of blood.
Hee that taketh away his neighbours living, slayeth him:
And hee that defraudeth the labourer of his hire, is a bloodshedder.
When one buildeth, and another pulleth downe,
What profite have they then but labour?
When one prayeth, and another curseth,
Whose voice will the Lorde heare?
He that washeth himselfe after the touching of a dead body, if he touch it againe,
What availeth his washing?
So is it with a man that fasteth for his sinnes,
And goeth againe and doeth the same:
Who will heare his prayer,
Or what doeth his humbling profit him?

CHAPTER XXXV

Sacrifices pleasing God.

HEE that keepeth the law, bringeth offerings enow:
He that taketh heed to the commandement, offereth a peace offering.
He that requiteth a good turne, offereth fine floure:
And he that giveth almes, sacrificeth praise.
To depart from wickednesse is a thing pleasing to the Lord:
And to forsake unrighteousnesse, is a propitiation.
Thou shalt not appeare emptie before the Lord:
For all these things [are to bee done] because of the commandement.

ECCLESIASTICUS

The offering of the righteous maketh the Altar fat,
And the sweete savour thereof is before the most high.
The sacrifice of a iust man is acceptable,
And the memoriall thereof shall never be forgotten.
Give the Lord his honour with a good eye,
And diminish not the first fruits of thine hands.
In all thy gifts shew a cheerefull countenance,
And dedicate thy tithes with gladnesse.
Give unto the most high, according as hee hath enriched thee,
And as thou hast gotten, give with a cheerefull eye.
For the Lord recompenseth,
And will give thee seven times as much.
Doe not thinke to corrupt with gifts, for such he will not receive :
And trust not to unrighteous sacrifices,
For the Lord is iudge,
And with him is no respect of persons.
Hee will not accept any person against a poore man :
But will heare the prayer of the oppressed.
He will not despise the supplication of the fatherlesse :
Nor the widowe when she powreth out her complaint.
Doeth not the teares run downe the widowes cheeks ?
And is not her crie against him that causeth them to fall ?
He that serveth the Lord, shall be accepted with favour,
And his prayer shall reach unto the cloudes.
The prayer of the humble pierceth the clouds :
And till it come nigh he will not be comforted :
And will not depart till the most High shall beholde
To iudge righteously, and execute iudgement.
For the Lord will not be slacke, neither will the mightie be patient towards them,
Till he hath smitten in sunder the loines of the unmercifull,
And repaid vengeance to the heathen :
Till he have taken away the multitude of the proud,
And broken the scepter of the unrighteous :
Till he have rendred to every man according to his deeds,
And to the works of men according to their devises,
Till he have iudged the cause of his people :
And made them to reioyce in his mercie.
Mercie is seasonable in the time of affliction,
As cloudes of raine in the time of drought.

CHAPTER XXXV

The prayer of the fatherlesse, of the widow, and of the humble in spirit.

Acceptable mercy.

ECCLESIASTICUS

CHAPTER XXXVI

<small>CHAPTER XXXVI
A prayer for the Church against the enemies thereof.</small>

Have mercie upon us, O Lord God of all, and behold us:
And send thy feare upon all the nations that seeke not after thee.
Lift up thy hand against the strange nations,
And let them see thy power.
As thou wast sanctified in us before them:
So be thou magnified among them before us.
And let them know thee, as we have knowen thee,
That there is no God, but onely thou, O God.
Shew new signes, and make other strange wonders:
Glorifie thy hand and thy right arme,
That they may set forth thy wonderous workes.
Raise up indignation, and powre out wrath:
Take away the adversarie and destroy the enemie:
Make the time short, remember the covenant,
And let them declare thy wonderfull works.
Let him that escapeth, be consumed by the rage of the fire,
And let them perish that oppresse the people.
Smite in sunder the heads of the rulers of the heathen,
That say, There is none other but we.
Gather all the tribes of Iacob together,
And inherit thou them, as from the beginning.
O Lord have mercie upon the people, that is called by thy name,
And upon Israel, whom thou hast named thy first borne.
O bee mercifull unto Ierusalem thy holy citie,
The place of thy rest.
Fill Sion with thine unspeakable oracles,
And thy people with thy glory.
Give testimonie unto those that thou hast possessed from the beginning,
And raise up prophets that have bin in thy name.
Reward them that wait for thee,
And let thy prophets be found faithfull.
O Lord heare the prayer of thy servants,
According to the blessing of Aaron over thy people,
That all they which dwel upon the earth, may know
That thou art the Lord, the eternall God.

<small>A good heart and a froward.</small>

The belly devoureth all meates,
Yet is one meat better then another.
As the palate tasteth divers kinds of venison:

ECCLESIASTICUS

So doth an heart of understanding false speeches.
A froward heart causeth heavinesse:
But a man of experience will recompense him.
A woman will receive every man,
Yet is one daughter better then another.
The beautie of a woman cheareth the countenance,
And a man loveth nothing better.
If there be kindnesse, meekenes, and comfort in her tongue,
Then is not her husband like other men.
He that getteth a wife, beginneth a possession,
A helpe like unto himselfe, and a pillar of rest.
Where no hedge is, there the possession is spoiled:
And he that hath no wife will wander up and downe mourning.
Who will trust a thiefe well appointed, that skippeth from citie to citie?
So [who will beleeve] a man that hath no house? and lodgeth wheresoever the night taketh him?

CHAPTER XXXVI

Of a good wife.

CHAPTER XXXVII

EVERY friend saieth, I am his friend also:
But there is a friend which is onely a friend in name.
Is it not a griefe unto death,
When a companion and friend is turned to an enemie?
O wicked imagination, whence camest thou in
To cover the earth with deceit?
There is a companion, which reioyceth in the prosperity of a friend:
But in the time of trouble will be against him.
There is a companion which helpeth his friend for the belly,
And taketh up the buckler against the enemie.
Forget not thy friend in thy minde,
And be not unmindfull of him in thy riches.
Every counseller extolleth counsell;
But there is some that counselleth for himselfe.
Beware of a counseller,
And know before what neede he hath
(For he will counsell for himselfe)
Lest hee cast the lot upon thee:
And say unto thee, Thy way is good:
And afterward he stand on the other side, to see what shall befall thee.

How to know friends and counsellers.

ECCLESIASTICUS

CHAPTER XXXVII

Consult not with one that suspecteth thee:
And hide thy counsell from such as envie thee.
Neither consult with a woman touching her of whom she is iealous;
Neither with a coward in matters of warre,
Nor with a merchant concerning exchange;
Nor with a buyer of selling;
Nor with an envious man of thankfulnesse;
Nor with an unmercifull man touching kindnesse;
Nor with the slouthfull for any worke;
Nor with an hireling for a yeere, of finishing worke;
Nor with an idle servant of much businesse:
Hearken not unto these in any matter of counsell.

The descretion and wisedome of a godly man blesseth him.

But be continually with a godly man,
Whom thou knowest to keepe the commandements of the Lord,
Whose minde is according to thy minde,
And will sorrow with thee, if thou shalt miscarry.
And let the counsell of thine owne heart stand:
For there is no man more faithfull unto thee then it.
For a mans minde is sometime wont to tell him
More then seven watchmen, that sit above in a high towre.
And above all this pray to the most high,
That he will direct thy way in trueth.
Let reason goe before every enterprise,
And counsell before every action.
The countenance is a signe of changing of the heart.
Foure maner of things appeare:
Good and evill, life and death:
But the tongue ruleth over them continually.
There is one that is wise and teacheth many,
And yet is unprofitable to himselfe.
There is one that sheweth wisedome in words, and is hated:
He shall be destitute of all foode.
For grace is not given him from the Lord:
Because he is deprived of all wisedome.
Another is wise to himselfe:
And the fruits of understanding are commendable in his mouth.
A wise man instructeth his people,
And the fruits of his understanding faile not.
A wise man shall be filled with blessing,
And all they that see him, shall count him happy.

ECCLESIASTICUS

The daies of the life of man may be numbred: CHAPTER
But the daies of Israel are innumerable: XXXVII
A wise man shall inherite glory among his people,
And his name shalbe perpetuall.
My sonne proove thy soule in thy life,   *Learne to refraine thine appetite.*
And see what is evill for it, and give not that unto it.
For all things are not profitable for all men,
Neither hath every soule pleasure in every thing.
Be not unsatiable in any dainty thing:
Nor too greedy upon meates.
For excesse of meates, bringeth sicknesse,
And surfetting will turne into choler.
By surfetting have many perished,
But hee that taketh heed, prolongeth his life.

CHAPTER XXXVIII

HONOUR a Phisitian with the honour due unto him,   *Honour due to the Phisitian, and why.*
    for the uses which you may have of him:
    For the Lord hath created him.
For of the most High commeth healing,
And he shall receive honour of the King.
The skill of the Phisitian shall lift up his head:
And in the sight of great men he shalbe in admiration.
The Lord hath created medicines out of the earth;
And he that is wise will not abhorre them.
Was not the water made sweet with wood,
That the vertue thereof might be knowen?
And he hath given men skill,
That hee might be honoured in his marveilous workes.
With such doeth he beale [men,]
And taketh away their paines.
Of such doeth the Apothecarie make a confection;
And of his workes there is no end,
And from him is peace over all the earth.
My sonne, in thy sickenesse be not negligent:
But pray unto the Lord, and he will make thee whole.
Leave off from sinne, and order thy hands aright,
And cleanse thy heart from all wickednesse.
Give a sweet savour, and a memoriall of fine flowre:
And make a fat offering, as not being.
Then give place to the phisitian, for the Lord hath created
    him:

ECCLESIASTICUS

CHAPTER XXXVIII

Let him not go from thee, for thou hast need of him.
There is a time when in their hands there is good successe.
For they shall also pray unto the Lord,
That hee would prosper that, which they give, for ease and remedy to prolong life.
He that sinneth before his maker,
Let him fal into the hand of the Phisitian.

How to weepe and mourne for the dead.

My sonne, let teares fall downe over the dead,
And begin to lament, as if thou hadst suffered great harme thy selfe:
And then cover his body according to the custome,
And neglect not his buriall.
Weepe bitterly, and make great moane,
And use lamentation, as hee is worthy,
And that a day or two, lest thou be evill spoken of:
And then comfort thy selfe for thy heavinesse.
For of heavinesse commeth death,
And the heavinesse of the heart, breaketh strength.
In affliction also sorrow remaineth:
And the life of the poore, is the curse of the heart.
Take no heavines to heart:
Drive it away, and remember the last end.
Forget it not, for there is no turning againe:
Thou shalt not doe him good, but hurt thy selfe.
Remember my iudgement: for thine also shall be so;
Yesterday for me, and to day for thee.
When the dead is at rest, let his remembrance rest,
And be comforted for him, when his spirit is departed from him.

The wisedome of the learned man, and of the Labourer and Artificer: with the use of them both.

The wisedome of a learned man commeth by opportunitie of leasure:
And he that hath litle busines shal become wise.
How can he get wisdome that holdeth the plough,
And that glorieth in the goad;
That driveth oxen, and is occupied in their labours,
And whose talke is of bullocks?
He giveth his minde to make furrowes:
And is diligent to give the kine fodder.
So every carpenter, and workemaster, that laboureth night and day:
And they that cut and grave seales,
And are diligent to make great variety,
And give themselves to counterfait imagerie,
And watch to finish a worke.

ECCLESIASTICUS

<small>CHAPTER XXXVIII</small>

The smith also sitting by the anvill,
And considering the iron worke;
The vapour of the fire wasteth his flesh,
And he fighteth with the heat of the furnace:
The noise of the hammer and the anvill is ever in his eares,
And his eies looke still upon the patterne of the thing that he maketh,
He setteth his mind to finish his worke,
And watcheth to polish it perfitly.
So doeth the potter sitting at his worke,
And turning the wheele about with his feet,
Who is alway carefully set at his worke:
And maketh all his worke by number.
He fashioneth the clay with his arme,
And boweth downe his strength before his feet:
He applieth himselfe to lead it over;
And he is diligent to make cleane the furnace.
All these trust to their hands:
And every one is wise in his worke.
Without these cannot a citie be inhabited:
And they shall not dwell where they will, nor goe up and downe.
They shall not be sought for in publike counsaile,
Nor sit high in the congregation:
They shal not sit on the Iudges seate,
Nor understand the sentence of iudgement:
They cannot declare iustice, and iudgement,
And they shall not be found where parables are spoken.
But they will maintaine the state of the world,
And [all] their desire is in the worke of their craft.

CHAPTER XXXIX

BUT hee that giveth his minde to the Law of the most high,
And is occupied in the meditation thereof,
Wil seeke out the wisdome of all the ancient,
And be occupied in prophecies.
Hee will keepe the sayings of the renowmed men:
And where subtile parables are, he will be there also.
Hee will seeke out the secrets of grave sentences,
And be conversant in darke parables.
He shall serve among great men,

<small>A description of him that is truely wise.</small>

ECCLESIASTICUS

<small>CHAPTER
XXXIX</small>

And appeare before princes:
He will travaile through strange countreys,
For hee hath tried the good, and the evill among men.
Hee will give his heart to resort early to the Lord that made him,
And will pray before the most high,
And will open his mouth in prayer,
And make supplication for his sinnes.
When the great Lord will,
He shall bee filled with the spirit of understanding:
He shal powre out wise sentences,
And give thankes unto the Lord in his prayer.
Hee shall direct his counsell and knowledge,
And in his secrets shall hee meditate.
Hee shall shew foorth that which he hath learned,
And shall glory in the Law of the covenant of the Lord.
Many shall commend his understanding,
And so long as the world endureth, it shall not be blotted out,
His memoriall shall not depart away,
And his name shall live from generation to generation.
Nations shall shewe foorth his wisedome,
And the congregation shall declare his praise.
If hee die, he shall leave a greater name then a thousand:
And if he live, he shall increase it.

<small>An exhortation to praise God for his workes, which are good to the good, and evill to them that are evill.</small>

Yet I have more to say which I have thought upon,
For I am filled as the Moone at the full.
Hearken unto me, ye holy children,
And budde foorth as a rose growing by the brooke of the field:
And give yee a sweete savour as frankincense,
And flourish as a lilly,
Send foorth a smell, and sing a song of praise,
Blesse the Lord in all his workes.
Magnifie his Name,
And shewe foorth his praise
With the songs of your lips, and with harpes,
And in praising him you shall say after this maner:
Al the works of the Lord are exceeding good,
And whatsoever hee commandeth, shalbe accomplished in due season.
And none may say, What is this? wherefore is that?
For at time convenient they shall all be sought out:
At his commaundement the waters stood as an heape,

ECCLESIASTICUS

And at the wordes of his mouth the receptacles of waters.
At his commandement is done whatsoever pleaseth him,
And none can hinder when he will save.
The workes of all flesh are before him,
And nothing can be hid from his eyes.
He seeth from everlasting to everlasting,
And there is nothing wonderfull before him.
A man neede not to say, What is this? wherefore is that?
For hee hath made all things for their uses.
His blessing covered the dry land as a river,
And watered it as a flood.
As hee hath turned the waters into saltnesse:
So shall the heathen inherite his wrath.
As his wayes are plaine unto the holy,
So are they stumbling blockes unto the wicked.
For the good, are good things created from the beginning:
So evill things for sinners.
The principall things for the whole use of mans life,
Are water, fire, yron, and salt,
Floure of wheate, honie, milke,
And the blood of the grape, and oyle, and clothing.
All these things are for good to the godly:
So to the sinners they are turned into evill.
There be spirits that are created for vengeance,
Which in their furie lay on sore strokes,
In the time of destruction they powre out their force,
And appease the wrath of him that made them.
Fire, and haile, and famine, and death:
All these were created for vengeance:
Teeth of wild beasts, and scorpions, serpents,
And the sword, punishing the wicked to destruction.
They shall reioice in his commandement,
And they shall bee ready upon earth when neede is,
And when their time is come, they shall not transgresse his word.
Therefore from the beginning I was resolved,
And thought upon these things, and have left them in writing.
All the workes of the Lord are good:
And he will give every needefull thing in due season.
So that a man cannot say, This is worse then that:
For in time they shall all be well approved.

CHAPTER XXXIX

ECCLESIASTICUS

CHAPTER XXXIX

And therefore praise ye the Lord with the whole heart and mouth,
And blesse the Name of the Lord.

CHAPTER XL

Many miseries in a mans life.

GREAT travaile is created for every man,
And an heavy yoke is upon the sons of Adam,
From the day that they goe out of their mothers wombe,
Till the day that they returne to the mother of all things.
Their imagination of things to come, and the day of death
[Trouble] their thoughts, and [cause] feare of heart:
From him that sitteth on a throne of glory,
Unto him that is humbled in earth and ashes.
From him that weareth purple, and a crown,
Unto him that is clothed with a linnen frocke.
Wrath, and envie, trouble and unquietnesse,
Feare of death, and anger, and strife,
And in the time of rest upon his bed,
His night sleepe doe change his knowledge.
A litle or nothing is his rest,
And afterward he is in his sleepe, as in a day of keeping watch,
Troubled in the vision of his heart,
As if he were escaped out of a battell:
When all is safe, he awaketh,
And marveileth that the feare was nothing.
[Such things happen] unto all flesh, both man and beast,
And that is seven fold more upon sinners.
Death and bloodshed, strife and sword,
Calamities, famine, tribulation, and the scourge:
These things are created for the wicked,
And for their sakes came the flood.
All things that are of the earth shal turne to the earth againe:
And that which is of the waters doeth returne into the Sea.

The reward of unrighteousnesse, and the fruit of true dealing.

All briberie and iniustice shall be blotted out:
But true dealing shall endure for ever.
The goods of the uniust shall bee dried up like a river,
And shall vanish with noise, like a great thunder in raine.
While he openeth his hand he shal reioyce:
So shall transgressours come to nought.

ECCLESIASTICUS

The children of the ungodly shall not bring forth many branches: {CHAPTER XL}
But are as uncleane roots upon a hard rocke.
The weed growing upon every water, and banke of a river,
Shall bee pulled up before all grasse.
Bountifulnes is as a most fruitfull garden,
And mercifulnesse endureth for ever.
To labour and to be content with that a man hath, is a sweet life: {A vertuous wife, and an honest frien rejoyce the heart, but the feare of the Lord is above all.}
But hee that findeth a treasure, is above them both.
Children and the building of a citie continue a mans name:
But a blamelesse wife is counted above them both.
Wine and musicke reioyce the heart:
But the love of wisedome is above them both.
The pipe and the psalterie make sweet melodie:
But a pleasant tongue is above them both.
Thine eye desireth favour and beautie:
But more then both, corne while it is greene.
A friend and companion never meet amisse:
But above both is a wife with her husband.
Brethren and helpe are against time of trouble:
But almes shall deliver more then them both.
Golde and silver make the foote stand sure:
But counsell is esteemed above them both.
Riches and strength lift up the heart:
But the feare of the Lord is above them both:
There is no want in the feare of the Lord,
And it needeth not to seeke helpe.
The feare of the Lord is a fruitfull garden,
And covereth him above all glory.
My sonne, lead not a beggers life: {A beggers life is hatefull.}
For better it is to die then to beg.
The life of him that dependeth on another mans table,
Is not to be counted for a life:
For he polluteth himselfe with other mens meate,
But a wise man well nurtured will beware thereof.
Begging is sweet in the mouth of the shamelesse:
But in his belly there shall burne a fire.

ECCLESIASTICUS

CHAPTER XLI

<small>CHAPTER XLI
The remembrance of Death.</small>

O DEATH, how bitter is the remembrance of thee to a man that liveth at rest in his possessions,
Unto the man that hath nothing to vexe him, and that hath prosperity in all things:
Yea unto him that is yet able to receive meate?
O death, acceptable is thy sentence unto the needy, and unto him whose strength faileth,
That is now in the last age, and is vexed with all things,
And to him that despaireth and hath lost patience.

<small>Death is not to be feared.</small>

Feare not the sentence of death,
Remember them that have beene before thee, and that come after,
For this is the sentence of the Lord over all flesh.
And why art thou against the pleasure of the most High?
There is no inquisition in the grave,
Whether thou have lived ten, or a hundred, or a thousand yeeres.

<small>The ungodly shall be accursed.</small>

The children of sinners, are abhominable children:
And they that are conversant in the dwelling of the ungodly.
The inheritance of sinners children shal perish,
And their posterity shal have a perpetuall reproch.
The children will complaine of an ungodly father,
Because they shall be reproched for his sake.
Woe be unto you ungodly men
Which have forsaken the law of the most high God:
For if you encrease, it shall be to your destruction.
And if you be borne, you shall be borne to a curse:
And if you die, a curse shall be your portion.
All that are of the earth shall turne to earth againe:
So the ungodly shall goe from a curse to destruction.

<small>Of an evill and a good name.</small>

The mourning of men is about their bodies:
But an ill name of sinners shall be blotted out.
Have regard to thy name:
For that shall continue with thee above a thousand great treasures of gold.
A good life hath but few daies:
But a good name endureth for ever.

<small>Wisedome is to be uttered.</small>

My children, keepe discipline in peace:
For wisedome that is hid, and a treasure that is not seene,
What profit is in them both?
A man that hideth his foolishnesse is better

ECCLESIASTICUS

Then a man that hideth his wisedome.
Therefore be shamefast according to my word:
For it is not good to retaine all shamefastnesse,
Neither is it altogether approoved in every thing.
Be ashamed of whoredome before father and mother,
And of a lie before a prince and a mighty man:
Of an offence before a iudge and ruler,
Of iniquitie before a congregation and people,
Of unlust dealing before thy partner and friend
And of theft in regard of the place where thou soiournest,
And in regard of the trueth of God and his covenant,
And to leane with thine elbow upon the meate,
And of scorning to give and take:
And of silence before them that salute thee,
And to look upon an harlot:
And to turne away thy face from thy kinsman,
Or to take away a portion or a gift,
Or to gaze upon another mans wife,
Or to bee overbusie with his maide, and come not neere her bed,
Or of upbraiding speaches before friends;
And after thou hast given, upbraide not:
Or of iterating and speaking againe that which thou hast heard,
And of revealing of secrets.
So shalt thou be truely shamefast,
And finde favour before all men.

CHAPTER XLI
Of what things we should be ashamed.

CHAPTER XLII

OF these things be not thou ashamed,
And accept no person to sinne thereby.
Of the Law of the most High, and his Covenant,
And of iudgement to iustifie the ungodly:
Of reckoning with thy partners and traveilers:
Or of the gift of the heritage of friends:
Of exactnesse of ballance, and waights:
Or of getting much or little
And of merchants indifferent selling,
Of much correction of children,
And to make the side of an evill servant to bleed.
Sure keeping is good where an evill wife is,
And shut up where many hands are.

Whereof we should not be ashamed.

ECCLESIASTICUS

<small>CHAPTER XLII</small>

Deliver all things in number and waight,
And put al in writing that thou givest out, or receivest in.
Be not ashamed to informe the unwise and foolish,
And the extreeme aged that contendeth with those that are yong,
Thus shalt thou bee truely learned
And approved of all men living.

<small>Be carefull of thy daughter.</small>

The father waketh for the daughter when no man knoweth,
And the care for her taketh away sleepe;
When shee is yong lest shee passe away the flowre of her age,
And being married, lest she should be hated:
In her virginitie lest she should be defiled,
And gotten with childe in her fathers house;
And having an husband, lest she should misbehave herselfe:
And when shee is married, lest shee should be barren.
Keepe a sure watch over a shamelesse daughter,
Lest shee make thee a laughing stocke to thine enemies,
And a by-word in the citie, and a reproch among the people,
And make thee ashamed before the multitude.

<small>Beware of a woman.</small>

Behold not every bodies beauty,
And sit not in the midst of women.
For from garments commeth a moth,
And from women wickednesse.
Better is the churlishnesse of a man, then a courteous woman,
A woman I say, which bringeth shame and reproch.

<small>The workes and greatnes of God.</small>

I will now remember the works of the Lord,
And declare the things that I have seene:
In the words of the Lord are his workes.
The Sunne that giveth light, looketh upon all things:
And the worke thereof is full of the glory of the Lord.
The Lord hath not given power to the Saints to declare all his marveilous workes,
Which the Almightie Lord firmely setled,
That whatsoever is, might be established for his glory.
He seeketh out the deepe and the heart,
And considereth their crafty devices:
For the Lord knoweth all that may be knowen,
And he beholdeth the signes of the world.
Hee declareth the things that are past, and for to come,
And reveileth the steps of hidden things.
No thought escapeth him,
Neither any word is hidden from him.
Hee hath garnished the excellent workes of his wisedome,

ECCLESIASTICUS

And hee is from everlasting to everlasting,
Unto him may nothing be added, neither can he be diminished,
And he hath no need of any counseller.
O how desireable are all his workes:
And that a man may see even to a sparke.
All these things live and remaine for ever, for all uses,
And they are all obedient.
All things are double one against another:
And hee hath made nothing unperfit.
One thing establisheth the good of another:
And who shalbe filled with beholding his glory?

CHAPTER XLII

CHAPTER XLIII

THE pride of the height, the cleare firmament,
The beautie of heaven, with his glorious shew;
The Sunne when it appeareth, declaring at his rising,
A marveilous instrument, the worke of the most High.
At noone it parcheth the country,
And who can abide the burning heate thereof?
A man blowing a furnace is in works of heat,
But the Sunne burneth the mountaines three times more;
Breathing out fiery vapours,
And sending foorth bright beames, it dimmeth the eyes.
Great is the Lord that made it,
And at his commandement it runneth hastily.
He made the Moone also to serve in her season,
For a declaration of times, and a signe of the world.
From the Moone is the signe of Feasts,
A light that decreaseth in her perfection.
The moneth is called after her name,
Encreasing wonderfully in her changing,
Being an instrument of the armies above,
Shining in the firmament of heaven,
The beautie of heaven, the glory of the starres,
An ornament giving light in the highest places of the Lord.
At the commandement of the holy One, they will stand in their order,
And never faint in their watches.
Looke upon the rainebow, and praise him that made it,
Very beautifull it is in the brightnesse thereof.
It compasseth the heaven about with a glorious circle,

The workes of God in heaven, and in earth, and in the sea, are exceeding glorious and wonderfull.

ECCLESIASTICUS

CHAPTER XLIII

And the hands of the most high have bended it.
By his commandement hee maketh the snow to fall apace,
And sendeth swiftly the lightnings of his iudgment.
Through this the treasures are opened,
And clouds flie forth as foules.
By his great power hee maketh the cloudes firme,
And the hailestones are broken small.
At his sight the mountaines are shaken,
And at his will the South wind bloweth.
The noise of the thunder maketh the earth to tremble :
So doth the Northren storme, and the whirlewinde :
As birds flying he scattereth the snow,
And the falling downe thereof, is as the lighting of grashoppers.
The eye marveileth at the beauty of the whitenesse thereof,
And the heart is astonished at the raining of it.
The hoare frost also as salt hee powreth on the earth,
And being congealed, it lieth on the toppe of sharpe stakes.
When the colde North-winde bloweth,
And the water is congealed into yce,
It abideth upon every gathering together of water,
And clotheth the water as with a brestplate.
It devoureth the mountaines, and burneth the wildernesse,
And consumeth the grasse as fire.
A present remedy of all is a miste coming speedily :
A dew comming after heate, refresheth.
By his counsell he appeaseth the deepe,
And planteth Ilands therein.
They that saile on the Sea, tell of the danger thereof,
And when wee heare it with our eares, wee marveile thereat.
For therein be strange and wonderous workes,
Varietie of all kindes of beasts, and whales created.
By him the ende of them hath prosperous successe,
And by his word all things consist.
We may speake much, and yet come short :
Wherefore in summe, he is all.
How shall wee be able to magnifie him?
For hee is great above all his workes.

Yet God himselfe in his power and wisedome is above all.

The Lord is terrible and very great,
And marveilous is his power.
When you glorifie the Lord exalt him as much as you can :
For even yet wil he farre exceed,
And when you exalt him, put foorth all your strength,

ECCLESIASTICUS

And be not weary: for you can never goe farre enough.
Who hath seene him, that hee might tell us?
And who can magnifie him as he is?
There are yet hid greater things then these be,
For wee have seene but a few of his workes:
For the Lord hath made all things,
And to the godly hath hee given wisedome.

CHAPTER XLIII

CHAPTER XLIIII

LET us now praise famous men,
   And our Fathers that begat us.
   The Lorde hath wrought great glory by them,
Through his great power from the beginning.
Such as did beare rule in their kingdomes,
Men renowmed for their power,
Giving counsell by their understanding,
And declaring prophecies:
Leaders of the people by their counsels,
And by their knowledge of learning meet for the people,
Wise and eloquent in their instructions.
Such as found out musical tunes,
And recited verses in writing.
Rich men furnished with abilitie,
Living peaceably in their habitations.
All these were honoured in their generations,
And were the glory of their times.
There be of them, that have left a name behind them,
That their praises might be reported.
And some there be, which have no memorial,
Who are perished as though they had never bene,
And are become as though they had never bene borne,
And their children after them.
But these were mercifull men,
Whose righteousnesse hath not beene forgotten.
With their seed shall continually remaine a good inheritance,
And their children are within the covenant.
Their seed stands fast,
And their children for their sakes.
Their seed shall remaine for ever,
And their glory shall not be blotted out.
Their bodies are buried in peace,
But their name liveth for evermore.

The praise of certaine holy men:

ECCLESIASTICUS

CHAPTER XLIIII

of Enoch,

The people will tell of their wisdome,
And the congregation will shew forth their praise.
Enoch pleased the Lord and was translated,
Being an example of repentance, to all generations.

Noah,

Noah was found perfect and righteous,
In the time of wrath, he was taken in exchange (for the world)
Therefore was he left as a remnant unto the earth, when the flood came.
An everlasting Covenant was made with him,
That all flesh should perish no more by the flood.

Abraham,

Abraham was a great father of many people:
In glory was there none like unto him:
Who kept the Law of the most High,
And was in covenant with him,
Hee established the Covenant in his flesh,
And when he was proved, he was found faithfull.
Therefore he assured him by an othe,
That he would blesse the nations in his seed,
And that he would multiply him, as the dust of the earth,
And exalt his seed as the starres,
And cause them to inherit from Sea to Sea,
And from the river unto the utmost part of the land.

Isaac,

With Isaac did he establish likewise [for Abraham his fathers sake]
The blessing of all men and the covenant,

and Iacob.

And made it rest upon the head of Iacob.
Hee acknowledged him in his blessing,
And gave him an heritage,
And divided his portions,
Among the twelve tribes did he part them.

CHAPTER XLV

The praise of Moses,

AND he brought out of him a mercifull man,
Which found favour in the sight of all flesh,
Even Moses beloved of God and men,
Whose memoriall is blessed:
He made him like to the glorious Saints,
And magnified him, so that his enemies stood in feare of him.
By his words he caused the wonders to cease,
And he made him glorious in the sight of kings,
And gave him a commaundement for his people,

ECCLESIASTICUS

And shewed him part of his glory.
He sanctified him in his faithfulnesse, and meekenesse,
And chose him out of all men.
He made him to heare his voyce,
And brought him into the darke cloud,
And gave him commandements before his face,
Even the law of life and knowledge,
That hee might teach Iacob his Covenants,
And Israel his iudgments.
He exalted Aaron an holy man like unto him,
Even his brother, of the tribe of Levi.
An everlasting covenant he made with him,
And gave him the priesthood among the people,
He beautified him with comely ornaments,
And clothed him with a robe of glory.
Hee put upon him perfect glory:
And strengthened him with rich garments,
With breeches, with a long robe, and the Ephod:
And he compassed him with pomegranates,
And with many golden bels round about,
That as he went, there might be a sound,
And a noise made that might be heard in the Temple,
For a memoriall to the children of his people.
With an holy garment, with gold and blew silke, and purple the worke of the embroiderer;
With a brestplate of iudgement, and with Urim and Thummim.
With twisted scarlet, the worke of the cunning workeman,
With precious stones graven like seales, and set in gold, the worke of the Ieweller,
With a writing engraved for a memoriall, after the number of the tribes of Israel.
He set a crowne of gold upon the miter, wherein was engraved holinesse
An ornament of honour, a costly worke,
The desires of the eies goodly and beautiful.
Before him there were none such,
Neither did ever any stranger put them on, but onely his children, and his childrens children perpetually.
Their sacrifices shall be wholy consumed
Every day twise continually.
Moises consecrated him,

CHAPTER XLV

Of Aaron,

ECCLESIASTICUS

<small>CHAPTER XLV</small>

And annointed him with holy oile,
This was appointed unto him by an everlasting covenant,
And to his seed so long as the heavens should remaine,
That they should minister unto him, and execute the office of the priesthood,
And blesse the people in his name.
He chose him out of all men living
To offer sacrifices to the Lord,
Incense and a sweet savour, for a memoriall,
To make reconciliation for his people.
He gave unto him his commandements,
And authority in the statutes of iudgements,
That he should teach Iacob the testimonies,
And informe Israel in his lawes.
Strangers conspired together against him,
And maligned him in the wildernesse,
Even the men that were of Dathans, and Abirons side,
And the congregation of Core with fury and wrath.
This the Lord saw and it displeased him,
And in his wrathfull indignation, were they consumed:
He did wonders upon them,
To consume them with the fiery flame.
But he made Aaron more honourable,
And gave him an heritage,
And divided unto him the first fruits of the encrease,
Especially he prepared bread in abundance:
For they eate of the sacrifices of the Lord,
Which he gave unto him and his seed:
Howbeit in the land of the people he had no inheritance,
Neither had he any portion among the people,
For the Lord himselfe is his portion and inheritance.

<small>and of Phinees.</small> The third in glory is Phinees the sonne of Eleazar,
Because he had zeale in the feare of the Lord,
And stood up with good courage of heart,
When the people were turned backe, and made reconciliation for Israel.
Therfore was there a covenant of peace made with him,
That he should be the cheefe of the sanctuary, and of his people,
And that he, and his posteritie
Should have the dignitie of the Priesthood for ever.
According to the covenant made with David sonne of Iesse, of the tribe of Iuda,

ECCLESIASTICUS

That the inheritance of the king should be to his posterity alone:
So the inheritance of Aaron should also be unto his seed.
God give you wisedome in your heart
To iudge his people in righteousnesse,
That their good things be not abolished,
And that their glory may endure for ever.

CHAPTER XLV

CHAPTER XLVI

IESUS the sonne of Nave was valiant in the wars,
    And was the successor of Moses in prophesies,
    Who according to his name was made great
For the saving of the elect of God,
And taking vengeance of the enemies that rose up against them,
That he might set Israel in their inheritance.
How great glory gat he when he did lift up his hands,
And stretched out his sword against the cities?
Who before him so stood to it?
For the Lord himselfe brought his enemies unto him.
Did not the Sunne goe backe by his meanes?
And was not one day as long as two?
He called upon the most high Lord,
When the enemies pressed upon him on every side,
And the great Lord heard him.
And with hailestones of mighty power
He made the battell to fall violently upon the nations,
And in the descent (of Bethoron) hee destroyed them that resisted,
That the nations might know all their strength,
Because hee fought in the sight of the Lord,
And he followed the mightie one.
In the time of Moses also, he did a worke of mercie,
Hee and Caleb the sonne of Iephunne,
In that they withstood the Congregation,
And withheld the people from sinne,
And appeased the wicked murmuring.
And of sixe hundred thousand people on foot, they two were preserved
To bring them into the heritage,
Even unto the land that floweth with milk and hony.
The Lord gave strength also unto Caleb,

The praise of Ioshua,

Of Caleb,

ECCLESIASTICUS

CHAPTER XLVI

Which remained with him unto his old age,
So that he entred upon the high places of the land,
And his seed obtained it for an heritage.
That all the children of Israel might see
That it is good to follow the Lord.
And concerning the Iudges, every one by name,
Whose heart went not a whoring,
Nor departed from the Lord,
Let their memory be blessed.
Let their bones flourish out of their place,
And let the name of them that were honoured, be continued upon their children.

Of Samuel. Samuel the Prophet of the Lord, beloved of his Lord,
Established a kingdom, and anointed princes over his people.
By the Law of the Lord hee iudged the Congregation,
And the Lord had respect unto Iacob.
By his faithfulnes he was found a true Prophet,
And by his word he was knowen to be faithfull in vision.
He called upon the mighty Lord,
When his enemies pressed upon him on every side,
When he offered the sucking lambe.
And the Lord thundered from heaven,
And with a great noise made his voice to be heard.
And he destroyed the rulers of the Tyrians,
And all the princes of the Philistines.
And before his long sleepe
Hee made protestations in the sight of the Lord, and his anoynted,
I have not taken any mans goods, so much as a shoe, and no man did accuse him.
And after his death he prophesied,
And shewed the King his end,
And lift up his voyce from the earth in prophesie,
To blot out the wickednesse of the people.

CHAPTER XLVII

The praise of Nathan, Of David,

AND after him rose up Nathan
To prophesie in the time of David.
As is the fat taken away from the peace offering,
So was David chosen out of the children of Israel.
Hee played with Lions as with kids,
And with beares as with lambs.

ECCLESIASTICUS

Slew he not a gyant when hee was yet but yong?   CHAPTER
And did he not take away reproch from the people,   XLVII
When he lifted up his hand with the stone in the sling,
And beat downe the boasting of Goliah?
For he called upon the most high Lord,
And he gave him strength in his right hand
To slay that mighty warriour,
And set up the horne of his people:
So the people honoured him with ten thousands,
And praised him in the blessings of the Lord,
In that hee gave him a crowne of glory.
For hee destroyed the enemies on every side,
And brought to nought the Philistines his adversaries,
And brake their horne in sunder unto this day.
In all his workes hee praised the holy one most High, with words of glory,
With his whole heart he sung songs,
And loved him that made him.
He set singers also before the Altar,
That by their voyces they might make sweet melody, and daily sing praises in their songs.
He beautified their feasts,
And set in order the solemne times, untill the ende,
That they might praise his holy Name,
And that the Temple might sound from morning.
The Lord tooke away his sinnes,
And exalted his horne for ever:
He gave him a covenant of kings,
And a throne of glory in Israel.
After him rose up a wise sonne,   Of Solomon
And for his sake he dwelt at large.   his glory, and
Salomon reigned in a peaceable time, and was honoured;   infirmities.
For God made all quiet round about him,
That hee might build an house in his Name,
And prepare his Sanctuary for ever.
How wise wast thou in thy youth,
And as a flood filled with understanding.
Thy soule covered the whole earth,
And thou filledst it with dark parables.
Thy name went farre unto the Ilands,
And for thy peace thou wast beloved.
The countreys marveiled at thee for thy Songs,
And Proverbs, and Parables, and interpretations.

ECCLESIASTICUS

<small>CHAPTER XLVII</small>

By the Name of the Lord God,
Which is called the Lord God of Israel,
Thou didst gather gold as tinne,
And didst multiply silver as lead.
Thou didst bow thy loines unto women,
And by thy body thou wast brought into subiection.
Thou didst staine thy honour, and pollute thy seed,
So that thou broughtest wrath upon thy children,
And wast grieved for thy folly.
So the kingdome was divided,
And out of Ephraim ruled a rebellious kingdome.
But the Lord will never leave off his mercy,
Neither shall any of his workes perish,
Neither will hee abolish the posterity of his elect,
And the seed of him that loveth him he will not take away:
Wherefore he gave a remnant unto Iacob,
And out of him a roote unto David.

<small>Of his end and punishment.</small>

Thus rested Solomon with his fathers,
And of his seede he left behinde him Roboam,
Even the foolishnesse of the people, and one that had no understanding;
Who turned away the people through his counsell:
There was also Ieroboam the sonne of Nabat,
Who caused Israel to sinne,
And shewed Ephraim the way of sinne:
And their sinnes were multiplied exceedingly,
That they were driven out of the land.
For they sought out all wickednes,
Till the vengeance came upon them.

CHAPTER XLVIII

<small>The praise of Elias,</small>

THEN stood up Elias the Prophet as fire,
And his word burnt like a lampe.
He brought a sore famine upon them,
And by his zeale he diminished their number.
By the word of the Lord he shut up the heaven,
And also three times brought downe fire.
O Elias, how wast thou honoured in thy wondrous deedes!
And who may glory like unto thee!
Who didst raise up a dead man from death,
And his soule from the place of the dead by the word of the most Hie.

ECCLESIASTICUS

Who broughtest kings to destruction,   CHAPTER
And honourable men from their bedde.   XLVIII
Who heardest the rebuke of the Lord in Sinai,
And in Horeb the iudgment of vengeance.
Who anointed kings to take revenge,
And Prophets to succeed after him:
Who wast taken up in a whirlewinde of fire,
And in a charet of fierie horses:
Who wast ordained for reproofes in their times,
To pacifie the wrath of the Lordes iudgement before it brake
    foorth into fury,
And to turne the heart of the father unto the sonne,
And to restore the tribes of Iacob.
Blessed are they that saw thee,
And slept in love,
For we shal surely live.
Elias it was, who was covered with a whirlewinde: of Elizeus,
And Elizeus was filled with his spirit:
Whilest he lived he was not mooved [with the presence] of
    any prince,
Neither could any bring him into subiection.
No word could overcome him,
And after his death his body prophecied.
He did wonders in his life,
And at his death were his works marveilous.
For all this the people repented not,
Neither departed they from their sinnes,
Till they were spoiled and caried out of their land,
And were scattered through all the earth:
Yet there remained a small people,
And a ruler in the house of David:
Of whom, some did that which was pleasing to God,
And some multiplied sinnes.
Ezekias fortified his citie,   and of Ezekias.
And brought in water into the midst thereof:
He digged the hard rocke with yron,
And made welles for waters.
In his time Sennacherib came up,
And sent Rabsaces,
And lift up his hand against Sion,
And boasted proudly.
Then trembled their hearts and handes,
And they were in paine as women in travell.

ECCLESIASTICUS

CHAPTER XLVIII

But they called upon the Lord which is mercifull,
And stretched out their hands towards him,
And immediatly the holy One heard them out of heaven,
And delivered them by the ministery of Esay.
He smote the hoste of the Assyrians,
And his Angel destroyed them.
For Ezekias had done the thing that pleased the Lord,
And was strong in the wayes of David his father,
As Esay the Prophet, who was great and faithfull in his vision, had commaunded him.
In his time the Sunne went backeward,
And hee lengthened the kings life.
Hee sawe by an excellent spirit what should come to passe at the last,
And hee comforted them that mourned in Sion.
He shewed what should come to passe for ever,
And secret things or ever they came.

CHAPTER XLIX

The praise of Iosias,

THE remembrance of Iosias is like the composition of the perfume
That is made by the arte of the Apothecarie:
It is sweete as hony in all mouthes,
And as musicke at a banquet of wine.
He behaved himselfe uprightly in the conversion of the people,
And tooke away the abominations of iniquitie.
He directed his heart unto the Lord,
And in the time of the ungodly he established the worship of God.

Of David and Ezekias,

All, except David and Ezechias, and Iosias, were defective:
For they forsooke the Law of the most High,
(Even) the kings of Iudah failed:
Therefore he gave their power unto others,
And their glory to a strange nation.

Of Ieremie,

They burnt the chosen citie of the Sanctuarie,
And made the streets desolate according to the prophecie of Ieremias:
For they entreated him evil,
Who neverthelesse was a prophet sanctified in his mothers wombe,

ECCLESIASTICUS

That he might root out and afflict and destroy, _{CHAPTER XLIX}
And that he might build up also and plant.
It was Ezechiel who sawe the glorious vision, _{Of Ezechiel,}
Which was shewed him upon the chariot of the Cherubims.
For he made mention of the enemies under [the figure of] the raine,
And directed them that went right.
And of the twelve prophets let the memorial be blessed,
And let their bones flourish againe out of their place:
For they comforted Iacob,
And delivered them by assured hope.
How shall we magnifie Zorobabel? _{Zorobabel,}
Even he was as a signet on the right hand.
So was Iesus the sonne of Iosedec: _{Iesus the sonne of Iosedec.}
Who in their time builded the house,
And set up an holy Temple to the Lord,
Which was prepared for everlasting glory.
And among the elect was Neemias whose renowme is great, _{Of Nehemiah, Enoch, Seth, Sem, and Adam.}
Who raised up for us, the walles that were fallen,
And set up the gates and the barres,
And raised up our ruines againe.
But upon the earth was no man created like Enoch,
For he was taken from the earth.
Neither was there a man borne like unto Ioseph,
A governour of his brethren, a stay of the people,
Whose bones were regarded of the Lord.
Sem and Seth were in great honour among men,
And so was Adam above every living thing in the creation.

CHAPTER L

SIMON the high priest the sonne of Onias, _{Of Simon the sonne of Onias.}
   Who in his life repaired the house againe,
   And in his dayes fortified the Temple:
And by him was built from the foundation the double height,
The high fortresse of the wall about the Temple.
In his dayes the cisterne to receive water being in compasse as the sea,
Was covered with plates of brasse.
He tooke care of the Temple that it should not fall,
And fortified the citie against besieging.
How was he honoured in the midst of the people,
In his comming out of the Sanctuarie?

ECCLESIASTICUS

CHAPTER L

He was as the morning starre in the midst of a cloud:
And as the moone at the full.
As the Sunne shining upon the Temple of the most High,
And as the rainebow giving light in the bright cloudes.
And as the flowre of roses in the spring of the yeere,
As lillies by the rivers of waters,
And as the branches of the frankincense tree in the time of summer.
As fire and incense in the censer,
And as a vessell of beaten gold
Set with all maner of precious stones,
And as a faire olive tree budding forth fruit,
And as a Cypresse tree which groweth up to the cloudes.
When he put on the robe of honour,
And was clothed with the perfection of glory,
When he went up to the holy altar,
He made the garment of holinesse honourable.
When he tooke the portions out of the priests hands,
Hee himselfe stood by the hearth of the altar,
Compassed with his brethren round about,
As a yong cedar in Libanus,
And as palme trees compassed they him round about.
So were all the sonnes of Aaron in their glory,
And the oblations of the Lord in their hands, before all the congregation of Israel.
And finishing the service at the altar,
That he might adorne the offring of the most high Almighty,
He stretched out his hand to the cup,
And powred of the blood of the grape,
He powred out at the foote of the altar,
A sweet smelling savour unto the most high King of all.
Then shouted the sonnes of Aaron,
And sounded the silver trumpets,
And made a great noise to be heard,
For a remembrance before the most High.
Then all the people together hasted,
And fell downe to the earth upon their faces
To worship their Lord God almighty the most High.
The singers also sang praises with their voices,
With great variety of sounds was there made sweete melodie.
And the people besought the Lord the most High
By prayer before him that is mercifull,
Till the solemnity of the Lord was ended,

ECCLESIASTICUS

And they had finished his service.
Then he went downe, and lifted up his hands
Over the whole congregation of the children of Israel,
To give the blessing of the Lord with his lips,
And to reioyce in his name.
And they bowed themselves downe to worship the second time,
That they might receive a blessing from the most High.
Now therefore blesse yee the God of all,
Which onely doth wonderous things every where,
Which exalteth our daies from the wombe,
And dealeth with us according to his mercy.
He grant us ioyfulnesse of heart,
And that peace may be in our daies in Israel for ever.
That hee would confirme his mercy with us,
And deliver us at his time.
There be two maner of nations which my heart abhorreth,
And the third is no nation.
They that sit upon the mountaine of Samaria, and they that dwell amongst the Philistines,
And that foolish people that dwell in Sichem.
Iesus the sonne of Sirach of Hierusalem hath written in this booke,
The instruction of understanding and knowledge,
Who out of his heart powred forth wisedome.
Blessed is he that shall be exercised in these things,
And hee that layeth them up in his heart, shall become wise.
For if he doe them, hee shall be strong to all things,
For the light of the Lord leadeth him,
Who giveth wisedome to the godly:
Blessed be the Lord for ever. Amen. Amen.

CHAPTER L

How the people were taught to praise God, and pray.

The conclusion.

CHAPTER LI

A Prayer of Iesus the sonne of Sirach.

I WILL thanke thee, O Lord and king,
And praise thee O God my Saviour,
I doe give praise unto thy name:
For thou art my defender, and helper,
And hast preserved my body from destruction,
And from the snare of the slanderous tongue,
And from the lippes that forge lies,

ECCLESIASTICUS

CHAPTER LI

And hast beene my helper against mine adversaries.
And hast delivered me according to the multitude of thy mercies, and greatnesse of thy name,
From the teeth of them that were ready to devoure me,
And out of the hands of such as sought after my life,
And from the manifold afflictions which I had:
From the choking of fire on every side,
And from the mids of the fire, which I kindled not:
From the depth of the belly of hel,
From an uncleane tongue,
And from lying words.
By an accusation to the king from an unrighteous tongue,
My soule drew neere even unto death,
My life was neere to the hell beneath:
They compassed me on every side,
And there was no man to helpe me:
I looked for the succour of men,
But there was none:
Then thought I upon thy mercy, O Lord,
And upon thy acts of old,
How thou deliverest such as waite for thee,
And savest them out of the hands of the enemies:
Then lifted I up my supplication from the earth,
And prayed for deliverance from death.
I called upon the Lord the father of my Lord,
That he would not leave me in the dayes of my trouble,
And in the time of the proud when there was no helpe.
I will praise thy Name continually,
And will sing praise with thanksgiving,
And so my prayer was heard:
For thou savedst me from destruction,
And deliverest mee from the evill time:
Therefore will I give thankes and praise thee,
And blesse thy Name, O Lord.
When I was yet yong,
Or ever I went abroad,
I desired wisedome openly in my prayer.
I prayed for her before the Temple,
And will seeke her out even to the end:
Even from the flowre till the grape was ripe, hath my heart delighted in her,
My foot went the right way,
From my youth up sought I after her.

ECCLESIASTICUS

CHAPTER LI

I bowed downe mine eare a litle and received her,
And gate much learning.
I profited therein, [therefore] will I ascribe the glory
Unto him that giveth me wisedome:
For I purposed to doe after her,
And earnestly I followed that which is good,
So shall I not be confounded:
My soule hath wrestled with her,
And in my doings I was exact,
I stretched foorth my hands to the heaven above,
And bewailed my ignorances of her.
I directed my soule unto her,
And I found her in purenesse,
I have had my heart ioyned with her from the beginning,
Therefore shall I not bee forsaken.
My heart was troubled in seeking her:
Therefore have I gotten a good possession.
The Lord hath given mee a tongue for my reward.
And I wil praise him therewith.
Draw neere unto me you unlearned,
And dwell in the house of learning.
Wherefore are you slow, and what say you of these things,
Seeing your soules are very thirstie?
I opened my mouth, and said,
Buy her for your selves without money.
Put your necke under the yoke,
And let your soule receive instruction,
She is hard at hand to finde.
Behold with your eies,
How that I have had but little labour,
And have gotten unto me much rest.
Get learning with a great summe of money,
And get much gold by her.
Let your soule reioyce in his mercy,
And be not ashamed of his praise.
Worke your worke betimes,
And in his time he will give you your reward.

BARUCH

BARUCH

CHAPTER I

<small>Baruch wrote a booke in Babylon.</small>

AND these are the wordes of the booke, which Baruch the sonne of Nerias, the sonne of Maasias, the sonne of Sedecias, the sonne of Asadias, the son of Chelcias, wrote in Babylon, in the fift yere, and in the seventh day of the moneth, what time as the Caldeans tooke Ierusalem, and burnt it with fire. And Baruch did reade the words of this booke, in the hearing of Iechonias, the sonne of Ioachim king of Iuda, and in the eares of all the people, that came to [heare] the booke. And in the hearing of the nobles, and of the kings sonnes, and in the hearing of the Elders, and of all the people from the lowest unto the highest, even of all them that dwelt at Babylon, <small>The Iewes there wept at the reading of it.</small> by the river Sud. Whereupon they wept, fasted, and prayed before the Lord. They made also a collection of money, according to every mans power. And they sent it to Ierusalem unto Ioachim <small>They sende money and the booke, to the brethren at Hierusalem.</small> the hie Priest the sonne of Chelcias, sonne of Salom, and to the Priestes, and to all the people which were found with him at Ierusalem, at the same time, when he received the vessels of the house of the Lord that were caried out of the Temple, to returne them into the land of Iuda the tenth day of the moneth Sivan, [namely] silver vessels, which Sedecias the sonne of Iosias king of Iuda had made, after that Nabuchodonosor king of Babylon had caried away Iechonias, and the Princes, and the captives, and the mightie men, and the people of the land from Ierusalem, and brought them unto Babylon: and they said, Behold, we have sent you money, to buy you burnt offerings, and sinne offerings, and incense, and prepare yee Manna, and offer upon the Altar of the Lord our God, and pray for the life of Nabuchodonosor king of Babylon, and for the life of Balthasar his sonne, that their dayes may be upon earth as the dayes of heaven. And the Lord wil give us strength, and lighten our eyes, and we shall live under the shadow of Nabuchodo-

240

BARUCH

nosor king of Babylon, and under the shadow of Balthasar his sonne, and wee shall serve them many dayes, and finde favour in their sight. Pray for us also unto the Lord our God, (for wee have sinned against the Lord our God, and unto this day the fury of the Lord, and his wrath is not turned from us) And yee shall reade this booke, which we have sent unto you, to make confession in the house of the Lord,.upon the feasts and solemne dayes. And yee shall say, To the Lord our God belongeth righteousnesse, but unto us the confusion of faces, as it is come to passe this day unto them of Iuda, and to the inhabitants of Ierusalem, and to our kings, and to our princes, and to our Priests, and to our Prophets, and to our fathers. For wee have sinned before the Lord, and disobeyed him, and have not hearkened unto the voice of the Lord our God, to walke in the commaundements that he gave us openly: since the day that the Lorde brought our forefathers out of the land of Egypt, unto this present day, wee have beene disobedient unto the Lord our God, and we have beene negligent in not hearing his voice. Wherefore the evils cleaved unto us, and the curse which the Lord appointed by Moses his servant, at the time that he brought our fathers out of the land of Egypt, to give us a land that floweth with milke and honie, like as it is to see this day. Neverthelesse we have not hearkened unto the voice of the Lord our God, according unto all the wordes of the Prophets, whom he sent unto us. But every man followed the imagination of his owne wicked heart, to serve strange gods, and to doe evill in the sight of the Lord our God.

CHAPTER I

CHAPTER II

THEREFORE the Lord hath made good his worde, which hee pronounced against us, and against our Iudges that iudged Israel, and against our kings, and against our princes, and against the men of Israel and Iuda, to bring upon us great plagues, such as never happened under the whole heaven, as it came to passe in Ierusalem, according to the things that were written in the Law of Moses, that a man should eat the flesh of his owne sonne, and the flesh of his owne daughter. Moreover, he hath delivered them to be in subiection to all the kingdomes that are round about us, to be as a reproch and desolation among all the people round about, where the Lord hath scattered them. Thus wee were cast downe and not exalted, because wee. have sinned against the Lord our God, and have not beene obedient unto his voice. To the Lord our God appertaineth righteousnesse: but

The prayer and confession which the Iewes at Babylon made, and sent in that booke unto the brethren in Ierusalem.

5 : HH   241

BARUCH

CHAPTER II

unto us and to our fathers open shame, as appeareth this day. For all these plagues are come upon us, which the Lord hath pronounced against us, yet have we not prayed before the Lord, that we might turne every one from the imaginations of his wicked heart. Wherefore the Lord watched over us for evill, and the Lord hath brought it upon us: for the Lord is righteous in all his works, which he hath commanded us. Yet we have not hearkened unto his voice, to walk in the commandements of the Lord, that he hath set before us. And now O Lord God of Israel, that hast brought thy people out of the land of Egypt with a mighty hand, and high arme, and with signes and with wonders, and with great power, and hast gotten thy selfe a name, as appeareth this day: O Lord our God, we have sinned, we have done ungodly, wee have dealt unrighteously in all thine ordinances. Let thy wrath turne from us: for we are but a few left among the heathen, where thou hast scattered us. Heare our prayers, O Lord, and our petitions, and deliver us for thine owne sake, and give us favour in the sight of them which have led us away: that all the earth may know that thou art the Lord our God, because Israel and his posterity is called by thy name. O Lord looke downe from thy holy house, and consider us: bow downe thine eare, O Lord, to heare us. Open thine eyes and behold: for the dead that are in the graves, whose soules are taken from their bodies, wil give unto the Lord neither praise nor righteousnesse. But the soule that is greatly vexed, which goeth stouping and feeble, and the eyes that faile, and the hungry soule wil give thee praise and righteousnes O Lord. Therfore wee doe not make our humble supplication before thee, O Lord our God, for the righteousnes of our fathers, and of our kings. For thou hast sent out thy wrath and indignation upon us, as thou hast spoken by thy servants the prophets, saying, Thus saith the Lord, bow down your shoulders to serve the king of Babylon: so shall ye remaine in the lande that I gave unto your fathers. But if ye will not heare the voice of the Lord to serve the king of Babylon, I will cause to cease out of the cities of Iuda, and from without Ierusalem the voice of mirth, and the voice of ioy: the voice of the bridegrome, and the voice of the bride, and the whole land shall be desolate of inhabitants. But we would not hearken unto thy voyce, to serve the king of Babylon: therefore hast thou made good the wordes that thou spakest by thy servants the prophets, namely that the bones of our kings, and the bones of our fathers should be taken out of their places. And loe, they are cast out to the heat of the day, and to the frost of the night, and they died in great miseries, by famine, by sword,

242

BARUCH

CHAPTER II

and by pestilence. And the house which is called by thy name (hast thou laid waste) as it is to be seene this day, for the wickednesse of the house of Israel, and the house of Iuda. O Lord our God, thou hast dealt with us after all thy goodnesse, and according to all that great mercie of thine. As thou spakest by thy servant Moses in the day when thou didst command him to write thy Law, before the children of Israel, saying, If ye will not heare my voyce, surely this very great multitude shalbe turned into a smal [number] among the nations, where I will scatter them. For I knew that they would not heare me: because it is a stiffenecked people: but in the land of their captivities, they shall remember themselves, and shall know that I am the Lord their God: For I give them an heart, and eares to heare. And they shal praise me in the land of their captivitie, and thinke upon my name, and returne from their stiffe neck, and from their wicked deeds: for they shal remember the way of their fathers which sinned before the Lord. And I will bring them againe into the land which I promised with an oath unto their fathers, Abraham, Isaac, and Iacob, and they shall bee lords of it, and I will increase them, and they shall not be diminished. And I will make an everlasting covenant with them, to be their God, and they shall be my people: and I will no more drive my people of Israel out of the land that I have given them.

CHAPTER III

O LORD almighty, God of Israel, the soule in anguish, the troubled spirit crieth unto thee. Heare O Lord, and have mercy: for thou art mercifull, and have pitty upon us, because we have sinned before thee. For thou endurest for ever, and we perish utterly. O Lord almighty, thou God of Israel, heare now the prayers of the dead Israelites, and of their children, which have sinned before thee, and not hearkened unto the voice of thee their God: for the which cause these plagues cleave unto us. Remember not the iniquities of our forefathers: but thinke upon thy power and thy name, now at this time. For thou art the Lord our God, and thee, O Lord, will we praise. And for this cause thou hast put thy feare in our hearts, to the intent that we should call upon thy name, and praise thee in our captivity: for we have called to minde all the iniquity of our forefathers that sinned before thee. Behold, we are yet this day in our captivity, where thou hast scattered us, for a reproch and a curse, and to be subiect to payments, according to all the iniquities of our fathers which departed from the Lord our God. *The rest of their prayer and confession contained in that book, which Baruch writ and sent to Hierusalem.*

BARUCH

CHAPTER III

Heare, Israel, the commandements of life,
Give eare to understand wisedome.
How happeneth it, Israel, that thou art in thine enemies land,
That thou art waxen old in a strange countrey,
That thou art defiled with the dead?
That thou art counted with them that goe downe into the grave?
Thou hast forsaken the fountaine of wisedome.
For if thou hadst walked in the way of God,
Thou shouldest have dwelled in peace for ever.
Learne where is wisedome, where is strength, where is understanding,
That thou mayest know also where is length of daies, and life,
Where is the light of the eyes and peace.
Who hath found out her place?
Or who hath come into her treasures?
Where are the princes of the heathen become,
And such as ruled the beasts upon the earth.
They that had their pastime with the foules of the aire,
And they that hoorded up silver
And gold wherein men trust,
And made no end of their getting?
For they that wrought in silver, and were so careful,
And whose workes are unsearchable,
They are vanished, and gone downe to the grave,
And others are come up in their steads.
Young men have seene light, and dwelt upon the earth:
But the way of knowledge have they not knowen,
Nor understood the pathes thereof,
Nor laid hold of it:
Their children were farre off from that way.
It hath not beene heard of in Chanaan:
Neither hath it beene seene in Theman.
The Agarenes that seek wisdome upon earth,
The marchants of Merran, and of Theman,
The authors of fables, and searchers out of understanding:
None of these have knowen the way of wisedome,
Or remember her pathes.
O Israel, how great is the house of God?
And how large is the place of his possession?
Great, and hath none end:
High, and unmeasurable.
There were the gyants, famous from the beginning,

BARUCH

That were of so great stature, and so expert in warre.
Those did not the Lord chuse,
Neither gave he the way of knowledge unto them.
But they were destroyed, because they had no wisedome,
And perished through their owne foolishnesse.
Who hath gone up into heaven and taken her,
And brought her downe from the clouds?
Who hath gone over the Sea, and found her,
And wil bring her for pure gold?
No man knoweth her way,
Nor thinketh of her path.
But he that knoweth all things, knoweth her,
And hath found her out with his understanding:
He that prepared the earth for evermore,
Hath filled it with fourefooted beasts.
He that sendeth forth light, and it goeth:
Calleth it againe, and it obeyeth him with feare.
The starres shined in their watches, and reioyced:
When he calleth them, they say, Here we be,
And so with cheerefulnesse they shewed light unto him that made them.
This is our God,
And there shall none other be accounted of in comparison of him.
He hath found out all the way of knowledge,
And hath given it unto Iacob his servant,
And to Israel his beloved.
Afterward did he shew himselfe upon earth,
And conversed with men.

CHAPTER III

Wisdome was shewed first to Iacob, and was seene upon the earth.

CHAPTER IIII

THIS is the Booke of the commandements of God:
And the Law that endureth for ever:
All they that keepe it shall come to life:
But such as leave it, shall die.
Turne thee, O Iacob, and take heed of it:
Walke in the presence of the light therof,
That thou mayest be illuminated.
Give not thine honour to another,
Nor the things that are profitable unto thee, to a strange nation.
O Israel, happie are wee:

The booke of Commandements, is that Wisdome which was commended in the former chapter.

245

BARUCH

CHAPTER IIII

For things that are pleasing to God, are made knowen unto us.
Be of good cheare, my people, the memoriall of Israel.
Ye were sold to the nations, not for [your] destruction:
But because you moved God to wrath, ye were delivered unto the enemies.
For yee provoked him that made you,
By sacrificing unto devils, and not to God.
Ye have forgotten the everlasting God, that brought you up,
And ye have grieved Ierusalem that noursed you.
For when shee saw the wrath of God comming upon you, she said;
Hearken, O ye that dwell about Sion:
God hath brought upon me great mourning.
For I saw the captivitie of my sonnes and daughters,
Which the everlasting brought upon them.
With ioy did I nourish them:
But sent them away with weeping and mourning.
Let no man reioyce over me a widow, and forsaken of many,
Who for the sinnes of my children, am left desolate:
Because they departed from the Law of God.
They knew not his statutes,
Nor walked in the waies of his Commandements,
Nor trode in the pathes of discipline in his righteousnesse.
Let them that dwell about Sion come,
And remember ye the captivity of my sonnes and daughters,
Which the everlasting hath brought upon them.
For he hath brought a nation upon them from far:
A shamelesse nation, and of a strange language,
Who neither reverenced old man, nor pitied childe.
These have caried away the deare beloved children of the widow,
And left her that was alone, desolate without daughters.
But what can I helpe you?
For he that brought these plagues upon you,
Will deliver you from the hands of your enemies.
Goe your way, O my children, goe your way:
For I am left desolate.
I have put off the clothing of peace,
And put upon me the sackcloth of my prayer.
I will cry unto the everlasting in my dayes.
Be of good cheare, O my children, cry unto the Lord:

BARUCH

And he shal deliver you from the power and hand of the enemies. CHAPTER IIII
For my hope is in the Everlasting that hee will save you,
And ioy is come unto me from the Holy one,
Because of the mercy which shall soone come unto you from the everlasting our Saviour.
For I sent you out with mourning and weeping:
But God will give you to mee againe, with ioy and gladnesse for ever.
Like as now the neighbours of Sion have seene your captivity:
So shall they see shortly your salvation from our God,
Which shall come upon you with great glory,
And brightnesse of the everlasting.
My children, suffer patiently the wrath that is come upon you from God: *The Iewes are mooved to patience, and to hope for the deliverance.*
For thine enemy hath persecuted thee:
But shortly thou shalt see his destruction,
And shalt tread upon his necke.
My delicate ones have gone rough wayes,
And were taken away as a flocke caught of the enemies.
Be of good comfort, O my children, and cry unto God:
For you shall be remembred of him that brought these things upon you.
For as it was your minde to goe astray from God:
So being returned seeke him ten times more.
For he that hath brought these plagues upon you,
Shall bring you everlasting ioy againe with your salvation.
Take a good heart, O Ierusalem:
For hee that gave thee that name, will comfort thee.
Miserable are they that afflicted thee,
And reioyced at thy fall.
Miserable are the cities which thy children served:
Miserable is she that received thy sonnes.
For as shee reioyced at thy ruine,
And was glad of thy fall:
So shall she be grieved for her owne desolation.
For I will take away the reioycing of her great multitude,
And her pride shalbe turned into mourning.
For fire shal come upon her from the everlasting, long to endure:
And she shal be inhabited of devils for a great time.
O Ierusalem, looke about thee toward the East,
And behold the ioy that commeth unto thee from God.

BARUCH

CHAPTER IIII

Loe, thy sonnes come whom thou sentest away:
They come gathered together from the East to the West,
By the word of the holy One,
Reioycing in the glory of God.

CHAPTER V

Ierusalem is moved to reioyce,

PUT off, O Ierusalem, the garment of thy mourning and affliction,
And put on the comelinesse of the glory that commeth from God for ever.
Cast about thee a double garment of the righteousnesse which commeth from God,
And set a diademe on thine head of the glory of the everlasting.
For God wil shew thy brightnesse unto every countrey under heaven.
For thy name shall bee called of God for ever,
The peace of righteousnesse, and the glory of Gods worship.

and to behold their returne out of captivity with glory.

Arise, O Ierusalem, and stand on high,
And looke about toward the East,
And behold thy children gathered from the West unto the East
By the word of the holy One,
Reioycing in the remembrance of God.
For they departed from thee on foote, and were ledde away of their enemies:
But God bringeth them unto thee exalted with glory,
As children of the kingdome.
For God hath appointed that every high hill, and banks of long continuance should be cast downe,
And valleys filled up, to make even the ground,
That Israel may goe safely in the glory of God.
Moreover, even the woods, and every sweet smelling tree, shall overshadow Israel
By the commandement of God.
For God shall leade Israel with ioy, in the light of his glory,
With the mercy and righteousnes that commeth from him.

BARUCH

The Epistle of Ieremie

CHAPTER VI

CHAPTER VI

A COPY of an Epistle which Ieremie sent unto them which were to be led captives into Babylon, by the king of the Babylonians, to certifie them as it was commanded him of God. <small>The cause of the captivity is their sinne.</small>

BECAUSE of the sinnes which ye have committed before God, ye shall be led away captives unto Babylon by Nabuchodonosor king of the Babylonians. So when ye be come unto Babylon, ye shal remaine there many yeeres, and for a long season, namely seven generations: and after that I will bring you away peaceably from thence. Now shal ye see in Babylon gods of silver, and of gold, and of wood, borne upon shoulders, which cause the nations to feare. Beware therefore that yee in no wise be like to strangers, neither be yee afraid of them, when yee see the multitude before them, and behinde them, worshipping them. But say yee in your hearts, O Lord, we must worship thee. For mine Angel is with you, and I my selfe caring for your soules. As for their tongue, it is polished by the workeman, and they themselves are guilded and laid over with silver, yet are they but false and cannot speake. And taking golde, as it were for a virgine that loves to go gay, they make crownes for the heads of their gods. Sometimes also the Priests convey from their gods golde and silver, and bestow it upon themselves. Yea they will give thereof to the common harlots, and decke them as men with garments [being] gods of silver, and gods of gold, and wood. Yet cannot these gods save themselves from rust and moths, though they be covered with purple raiment. They wipe their faces because of the dust of the Temple, when there is much upon them. And he that cannot put to death one that offendeth him, holdeth a scepter as though hee were a iudge of the countrey. Hee hath also in his right hand a dagger, and an axe: but cannot deliver himselfe from warre and theeves. Whereby they are knowen not to bee gods, therefore feare them not. For like as a vessell that a man useth, is nothing worth when it is broken: even so it is with their gods: when they be set up in the Temple, their eyes be full of dust, thorow the feet of them that come in. And as the doores are made sure on every side, upon him that offendeth the king, as being committed to suffer death: even so the priests make fast their temples, with doores, with lockes and barres, lest their gods bee spoiled with robbers. They light them candles, yea, more then for themselves, whereof <small>The place whereto they were caried, is Babylon: the vanitie of whose idols and idolatry are set foorth at large in this Chapter.</small>

BARUCH

CHAPTER VI

they cannot see one. They are as one of the beames of the temple, yet they say, their hearts are gnawed upon by things creeping out of the earth, and when they cate them and their clothes, they feele it not. Their faces are blacked, thorow the smoke that comes out of the temple. Upon their bodies and heads, sit battes, swallowes, and birds, and the cats also. By this you may know that they are no gods: therefore feare them not. Notwithstanding the gold that is about them, to make them beautifull, except they wipe off the rust they will not shine: for neither when they were molten did they feele it. The things wherein there is no breath, are bought for a most hie price. They are borne upon shoulders, having no feete, whereby they declare unto men that they be nothing worth. They also that serve them, are ashamed: for if they fall to the ground at any time, they cannot rise up againe of themselves: neither if one set them upright can they move of themselves: neither if they be bowed downe, can they make themselves streight: but they set gifts before them as unto dead men. As for the things that are sacrificed unto them, their priests sell and abuse: in like maner their wives lay up part thereof in salt: but unto the poore and impotent, they give nothing of it. Menstruous women, and women in childbed eate their sacrifices: by these things ye may know that they are no gods: feare them not. For how can they be called gods? because women set meate before the gods of silver, gold, and wood. And the priests sit in their temples, having their clothes rent, and their heads and beards shaven, and nothing upon their heads. They roare and crie before their gods: as men doe at the feast when one is dead. The priestes also take off their garments, and clothe their wives and children. Whether it be evill that one doth unto them, or good: they are not able to recompense it: they can neither set up a king, nor put him downe. In like maner, they can neither give riches nor money: though a man make a vowe unto them, and keepe it not, they will not require it. They can save no man from death, neither deliver the weake from the mightie. They cannot restore a blind man to his sight, nor helpe any man in his distresse. They can shew no mercie to the widow: nor doe good to the fatherlesse. Their gods of wood, and which are overlaid with gold, and silver, are like the stones that be hewen out of the mountaine: they that worship them shall be confounded. How should a man then thinke and say that they are gods? when even the Chaldeans themselves dishonour them. Who if they shall see one dumbe that cannot speake, they bring him and intreate Bel that he may speake, as

BARUCH

CHAPTER VI

though he were able to understand. Yet they cannot understand this themselves, and leave them: for they have no knowledge. The women also with cordes about them, sitting in the wayes, burne branne for perfume: but if any of them drawen by some that passeth by, lie with him, she reproacheth her fellow that she was not thought as worthy as her selfe, nor her cord broken. Whatsoever is done among them is false: how may it then be thought or said that they are gods? They are made of carpenters, and goldsmiths, they can be nothing else, then the workman will have them to be. And they themselves that made them, can never continue long, how should then the things that are made of them, be gods? For they left lies and reproaches to them that come after. For when there commeth any warre or plague upon them, the priests consult with themselves, where they may be hidden with them. How then cannot men perceive, that they be no gods, which can neither save themselves from warre nor from plague? For seeing they be but of wood, and overlaide with silver and golde: it shall be knowen heereafter that they are false. And it shall manifestly appeare to all nations and kings, that they are no gods: but the workes of mens hands, and that there is no worke of God in them. Who then may not know that they are no gods? For neither can they set up a king in the land, nor give raine unto men. Neither can they iudge their owne cause, nor redresse a wrong being unable: for they are as crowes between heaven and earth. Whereupon when fire falleth upon the house of gods of wood, or layd over with gold or silver, their priests will fly away, and escape: but they themselves shall be burnt asunder like beames. Moreover they cannot withstand any king or enemies: how can it then be thought or said that they be gods? Neither are those gods of wood, and layd over with silver or gold able to escape either from theeves or robbers. Whose gold, and silver, and garments wherwith they are clothed, they that are strong doe take, and goe away withall: neither are they able to helpe themselves. Therefore it is better to be a king that sheweth his power, or else a profitable vessell in an house, which the owner shall have use of, then such false gods: or to be a doore in an house to keepe such things safe as be therein, then such false gods: or a pillar of wood in a palace, then such false gods. For Sunne, Moone, and starres, being bright and sent to doe their offices, are obedient. In like maner the lightning when it breaketh forth is easie to bee seene, and after the same maner the wind bloweth in every country. And when God commandeth the clouds to goe over the whole world: they doe as they are bidden: and the fire sent

THE SONG OF

CHAPTER VI

from above to consume hilles and woods, doth as it is commanded: but these are like unto them neither in shew, nor power. Wherefore it is neither to be supposed nor said, that they are gods, seeing they are able, neither to iudge causes, nor to doe good unto men. Knowing therefore that they are no gods, feare them not. For they can neither curse nor blesse kings. Neither can they shew signes in the heavens among the heathen: nor shine as the Sunne, nor give light as the Moone. The beasts are better then they: for they can get under a covert, and helpe themselves. It is then by no meanes manifest unto us that they are gods: therefore feare them not. For as a scarcrow in a garden of Cucumbers keepeth nothing: so are their gods of wood, and laid over with silver and gold. And likewise their gods of wood, and laid over with silver and gold, are like to a white thorne in an orchard that every bird sitteth upon: as also to a dead body, that is cast into the darke. And you shall know them to be no gods, by the bright purple that rotteth upon them: and they themselves afterward shall be eaten, and shall be a reproach in the country. Better therefore is the iust man that hath none idoles: for he shall be farre from reproach.

THE SONG OF THE THREE HOLY CHILDREN,

which followeth in the third Chapter of Daniel after this place, [And they walked in the midst of the fire, praising God, and blessing the Lord.] That which followeth is not in the Hebrew; to wit, [Then Azarias stood up] unto these wordes, [And Nabuchodonosor.]

Azarias his praier and confession in the flame,

THEN Azarias stood up and prayed on this manner, and opening his mouth in the midst of the fire, said, Blessed art thou, O Lord God of our fathers: thy Name is worthy to be praised, and glorified for evermore. For thou art righteous in all the things that thou hast done to us: yea, true are all thy workes: thy wayes are right, and all thy iudgements trueth. In all the things that thou hast brought upon us, and upon the holy citie of our fathers, even Ierusalem, thou hast

THE THREE CHILDREN

executed true iudgement: for according to trueth and iudgement, didst thou bring all these things upon us, because of our sinnes. For wee have sinned and committed iniquitie, departing from thee. In all things have we trespassed, and not obeyed thy Commandements, nor kept them, neither done as thou hast commanded us, that it might goe well with us. Wherefore all that thou hast brought upon us, and every thing that thou hast done to us, thou hast done in true iudgement. And thou didst deliver us into the hands of lawlesse enemies, most hatefull forsakers [of God] and to an uniust King, and the most wicked in all the world. And now wee can not open our mouthes, we are become a shame, and reproch to thy servants, and to them that worship thee. Yet deliver us not up wholy for thy Names sake, neither disanull thou thy Covenant: and cause not thy mercy to depart from us: for thy beloved Abrahams sake: for thy servant Isaacs sake, and for thy holy Israels sake. To whom thou hast spoken and promised, That thou wouldest multiply their seed as the starres of heaven, and as the sand that lyeth upon the sea shore. For we, O Lord, are become lesse then any nation, and bee kept under this day in all the world, because of our sinnes. Neither is there at this time, Prince, or Prophet, or leader, or burnt offering, or sacrifice, or oblation, or incense, or place to sacrifice before thee, and to finde mercie. Nevertheless in a contrite heart, and an humble spirit, let us be accepted. Like as in the burnt offering of rammes and bullockes, and like as in ten thousands of fat lambes: so let our sacrifice bee in thy sight this day, and [grant] that wee may wholy goe after thee: for they shall not bee confounded that put their trust in thee. And now wee follow thee, with all our heart, wee feare thee, and seeke thy face. Put us not to shame: but deale with us after thy loving kindenesse, and according to the multitude of thy mercies. Deliver us also according to thy marveilous workes, and give glory to thy Name, O Lord, and let all them that doe thy servants hurt be ashamed. And let them be confounded in all their power and might, and let their strength be broken. And let them know that thou art Lord, the onely God, and glorious over the whole world. And the kings servants that put them in, ceased not to make the oven hote with rosin, pitch, towe, and small wood. So that the flame streamed forth above the fornace, wherewith the fourtie and nine cubites: and it passed through, and burnt those Chaldeans about the Caldeans it found about the fornace. But the Angel of the Lord oven were came downe into the oven, together with Azarias and his fellowes, consumed, but the three chiland smote the flame of the fire out of the oven: and made the dren within it mids of the fornace, as it had bene a moist whistling wind, so that were not hurt.

253

THE SONG OF

the fire touched them not at all, neither hurt nor troubled them. Then the three, as out of one mouth, praised, glorified, and blessed God in the fornace, saying;

The Song of the three children in the oven.

BLESSED art thou, O Lord God of our fathers:
And to be praised and exalted above all for ever.
And blessed is thy glorious and holy Name:
And to be praised and exalted above all for ever.
Blessed art thou in the temple of thine holy glory:
And to be praised and glorified above all for ever.
Blessed art thou that beholdest the depths,
And sittest upon the Cherubims,
And to be praised and exalted above all for ever.
Blessed art thou on the glorious Throne of thy kingdome:
And to bee praised and glorified above all for ever.
Blessed art thou in the firmament of heaven:
And above all to be praised and glorified for ever.
O all yee workes of the Lorde, blesse ye the Lord:
Praise and exalt him above all for ever.
O ye heavens, blesse ye the Lord:
Praise and exalt him above all for ever.
O yee Angels of the Lord, blesse ye the Lord:
Praise and exalt him above all for ever.
O all ye waters that be above the heaven, blesse yee the Lord:
Praise and exalt him above all for ever.
O all yee powers of the Lord, blesse ye the Lord:
Praise and exalt him above all for ever.
O yee Sunne and Moone, blesse ye the Lord:
Praise and exalt him above all for ever.
O ye starres of heaven, blesse ye the Lord:
Praise and exalt him above all for ever.
O every showre and dew, blesse ye the Lord:
Praise and exalt him above all for ever.
O all ye windes, blesse yee the Lord:
Praise and exalt him above all for ever.
O yee fire and beate, blesse ye the Lord:
Praise and exalt him above all for ever.
O yee Winter and Summer, blesse ye the Lord:
Praise and exalt him above all for ever.
O ye dewes and stormes of snow, blesse ye the Lord:
Praise and exalt him above all for ever.
O ye nights and dayes, blesse ye the Lord:
Praise and exalt him above all for ever.

THE THREE CHILDREN

O ye light and darkenesse, blesse ye the Lord:
Praise and exalt him above all for ever.
O yee yce and colde, blesse ye the Lord:
Praise and exalt him above all for ever.
O ye frost and snow, blesse ye the Lord:
Praise and exalt him above all for ever.
O ye lightnings and clouds, blesse ye the Lord:
Praise and exalt him above all for ever.
O let the earth blesse the Lord:
Praise and exalt him above all for ever.
O ye mountaines and little hils, blesse ye the Lord
Praise and exalt him above all for ever.
O all ye things that grow on the earth, blesse ye the Lord:
Praise and exalt him above all for ever.
O yee fountaines, blesse yee the Lord:
Praise and exalt him above all for ever.
O ye seas and rivers, blesse ye the Lord:
Praise and exalt him above all for ever.
O ye whales and all that moove in the waters, blesse ye the Lord:
Praise and exalt him above all for ever.
O all ye foules of the aire, blesse ye the Lord:
Praise and exalt him above all for ever.
O all ye beasts and cattell, blesse ye the Lord:
Praise and exalt him above all for ever.
O ye children of men, blesse yee the Lord:
Praise and exalt him above all for ever.
O Israel blesse ye the Lord:
Praise and exalt him above all for ever.
O ye priests of the Lord, blesse ye the Lord:
Praise and exalt him above all for ever.
O ye servants of the Lord, blesse ye the Lord:
Praise and exalt him above all for ever.
O ye spirits and soules of the righteous, blesse ye the Lord:
Praise and exalt him above all for ever.
O ye holy and humble men of heart, blesse ye the Lord:
Praise and exalt him above all for ever.
O Ananias, Azarias, and Misael, blesse ye the Lord,
Praise and exalt him above all for ever:
For hee hath delivered us from hell,
And saved us from the hand of death,
And delivered us out of the mids of the furnace, [and] burning flame:

SUSANNA

Even out of the mids of the fire hath he delivered us.
O give thanks unto the Lord, because he is gracious:
For his mercie endureth for ever.
O all ye that worship the Lord, blesse the God of gods,
Praise him, and give him thanks:
For his mercie endureth for ever.

THE HISTORIE OF SUSANNA,
set apart from the beginning of Daniel, because it is not in Hebrew, as neither the narration of BEL AND THE DRAGON.

THERE dwelt a man in Babylon, called Ioacim. And hee tooke a wife, whose name was Susanna, the daughter of Chelcias, a very faire woman, and one that feared the Lord. Her parents also were righteous, and taught their daughter according to the Law of Moses. Now Ioacim was a great rich man, and had a faire garden ioyning unto his house, and to him resorted the Iewes: because he was more honourable then all others. The same yeere were appointed two of the Ancients of the people to be iudges, such as the Lord spake of, that wickednesse came from Babylon from ancient iudges, who seemed to governe the people. These kept much at Ioacims house: and all that had any suits in lawe, came unto them. Now when the people departed away at noone, Susanna went into her husbands garden to walke. And the two Elders saw her going in every day and walking: so that their lust was inflamed toward her. And they perverted their owne mind, and turned away their eyes, that they might not looke unto heaven, nor remember iust iudgements. And albeit they both were wounded with her love: yet durst not one shew another his griefe. For they were ashamed to declare their lust, that they desired to have to doe with her. Yet they watched diligently from day to day to see her. And the one said to the other, Let us now goe home: for it is dinner time. So when they were gone out, they parted the one from the other, and turning backe againe they came to the same place, and after that they had asked one another the cause, they acknowledged

SUSANNA

their lust: then appointed they a time both together, when they might find her alone. And it fell out as they watched a fit time, she went in as before, with two maids onely, and she was desirous to wash her selfe in the garden: for it was hot. And there was no body there save the two Elders, that had hid themselves, and watched her. Then she said to her maids, Bring me oile and washing bals, and shut the garden doores, that I may wash me. And they did as she bad them, and shut the garden doores, and went out themselves at privie doores to fetch the things that she had commaunded them: but they saw not the Elders, because they were hid. Now when the maids were gone forth, the two Elders rose up, and ran unto her, saying, Behold, the garden doores are shut, that no man can see us, and we are in love with thee: therefore consent unto us, and lie with us. If thou wilt not, we will beare witnesse against thee, that a young man was with thee: and therefore thou didst send away thy maides from thee. Then Susanna sighed and said, I am straited on every side: for if I doe this thing, it is death unto me: and if I doe it not, I cannot escape your hands. It is better for me to fall into your hands, and not doe it: then to sinne in the sight of the Lord. With that Susanna cried with a loud voice: and the two Elders cried out against her. Then ranne the one, and opened the garden doore. So when the servants of the house heard the crie in the garden, they rushed in at a privie doore to see what was done unto her. But when the Elders had declared their matter, the servants were greatly ashamed: for there was never such a report made of Susanna. And it came to passe the next day, when the people were assembled to her husband Ioacim, the two Elders came also full of mischievous imagination against Susanna to put her to death, and said before the people, Send for Susanna, the daughter of Chelcias, Ioacims wife. And so they sent. So she came with her father and mother, her children and all her kinred. Now Susanna was a very delicate woman and beauteous to behold. And these wicked men commanded to uncover her face (for she was covered) that they might be filled with her beautie. Therefore her friends, and all that saw her, wept. Then the two Elders stood up in the mids of the people, and laid their hands upon her head. And she weeping looked up towards heaven: for her heart trusted in the Lord. And the Elders said, As we walked in the garden alone, this woman came in, with two maides, and shut the garden doores, and sent the maides away. Then a young man who there was hid, came unto her and lay with her. Then we that stood in a corner of the garden, seeing this wickednesse, ran unto them.

Two Iudges hide themselves in the garden of Susanna to have their pleasure of her:

which when they could not obteine, they accuse and cause her to be condemned for adulterie,

SUSANNA

And when we saw them together, the man we could not hold: for he was stronger then we, and opened the doore, and leaped out. But having taken this woman, we asked who the young man was: but she would not tell us: these things doe we testifie. Then the assembly beleeved them, as those that were the Elders and Iudges of the people: so they condemned her to death. Then Susanna cried out with a loud voice and said: O everlasting God that knowest the secrets, and knowest all things before they be: thou knowest that they have borne false witnesse against me, and behold I must die: whereas I never did such things, as these men have maliciously invented against me. And the Lord heard her voice. Therefore when she was led to be put to death: the Lord raised up the holy spirit of a young youth, whose name was Daniel, who *but Daniel examineth the matter againe, and findeth the two iudges false.* cried with a loud voice: I am cleare from the blood of this woman. Then all the people turned them towards him, and said: What meane these words that thou hast spoken? So he standing in the mids of them, said, Are ye such fooles ye sonnes of Israel, that without examination or knowledge of the truth, ye have condemned a daughter of Israel? Returne againe to the place of iudgement: for they have borne false witnesse against her. Wherefore all the people turned againe in hast, and the Elders said unto him, Come sit downe among us, and shew it us, seeing God hath given thee the honour of an Elder. Then said Daniel unto them, Put these two aside one farre from another, and I will examine them. So when they were put asunder one from another, hee called one of them, and said unto him, O thou that art waxen old in wickednesse: now thy sinnes which thou hast committed aforetime, are come [to light.] For thou hast pronounced false iudgement, and hast condemned the innocent, and hast let the guiltie goe free, albeit the Lord saith, The innocent and righteous shalt thou not slay. Now then if thou hast seene her: tell me, Under what tree sawest thou them companying together? who answered, Under a masticke tree. And Daniel said, Very wel; Thou hast lied against thine owne head: for even now the Angel of God hath received the sentence of God, to cut thee in two. So hee put him aside, and commanded to bring the other, and said unto him, O thou seed of Chanaan, and not of Iuda, beauty hath deceived thee, and lust hath perverted thine heart. Thus have yee dealt with the daughters of Israel, and they for feare companied with you: but the daughter of Iuda would not abide your wickednesse. Now therefore tell mee, Under what tree didst thou take them companying together? who answered, Under a holme tree. Then said Daniel unto him, Well: thou hast also lied against thine owne head: for the Angel

SUSANNA

of God waiteth with the sword to cut thee in two, that he may destroy you. With that all the assembly cried out with a lowd voice, and praised God who saveth them that trust in him. And they arose against the two Elders, (for Daniel had convicted them of false witnesse by their owne mouth) and according to the Law of Moses, they did unto them in such sort as they malitiously intended to doe to their neighbour: And they put them to death. Thus the innocent blood was saved the same day. Therefore Chelcias and his wife praised God for their daughter Susanna, with Ioacim her husband, and all the kinred: because there was no dishonestie found in her. From that day foorth was Daniel had in great reputation in the sight of the people.

THE HISTORY OF THE DESTRUCTION OF BEL AND THE DRAGON, cut off from the end of Daniel.

AND King Astyages was gathered to his fathers, and Cyrus of Persia received his kingdome. And Daniel conversed with the king, and was honored above all his friends. Now the Babylonians had an Idol called Bel, and there were spent upon him every day twelve great measures of fine flowre, and fourtie sheepe, and sixe vessels of wine. And the king worshipped it, and went daily to adore it: but Daniel worshipped his owne God. And the king said unto him, Why doest not thou worship Bel? Who answered and said, Because I may not worship idols made with hands, but the living God, who hath created the heaven, and the earth, and hath soveraigntie over all flesh. Then saide the King unto him, Thinkest thou not that Bel is a living god? seest thou not how much he eateth and drinketh every day? Then Daniel smiled, and said, O king, be not deceived: for this is but clay within, and brasse without, and did never eate or drinke any thing. So the king was wroth,

BEL AND THE DRAGON

and called for his Priests, and said unto them, If yee tell me not who this is that devoureth these expenses, ye shall die. But if ye can certifie me that Bel devoureth them, then Daniel shall die: for hee hath spoken blasphemie against Bel. And Daniel sayd unto the king, Let it be according to thy word. (Now the Priests of Bel were threescore and tenne, beside their wives and children) and the king went with Daniel into the temple of Bel. So Bels Priests said, Loe, wee goe out: but thou, O king, set on the meate, and make ready the wine, and shut the doore fast, and seale it with thine owne signet: and to morrow, when thou commest in, if thou findest not that Bel hath eaten up all, wee will suffer death; or else Daniel, that speaketh falsely against us. And they little regarded it: for under the table they had made a privie entrance, whereby they entred in continually, and consumed those things. So when they were gone forth, the king set meates before Bel. Now Daniel had commanded his servants to bring ashes, and those they strewed throughout all the temple, in the presence of the king alone: then went they out and shut the doore, and sealed it with the kings signet, and so departed. Now in the night came the Priests with their wives and children (as they were woont to doe) and did eate and drinke up all. In the morning betime the king arose, and Daniel with him. And the king said, Daniel, are the seales whole? And he said, Yea, O king, they be whole. And assoone as he had opened the doore, the king looked upon the table, and cried with a loude voice, Great art thou, O Bel, and with thee is no deceit at all. Then laughed Daniel, and helde the king that he should not goe in, and sayd, Behold now the pavement, and marke well whose footsteps are these. And the king said, I see the footsteps of men, women and children: and then the king was angry, and tooke the Priests, with their wives and children, who shewed him the privy doores, where they came in, and consumed such things as were upon the table. Therefore the king slewe them, and delivered Bel into Daniels power, who destroyed him and his temple. And in that same place there was a great Dragon, which they of Babylon worshipped. And the king said unto Daniel, Wilt thou also say that this is of brasse? loe, he liveth, he eateth and drinketh, thou canst not say, that he is no living God: therefore worship him. Then said Daniel unto the king, I will worship the Lord my God: for he is the living God. But give me leave, O king, and I shall slay this dragon without sword or staffe. The king sayde, I give thee leave. Then Daniel tooke pitch, fat, and haire, and did seethe them together, and made lumpes thereof: this hee put in the

The fraud of Bels Priests, is discovered by Daniel,

BEL AND THE DRAGON

Dragons mouth, and so the Dragon burst in sunder: and Daniel *and the Dragon* said, Loe, these are the gods you worship. When they of *slaine, which was worshipped.* Babylon heard that, they tooke great indignation, and conspired against the king, saying, The king is become a Iew, and he hath destroyed Bel, he hath slaine the Dragon, and put the Priests to death. So they came to the king, and said, Deliver us Daniel, or else we will destroy thee and thine house. Now when the king sawe that they pressed him sore, being constrained, he delivered Daniel unto them: who cast him into the lions den, where he was sixe dayes. And in the den there were seven lyons, and they had given them every day two carkeises, and two sheepe: which then were not given to them, to the intent they might devoure Daniel. Now there was in Iury a Prophet called Habacuc, who *Daniel is preserved in the Lions denne.* had made pottage, and had broken bread in a boule, and was going into the field, for to bring it to the reapers. But the Angel of the Lord said unto Habacuc, Goe carrie the dinner that thou hast into Babylon unto Daniel, who is in the lions denne. And Habacuc said, Lord, I never saw Babylon: neither do I know where the denne is. Then the Angel of the Lord tooke him by the crown, and bare him by the haire of his head, and through the vehemencie of his spirit, set him in Babylon over the den. And Habacuc cryed, saying, O Daniel, Daniel, take the dinner which God hath sent thee. And Daniel saide, Thou hast remembred mee, O God: neither hast thou forsaken them that seeke thee, and love thee. So Daniel arose and did cate: and the Angel of the Lord set Habacuc in his owne place againe immediatly. Upon the seventh day the king went to bewaile Daniel: and when he came to the den, he looked in, and behold, Daniel was sitting. Then cried the king with a loude voyce, saying, Great art thou, *The King doeth acknowledge the God of Daniel, and casteth his enemies into the same denne.* O Lord God of Daniel, and there is none other besides thee. And he drew him out: and cast those that were the cause of his destruction into the den: and they were devoured in a moment before his face.

261

MANASSES HIS PRAYER

THE PRAYER OF MANASSES
KING OF IUDA, when he was holden captive in BABYLON.

LORD, Almightie God of our Fathers,
Abraham, Isaac, and Iacob,
And of their righteous seed:
Who hast made heaven and earth, with all the ornament thereof:
Who hast bound the Sea by the word of thy Commandement:
Who hast shut up the deepe, and sealed it by thy terrible and glorious Name,
Whome all men feare, and tremble before thy power:
For the Maiestie of thy glory cannot bee borne,
And thine angry threatning towards sinners is importable:
But thy mercifull promise is unmeasurable and unsearchable:
For thou art the most High Lord, of great compassion, long suffering, very mercifull,
And repentest of the evils of men.
Thou, O Lord, according to thy great goodnesse hast promised repentance, and forgivenesse to them that have sinned against thee:
And of thine infinite mercies hast appointed repentance unto sinners that they may be saved.
Thou therefore, O Lord, that art the God of the iust, hast not appointed repentance to the iust,
As to Abraham, and Isaac, and Iacob, which have not sinned against thee:
But thou hast appointed repentance unto me that am a sinner:
For I have sinned above the number of the sands of the Sea.
My transgressions, O Lord, are multiplied: my transgressions are multiplied,
And I am not worthy to behold and see the height of heaven,
For the multitude of mine iniquitie.

MANASSES HIS PRAYER

I am bowed downe with many yron bands,
That I cannot lift up mine head,
Neither have any release:
For I have provoked thy wrath, and done evill before thee,
I did not thy will, neither kept I thy Commandements:
I have set up abominations, and have multiplied offences.
Now therefore I bow the knee of mine heart, beseeching
    thee of grace:
I have sinned, O Lord, I have sinned, and I acknowledge
    mine iniquities:
Wherefore I humbly beseech thee, forgive me, O Lord,
    forgive me,
And destroy me not with mine iniquities.
Be not angry with me for ever, by reserving evill for me,
Neither condemne mee into the lower parts of the earth.
For thou art the God, even the God of them that repent:
And in me thou wilt shew all thy goodnesse:
For thou wilt save me that am unworthy, according to thy
    great mercie.
Therefore I will praise thee for ever all the dayes of my life:
For all the powers of the heavens doe praise thee,
And thine is the glory for ever and ever.   Amen.

The First Booke of
THE MACCABEES

CHAPTER I

AND it happened, after that Alexander sonne of Philip, the Macedonian, who came out of the land of Chettiim, had smitten Darius king of the Persians and Medes, that hee reigned in his stead, the first over Greece, and made many wars, and wan many strong holds, and slew the kings of the earth, and went through to the ends of the earth, and tooke spoiles of many nations, insomuch, that the earth was quiet before him, whereupon he was exalted, and his heart was

I. MACCABEES

CHAPTER I — lifted up. And he gathered a mighty strong hoste, and ruled over countries, and nations and kings, who became tributaries unto him. And after these things he fell sicke, and perceived that he should die. Wherefore he called his servants, such as were honourable, and had bin brought up with him from his youth, and parted his kingdome among them, while he was yet alive: so Alexander reigned twelve yeeres, and (then) died. And his servants bare rule every one in his place. And after his death they all put crownes [upon themselves] so did their sonnes after them, many yeeres, and evils were multiplied in the earth. And there came out of them a wicked roote, Antiochus [surnamed] Epiphanes, sonne of Antiochus the king, who had beene an hostage at Rome, and he reigned in the hundreth and thirty and seventh yeere of the kingdome of the Greekes. In those daies went there out of Israel wicked men, who perswaded many, saying, Let us goe, and make a covenant with the heathen, that are round about us: for since we departed from them, we have had much sorrow. So this devise pleased them well. Then certaine of the people were so forward heerein, that they went to the king, who gave them licence to doe after the ordinances of the heathen. Whereupon they built a place of exercise at Ierusalem, according to the customes of the heathen, and made themselves, uncircumcised, and forsooke the holy covenant, and ioyned themselves to the heathen, and were sold to doe mischiefe.

Antiochus gave leave to set up the fashions of the Gentiles in Hierusalem,

Now when the kingdome was established, before Antiochus, hee thought to reigne over Egypt, that he might have the dominion of two realms: wherefore he entred into Egypt with a great multitude, with chariots, and elephants, and horsemen, and a great navie, and made warre against Ptolomee king of Egypt, but Ptolomee was afraide of him, and fled: and many were wounded to death. Thus they got the strong cities in the land of Egypt, and hee tooke the spoiles thereof. And after that Antiochus had smitten Egypt, he returned againe in the hundreth fortie and third yeere, and went up against Israel and Ierusalem with a great multitude, and entred proudly into the sanctuarie, and tooke away the golden altar, and the candlesticke of light, and all the vessels thereof, and the table of the shewbread, and the powring vessels, and the vials, and the censers of gold, and the vaile, and the crownes, and the golden ornaments that were before the temple, all which he pulled off. Hee tooke also the silver and the gold, and the pretious vessels: also he tooke the hidden treasures which he found: and when hee had taken all away, he went into his owne land, having made a great massacre, and spoken very proudly. Therfore

And spoiled it, and the temple in it,

I. MACCABEES

there was great mourning in Israel, in every place where they were; so that the Princes and Elders mourned, the virgines and yong men were made feeble, and the beautie of women was changed. Every bridegrome tooke up lamentation, and she that sate in the marriage chamber, was in heavinesse. The land also was moved for the inhabitants thereof, and all the house of Iacob was covered with confusion. And after two yeeres fully expired, the king sent his chiefe collectour of tribute unto the cities of Iuda, who came unto Ierusalem with a great multitude, and spake peaceable wordes unto them, but [all was] deceit: for when they had given him credence, he fell suddenly upon the citie, and smote it very sore, and destroyed much people of Israel. And when hee had taken the spoiles of the citie, hee set it on fire, and pulled downe the houses, and walles thereof on every side. But the women and children tooke they captive, and possessed the cattell. Then builded they the citie of David with a great and strong wall, [and] with mightie towers, and made it a strong hold for them, and they put therein a sinfull nation, wicked men, and fortified [themselves] therein. They stored it also with armour and victuals, and when they had gathered together the spoiles of Ierusalem, they layd them up there, and so they became a sore snare: for it was a place to lie in wait against the Sanctuary, and an evill adversary to Israel. Thus they shed innocent blood on every side of the Sanctuary, and defiled it. In so much that the inhabitants of Ierusalem fledde because of them, whereupon [the citie] was made an habitation of strangers, and became strange to those that were borne in her, and her owne children left her: her Sanctuary was laid waste like a wildernesse, her feasts were turned into mourning, her Sabbaths into reproch, her honour into contempt. As had bene her glory, so was her dishonour encreased, and her excellencie was turned into mourning. Moreover king Antiochus wrote to his whole kingdome, that all should be one people, and every one should leave his lawes: so all the heathen agreed, according to the commandement of the king. Yea many also of the Israelites consented to his religion, and sacrificed unto idols, and prophaned the Sabbath. For the king had sent letters by messengers unto Ierusalem, and the cities of Iuda, that they should follow the strange lawes of the land, and forbid burnt offerings, and sacrifice, and drinke offerings in the temple; and that they should prophane the Sabbaths, and festivall dayes: and pollute the Sanctuarie and holy people: set up altars, and groves, and chappels of idols, and sacrifice swines flesh, and uncleane beasts: that they should also leave their children uncircumcised, and

CHAPTER
I

I. MACCABEES

CHAPTER I

And set up therin the abomination of desolation,

And slew those that did circumcise their children.

make their soules abominable with all maner of uncleannesse, and prophanation: to the end they might forget the Law, and change all the ordinances. And whosoever would not doe according to the commandement of the king [he said] he should die. In the selfe same maner wrote he to his whole kingdome, and appointed overseers over all the people, commanding the cities of Iuda to sacrifice, citie by citie. Then many of the people were gathered unto them, to wit, every one that forsooke the Lawe, and so they committed evils in the land: and drove the Israelites into secret places, even wheresoever they could flie for succour. Now the fifteenth day of the moneth Casleu, in the hundreth fourtie and fift yeere, they set up the abomination of desolation upon the Altar, and builded idole altars throughout the cities of Iuda, on every side: and burnt incense at the doores of their houses, and in the streetes. And when they had rent in pieces the bookes of the Lawe which they found, they burnt them with fire. And wheresoever was found with any, the booke of the Testament, or if any consented to the Lawe, the kings commandement was, that they should put him to death. Thus did they by their authority, unto the Israelites every moneth, to as many as were found in the cities. Now the five and twentieth day of the moneth, they did sacrifice upon the idole altar, which was upon the Altar of God. At which time, according to the commandement, they put to death certaine women that had caused their children to be circumcised. And they hanged the infants about their neckes, and rifled their houses, and slewe them that had circumcised them. Howbeit, many in Israel were fully resolved and confirmed in themselves, not to eate any uncleane thing. Wherfore they chose rather to die, that they might not be defiled with meats, and that they might not profane the holy Covenant: So then they died. And there was very great wrath upon Israel.

CHAPTER II

Mattathias lamenteth the case of Ierusalem.

IN those daies arose Mattathias the son of Iohn, the sonne of Simeon, a Priest of the sonnes of Ioarib, from Ierusalem, and dwelt in Modin. And he had five sonnes, Ioannan called Caddis: Simon, called Thassi: Iudas, who was called Maccabeus: Eleazar, called Avaran, and Ionathan, whose surname was Apphus. And when hee saw the blasphemies that were committed in Iuda and Ierusalem, he said, Woe is me, wherfore was I borne to see this misery of my people, and of the holy citie, and to dwell there, when it was delivered into the hand of the enemie, and the

I. MACCABEES

Sanctuary into the hand of strangers? Her Temple is become as a man without glory. Her glorious vessels are caried away into captivitie, her infants are slaine in the streets, her yong men with the sword of the enemie. What nation hath not had a part in her kingdome, and gotten of her spoiles? All her ornaments are taken away, of a free-woman shee is become a bondslave. And behold, our Sanctuarie, even our beautie, and our glory is laid waste, and the Gentiles have profaned it. To what ende therefore shall we live any longer? Then Mattathias and his sons rent their clothes, and put on sackcloth, and mourned very sore. In the meane while the kings officers, such as compelled the people to revolt, came into the city Modin to make them sacrifice. And when many of Israel came unto them, Mattathias also and his sonnes came together. Then answered the kings officers, and said to Mattathias on this wise; Thou art a ruler, and an honourable and great man in this citie, and strengthened with sons and brethren: now therefore come thou first and fulfill the kings commandement, like as all the heathen have done; yea and the men of Iuda also, and such as remaine at Ierusalem: so shalt thou and thine house be in the number of the kings friends, and thou and thy children shall be honoured with silver, and golde, and many rewards. Then Mattathias answered, and spake with a loude voice, Though all the nations that are under the kings dominion obey him, and fall away every one from the religion of their fathers, and give consent to his commandements: yet will I, and my sonnes, and my brethren walke in the covenant of our fathers. God forbid that we should forsake the Law, and the ordinances: we will not hearken to the kings words, to goe from our religion, either on the right hand, or the left. Now when he had left speaking these words, there came one of the Iewes in the sight of all, to sacrifice on the altar, which was at Modin, according to the kings commandement. Which thing when Mattathias saw, he was inflamed with zeale, and his reines trembled, neither could hee forbeare to shew his anger according to iudgement: wherefore he ranne, and slew him upon the altar. Also the kings commissioner who compelled men to sacrifice, he killed at that time, and the altar he pulled downe. Thus dealt he zealously for the Law of God, like as Phineas did unto Zambri the sonne of Salom. And Mattathias cried throughout the citie with a loud voyce, saying, Whosoever is zealous of the Law, and maintaineth the covenant, let him follow me. So he and his sonnes fled into the mountaines, and left all that ever they had in the citie. Then many that sought after iustice and iudgement, went downe into

CHAPTER II

He slayeth a Iewe that did sacrifice to Idoles in his presence, and the Kings messenger also.

I. MACCABEES

CHAPTER II

the wildernesse to dwell there. Both they and their children, and their wives, and their cattell, because afflictions increased sore upon them. Now when it was told the kings servants, and the hoste that was at Ierusalem, in the citie of David, that certaine men, who had broken the kings commandement, were gone downe into the secret places in the wildernesse, they pursued after them, a great number, and having overtaken them, they camped against them, and made war against them on the Sabbath day. And they said unto them, Let that which you have done hitherto, suffice: Come foorth, and doe according to the commandement of the king, and you shall live. But they said, We will not come forth, neither will we do the kings commandement to profane the Sabbath day. So then they gave them the battell with all speed. Howbeit, they answered them not, neither cast they a stone at them, nor stopped the places where they lay hid, but said, Let us die all in our innocencie: heaven and earth shall testifie for us, that you put us to death wrongfully. So they rose up against them in battell on the Sabbath, and they slew them with their wives and children, and their cattell, to the number of a thousand people. Now when Mattathias and his friends understood hereof, they mourned for them right sore. And one of them said to another: If we all do as our brethren have done, and fight not for our lives, and lawes against the heathen, they wil now quickly root us out of the earth. At that time therfore they decreed, saying, Whosoever shall come to make battell with us on the Sabbath day, we will fight against him, neither will wee die all, as our brethren that were murdered in the secret places. Then came there unto him a company of Assideans, who were mightie men of Israel, even all such as were voluntarily devoted unto the Lawe. Also all they that fled for persecution ioyned themselves unto them, and were a stay unto them. So they ioyned their forces, and smote sinfull men in their anger, and wicked men in their wrath: but the rest fled to the heathen for succour. Then Mattathias and his friends went round about, and pulled downe the altars. And what children soever they found within the coast of Israel uncircumcised, those they circumcised valiantly. They pursued also after the proud men, and the work prospered in their hand. So they recovered the Law out of the hand of the Gentiles, and out of the hande of Kings, neither suffered they the sinner to triumph. Now when the time drew neere, that Mattathias should die, he said unto his sonnes, Now hath pride and rebuke gotten strength, and the time of destruction, and the wrath of indignation: now therefore, my sonnes, be ye

He and his are assailed upon the Sabbath, and make no resistance.

I. MACCABEES

zealous for the Law, and give your lives for the covenant of your fathers. Call to remembrance what actes our fathers did in their time, so shall ye receive great honour, and an everlasting name. Was not Abraham found faithfull in tentation, and it was imputed unto him for righteousnesse? Ioseph in the time of his distresse kept the commaundement, and was made Lord of Egypt. Phineas our father in being zealous and fervent, obtained the covenant of an everlasting priesthood. Iesus for fulfilling the word, was made a iudge in Israel. Caleb for bearing witnesse, before the congregation, received the heritage of the land. David for being mercifull, possessed the throne of an everlasting kingdome. Elias for being zealous and fervent for the law, was taken up into heaven. Ananias, Azarias, and Misael, by beleeving were saved out of the flame. Daniel for his innocencie was delivered from the mouth of Lyons. And thus consider ye throughout all ages, that none that put their trust in him shall be overcome. Feare not then the words of a sinfull man: for his glory shall bee dung and wormes. To day he shall be lifted up, and to morrow hee shall not be found, because he is returned into his dust, and his thought is come to nothing. Wherefore you my sonnes be valiant, and shew your selves men in the behalfe of the law, for by it shall you obtaine glory. And behold, I know that your brother Simon is a man of counsell, give eare unto him alway: he shall be a father unto you. As for Iudas Maccabeus hee hath bin mighty and strong, even from his youth up, let him be your captaine, and fight the battaile of the people. Take also unto you, all those that observe the law, and avenge ye the wrong of your people. Recompence fully the heathen, and take heed to the commandements of the law. So he blessed them, and was gathered to his fathers. And he died in the hundreth fortie, and sixth yeere, and his sonnes buried him in the Sepulchre of his fathers, at Modin, and all Israel made great lamentation for him.

CHAPTER II

Hee dieth, and instructeth his sons:

and maketh their brother Iudas Maccabeus generall.

CHAPTER III

THEN his sonne Indas, called Maccabeus, rose up in his stead. And all his brethren helped him, and so did all they that held with his father, and they fought with cheerefulnesse, the battaile of Israel. So he gate his people great honor, and put on a brestplate as a giant, and girt his warlike harnesse about him, and he made battels, protecting the host with his sword. In his acts he was like a lyon, and like a lyons whelp roaring for his pray. For hee pursued the wicked, and

The valour and fame of Iudas Maccabeus.

I. MACCABEES

CHAPTER III

He overthroweth the forces of Samaria and Syria.

sought them out, and burnt up those that vexed his people. Wherefore the wicked shrunke for feare of him, and all the workers of iniquity were troubled, because salvation prospered in his hand. He grieved also many kings, and made Iacob glad with his acts, and his memoriall is blessed for ever. Moreover he went through the citties of Iuda, destroying the ungodly out of them, and turning away wrath from Israel. So that he was renowned unto the utmost part of the earth, and he received unto him such as were ready to perish. Then Apollonius gathered the Gentiles together, and a great host out of Samaria to fight against Israel. Which thing when Iudas perceived he went forth to meete him, and so he smote him, and slew him, many also fell downe slaine, but the rest fled. Wherefore Iudas tooke their spoiles, and Apollonius sword also, and therewith he fought, all his life long. Now when Seron a prince of the armie of Syria, heard say that Iudas had gathered unto him a multitude and company of the faithfull, to goe out with him to warre, he said, I will get me a name and honour in the kingdome, for I will goe fight with Iudas, and them that are with him, who despise the kings commandement. So he made him ready to goe up, and there went with him a mighty host of the ungodly to helpe him, and to be avenged of the children of Israel. And when hee came neere to the going up of Bethoron, Iudas went forth to meet him with a smal company. Who when they saw the host comming to meet them, said unto Iudas; How shall wee be able, being so few to fight against so great a multitude, and so strong, seeing wee are ready to faint with fasting all this day? Unto whom Iudas answered: It is no hard matter for many to bee shut up in the hands of a few; and with the God of heaven it is all one, to deliver with a great multitude, or a small company: for the victory of battell standeth not in the multitude of an hoste, but strength commeth from heaven. They come against us in much pride and iniquitie to destroy us, and our wives and children, and to spoile us: but wee fight for our lives, and our Lawes. Wherefore the Lord himselfe will overthrow them before our face: and as for you, be ye not afraid of them. Now as soone as hee had left off speaking, he lept suddenly upon them, and so Seron and his host was overthrowen before him. And they pursued them from the going downe of Bethoron, unto the plaine, where were slaine about eight hundred men of them; and the residue fledde into the land of the Philistines. Then began the feare of Iudas and his brethren, and an exceeding great dread to fall upon the nations round about them: in so much, as his fame came unto the king, and all nations talked

I. MACCABEES

of the battels of Iudas. Now when King Antiochus heard these things, he was full of indignation: wherefore hee sent and gathered together all the forces of his realme [even] a very strong armie. He opened also his treasure, and gave his souldiers pay for a yeere, commanding them to be ready, whensoever he should need them. Neverthelesse, when he saw that the money of his treasures failed, and that the tributes in the countrey were small, because of the dissention, and plague which he had brought upon the land, in taking away the Lawes which had bene of old time, hee feared that he should not be able to beare the charges any longer, nor to have such gifts to give so liberally, as he did before: for hee had abounded above the Kings that were before him. Wherefore, being greatly perplexed in his minde, hee determined to goe into Persia, there to take the tributes of the countreys, and to gather much money. So hee left Lysias a noble man, and one of the blood royall, to oversee the affaires of the King, from the river Euphrates, unto the borders of Egypt: and to bring up his sonne Antiochus, untill he came againe. Moreover he delivered unto him the halfe of his forces, and the Elephants, and gave him charge of all things that he would have done, as also concerning them that dwelt in Iuda and Ierusalem. To wit, that he should send an armie against them, to destroy and root out the strength of Israel, and the remnant of Ierusalem, and to take away their memoriall from that place: and that he should place strangers in all their quarters, and divide their land by lot. So the king tooke the halfe of the forces that remained, and departed from Antioch his royall city, the hundreth fourtie and seventh yeere, and having passed the river Euphrates, hee went through the high countreys. Then Lysias chose Ptoleme, the son of Dorymenes and Nicanor, and Gorgias, mighty men of the kings friends: and with them hee sent fourtie thousand footmen, and seven thousand horsemen to goe into the land of Iuda, and to destroy it as the king commanded. So they went forth with all their power, and came and pitched by Emmaus in the plaine countrey. And the merchants of the countrey, hearing the fame of them, tooke silver, and gold very much, with servants, and came into the campe to buy the children of Israel for slaves; A power also of Syria, and of the land of the Philistines, ioyned themselves unto them. Now when Iudas and his brethren saw that miseries were multiplied, and that the forces did encampe themselves in their borders, (for they knewe how the king had given commaundement to destroy the people, and utterly abolish them,) they said one to another, Let us restore the decayed

CHAPTER III
Antiochus sendeth a great power against him.

I. MACCABEES

CHAPTER III

He and his fall to fasting and prayer,

estate of our people, and let us fight for our people and the Sanctuarie. Then was the congregation gathered together, that they might be ready for battell, and that they might pray, and aske mercy and compassion. Now Ierusalem lay voide as a wildernesse, there was none of her children that went in or out: the Sanctuarie also was troden downe, and aliens kept the strong holde: the heathen had their habitation in that place, and ioy was taken from Iacob, and the pipe with the harpe ceased. Wherefore the Israelites assembled themselves together, and came to Maspha over-against Ierusalem; for in Maspha was the place where they prayed aforetime in Israel. Then they fasted that day, and put on sackecloth, and cast ashes upon their heads, and rent their clothes: and laide open the booke of the Law, wherein the heathen had sought to paint the likenesse of their images. They brought also the Priestes garments, and the first fruits, and the tithes, and the Nazarites they stirred up, who had accomplished their dayes. Then cried they with a loude voice toward heaven, saying, What shall we doe with these, and whither shall wee cary them away? For thy Sanctuarie is troden downe and profaned, and thy Priestes are in heavinesse, and brought low. And loe, the heathen are assembled together against us, to destroy us: what things they imagine against us, thou knowest. How shall wee be able to stand against them, except thou (O God) be our helpe? Then sounded they with trumpets, and cryed with a loude voice. And after this, Iudas ordained captains over the people, even captains over thousands, and over hundreds, and over fifties, and over tennes. But as for such as were building houses, or had betrothed wives, or were planting vineyards, or were fearefull, those hee commanded that they should returne, every man to his owne house, according to the Law. So the campe remooved, and pitched upon the South side of Emmaus.

and are encouraged.

And Indas sayde, Arme your selves, and be valiant men, and see that ye be in readinesse against the morning, that yee may fight with these nations, that are assembled together against us, to destroy us and our Sanctuarie. For it is better for us to die in battell, then to behold the calamities of our people, and our Sanctuarie. Neverthelesse, as the will [of God] is in heaven, so let him doe.

I. MACCABEES
CHAPTER IIII

THEN tooke Gorgias five thousand footmen, and a thousand of the best horsemen, and remooved out of the campe by night: to the end he might rush in upon the camp of the Iewes, and smite them suddenly. And the men of the fortresse were his guides. Now when Iudas heard thereof, hee himselfe remooved, and the valiant men with him, that hee might smite the Kings armie which was at Emmaus, while as yet the forces were dispersed from the campe. In the meane season came Gorgias by night into the campe of Iudas: and when hee found no man there, hee sought them in the mountaines: for said hee, these fellowes flee from us. But assoone as it was day, Iudas shewed himselfe in the plaine with three thousand men, who neverthelesse had neither armour, nor swordes to their mindes. And they sawe the campe of the heathen, that it was strong, and well harnessed, and compassed round about with horsemen; and these were expert of warre. Then said Iudas to the men that were with him: feare ye not their multitude, neither be ye afraid of their assault. Remember how our fathers were delivered in the red Sea, when Pharao pursued them with an armie. Now therfore let us crie unto heaven, if peradventure the Lord wil have mercie upon us, and remember the covenant of our fathers, and destroy this hoste before our face this day. That so all the heathen may know that there is one, who delivereth and saveth Israel. Then the strangers lift up their eyes, and saw them comming over against them. Wherefore they went out of the campe to battell, but they that were with Iudas sounded their trumpets. So they ioyned battell, and the heathen being discomfited, fled into the plaine. Howbeit all the hindmost of them were slaine with the sword: for they pursued them unto Gazera, and unto the plaines of Idumea, and Azotus, and Iamnia, so that there were slaine of them, upon a three thousand men. This done, Iudas returned againe with his hoste from pursuing them, and said to the people, Bee not greedie of the spoiles, in as much as there is a battell before us, and Gorgias and his hoste are here by us in the mountaine, but stand ye now against your enemies, and overcome them, and after this you may boldly take the spoiles. As Iudas was yet speaking these words, there appeared a part of them looking out of the mountaine. Who when they perceived that the Iewes had put their hoste to flight, and were burning the tents: (for the smoke that was seene declared what was done) when therefore they perceived these things, they were sore afraid, and seeing also the hoste of Iudas in the plaine ready

Iudas defeateth the plot.

and forces of Gorgias,

I. MACCABEES

CHAPTER IIII

and spoileth their tents,

to fight: they fled every one into the land of strangers. Then Iudas returned to spoile the tents, where they got much golde, and silver, and blew silke, and purple of the sea, and great riches. After this, they went home, and sung a song of thankesgiving, and praised the Lord in heaven: because it is good, because his mercie endureth for ever. Thus Israel had a great deliverance that day. Now all the strangers that had escaped, came and told Lysias what had happened. Who when hee heard thereof, was confounded, and discouraged, because neither such things as he would, were done unto Israel, nor such things as the king commanded him were come to passe. The next yeere therefore following, Lysias gathered together threescore thousand choice men of foote, and five thousand horsemen, that he might subdue them. So they came into Idumea, and pitched their tents at Bethsura, and Iudas met them with ten thousand men. And when he saw that mighty armie, he prayed, and said, Blessed art thou, O saviour of Israel, who diddest quaile the violence of the mighty man by the hand of thy servant David, and gavest the host of strangers into the hands of Ionathan the sonne of Saul, and his armour bearer. Shut up this armie in the hand of thy people Israel, and let them be confounded in their power and horsemen. Make them to be of no courage, and cause the boldnesse of their strength to fall away, and let them quake at their destruction. Cast them downe with the sword of them that love thee, and let all those that know thy name, praise thee with thanksgiving. So they ioyned battaile, and there were slaine of the host of Lysias about five thousand men, even before them were they slaine. Now when Lysias saw his armie put to flight, and the manlinesse of Iudas souldiers, and how they were ready, either to live or die valiantly, he went into Antiochia, and gathered together a company of strangers, and having made his armie greater then it was, he purposed to come againe into Iudea. Then saide Iudas and his brethren, Behold our enemies are discomfited: let us goe up to cleanse, and dedicate the Sanctuarie. Upon this all the host assembled themselves together, and went up into mount Sion. And when they saw the sanctuarie desolate, and the altar prophaned, and the gates burnt up, and shrubs growing in the courts, as in a forrest, or in one of the mountaines, yea and the priests chambers pulled downe, they rent their clothes, and made great lamentation, and cast ashes upon their heads, and fell downe flat to the ground upon their faces, and blew an alarme with the trumpets, and cried towards heaven. Then Iudas appointed certaine men to fight against those that were in the fortresse, untill he had clensed the Sanctuarie. So he

and over-throweth Lysias.

I. MACCABEES

chose priests of blamelesse conversation, such as had pleasure in the law. Who cleansed the Sanctuarie, and bare out the defiled stones into an uncleane place. And when as they consulted what to doe with the altar of burnt offrings which was prophaned, they thought it best to pull it downe, lest it should be a reproch to them, because the heathen had defiled it; wherefore they pulled it downe, and laide up the stones in the mountaine of the temple in a convenient place, untill there should come a Prophet, to shew what should be done with them. Then they tooke whole stones according to the law, and built a new altar, according to the former: and made up the Sanctuarie, and the things that were within the temple, and hallowed the courts. They made also new holy vessels, and into the temple they brought the candlesticke, and the altar of burnt offerings, and of incense, and the table. And upon the altar they burnt incense, and the lamps that were upon the candlesticke they lighted, that they might give light in the temple. Furthermore they set the loaves upon the table, and spread out the veiles, and finished all the workes which they had begunne to make. Now on the five and twentieth day of the ninth moneth, (which is called the moneth Casleu) in the hundreth fourty and eight yeere they rose up betimes in the morning, and offered sacrifice according to the law upon the new altar of burnt offerings, which they had made. Looke at what time, and what day the heathen had prophaned it, even in that was it dedicated with songs, and cittherns, and harpes, and cimbals. Then all the people fell upon their faces, worshipping and praising the God of heaven, who had given them good successe. And so they kept the dedication of the altar eight dayes, and offered burnt offerings with gladnesse, and sacrificed the sacrifice of deliverance and praise. They deckt also the forefront of the temple with crownes of gold; and with shields, and the gates, and the chambers they renewed and hanged doores upon them. Thus was there very great gladnesse among the people, for that the reproch of the heathen was put away. Moreover Iudas and his brethren with the whole congregation of Israel ordained that the daies of the dedication of the altar, should be kept in their season from yeere to yeere by the space of eight dayes, from the five and twentieth day of the moneth Casleu, with mirth and gladnesse. At that time also they builded up the mount Sion with high walles, and strong towres round about, lest the Gentiles should come and tread it downe, as they had done before. And they set there a garison to keepe it: and fortified Bethsura to preserve it, that the people might have a defence against Idumea.

CHAPTER IIII

He pulleth downe the Altar which the heathen had prophaned, and setteth up a newe,

and maketh a wall about Sion.

I. MACCABEES

CHAPTER V

Iudas smiteth the children of Dan, Bean, and Ammon.

NOW when the nations round about heard that the Altar was built, and the Sanctuarie renewed as before, it displeased them very much. Wherfore they thought to destroy the generation of Iacob that was among them, and thereupon they began to slay and destroy the people. Then Iudas fought against the children of Esau in Idumea at Arabattine, because they besieged Israel: and hee gave them a great overthrow, and abated their courage, and tooke their spoiles. Also he remembred the iniurie of the children of Bean, who had bene a snare and an offence unto the people, in that they lay in waite for them in the wayes. Hee shut them up therefore in the towres, and incamped against them, and destroyed them utterly, and burnt the towers of that place with fire, and all that were therein. Afterward he passed over to the children of Ammon, where he found a mighty power, and much people, with Timotheus their captaine. So he fought many battels with them, till at length they were discomfited before him; and he smote them. And when hee had taken Iazar, with the townes belonging thereto, he returned into Iudea. Then the heathen that were at Galead, assembled themselves together against the Israelites that were in their quarters to destroy them: but they fled to the fortresse of Dathema; and sent letters unto Iudas and his brethren: The heathen that are round about us, are assembled together against us to destroy us; and they are preparing to come and take the fortresse whereunto wee are fled, Timotheus being captaine of their host. Come now therefore and deliver us from their handes, for many of us are slaine. Yea all our brethren that were in the places of Tobie, are put to death, their wives and their children; Also they have caried away captives, and borne away their stuffe, and they have destroied there about a thousand men. While these letters were yet reading, behold there came other messengers from Galilee with their clothes rent, who reported on this wise, and said: They of Ptolemais, and of Tyrus, and Sidon, and all Galilee of the Gentiles are assembled together against us to consume us. Now when Iudas and the people heard these wordes, there assembled a great congregation together, to consult what they should doe for their brethren, that were in trouble and assaulted of them. Then said Iudas unto Simon his brother,

Simon is sent into Galile.

Choose thee out men, and goe, and deliver thy brethren that are in Galilee, for I and Ionathan my brother, will goe into the countrey of Galaad. So hee left Ioseph the sonne of Zacharias, and Azarias captaines of the people, with the remnant of the hoste in Iudea to

I. MACCABEES

keepe it, unto whom he gave commandement, saying, Take yee the charge of this people, and see that you make not warre against the heathen, untill the time that we come againe. Now unto Simon were given three thousand men to goe into Galilee, and unto Indas eight thousand men for the countrey of Galaad. Then went Simon into Galilee, where hee fought many battels with the heathen, so that the heathen were discomfited by him. And hee pursued them unto the gate of Ptolemais; And there were slaine of the heathen about three thousand men, whose spoiles he tooke. And those that were in Galilee and in Arbattis, with their wives and their children, and all that they had, tooke he away [with him] and brought them into Iudea, with great ioy. Iudas Maccabeus also and his brother Ionathan, went over Iordan, and travailed three dayes iourney in the wildernesse, where they met with the Nabathites, who came unto them in peaceable maner, and told them every thing that had happened to their brethren in the land of Galaad, and how that many of them were shut up in Bosora, and Bosor, in Alema, Casphor, Maked and Carnaim (all these cities are strong and great.) And that they were shut up in the rest of the cities of the countrey of Galaad, and that against to morrow they had appointed to bring their host against the forts, and to take them, and to destroy them all in one day. Hereupon Iudas and his host turned suddenly by the way of the wildernesse unto Bosorra, and when he had wonne the citie, hee slew all the males with the edge of the sword, and tooke all their spoiles, and burnt the citie with fire. From whence hee remooved by night, and went till he came to the fortresse. And betimes in the morning they looked up, and behold, there was an innumerable people bearing ladders, and other engines of warre, to take the fortresse : for they assaulted them. When Iudas therefore saw that the battaile was begun, and that the cry of the citie went up to heaven, with trumpets, and a great sound, he said unto his hoste, Fight this day for your brethren. So he went foorth behinde them in three companies, who sounded their trumpets, and cryed with prayer. Then the hoste of Timotheus knowing that it was Maccabeus, fled from him: wherefore hee smote them with a great slaughter : so that there were killed of them that day about eight thousand men. This done, Iudas turned aside to Maspha, and after he had assaulted it, hee tooke it, and slewe all the males therein, and received the spoiles therof, and burnt it with fire. From thence went he, and tooke Casphon, Maged, Bosor, and the other cities of the countrey of Galaad. After these things, gathered Timotheus another hoste, and encamped against Raphon beyond the brooke. So Iudas sent [men] to espie the hoste, who

CHAPTER V

The exploits of Iudas in Galaad.

I. MACCABEES

CHAPTER V

brought him word, saying; All the heathen that be round about us, are assembled unto them, even a very great hoste. Hee hath also hired the Arabians to helpe them, and they have pitched their tents beyond the brooke, readie to come and fight against thee: upon this Iudas went to meet them. Then Timotheus said unto the captaines of his hoste, When Indas and his hoste come neere the brooke, if he passe over first unto us, we shall not be able to withstand him, for hee will mightily prevaile against us. But if he be afraid, and campe beyond the river, we shall goe over unto him, and prevaile against him. Now when Iudas came neere the brooke, he caused the Scribes of the people to remaine by the brooke: unto whom hee gave commandement, saying, Suffer no man to remaine in the campe, but let all come to the battell. So he went first over unto them, and all the people after him: then all the heathen being discomfited before him, cast away their weapons, and fled unto the Temple that was at Carnaim. But they tooke the citie, and burnt the Temple, with all that were therein. Thus was Carnaim subdued, neither could they stand any longer before Iudas. Then Iudas gathered together all the Israelites that were in the countrey of Galaad from the least unto the greatest, even their wives and their children, and their stuffe, a very great hoste, to the ende they might come into the land of Iudea. Now when they came unto Ephron (this was a great city in the way as they should goe, very well fortified) they could not turne from it, either on the right hand or the left, but must needs passe through the midst of it. Then they of the city shut them out, and stopped up the gates with stones. Whereupon Iudas sent unto them in peaceable maner, saying; Let us passe through your land to goe into our owne countrey, and none shall doe you any hurt, we will onely passe thorow on foote: howbeit they would not open unto him. Wherefore Iudas commaunded a proclamation to be made throughout the hoste, that every man should pitch his tent in the place where he was. So the souldiers pitched, and assaulted the city all that day, and all that night, till at the length the city was delivered

He destroyeth Ephron, for denying him to passe through it.

into his hands: who then slew all the males with the edge of the sword, and rased the city, and tooke the spoiles therof, and passed through the city over them that were slaine. After this went they over Iordan, into the great plaine before Bethsan. And Iudas gathered together those that came behind, and exhorted the people all the way through, till they came into the land of Iudea. So they went up to mount Sion with ioy and gladnesse, where they offered burnt offerings, because not one of them were slaine, untill they had returned in peace. Now what time as Iudas and Ionathan

278

I. MACCABEES

were in the land of Galaad, and Simon his brother in Galilee before Ptolemais, Ioseph the sonne of Zacharias, and Azarias, captaines of the garisons, heard of the valiant actes and warlike deeds which they had done. Wherefore they said, Let us also get us a name, and goe fight against the heathen that are round about us. So when they had given charge unto the garison that was with them, they went towards Iamnia. Then came Gorgias and his men out of the citie to fight against them. And so it was, that Ioseph and Azarias were put to flight, and pursued unto the borders of Iudea, and there were slaine that day of the people of Israel about two thousand men. Thus was there a great overthrow among the children of Israel, because they were not obedient unto Iudas, and his brethren, but thought to doe some valiant act. Moreover these men came not of the seed of those, by whose hand deliverance was given unto Israel. Howbeit the man Iudas and his brethren were greatly renowned in the sight of all Israel, and of all the heathen wheresoever their name was heard of, insomuch as the people assembled unto them with ioyfull acclamations. Afterward went Iudas foorth with his brethren, and fought against the children of Esau in the land toward the South, where he smote Hebron, and the townes thereof, and pulled downe the fortresse of it, and burnt the townes thereof round about. From thence he removed to goe into the land of the Philistines, and passed through Samaria. At that time certaine priests desirous to shew their valour, were slaine in battell, for that they went out to fight unadvisedly. So Iudas turned to Azotus in the land of the Philistines, and when he had pulled downe their altars, and burnt their carved images with fire, and spoiled their cities, he returned into the land of Iudea.

CHAPTER V

Diverse, that in Iudas absence would fight with their enemies, are slaine.

CHAPTER VI

ABOUT that time king Antiochus travailing through the high countreys, heard say that Elimais in the countrey of Persia, was a citie greatly renowned for riches, silver, and gold, and that there was in it a very rich temple, wherein were coverings of gold, and brestplates, and shields which Alexander sonne of Philippe the Macedonian King, who reigned first among the Grecians, had left there. Wherefore he came and sought to take the citie, and to spoile it, but he was not able, because they of the citie having had warning thereof, rose up against him in battell: So he fled and departed thence with great heavinesse, and returned to Babylon. Moreover there came one, who brought in tidings into Persia, that the armies which went against the land of Iudea,

I. MACCABEES

CHAPTER VI

Antiochus dieth,

and confesseth that he is plagued for the wrong done to Ierusalem.

Iudas besiegeth those in the towre at Hierusalem.

were put to flight: and that Lysias who went forth first with a great power, was driven away of the Iewes, and that they were made strong by the armour, and power, and store of spoiles, which they had gotten of the armies, whom they had destroyed. Also that they had pulled downe the abomination which hee had set up upon the altar in Ierusalem, and that they had compassed about the Sanctuarie with high wals as before, and his citie Bethsura. Now when the king heard these words, he was astonished, and sore moved, whereupon hee laide him downe upon his bedde, and fell sicke for griefe, because it had not befallen him, as hee looked for. And there hee continued many dayes: for his griefe was ever more and more, and he made account that he should die. Wherefore he called for all his friends, and said unto them, The sleepe is gone from mine eyes, and my heart faileth for very care. And I thought with my selfe: Into what tribulation am I come, and how great a flood [of miserie] is it wherein now I am? for I was bountifull, and beloved in my power. But now I remember the evils that I did at Ierusalem, and that I tooke all the vessels of gold and silver that were therein, and sent to destroy the inhabitants of Iudea without a cause. I perceive therefore that for this cause these troubles are come upon me, and behold I perish through great griefe in a strange land. Then called he for Philip one of his friends whom he made ruler over all his realme: and gave him the crowne and his robe, and his signet, to the end hee should bring up his sonne Antiochus, and nourish him up for the kingdome. So king Antiochus died there in the hundreth forty and ninth yeere. Now when Lysias knew that the king was dead, he set up Antiochus his sonne (whom he had brought up being yong) to reigne in his stead, and his name he called Eupator. About this time they that were in the towre shut up the Israelites round about the Sanctuarie, and sought alwayes their hurt, and the strengthening of the heathen. Wherefore Iudas purposing to destroy them, called all the people together to besiege them. So they came together, and besieged them in the hundred and fiftith yeere, and he made mounts for shot against them, and [other] engines: howbeit certaine of them that were besieged got forth, unto whom some ungodly men of Israel ioyned themselves. And they went unto the king and said, How long will it be ere thou execute iudgement, and avenge our brethren? We have beene willing to serve thy father, and to doe as he would have us, and to obey his commandements. For which cause they of our nation besiege the towre, and are alienated from us: Moreover as many of us as they could light on, they slew, and spoiled our inheritance. Neither have they

I. MACCABEES

stretched out their hand against us only, but also against all their borders. And behold this day are they besieging the towre at Ierusalem to take it: the Sanctuary also, and Bethsura have they fortified. Wherefore if thou doest not prevent them quickly, they wil doe greater things then these, neither shalt thou be able to rule them. Now when the king heard this, he was angry, and gathered together all his friends, and the captaines of his armie, and those that had charge of the horse. There came also unto him from other kingdomes, and from Isles of the Sea bands of hired souldiers. So that the number of his armie was an hundred thousand foote men, and twentie thousand horsemen, and two and thirty Elephants exercised in battell. These went through Idumea, and pitched against Bethsura which they assaulted many daies, making engines of warre: but they [of Bethsura] came out, and burnt them with fire, and fought valiantly. Upon this Iudas removed from the towre, and pitched in Bathzacharias, over against the kings campe. Then the king rising very earely marched fiercely with his host toward Bathzacharias, where his armies made them ready to battell, and sounded the trumpets. And to the end they might provoke the elephants to fight, they shewed them the blood of grapes and mulberies. Moreover, they divided the beasts among the armies, and for every elephant they appointed a thousand men, armed with coats of male, and with helmets of brasse on their heads, and besides this, for every beast were ordained five hundred horsemen of the best. These were ready at every occasion: wheresoever the beast was, and whithersoever the beast went, they went also, neither departed they from him. And upon the beastes were there strong towres of wood, which covered every one of them, and were girt fast unto them with devices: there were also upon every one two and thirtie strong men that fought upon them, besides the Indian that ruled him. As for the remnant of the horsemen they set them on this side, and that side, at the two parts of the host giving them signes what to do, and being harnessed all over amidst the rankes. Now when the Sunne shone upon the shields of golde, and brasse, the mountaines glistered therewith, and shined like lampes of fire. So part of the kings armie being spred upon the high mountaines, and part on the valleyes below, they marched on safely, and in order. Wherefore all that heard the noise of their multitude, and the marching of the company, and the ratling of the harnesse, were moved: for the army was very great and mighty. Then Iudas and his host drew neere, and entred into battell, and there were slaine of the kings army, sixe hundred men.

CHAPTER VI

They procure Antiochus the yonger to come into Iudea.

I. MACCABEES

CHAPTER VI

He besiegeth Sion,

and maketh peace with Israel:

Eleazar also (syrnamed) Savaran, perceiving that one of the beasts, armed with royall harnesse, was higher then all the rest, and supposing that the king was upon him, put himselfe in ieopardie, to the end hee might deliver his people, and get him a perpetuall name: wherefore hee ranne upon him courageously through the midst of the battell, slaying on the right hand, and on the left, so that they were divided from him on both sides. Which done, he crept under the Elephant, and thrust him under and slew him: whereupon the Elephant fell downe upon him and there he died. How be it [the rest of the Iewes] seeing the strength of the king, and the violence of his forces, turned away from them.

Then the kings armie went up to Ierusalem to meet them, and the king pitched his tents against Iudea, and against mount Sion. But with them that were in Bethsura hee made peace: for they came out of the citie, because they had no victuals there, to endure the siege, it being a yeere of rest to the land. So the King tooke Bethsura, and set a garison there to keepe it. As for the Sanctuarie hee besieged it many dayes: and set there artillerie with engins, and instruments to cast fire and stones, and pieces to cast darts, and slings. Whereupon they also made engins, against their engins, and helde them battell a long season. Yet at the last their vessels being without victuals, (for that it was the seventh yeere, and they in Iudea that were delivered from the Gentiles, had eaten up the residue of the store) there were but a few left in the Sanctuary, because the famine did so prevaile against them, that they were faine to disperse themselves, every man to his owne place. At that time Lysias heard say, that Philip (whom Antiochus the King whiles hee lived had appointed to bring up his sonne Antiochus, that he might be king) was returned out of Persia, and Media, and the Kings host also that went with him, and that hee sought to take unto him the ruling of the affaires. Wherefore hee went in all haste, and said to the King, and the captaines of the host, and the company, Wee decay dayly, and our victuals are but small, and the place wee lay siege unto is strong: and the affaires of the kingdome lie upon us. Now therefore let us be friends with these men, and make peace with them, and with all their nation. And covenant with them, that they shall live after their Lawes, as they did before: for they are therefore displeased, and have done all these things because wee abolished their Lawes. So the King and the Princes were content: wherefore hee sent unto them to make peace, and they accepted thereof. Also the King and the Princes made an oath unto them: whereupon they went out of the strong hold. Then

I. MACCABEES

the King entred into mount Sion, but when hee saw the strength of the place, hee brake his oath that hee had made, and gave commandement to pull downe the wall round about. Afterward departed hee in all haste, and returned unto Antiochia, where hee found Philip to bee master of the citie; So he fought against him, and tooke the citie by force. CHAPTER VI yet over-throweth the wall of Sion.

CHAPTER VII

IN the hundreth and one and fiftieth yeere, Demetrius the sonne of Seleucus departed from Rome, and came up with a fewe men unto a citie of the Sea coast, and reigned there. And as he entred into the palace of his ancestors, so it was, that his forces had taken Antiochus and Lysias to bring them unto him. Wherefore when he knew it, hee said; Let me not see their faces. So his hoste slewe them. Now when Demetrius was set upon the throne of his kingdome, there came unto him all the wicked and ungodly men of Israel, having Alcimus (who was desirous to be high Priest) for their captaine. And they accused the people to the king, saying; Iudas and his brethren have slaine all thy friends, and driven us out of our owne land. Now therefore send some man whom thou trustest, and let him goe and see what havocke he hath made amongst us, and in the kings land, and let him punish them with all them that aide them. Then the king chose Bacchides a friend of the king, who ruled beyond the flood, and was a great man in the kingdome, and faithfull to the king. And him hee sent with that wicked Alcimus, whom hee made high Priest, and commanded that he should take vengeance of the children of Israel. So they departed, and came with a great power into the land of Iudea, where they sent messengers to Iudas and his brethren with peaceable words deceitfully. But they gave no heede to their words, for they sawe that they were come with a great power. Then did there assemble unto Alcimus and Bacchides a company of Scribes, to require iustice. Now the Assideans were the first among the children of Israel, that sought peace of them: For, said they, one that is a Priest of the seede of Aaron, is come with this armie, and he will doe us no wrong. So he spake unto them peaceably, and sware unto them, saying; We will procure the harme neither of you nor your friends. Whereupon they beleeved him: howbeit hee tooke of them threescore men, and slewe them in one day, according to the words which he wrote: The flesh of thy Saints [have they cast out] and their blood have they shed round about Ierusalem, and there was none to bury them. Where- Antiochus is slaine, and Demetrius reigneth in his stead.
Alcimus would be hie Priest, and complaineth of Iudas to the king.
He slayeth threescore Asideans.

I. MACCABEES

CHAPTER VII

fore the feare and dread of them fell upon all the people, who said, There is neither trueth, nor righteousnesse in them; for they have broken the covenant and othe that they made. After this remooved Bacchides from Ierusalem, and pitched his tents in Bezeth, where he sent and tooke many of the men that had forsaken him, and certaine of the people also, and when he had slaine them, [he cast them] into the great pit. Then committed he the countrey to Alcimus, and left with him a power to aide him: so Bacchides went unto the king. But Alcimus contended for the high Priesthood. And unto him resorted all such as troubled the people, who after they had gotten the land of Iuda into their power, did much hurt in Israel. Now when Iudas saw all the mischiefe that Alcimus and his company had done among the Israelites, even above the heathen, he went out into all the coast of Iudea round about, and tooke vengeance of them that had revolted from him, so that they durst no more goe foorth into the countrey. On the other side, when Alcimus saw that Iudas and his company had gotten the upper hand, and knew that he was not able to abide their force, he went againe to the king, and said all the worst of them that he could. Then the king sent Nicanor one of his honourable princes, a man that bare deadly hate unto Israel, with commandement to destroy the people. So Nicanor came to Ierusalem with a great force: and sent unto Iudas and his brethren deceitfully with friendly words, saying, Let there be no battell betweene me and you, I will come with a fewe men, that I may see you in peace. He came therefore to Iudas, and they saluted one another peaceably. Howbeit the enemies were prepared to take away Iudas by violence. Which thing after it was knowen to Indas (to wit) that he came unto him with deceit, he was sore afraid of him, and would see his face no more. Nicanor also when he saw that his counsell was discovered, went out to fight against Indas besides Capharsalama. Where there were slaine of Nicanors side, about five thousand men, and [the rest] fled into the citie of David. After this went Nicanor up to mount Sion, and there came out of the Sanctuarie certaine of the priestes, and certaine of the elders of the people to salute him peaceably, and to shewe him the burnt sacrifice that was offred for the king. But he mocked them, and laughed at them, and abused them shamefully, and spake proudly, and swore in his wrath, saying, Unlesse Iudas and his hoste be now delivered into my hands, if ever I come againe in safetie, I will burne up this house: and with that he went out in a great rage. Then the priests entred in, and stood before the altar, and the

I. MACCABEES

Temple, weeping, and saying, Thou O Lord didst choose this house, to be called by thy Name, and to be a house of prayer and petition for thy people. Be avenged of this man and his hoste, and let them fall by the sword: Remember their blasphemies, and suffer them not to continue any longer. So Nicanor went out of Ierusalem, and pitched his tents in Bethoron, where an hoste out of Syria met him. But Iudas pitched in Adasa with three thousand men, and there he prayed, saying, O Lord, when they that were sent from the king of the Assyrians blasphemed, thine Angel went out, and smote a hundred, fourescore, and five thousand of them. Even so destroy thou this host before us this day, that the rest may know that he hath spoken blasphemously against thy Sanctuary, and iudge thou him according to his wickednesse. So the thirteenth day of the moneth Adar, the hostes ioyned battell, but Nicanors host was discomfited, and he himselfe was first slaine in the battell. Now when Nicanors host saw that he was slaine, they cast away their weapons, and fled. Then they pursued after them a dayes iourney from Adasa, unto Gasera, sounding an alarme after them with their trumpets. Whereupon they came forth out of all the townes of Iudea round about, and closed them in, so that they turning backe upon them that pursued them, were all slaine with the sword, and not one of them was left. Afterwards they tooke the spoiles, and the pray, and smote off Nicanors head, and his right hand, which he stretched out so proudly, and brought them away, and hanged them up, towards Ierusalem. For this cause the people reioyced greatly, and they kept that day, a day of great gladnesse. Moreover they ordeined to keepe yeerely this day, being the thirteenth of Adar. Thus the land of Iuda was in rest a litle while.

CHAPTER VII

Nicanor is slaine, and the kings forces are defeated by Iudas.

The day of this victorie is kept holy every yeere.

CHAPTER VIII

NOW Iudas had heard of the fame of the Romanes, that they were mighty and valiant men, and such as would lovingly accept all that ioyned themselves unto them, and make a league of amitie with all that came unto them, and that they were men of great valour: It was told him also of their warres and noble acts which they had done amongst the Galatians, and how they had conquered them, and brought them under tribute. And what they had done in the countrey of Spaine, for the winning of the mines of the silver and gold which is there. And that by their policie and patience, they had conquered all that place (though it were very

Iudas is informed of the power and policie of the Romanes,

I. MACCABEES

CHAPTER VIII

farre from them) and the kings also that came against them from the uttermost part of the earth, till they had discomfited them, and given them a great overthrow, so that the rest did give them tribute every yere. Besides this, how they had discomfited in battell Philip, and Perseus king of the Citims, with others that lift up themselves against them, and had overcome them. How also Antiochus the great king of Asia that came against them in battaile, having an hundred and twentie Elephants with horsemen and chariots, and a very great armie, was discomfited by them. And how they tooke him alive, and covenanted that hee and such as reigned after him, should pay a great tribute, and give hostages, and that which was agreed upon, and the country of India, and Media, and Lidia, and of the goodliest countries: which they tooke of him, and gave to king Eumenes. Moreover how the Grecians had determined to come and destroy them. And that they having knowledge thereof sent against them a certaine captaine, and fighting with them slew many of them, and caried away captives, their wives, and their children, and spoiled them, and tooke possession of their lands, and pulled downe their strong holds, and brought them to be their servants unto this day. [It was told him besides] how they destroyed and brought under their dominion, all other kingdomes and isles that at any time resisted them. But with their friends, and such as relied upon them they kept amitie: and that they had conquered kingdomes both farre and nigh, insomuch as all that heard of their name were afraid of them. Also that whom they would helpe to a kingdome, those raigne, and whom againe they would, they displace: finally that they were greatly exalted. Yet for all this, none of them wore a crowne, or was clothed in purple to be magnified thereby. Moreover how they had made for themselves a senate house, wherin three hundred and twentie men sate in counsell daily, consulting alway for the people, to the end they might be wel ordered. And that they committed their government to one man every yeere, who ruled over all their countrie, and that all were obedient to that one, and that there was neither envy, nor emulation amongst them. In consideration of these things Iudas chose Eupolemus the sonne of Iohn, the sonne of Accas, and Iason the sonne of Eleazar, and sent them to Rome to make a league of amitie and confederacie with them, [and to intreate them] that they would take the yoke from them, for they saw that the kingdome of the Grecians did oppresse Israel with servitude.

and maketh a league with them.

They went therefore to Rome (which was a very great iourney) and came into the Senate, where they spake and said, Iudas Maccabeus with his brethren, and the people of the Iewes,

I. MACCABEES

have sent us unto you, to make a confederacie, and peace with you, and that we might be registred, your confederats and friends. So that matter pleased the Romanes well. And this is the copie of the Epistle which (the Senate) wrote backe againe, in tables of brasse: and sent to Ierusalem, that there they might have by them a memorial of peace and confederacy. Good successe be to the Romans and to the people of the Iewes, by Sea, and by land for ever: the sword also and enemie, be farre from them. If there come first any warre upon the Romans or any of their confederats throughout all their dominion, the people of the Iewes shall helpe them, as the time shall be appointed, with all their heart. Neither shal they give any thing, unto them that make war upon them, or aide them with victuals, weapons, money, or ships, as it hath seemed good unto the Romans, but they shall keepe their covenant without taking any thing therefore. In the same maner also, if warre come first upon the nation of the Iewes, the Romans shall helpe them with all their heart, according as the time shall be appointed them. Neither shal victuals be given to them that take part against them, or weapons, or money, or ships, as it hath seemed good to the Romanes; but they shall keepe their covenants, and that without deceit. According to these articles did the Romanes make a covenant with the people of the Iewes. Howbeit, if hereafter the one partie or the other, shall thinke meete to adde or diminish any thing, they may doe it at their pleasures, and whatsoever they shall adde or take away, shalbe ratified. And as touching the evils that Demetrius doeth to the Iewes, wee have written unto him, saying, Wherefore hast thou made thy yoke heavie upon our friends, and confederats the Iewes? If therefore they complaine any more against thee: wee will doe them iustice, and fight with thee by sea and by land.

CHAPTER VIII

The articles of that league.

CHAPTER IX

FURTHERMORE, when Demetrius heard that Nicanor and his hoste were slaine in battell, hee sent Bacchides and Alcimus into the land of Iudea the second time, and with them the chiefe strength of his hoste. Who went forth by the way that leadeth to Galgala, and pitched their tents before Masaloth, which is in Arbela, and after they had wonne it, they slew much people. Also the first moneth of the hundred fiftie and second yeere, they encamped before Ierusalem. From whence they removed and went to Berea, with twentie thousand footmen, and two thousand horsemen. Now Iudas had pitched his tents at Eleasa, and three

Alcimus and Bacchides come againe with new forces into Iudea.

I. MACCABEES

CHAPTER IX

The armie of Iudas flee from him,

thousand chosen men with him. Who seeing the multitude of the other army to be so great, were sore afraide, whereupon many conveyed themselves out of the hoste, insomuch as there abode of them no moe but eight hundred men. When Iudas therefore saw that his hoste slipt away, and that the battell pressed upon him, he was sore troubled in mind, and much distressed, for that he had no time to gather them together. Nevertheless unto them that remained, he said; Let us arise and goe up against our enemies, if peradventure we may be able to fight with them. But they dehorted him, saying, Wee shall never be able: Let us now rather save our lives, and hereafter we will returne with our brethren, and fight against them: for we are but few. Then Iudas said, God forbid that I should doe this thing, and flee away from them: If our time be come, let us die manfully for our brethren, and let us not staine our honour. With that the hoste [of Bacchides] removed out of their tents, and stood over against them, their horsemen being divided into two troupes, and their slingers and archers going before the hoste, and they that marched in the foreward were all mighty men. As for Bacchides, hee was in the right wing, so the hoste drew neere on the two parts, and sounded their trumpets. They also of Iudas side, even they sounded their trumpets also, so that the earth shooke at the noise of the armies, and the battell continued from morning till night. Now when Iudas perceived that Bacchides and the strength of his armie were on the right side, he tooke with him all the hardy men, who discomfited the right wing, and pursued them unto the mount Azotus. But when they of the left wing saw that they of the right wing were discomfited, they followed upon Iudas and those

and he is slaine. that were with him hard at the heeles from behinde: whereupon there was a sore battell, insomuch as many were slaine on both parts. Iudas also was killed, and the remnant fled. Then Ionathan and Simon tooke Iudas their brother, and buried him in the sepulchre of his fathers in Modin. Moreover they bewailed him, and all Israel made great lamentation for him, and mourned many dayes, saying; How is the valiant man fallen, that delivered Israel? As for the other things concerning Iudas and his warres, and the noble actes which he did, and his greatnesse, they are not written: for they were very many.

Now after the death of Iudas, the wicked began to put foorth their heads in all the coasts of Israel, and there rose up all such as wrought iniquitie. In those dayes also was there a very great famine, by reason whereof the countrey revolted, and went with them. Then Bacchides chose the wicked men,

I. MACCABEES

and made them lordes of the countrey. And they made enquirie and search for Iudas friends, and brought them unto Bacchides, who tooke vengeance of them, and used them despitefully. So was there a great affliction in Israel, the like whereof was not since the time that a Prophet was not seene amongst them. For this cause all Iudas friends came together, and said unto Ionathan, Since thy brother Iudas died, we have no man like him to goe foorth against our enemies, and Bacchides, and against them of our nation that are adversaries to us. Now therefore wee have chosen thee this day to be our prince, and captaine in his stead, that thou mayest fight our battels. Upon this, Ionathan tooke the governance upon him at that time, and rose up in stead of his brother Iudas. But when Bacchides gat knowledge thereof, he sought for to slay him. Then Ionathan and Simon his brother, and all that were with him, perceiving that, fled into the wildernes of Thecoe, and pitched their tents by the water of the poole Asphar. Which when Bacchides understood, he came neere to Iordan with all his hoste upon the Sabbath day. Now Ionathan had sent his brother [Iohn] a captaine of the people, to pray his friendes the Nabbathites that they might leave with them their cariage, which was much. But the children of Iambri came out of Medaba, and tooke Iohn and all that hee had, and went their way with it. After this came word to Ionathan and Simon his brother, that the children of Iambri made a great mariage, and were bringing the bride from Nadabatha with a great traine, as being the daughter of one of the great princes of Canaan. Therfore they remembred Iohn their brother, and went up and hidde themselves under the covert of the mountaine. Where they lift up their eyes, and looked, and behold, there was much adoe and great cariage: and the bridegrome came foorth, and his friends and brethren to meet them with drums and instruments of musicke, and many weapons. Then Ionathan and they that were with him, rose up against them from the place where they lay in ambush, and made a slaughter of them in such sort, as many fell downe dead, and the remnant fledde into the mountaine, and they tooke all their spoiles. Thus was the mariage turned into mourning, and the noise of their melody into lamentation. So when they had avenged fully the blood of their brother, they turned againe to the marish of Iordan. Now when Bacchides heard hereof, hee came on the Sabbath day unto the banks of Iordan with a great power. Then Ionathan sayde to his company, Let us goe up now and fight for our lives, for it standeth not with us to day, as in time past: for behold, the battell is before us and behinde us, and the water of Iordan on

CHAPTER IX

Ionathan is in his place,

and revengeth his brother Iohns quarrell.

I. MACCABEES

CHAPTER IX

this side and that side, the marish likewise and wood, neither is there place for us to turne aside. Wherefore cry ye now unto heaven, that ye may be delivered from the hand of your enemies. With that they ioyned battel, and Ionathan stretched foorth his hand to smite Bacchides, but hee turned backe from him. Then Ionathan and they that were with him, leapt into Iordan, and swamme over unto the farther banke : howbeit the other passed not over Iordan unto them. So there were slaine of Bacchides side that day about a thousand men. Afterward returned [Bacchides] to Ierusalem, and repaired the strong cities in Iudea : the fort in Iericho, and Emmaus, and Bethoron, and Bethel, and Thamnatha, Pharathoni, and Taphon (these did he strengthen with high wals, with gates, and with barres.) And in them he set a garison, that they might worke malice upon Israel. He fortified also the citie Bethsura, and Gazara, and the towre, and put forces in them, and provision of victuals. Besides, he tooke the chiefe mens sonnes in the country for hostages, and put them into the towre at Ierusalem to be kept. Moreover, in the hundred, fiftie and third yere, in the second moneth, Alcimus commanded that the wall of the inner court of the Sanctuarie should be pulled

Alcimus is plagued, and dieth.

downe, he pulled downe also the works of the prophets. And as he began to pull downe, even at that time was Alcimus plagued, and his enterprises hindered : for his mouth was stopped, and he was taken with a palsie, so that hee could no more speake any thing, nor give order concerning his house. So Alcimus died at that time with great torment. Now when Bacchides saw that Alcimus was dead, he returned to the king, whereupon the land of Iudea was in rest two yeere. Then all the ungodly men held a counsell, saying, Behold, Ionathan and his companie are at ease, and dwell without care : now therefore wee will bring Bacchides hither, who shall take them all in one night. So they went, and consulted with him. Then removed he, and came with a great hoste, and sent letters privily to his adherents in Iudea, that they should take Ionathan, and those that were with him : Howbeit they could not, because their counsell was knowen unto them. Wherefore they tooke of the men of the countrey that were authours of that mischiefe, about fiftie persons, and slew them. Afterward Ionathan and Simon, and they that were with him, got them away to Bethbasi, which is in the wildernesse, and they repaired the decayes thereof, and made it strong. Which thing when Bacchides knew, he gathered together all his host, and sent word to them that were of Iudea. Then went he and laid siege against Bethbasi, and they fought against it a long season, and

I. MACCABEES

made engines of warre. But Ionathan left his brother Simon in the citie, and went forth himselfe into the countrey, and with a certaine number went he forth. And he smote Odonarkes and his brethren, and the children of Phasiron in their tent. And when he began to smite them, and came up with his forces, Simon and his company went out of the citie, and burnt up the engines of warre, and fought against Bacchides, who was discomfited by them, and they afflicted him sore. For his counsell and travaile was in vaine. Wherefore he was very wroth at the wicked men that gave him counsell to come into the countrey, insomuch as he slew many of them, and purposed to returne into his owne countrey. Whereof when Ionathan had knowledge, he sent ambassadours unto him, to the end he should make peace with him, and deliver them the prisoners. Which thing hee accepted, and did according to his demaunds, and sware unto him that hee would never doe him harme all the dayes of his life. When therefore hee had restored unto him the prisoners that he had taken aforetime out of the land of Iudea, he returned and went his way into his owne land, neither came he any more into their borders. Thus the sword ceased from Israel: but Ionathan dwelt at Machmas, and began to governe the people, and he destroyed the ungodly men out of Israel.

CHAPTER IX

Bacchides maketh peace with Ionathan.

CHAPTER X

IN the hundreth and sixtieth yere, Alexander the sonne of Antiochus surnamed Epiphanes, went up and tooke Ptolemais: for the people had received him, by meanes whereof he reigned there. Now when king Demetrius heard thereof, he gathered together an exceeding great host, and went foorth against him to fight. Moreover Demetrius sent letters unto Ionathan with loving wordes, so as he magnified him. For, said hee, Let us first make peace with him before he ioyne with Alexander against us. Else he wil remember all the evils that we have done against him, and against his brethren and his people. Wherefore he gave him authority to gather together an host, and to provide weapons that hee might aide him in battell: he commaunded also that the hostages that were in the towre, should be delivered him. Then came Ionathan to Ierusalem, and read the letters in the audience of all the people, and of them that were in the towre. Who were sore afraid when they heard that the king had given him authoritie to gather together an host. Whereupon they of the towre delivered their hostages unto Ionathan, and he delivered them unto their

Demetrius maketh large offers to have peace with Ionathan.

I. MACCABEES

CHAPTER X

parents. This done, Ionathan setled himselfe in Ierusalem, and began to build and repaire the citie. And he commaunded the workemen to build the wals, and the mount Sion round about with square stones, for fortification, and they did so. Then the strangers that were in the fortresses which Bacchides had built, fled away: insomuch as every man left his place, and went into his owne country. Onely at Bethsura certaine of those that had forsaken the law, and the commaundements remained still: for it was their place of refuge. Now when king Alexander had heard what promises Demetrius had sent unto Ionathan: when also it was told him of the battels and noble acts which he and his brethren had done, and of the paines that they had indured, he said, Shal we find such another man? Now therefore we will make him our friend, and confederate. Upon this he wrote a letter and sent it unto him according to these words, saying: King Alexander to his brother Ionathan, sendeth greeting: We have heard of thee, that thou art a man of great power, and meete to be our friend. Wherefore now this day we ordaine thee to bee the high priest of thy nation, and to be called the kings friend, (and therewithall he sent him a purple robe and a crowne of gold) [and require thee] to take our part, and keepe friendship with us. So in the seventh moneth of the hundreth and sixtieth yere, at the feast of the Tabernacles, Ionathan put on the holy robe, and gathered together forces, and provided much armour. Wherof when Demetrius heard, he was very sory, and said, What have we done that Alexander hath prevented us, in making amity with the Iewes to strengthen himself? I also will write unto them words of encouragement [and promise them] dignities and gifts, that I may have their ayde. He sent unto him therefore, to this effect: King Demetrius unto the people of the Iewes, sendeth greeting: Whereas you have kept covenants with us, and continued in our friendship, not ioyning your selves with our enemies, we have heard hereof, and are glad: Wherefore now continue yee still to be faithful unto us, and we will well recompence you for the things you doe in our behalfe, and will grant you many immunities, and give you rewards. And now I doe free you, and for your sake I release all the Iewes from tributes, and from the customes of salt, and from crowne taxes, and from that which apperteineth unto me to receive for the third part of the seed, and the halfe of the fruit of the trees, I release it from this day forth, so that they shall not be taken of the land of Iudea, nor of the three governments which are added thereunto out of the country of Samaria and Galile, from this day forth for evermore. Let Ierusalem also bee holy and free,

His letters to the Iewes.

I. MACCABEES

CHAPTER X

with the borders thereof, both from tenths and tributes. And as for the towre which is at Ierusalem, I yeeld up my authoritie over it, and give it to the high Priest, that he may set in it such men as he shall choose to keepe it. Moreover I freely set at libertie every one of the Iewes that were carried captives out of the land of Iudea, into any part of my kingdome, and I will that all my officers remit the tributes, even of their cattell. Furthermore, I will that all the Feasts and Sabbaths, and New moones and solemne dayes, and the three dayes before the Feast, and the three dayes after the Feast, shall be all dayes of immunitie and freedom for all the Iewes in my realme. Also no man shall have authoritie to meddle with them, or to molest any of them in any matter. [I will further] that there be enrolled amongst the kings forces about thirtie thousand men of the Iewes, unto whom pay shall be given as belongeth to all the kings forces. And of them some shalbe placed in the kings strong holds, of whom also some shall be set over the affaires of the kingdome, which are of trust: and I will that their overseers and governours be of themselves, and that they live after their owne lawes, even as the King hath commanded in the land of Iudea. And concerning the three governments that are added to Iudea from the countrey of Samaria, let them be ioyned with Iudea, that they may be reckoned to be under one, nor bound to obey other authoritie then the high priests. As for Ptolemais and the land pertaining thereto, I give it as a free gift to the Sanctuary at Ierusalem, for the necessary expences of the Sanctuary. Moreover, I give every yeere fifteene thousand shekels of silver, out of the Kings accompts from the places appertaining. And all the overplus which the officers payed not in as in former time, from henceforth shalbe given towards the workes of the Temple. And besides this, the five thousand shekels of silver, which they tooke from the uses of the Temple out of the accompts yeere by yeere, even those things shall be released, because they appertaine to the Priests that minister. And whosoever they be that flee unto the Temple at Ierusalem, or be within the liberties thereof, being indebted unto the King, or for any other matter, let them be at libertie, and all that they have in my realme. For the building also and repairing of the workes of the Sanctuary, expences shalbe given of the Kings accompts. Yea, and for the building of the walles of Ierusalem, and the fortifying thereof round about, expences shall bee given out of the Kings accompts, as also for building of the walles in Iudea. Now when Ionathan and the people heard these words, they gave no credite unto them, nor received them, because they remembred the great evill that he had done in Israel;

I. MACCABEES

CHAPTER X

Ionathan maketh peace with Alexander,

Who killeth Demetrius,

and marieth the daughter of Ptolomeus.

Ionathan is sent for by him, and much honoured,

for hee had afflicted them very sore. But with Alexander they were well pleased, because hee was the first that entreated of peace with them, and they were confederate with him alwayes. Then gathered King Alexander great forces, and camped over against Demetrius. And after the two Kings had ioyned battell, Demetrius hoste fled: but Alexander followed after him, and prevailed against them. And he continued the battell very sore untill the Sunne went downe, and that day was Demetrius slaine. Afterward Alexander sent Embassadors to Ptoleme king of Egypt, with a message to this effect; Forsomuch as I am come againe to my realme, and am set in the throne of my progenitors, and have gotten the dominion, and overthrowen Demetrius, and recovered our countrey, (for after I had ioyned battell with him, both he, and his hoste was discomfited by us, so that we sit in the throne of his kingdome) now therefore let us make a league of amitie together, and give me now thy daughter to wife: and I will be thy son in law, and will give both thee and her, gifts according to thy dignity. Then Ptoleme the king gave answere, saying, Happy be the day wherein thou diddest returne into the land of thy fathers, and satest in the throne of their kingdome. And now will I doe to thee, as thou hast written: meet me therefore at Ptolemais, that wee may see one another, for I will marry my daughter to thee according to thy desire. So Ptolome went out of Egypt with his daughter Cleopatra, and they came unto Ptolemais in the hundred threescore and second yeere. Where king Alexander meeting him, gave unto him his daughter Cleopatra, and celebrated her marriage at Ptolemais with great glory, as the maner of kings is. Now king Alexander had written unto Ionathan, that hee should come and meete him. Who thereupon went honourably to Ptolemais, where he met the two kings, and gave them and their friends silver and golde, and many presents, and found favour in their sight. At that time certaine pestilent fellowes of Israel, men of a wicked life, assembled themselves against him, to accuse him: but the king would not heare them. Yea more then that, the king commanded to take off his garments, and clothe him in purple: and they did so. Also he made him sit by himselfe, and said unto his princes, Goe with him into the midst of the city, and make proclamation, that no man complaine against him of any matter, and that no man troble him for any maner of cause. Now when his accusers sawe that he was honoured according to the proclamation, and clothed in purple, they fled all away. So the king honoured him, and wrote him amongst his chiefe friends, and made him a duke, and partaker of his dominion. Afterward Ionathan returned to Ierusalem with

I. MACCABEES

peace and gladnes. Furthermore, in the hundreth threescore and fifth yeere, came Demetrius sonne of Demetrius, out of Crete into the land of his fathers. Whereof when king Alexander heard tell, he was right sory, and returned into Antioch. Then Demetrius made Apollonius the governour of Coelosyria his general, who gathered together a great hoste, and camped in Iamnia, and sent unto Ionathan the high Priest, saying, Thou alone liftest up thy selfe against us, and I am laughed to scorne for thy sake, and reproched, and why doest thou vaunt thy power against us in the mountaines? Now therefore if thou trustest in thine owne strength, come downe to us into the plaine field, and there let us trie the matter together, for with me is the power of the cities. Aske and learne who I am, and the rest that take our part, and they shal tel thee that thy foot is not able to stand before our face; for thy fathers have bene twice put to flight in their owne land. Wherefore now thou shalt not be able to abide the horsemen and so great a power in the plaine, where is neither stone nor flint, nor place to flee unto. So when Ionathan heard these words of Apollonius, he was moved in his mind, and choosing ten thousand men, he went out of Ierusalem, where Simon his brother met him for to helpe him. And hee pitched his tents against Ioppe: but they of Ioppe shut him out of the citie, because Apollonius had a garison there. Then Ionathan laid siege unto it: whereupon they of the citie let him in for feare: and so Ionathan wan Ioppe. Wherof when Apollonius heard, he tooke three thousand horsemen with a great hoste of footmen, and went to Azotus as one that iourneyed, and therewithal drew him forth into the plaine, because he had a great number of horsemen, in whom he put his trust. Then Ionathan followed after him to Azotus, where the armies ioyned battell. Now Apollonius had left a thousand horsemen in ambush. And Ionathan knew that there was an ambushment behinde him; for they had compassed in his host, and cast darts at the people, from morning till evening. But the people stood still, as Ionathan had commanded them: and so the enemies horses were tired. Then brought Simon forth his hoste, and set them against the footmen, (for the horsmen were spent) who were discomfited by him, and fled. The horsemen also being scattered in the field, fled to Azotus, and went into Bethdagon their idols temple for safety. But Ionathan set fire on Azotus, and the cities round about it, and tooke their spoiles, and the temple of Dagon, with them that were fled into it, he burnt with fire. Thus there were burnt and slaine with the sword, well nigh eight thousand men. And from thence Ionathan removed

CHAPTER X

and prevaileth against the forces of Demetrius the yonger,

and burneth the temple of Dagon.

I. MACCABEES

CHAPTER X — his hoste, and camped against Ascalon, where the men of the city came forth, and met him with great pompe. After this, returned Ionathan and his hoste unto Ierusalem, having many spoiles. Now when king Alexander heard these things, he honoured Ionathan yet more, and sent him a buckle of golde, as the use is to be given to such as are of the kings blood : he gave him also Accaron with the borders thereof in possession.

CHAPTER XI

AND the king of Egypt gathered together a great host like the sand that lieth upon the Sea shore, and many ships, and went about through deceit to get Alexanders kingdome, and ioyne it to his owne. Whereupon he tooke his iourney into Syria in peaceable maner, so as they of the cities opened unto him, and met him : for king Alexander had commanded them so to doe, because he was his father in law. Now as Ptolomee entred into the cities, he set in every one of them a garison of souldiers to keepe it. And when he came neere to Azotus, they shewed him the temple of Dagon that was burnt, and Azotus, and the suburbs thereof that were destroyed, and the bodies that were cast abroad, and them that he had burnt in the battell, for they had made heapes of them by the way where he should passe. Also they told the king whatsoever Ionathan had done, to the intent he might blame him : but the king helde his peace. Then Ionathan met the king with great pompe at Ioppa, where they saluted one another, and lodged. Afterward Ionathan when he had gone with the king to the river called Eleutherus, returned againe to Ierusalem. King Ptolomee therefore having gotten the dominion of the cities by the sea, unto Seleucia upon the sea coast, imagined wicked counsels against Alexander. Whereupon he sent embassadours unto king Demetrius, saying, Come, let us make a league betwixt us, and I will give thee my daughter whome Alexander hath, and thou shalt reigne in thy fathers kingdome : for I repent that I gave my daughter unto him, for he sought to slay me. Thus did he slander him, because he was desirous of his kingdome.

Ptolomeus taketh away his daughter from Alexander, and entreth upon his kingdome.

Wherefore he tooke his daughter from him, and gave her to Demetrius, and forsooke Alexander, so that their hatred was openly knowen. Then Ptolomee entred into Antioch, where he set two crownes upon his head, the crowne of Asia, and of Egypt. In the meane season was king Alexander in Cilicia, because those that dwelt in those parts, had revolted from him. But when Alexander heard of this, hee came to warre against him, whereupon king

I. MACCABEES

CHAPTER XI

Ptolomee brought forth his hoste, and met him with a mightie power, and put him to flight. So Alexander fled into Arabia, there to be defended, but king Ptolomee was exalted. For Zabdiel the Arabian tooke off Alexanders head, and sent it unto Ptolomee. King Ptolemee also died the third day after, and they that were in the strong holds, were slaine one of another. By this meanes Demetrius reigned in the hundreth, threescore and seventh yeere. At the same time Ionathan gathered together them that were in Iudea, to take the towre that was in Ierusalem, and he made many engines of warre against it. Then certaine ungodly persons who hated their owne people, went unto the king, and told him that Ionathan besieged the towre. Whereof when he heard, he was angry, and immediately removing, he cam to Ptolemais, and wrote unto Ionathan, that he should not lay siege to the towre, but come and speake with him at Ptolemais in great haste. Neverthelesse Ionathan when he heard this, commanded to besiege it [still] and he chose certaine of the Elders of Israel, and the priests, and put himselfe in perill, and tooke silver and gold, and rayment, and divers presents besides, and went to Ptolemais, unto the king, where he found favour in his sight. And though certaine ungodly men of the people, had made complaints against him, yet the king entreated him as his predecessors had done before, and promoted him in the sight of all his friends, and confirmed him in the high priesthood, and in all the honours that hee had before, and gave him preeminence among his chiefe friends. Then Ionathan desired the king, that hee would make Iudea free from tribute, as also the three governments with the countrey of Samaria, and he promised him three hundred talents. So the king consented and wrote letters unto Ionathan, of all these things after this maner. King Demetrius unto his brother Ionathan, and unto the nation of the Iewes, sendeth greeting. We send you heere a copie of the letter, which we did write unto our cousin Lasthenes, concerning you, that you might see it. King Demetrius unto his father Lasthenes, sendeth greeting : We are determined to doe good to the people of the Iewes, who are our friends, and keepe covenants with us, because of their good will towards us. Wherefore we have ratified unto them the borders of Iudea, with the three governments of Apherema, and Lidda, and Ramathem, that are added unto Iudea, from the countrie of Samaria, and all things appertaining unto them, for all such, as doe sacrifice in Ierusalem, in stead of the paiments, which the king received of them yeerely aforetime out of the fruits of the earth, and of trees. And as for other things

Alexander is slaine, and Ptolemeus dieth within three dayes.

Ionathan besiegeth the towre at Ierusalem.

The Iewes and he are much honoured by Demetrius,

I. MACCABEES

CHAPTER XI

that belong unto us of the tithes and customes pertaining unto us, as also the salt pits, and the crowne taxes, which are due unto us, we discharge them of them all for their reliefe. And nothing heereof shall be revoked from this time foorth for ever. Now therefore see that thou make a copie of these things, and let it be delivered unto Ionathan, and set upon the holy mount in a conspicuous place. After this, when king Demetrius saw that the land was quiet before him, and that no resistance was made against him, he sent away all his forces every one to his owne place, except certaine bands of strangers, whom he had gathered from the iles of the heathen, wherefore all the forces of his fathers hated him. Moreover there was one Tryphon, that had beene of Alexanders part afore, who seeing that all the hoste murmured against Demetrius, went to Simalcue the Arabian, that brought up Antiochus the yong sonne of Alexander, and lay sore upon him, to deliver him [this young Antiochus] that he might raigne in his fathers stead: he told him therefore all that Demetrius had done, and how his men of warre were at enmitie with him, and there he remained a long season. In the meane time Ionathan sent unto king Demetrius, that hee would cast those of the towre out of Ierusalem, and those also in the fortresses. For they fought against Israel. So Demetrius sent unto Ionathan, saying, I will not onely doe this for thee, and thy people, but I will greatly honour thee and thy nation, if opportunitie serve. Now therefore thou shalt do wel if thou send me men to helpe me; for all my forces are gone from me. Upon this Ionathan sent him three thousand strong men unto Antioch, and when they came to the king, the king was very glad of their comming. Howbeit, they that were of the citie, gathered themselves together into the midst of the citie, to the number of an hundreth and twentie thousand men, and would have slaine the king. Wherefore the king fled into the court, but they of the citie kept the passages of the citie, and began to fight. Then the king called to the Iewes for helpe, who came unto him all at once, and dispersing themselves through the city, slew that day in the citie to the number of an hundred thousand. Also they set fire on the citie, and gat many spoiles that day, and delivered the king. So when they of the city saw, that the Iewes had got the city as they would, their courage was abated, wherefore they made supplication to the king, and cried, saying: Graunt us peace, and let the Iewes cease from assaulting us and the citie. With that they cast away their weapons, and made peace, and the Iewes were honoured in the sight of the king, and in the sight of all

Who is rescued by the Iewes from his owne subiects in Antioch.

298

I. MACCABEES

that were in his realme, and they returned to Ierusalem having great spoiles. So king Demetrius sate on the throne of his kingdome, and the land was quiet before him. Neverthelesse hee dissembled in all that ever hee spake, and estranged himselfe from Ionathan, neither rewarded he him, according to the benefits which hee had received of him, but troubled him very sore. After this returned Tryphon, and with him the yong childe Antiochus, who reigned and was crowned. Then there gathered unto him all the men of warre whom Demetrius had put away, and they fought against Demetrius, who turned his backe and fled. Moreover Triphon tooke the Elephants, and wonne Antioch. At that time yong Antiochus wrote unto Ionathan, saying; I confirme thee in the high Priesthood, and appoint thee ruler over the foure governments, and to be one of the kings friends. Upon this he sent him golden vessels to be served in, and gave him leave to drinke in gold, and to bee clothed in purple, and to weare a golden buckle. His brother Simon also he made captaine from the place called the ladder of Tyrus, unto the borders of Egypt. Then Ionathan went foorth and passed through the cities beyond the water, and all the forces of Syria, gathered themselves unto him for to helpe him: and when he came to Ascalon, they of the city met him honorably. From whence he went to Gaza, but they of Gaza shut him out; wherefore hee layd siege unto it, and burned the suburbs thereof with fire, and spoiled them. Afterward when they of Gaza made supplication unto Ionathan, he made peace with them, and tooke the sonnes of the chiefe men for hostages, and sent them to Ierusalem, and passed through the countrey unto Damascus. Now when Ionathan heard that Demetrius Princes were come to Cades which is in Galilee, with a great power, purposing to remove him out of the countrey, hee went to meet them, and left Simon his brother in the countrey. Then Simon encamped against Bethsura, and fought against it a long season, and shut it up: but they desired to have peace with him, which he granted them, and then put them out from thence, and tooke the city, and set a garrison in it. As for Ionathan and his hoste, they pitched at the water of Gennesar, from whence betimes in the morning they gate them to the plaine of Nasor. And behold, the hoste of strangers met them in the plaine, who having layed men in ambush for him in the mountaines, came themselves over against him. So when they that lay in ambush rose out of their places, and ioyned battel, al that were of Ionathans side fled. In so much as there was not one of them left, except Mattathias the sonne of Absolon, and Indas the sonne of Calphi

CHAPTER XI

Antiochus the yonger honoureth Ionathan.

His exploits in divers places.

299

I. MACCABEES

CHAPTER XI — the captaines of the hoste. Then Ionathan rent his clothes, and cast earth upon his head, and prayed. Afterwards turning againe to battell, he put them to flight, and so they ranne away. Now when his owne men that were fled saw this, they turned againe unto him, and with him pursued them to Cades, even unto their owne tents, and there they camped. So there were slaine of the heathen that day, about three thousand men, but Ionathan returned to Ierusalem.

CHAPTER XII

Ionathan reneweth his league with the Romanes and Lacedemonians.

NOWE when Ionathan saw that the time served him, he chose certaine men and sent them to Rome, for to confirme and renew the friendship that they had with them. He sent letters also to the Lacedemonians, and to other places, for the same purpose. So they went unto Rome, and entred into the Senate, and said, Ionathan the high Priest, and the people of the Iewes sent us unto you, to the end you should renew the friendship which you had with them, and league, as in former time. Upon this the Romanes gave them letters unto the governours of every place, that they should bring them into the land of Iudea peaceably. And this is the copy of the letters which Ionathan wrote to the Lacedemonians: Ionathan the hie Priest, and the Elders of the nation, and the Priestes and the other people of the Iewes, unto the Lacedemonians their brethren, send greeting. There were letters sent in times past unto Onias the high Priest from Darius, who reigned then among you, to signifie that you are our brethren, as the copy here under-written doeth specific. At which time Onias intreated the Embassador that was sent, honourably, and received the letters, wherein declaration was made of the league and friendship. Therefore we also, albeit we need none of these things, for that wee have the holy bookes of Scripture in our hands to comfort us, have neverthelesse attempted to send unto you, for the renewing of brotherhood and friendship, lest we should become strangers unto you altogether: for there is a long time passed since you sent unto us. We therefore at all times without ceasing, both in our Feasts, and other convenient dayes, doe remember you in the sacrifices which we offer, and in our prayers, as reason is, and as it becommeth us to thinke upon our brethren: and wee are right glad of your honour. As for our selves, wee have had great troubles and warres on every side, forsomuch as the kings that are round about us have fought against us. Howbeit wee would not be troublesome unto you, nor to others of our confederates and friends in these warres: for wee

I. MACCABEES

have helpe from heaven that succoureth us, so as we are delivered from our enemies, and our enemies are brought under foote. For this cause we chose Numenius the son of Antiochus, and Antipater the sonne of Iason, and sent them unto the Romanes, to renew the amitie that we had with them, and the former league. We commanded them also to goe unto you, and to salute you, and to deliver you our letters, concerning the renewing of our brotherhood. Wherefore now ye shall doe well to give us an answere thereto. And this is the copy of the letters which Omiares sent: Areus king of the Lacedemonians, to Onias the hie Priest, greeting. It is found in writing, that the Lacedemonians and Iewes are brethren, and that they are of the stocke of Abraham: now therefore, since this is come to our knowledge, you shall doe well to write unto us of your prosperitie. We doe write backe againe to you, that your cattell and goods are ours, and ours are yours. We doe command therefore [our Embassadours] to make report unto you on this wise. Now when Ionathan heard that Demetrius princes were come to fight against him with a greater hoste then afore, hee remooved from Ierusalem, and met them in the land of Amathis: for he gave them no respite to enter his countrey. He sent spies also unto their tents, who came againe, and tolde him, that they were appointed to come upon them in the night season. Wherefore so soone as the Sunne was downe, Ionathan commaunded his men to watch, and to be in armes, that all the night long they might bee ready to fight: Also he sent foorth sentinels round about the hoste. But when the adversaries heard that Ionathan and his men were ready for battell, they feared, and trembled in their hearts, and they kindled fires in their campe. Howbeit Ionathan and his company knew it not till the morning: for they saw the lights burning. Then Ionathan pursued after them, but overtooke them not: for they were gone over the river Eleutherus. Wherefore Ionathan turned to the Arabians, who were called Zabadeans, and smote them, and tooke their spoiles. And removing thence, he came to Damascus, and so passed through all the countrey. Simon also went foorth, and passed through the countrey unto Ascalon, and the holds there adioyning, from whence he turned aside to Ioppe, and wanne it. For he had heard that they would deliver the hold unto them that tooke Demetrius part, wherefore he set a garison there to keepe it. After this came Ionathan home againe, and calling the Elders of the people together, hee consulted with them about building strong holdes in Iudea, and making the walles of Ierusalem higher, and raising a great mount betweene the towre and the city, for to

CHAPTER XII

The forces of Demetrius thinking to surprise Ionathan, flee away for feare.

Ionathan fortifieth the castles in Iudea.

I. MACCABEES

CHAPTER XII / separate it from the city, that so it might be alone, that men might neither sell nor buy in it. Upon this they came together, to build up the citie forasmuch as [part of] the wall toward the brooke on the East side was fallen down, and they repaired that which was called Caphenatha. Simon also set up Adida, in Sephela, and made it strong with gates and barres. Now Tryphon went about to get the kingdome of Asia, and to kill Antiochus the king, that hee might set the crowne upon his owne head. Howbeit, he was afraid that Ionathan would not suffer him, and that he would fight against him, wherefore he sought a way, howe to take Ionathan, that he might kill him. So he removed, and came to Bethsan. Then Ionathan went out to meet him with fourtie thousand men, chosen for the battell, and came to Bethsan. Now when Tryphon saw that Ionathan came with so great a force, hee durst not stretch his hande against him, but received him honourably, and commended him unto all his friends, and gave him gifts, and commaunded his men of warre to be as obedient unto him, as to himselfe. Unto Ionathan also hee said, Why hast thou put all this people to so great trouble, seeing there is no warre betwixt us? Therefore send them now home againe, and chuse a few men to waite on thee, and come thou with me to Ptolemais, for I will give it thee and the rest of the strong holds and forces, and all that have any charge: as for me, I will returne and depart: for this is the cause of my comming. So Ionathan beleeving him, did as he bade him, and sent away his host, who went into the land of Iudea. And with himselfe hee retained but three thousand men, of whome he sent two thousand

and is shut up by the fraud of Tryphon in Ptolemais. / into Galile, and one thousand went with him. Now assoone as Ionathan entred into Ptolemais, they of Ptolemais shut the gates, and tooke him, and all them that came with him, they slewe with the sword. Then sent Tryphon an hoste of footmen, and horsemen into Galile, and into the great plaine, to destroy all Ionathans company. But when they knew that Ionathan and they that were with him were taken and slaine, they encouraged one another, and went close together, prepared to fight. They therfore that followed upon them, perceiving that they were ready to fight for their lives, turned back againe. Whereupon they all came into the land of Iudea peaceably, and there they bewailed Ionathan and them that were with him, and they were sore afraid, wherfore all Israel made great lamentation. Then all the heathen that were round about them, sought to destroy them. For, said they, they have no captaine, nor any to helpe them. Now therfore let us make war upon them, and take away their memorial from amongst men.

I. MACCABEES

CHAPTER XIII

NOW when Simon heard that Tryphon had gathered together a great hoste to invade the land of Iudea, and destroy it, and saw that the people was in great trembling and feare, he went up to Ierusalem, and gathered the people together, and gave them exhortation, saying: Yee your selves know, what great things I and my brethren, and my fathers house have done for the lawes, and the Sanctuarie, the battels also, and troubles which we have seene, by reason whereof all my brethren are slaine for Israels sake, and I am left alone. Now therefore be it farre from me, that I should spare mine owne life in any time of trouble: for I am no better then my brethren. Doubtlesse I will avenge my nation and the Sanctuarie, and our wives, and our children: for all the heathen are gathered to destroy us, of very malice. Now as soone as the people heard these words, their spirit revived. And they answered with a loud voice, saying, Thou shalt bee our leader in stead of Iudas and Ionathan thy brother. Fight thou our battels, and what soever thou commandest us, that will we doe. *Simon is made captaine in his brother Ionathans roume.* So then he gathered together all the men of warre, and made hast to finish the walles of Ierusalem, and he fortified it round about. Also he sent Ionathan, the sonne of Absolom, and with him a great power to Ioppe, who casting out them that were therein, remained there in it. So Tryphon removed from Ptolemais, with a great power to invade the land of Iudea, and Ionathan was with him in warde. But Simon pitched his tents at Adida, over against the plaine. Now when Tryphon knew that Simon was risen up in stead of his brother Ionathan, and meant to ioyne battell with him, he sent messengers unto him, saying, Whereas we have Ionathan thy brother in hold, it is for money that he is owing unto the kings treasure, concerning the businesse that was committed unto him. Wherefore, now send an hundred talents of silver, and two of his sonnes for hostages, that when he is at liberty he may not revolt from us, and we will let him goe. Heereupon Simon, albeit he perceived that they spake deceiptfully unto him, yet sent he the money, and the children, lest peradventure he should procure to himselfe great hatred of the people: who might have said, Because I sent him not the money, and the children, therefore is [Ionathan] dead. So he sent them the children, and the hundred talents: Howbeit [Tryphon] dissembled, neither would he let Ionathan goe. And after this came Tryphon to invade the land, and destroy it, going round about by the way that leadeth unto Adora, but Simon and *Tryphon getteth two of Ionathans sonnes into his hands, and slayeth their father.*

I. MACCABEES

CHAPTER XIII

his host marched against him in every place wheresoever he went. Now they that were in the towre, sent messengers unto Tryphon, to the end that he should hasten his comming unto them by the wildernesse, and send them victuals. Wherefore Tryphon made readie all his horsemen to come that night, but there fell a very great snow, by reason whereof he came not: So he departed and came into the countrey of Galaad. And when he came neere to Bascama, he slew Ionathan, who was buried there. Afterward Tryphon returned, and went into his owne land. Then sent Simon and tooke the bones of Ionathan his brother, and buried them in Modin the citie of his fathers. And all Israel made great lamentation for him, and bewailed him many daies. Simon also built a monument upon the Sepulchre of his father and his brethren, and raised it aloft to the sight, with hewen stone behind and before. Moreover hee set up seven pyramides one against another, for his father and his mother, and his foure brethren. And in these he made cunning devices, about the which he set great pillars, and upon the pillars he made all their armour for a perpetuall memory, and by the armour, ships carved, that they might be seene of all that saile on the sea. This is the Sepulchre which he made at Modin, and it standeth yet unto this day. Now Tryphon dealt deceitfully with the yong king Antiochus, and slew him, and he raigned in his stead, and crowned himselfe king of Asia, and brought a great calamitie upon the land. Then Simon built up the strong holds in Iudea, and fensed them about with high towres, and great walles and gates and barres, and layd up victuals therein. Moreover Simon chose men, and sent to king Demetrius, to the end he should give the land an immunitie, because all that Tryphon did, was to spoyle. Unto whom king Demetrius answered and wrote after this maner. King Demetrius unto Simon the high Priest, and friend of kings, as also unto the Elders and nation of the Iewes, sendeth greeting. The golden crowne, and the scarlet robe which ye sent unto us, we have received, and wee are ready to make a stedfast peace with you, yea and to write unto our officers to confirme the immunities which we have granted. And whatsoever covenants we have made with you, shall stand, and the strong holdes which yee have builded shalbe your owne. As for any oversight or fault committed unto this day, we forgive it, and the crowne taxe also which yee owe us, if there were any other tribute paide in Ierusalem, it shall no more be paide. And looke who are meet among you to be in our court, let them be inrolled, and let there be peace betwixt us. Thus the yoke of the heathen was taken away from Israel, in the

The tombe of Ionathan.

Simon is favoured by Demetrius,

I. MACCABEES

hundred and seventieth yeere. Then the people of Israel began to write in their instruments, and contracts, in the first yeere of Simon the high Priest, the governour, and leader of the Iewes. In those dayes Simon camped against Gaza, and besieged it round about; he made also an engine of warre, and set it by the city, and battered a certaine towre, and tooke it. And they that were in the Engine leapt into the citie, whereupon there was a great uproare in the citie: insomuch as the people of the citie rent their clothes, and climed upon the walles, with their wives and children, and cried with a lowd voice, beseeching Simon to grant them peace. And they said, Deale not with us according to our wickednesse, but according to thy mercy. So Simon was appeased towards them, and fought no more against them, but put them out of the citie, and cleansed the houses wherein the idols were: and so entred into it, with songs, and thanksgiving. Yea, he put all uncleannesse out of it, and placed such men there, as would keepe the Law, and made it stronger then it was before, and built therein a dwelling place for himselfe. They also of the towre in Ierusalem were kept so strait, that they could neither come foorth, nor goe into the countrey, nor buy, nor sell, wherefore they were in great distresse for want of victuals, and a great number of them perished through famine. Then cried they to Simon, beseeching him to bee at one with them, which thing hee graunted them, and when he had put them out from thence, he cleansed the towre from pollutions: and entred into it the three and twentieth day of the second moneth, in the hundred seventie and one yere, with thanksgiving, and branches of palme trees, and with harpes, and cymbals, and with viols and hymnes, and songs: because there was destroyed a great enemy out of Israel. Hee ordained also that that day should be kept every yeere with gladnes. Moreover, the hill of the Temple that was by the towre he made stronger then it was, and there hee dwelt himselfe with his company. And when Simon sawe that Iohn his sonne was a valiant man, he made him captaine of all the hostes and dwelt in Gazara.

CHAPTER XIII

and winneth Gaza, and the towre at Hierusalem.

CHAPTER XIIII

NOW in the hundred three-score and twelfth yeere, king Demetrius gathered his forces together, and went into Media, to get him helpe to fight against Tryphon. But when Arsaces the king of Persia and Media, heard that Demetrius was entred within his borders, he sent one of his princes to take

I. MACCABEES

CHAPTER XIIII

Demetrius is taken by the King of Persia.

The good deedes of Simon to his countrey.

him alive. Who went and smote the hoste of Demetrius, and tooke him and brought him to Arsaces, by whom hee was put in warde. As for the land of Iudea, that was quiet all the dayes of Simon: for he sought the good of his nation, in such wise, as that evermore his authoritie and honour pleased them well. And as he was honourable (in all his acts) so in this, that he tooke Ioppe for an haven, and made an entrance to the yles of the Sea, and enlarged the boundes of his nation, and recovered the countrey, and gathered together a great number of captives, and had the dominion of Gazara and Bethsura, and the towre, out of the which he tooke all uncleannesse, neither was there any that resisted him. Then did they till their ground in peace, and the earth gave her increase, and the trees of the field their fruit. The ancient men sate all in the streetes, communing together of good things, and the young men put on glorious and warrelike apparell. He provided victuals for the cities, and set in them all maner of munition, so that his honourable name was renowmed unto the end of the world. He made peace in the land, and Israel reioyced with great ioy: for every man sate under his vine, and his figge-tree, and there was none to fray them: neither was there any left in the lande to fight against them: yea, the Kings themselves were overthrowen in those dayes. Moreover hee strengthened all those of his people that were brought low: the Law he searched out, and every contemner of the Law, and wicked person, he tooke away. He beautified the Sanctuary, and multiplied the vessels of the Temple. Now when it was heard at Rome, and as far as Sparta, that Ionathan was dead, they were very sorie. But assoone as they heard that his brother Simon was made high Priest in his stead, and ruled the countrey, and the cities therein,

The Lacedemonians and Romans renew their league with him.

they wrote unto him in tables of brasse, to renew the friendship and league which they had made with Iudas and Ionathan his brethren: which writings were read before the Congregation at Ierusalem. And this is the copy of the letters that the Lacedemonians sent: The rulers of the Lacedemonians, with the city, unto Simon the high Priest, and the Elders and Priestes, and residue of the people of the Iewes, our brethren, send greeting. The Embassadors that were sent unto our people, certified us of your glory and honour, wherefore we were glad of their comming, and did register the things that they spake, in the counsell of the people, in this maner: Numenius sonne of Antiochus, and Antipater sonne of Iason, the Iewes Embassadours, came unto us, to renew the friendship they had with us. And it pleased the people to entertaine the men honourably, and to put the copy of

I. MACCABEES

their embassage in publike records, to the end the people of the Lacedemonians might have a memoriall therof: furthermore we have written a copy thereof unto Simon the hie Priest. After this, Simon sent Numenius to Rome, with a great shield of golde of a thousand pound weight, to confirme the league with them. Whereof when the people heard, they said, What thankes shall wee give to Simon and his sonnes? For hee and his brethren, and the house of his father, have established Israel, and chased away in fight their enemies from them, and confirmed their libertie. So then they wrote [it] in tables of brasse, which they set upon pillars in mount Sion, and this is the copie of the writing. The eighteenth day of the moneth Elul, in the hundred threescore and twelft yeere, being the third yeere of Simon the hie priest, at Saramel in the great congregation of the priests and people, and rulers of the nation, and elders of the country, were these things notified unto us. Forsomuch as often times there have bin warres in the countrey, wherin for the maintenance of their Sanctuarie, and the law, Simon the sonne of Mattathias of the posteritie of Iarib, together with his brethren, put themselves in ieopardie, and resisting the enemies of their nation, did their nation great honour. (For after that Ionathan having gathered his nation together, and bene their hie priest, was added to his people, their enemies purposed to invade their countrey that they might destroy it, and lay hands on the Sanctuary. At which time Simon rose up, and fought for his nation, and spent much of his own substance, and armed the valiant men of his nation, and gave them wages, and fortified the cities of Iudea, together with Bethsura that lieth upon the borders of Iudea, where the armour of the enemies had bin before, but he set a garison of Iewes there. Moreover, hee fortified Ioppe which lieth upon the Sea, and Gazara that bordereth upon Azotus, where the enemies had dwelt before: but hee placed Iewes there, and furnished them with all things convenient for the reparation thereof.) The people therefore seeing the acts of Simon, and unto what glory he thought to bring his nation, made him their governor and chiefe priest, because he had done all these things, and for the iustice and faith which hee kept to his nation, and for that hee sought by all meanes to exalt his people. For in his time things prospered in his hands, so that the heathen were taken out of their countrey, and they also that were in the citie of David in Ierusalem, who had made themselves a towre, out of which they issued, and polluted all about the Sanctuarie, and did much hurt in the holy place. But he placed Iewes therein, and fortified it for the safetie of the countrey, and the city, and

CHAPTER XIIII

A memoriall of his actes is set up in Sion.

I. MACCABEES

CHAPTER XIIII

raised up the wals of Ierusalem. King Demetrius also confirmed him in the high priesthood, according to those things, and made him one of his friends, and honoured him with great honour. For he had heard say, that the Romanes had called the Iewes their friends, and confederates, and brethren, and that they had entertained the Embassadours of Simon honourably. Also that the Iewes and priests were wel pleased that Simon should be their governour, and high priest for ever until there should arise a faithfull prophet. Moreover, that he should be their captaine, and should take charge of the Sanctuarie, to set them over their workes, and over the countrey, and over the armour, and over the fortresses, that (I say) he should take charge of the Sanctuarie. Besides this, that he should be obeyed of every man, and that all the writings in the countrey should be made in his name, and that he should be clothed in purple, and weare gold. Also that it should be lawfull for none of the people or priests, to breake any of these things, or to gainesay his words, or to gather an assembly in the countrey without him, or to bee clothed in purple, or weare a buckle of gold. And whosoever should do otherwise, or breake any of these things, he should be punished. Thus it liked all the people to deale with Simon, and to do as hath bene said. Then Simon accepted hereof, and was well pleased to be high Priest, and captaine, and governour of the Iewes, and priests, and to defend them all. So they commanded that this writing should be put in tables of brasse, and that they should be set up within the compasse of the Sanctuary in a conspicuous place. Also that the copies therof should be laid up in the treasurie, to the ende that Simon and his sonnes might have them.

CHAPTER XV

MOREOVER Antiochus sonne of Demetrius the king, sent letters from the isles of the Sea, unto Simon the priest, and prince of the Iewes, and to all the people. The contents whereof were these: King Antiochus, to Simon the high Priest, and prince of his nation, and to the people of the Iewes, greeting, For as much as certaine pestilent men, have usurped the kingdome of our fathers, and my purpose is to chalenge it againe, that I may restore it to the old estate, and to that end have gathered a multitude of forraine souldiers together, and prepared shippes of warre, my meaning also being to goe through the countrey, that I may be avenged of them that have destroyed it, and made many cities in the kingdome desolate: Now therefore I

Antiochus desireth leave to passe through Iudea, and granteth great honours to Simon and the Iewes.

I. MACCABEES

confirme unto thee, all the oblations which the kings before me granted thee, and whatsoever gifts besides they granted. I give thee leave also to coine money for thy countrey with thine owne stampe. And as concerning Ierusalem, and the Sanctuarie, let them be free, and al the armour that thou hast made, and fortresses that thou hast built, and keepest in thy hands, let them remaine unto thee. And if any thing bee, or shall be owing to the king, let it be forgiven thee, from this time forth for evermore. Furthermore, when we have obtained our kingdome, we will honour thee, and thy nation, and thy temple with great honour, so that your honour shall bee knowen throughout the world. In the hundred threescore and fourteenth yeere, went Antiochus into the land of his fathers, at which time all the forces came together unto him, so that few were left with Tryphon. Wherefore being pursued by king Antiochus, he fled unto Dora, which lieth by the Sea side. For he saw, that troubles came upon him all at once, and that his forces had forsaken him. Then camped Antiochus against Dora, having with him, an hundred and twentie thousand men of warre, and eight thousand horsemen. And when he had compassed the citie round about, and ioyned ships close to the towne on the Sea side, hee vexed the citie by land, and by Sea, neither suffered he any to goe out or in. In the meane season came Numenius, and his company from Rome having letters to the kings and countries, wherein were written these things. Lucius, Consul of the Romanes, unto king Ptolomee greeting. The Iewes Embassadors our friends and confederates, came unto us to renew the old friendship and league, being sent from Simon the high Priest, and from the people of the Iewes. And they brought a shield of gold, of a thousand pound: we thought it good therefore, to write unto the kings and countries, that they should doe them no harme, nor fight against them, their cities, or countries, nor yet aide their enemies against them. It seemed also good to us, to receive the shield of them. If therefore there be any pestilent fellowes, that have fled from their countrie unto you, deliver them unto Simon the high priest, that hee may punish them according to their owne lawe. The same thing wrote hee likewise unto Demetrius the king, and Atalus, to Ariarathes, and Arsaces, and to all the countries, and to Sampsames, and the Lacedemonians, and to Delus, and Myndus, and Sycion, and Caria, and Samos, and Pamphylia, and Lycia, and Halicarnassus, and Rhodus, and Phaseilis, and Cos, and Sidee, and Aradus, and Gortina, and Cnidus, and Cyprus, and Cyrene. And the copy heereof they wrote, to Simon the high Priest. So

CHAPTER XV

The Romanes write to diverse kings and nations to favour the Iewes.

I. MACCABEES

CHAPTER XV

Antiochus quarrelleth with Simon,

Antiochus the king camped against Dora, the second day, assaulting it continually, and making engins, by which meanes he shut up Tryphon, that he could neither goe out nor in. At that time Simon sent him two thousand chosen men to aide him: silver also, and gold, and much armour. Neverthelesse, he would not receive them, but brake all the covenants which he had made with him afore, and became strange unto him. Furthermore hee sent unto him Athenobius, one of his friends to commune with him and say: You withhold Ioppe and Gazara with the towre that is in Ierusalem, which are cities of my realme. The borders thereof yee have wasted and done great hurt in the land, and got the dominion of many places within my kingdome. Now therefore deliver the cities which ye have taken, and the tributes of the places whereof yee have gotten dominion without the borders of Iudea. Or else give me for them five hundred talents of silver, and for the harme that you have done, and the tributes of the cities other five hundred talents: if not, we wil come and fight against you. So Athenobius the kings friend came to Ierusalem, and when hee saw the glory of Simon, and the cupboard of gold, and silver plate, and his great attendance, he was astonished and told him the kings message. Then answered Simon, and said unto him, We have neither taken other mens land, nor holden that which apperteineth to others, but the inheritance of our fathers, which our enemies had wrongfully in possession a certaine time. Wherefore we having opportunitie, hold the inheritance of our fathers. And whereas thou demaundest Ioppe and Gazara; albeit they did great harme unto the people in our countrey, yet will we give an hundred talents for them. Hereunto Athenobius answered him not a word, but returned in a rage to the king, and made report unto him of these speaches, and of the glory of Simon, and of all that hee had seene: whereupon the king was exceeding wroth.

and sendeth some to annoy Iudea.

In the meane time fled Tryphon by ship unto Orthosias. Then the king made Cendebeus captaine of the sea coast, and gave him an hoste of footmen and horsemen, and commanded him to remove his hoste toward Iudea: also hee commanded him to build up Cedron, and to fortifie the gates, and to warre against the people, but as for the king [himselfe] he pursued Tryphon. So Cendebeus came to Iamnia, and began to provoke the people, and to invade Iudea, and to take the people prisoners, and slay them. And when hee had built up Cedron, he set horsemen there, and an host [of footmen] to the end that issuing out, they might make outroades upon the wayes of Iudea, as the king had commanded him.

I. MACCABEES

CHAPTER XVI

THEN came up Iohn from Gazara, and told Simon his father, what Cendebeus had done. Wherefore Simon called his two eldest sonnes, Iudas and Iohn, and said unto them, I and my brethren, and my fathers house have ever from our youth unto this day fought against the enemies of Israel, and things have prospered so well in our hands, that wee have delivered Israel oftentimes. But now I am old, and yee [by Gods mercy] are of a sufficient age: Be ye in stead of mee, and my brother, and goe and fight for our nation, and the helpe from heaven be with you. *Iudas and Iohn prevaile against the forces sent by Antiochus.* So hee chose out of the countrey twentie thousand men of warre with horsemen, who went out against Cendebeus, and rested that night at Modin. And when as they rose in the morning, and went into the plaine, behold, a mighty great hoste both of footmen, and horsmen, came against them: Howbeit there was a water brooke betwixt them. So hee and his people pitched over against them, and when hee saw that the people were afraid to goe over the water brooke, hee went first over himselfe, and then the men seeing him, passed through after him. [That done] he divided his men, and set the horsemen in the midst of the footemen: for the enemies horsemen were very many. Then sounded they with the holy Trumpets: whereupon Cendebeus and his hoste were put to flight, so that many of them were slaine, and the remnant gat them to the strong hold. At that time was Iudas Iohns brother wounded: But Iohn still followed after them, untill he came to Cedron which [Cendebeus] had built. So they fled even unto the towres in the fields of Azotus, wherefore hee burnt it with fire: So that there were slaine of them about two thousand men. Afterward hee returned into the land of Iudea in peace. Moreover, in the plaine of Iericho was Ptolomeus the sonne of Abubus made captaine, and hee had abundance of silver and golde. For he was the hie Priests sonne in lawe. Wherefore his heart being lifted up, hee thought to get the countrey to himselfe, and thereupon consulted deceitfully against Simon and his sons, to destroy them. *The captaine of Hierico inviteth Simon and two of his sonnes into his castle, and there treacherously murdereth them.* Now Simon was visiting the cities that were in the countrey, and taking care for the good ordering of them, at which time hee came downe himselfe to Iericho with his sons, Mattathias and Iudas, in the hundreth threescore and seventh yeere, in the eleventh moneth called Sabat. Where the sonne of Abubus receiving them deceitfully into a little holde called Docus, which he had built, made them a great banquet: howbeit he had hidde men there. So when Simon and his sonnes had drunke largely,

311

I. MACCABEES

CHAPTER XVI

Ptolome and his men rose up, and tooke their weapons, and came upon Simon into the banketting place, and slewe him and his two sonnes, and certaine of his servants. In which doing, he committed a great treachery, and recompensed evill for good. Then Ptolome wrote these things, and sent to the king, that he should send him an hoste to aide him, and he would deliver him the countrey, and cities.

Iohn is sought for,

He sent others also to Gazara to kill Iohn, and unto the tribunes he sent letters to come unto him, that he might give them silver, and golde, and rewards. And others he sent to take Ierusalem, and the mountaine of the temple. Now one had runne afore to Gazara, and tolde Iohn that his father and brethren were slaine, and [quoth he] Ptolome hath sent to slay thee also.

and escapeth, and killeth those that sought for him.

Hereof when he heard, hee was sore astonished: So he laide hands on them that were come to destroy him, and slew them, for hee knew that they sought to make him away. As concerning the rest of the actes of Iohn, and his wars and worthy deeds which hee did, and the building of the walles which he made, and his doings, behold, these are written in the Chronicles of his Priesthood, from the time he was made high Priest after his father.

The Second Booke of
THE MACCABEES

CHAPTER I

A letter of the Iewes from Ierusalem to them of Egypt, to thanke God for the death of Antiochus.

THE brethren the Iewes that bee at Ierusalem, and in the lande of Iudea, wish unto the brethren the Iewes that are throughout Egypt, health and peace. God be gracious unto you, and remember his Covenant that hee made with Abraham, Isaac, and Iacob, his faithfull servants: and give you all an heart to serve him, and to doe his will, with a good courage, and a willing minde: and open your hearts in his law and commandements, and send you peace: and heare your prayers, and be at one with you, and never forsake you in time of

312

II. MACCABEES

trouble. And now wee be here praying for you. What time as Demetrius reigned, in the hundred threescore and ninth yeere, wee the Iewes wrote unto you, in the extremitie of trouble, that came upon us in those yeeres, from the time that Iason and his company revolted from the holy land, and kingdome, and burnt the porch, and shed innocent blood. Then we prayed unto the Lord, and were heard: we offered also sacrifices, and fine flowre, and lighted the lampes, and set forth the loaves. And now see that ye keepe the feast of Tabernacles in the moneth Casleu. In the hundreth, fourescore, and eight yeere, the people that were at Ierusalem, and in Iudea, and the counsel, and Iudas, sent greeting and health unto Aristobulus, king Ptolomeus master, who was of the stock of the anointed priests, and to the Iewes that were in Egypt. Insomuch as God hath delivered us from great perils, wee thanke him highly, as having bin in battell against a king. For he cast them out that fought within the holy citie. For when the leader was come into Persia, and the armie with him that seemed invincible, they were slaine in the temple of Nanea, by the deceit of Naneas priests. For Antiochus, as though hee would marrie her, came into the place, and his friends that were with him, to receive money in name of a dowrie. Which when the priests of Nanea had set forth, and he was entred with a small company into the compasse of the temple, they shut the temple assoone as Antiochus was come in. And opening a privie doore of the roofe, they threw stones like thunderbolts, and stroke downe the captaine, hewed them in pieces, smote off their heads, and cast them to those that were without. Blessed be our God in all things, who hath delivered up the ungodly. Therefore whereas we are nowe purposed to keep the purification of the Temple upon the five and twentieth day of the moneth Casleu, we thought it necessary to certifie you thereof, that ye also might keepe it, as the [feast] of the tabernacles, and of the fire [which was given us] when Neemias offered sacrifice, after that he had builded the Temple, and the Altar. For when our fathers were led into Persia, the Priests that were then devout, took the fire of the Altar privily, and hid it in a hollow place of a pit without water, where they kept it sure, so that the place was unknowen to all men. Now after many yeeres, when it pleased God, Neemias being sent from the king of Persia, did send of the posteritie of those Priests that had hid it, to the fire: but when they tolde us they found no fire, but thicke water, then commanded he them to draw it up, and to bring it: and when the sacrifices were laid on, Neemias commanded the Priests to sprinkle the wood, and the

CHAPTER I

Of the fire that was hidde in the pit.

II. MACCABEES

CHAPTER I

The prayer of Nehemias.

things laid therupon with the water. When this was done, and the time came that the Sun shone which afore was hid in the cloude, there was a great fire kindled, so that every man marveiled. And the Priests made a prayer whilest the sacrifice was consuming, [I say] both the Priests, and all the rest, Ionathan beginning, and the rest answering thereunto, as Neemias did. And the prayer was after this maner, O Lord, Lord God, Creatour of all things, who art fearefull, and strong, and righteous, and mercifull, and the onely, and gracious king, the onely giver of all things, the onely iust, almightie and everlasting, thou that deliverest Israel from al trouble, and didst choose the fathers, and sanctifie them: receive the sacrifice for thy whole people Israel, and preserve thine owne portion, and sanctifie it. Gather those together that are scattered from us, deliver them that serve among the heathen, looke upon them that are despised and abhorred, and let the heathen know that thou art our God. Punish them that oppresse us, and with pride doe us wrong. Plant thy people againe in thy holy place, as Moises hath spoken. And the Priests sung psalmes of thanksgiving. Now when the sacrifice was consumed, Neemias commanded the water that was left, to bee powred on the great stones. When this was done, there was kindled a flame: but it was consumed by the light that shined from the Altar. So when this matter was knowen, it was told the king of Persia, that in the place, where the Priests that were led away, had hid the fire, there appeared water, and that Neemias had purified the sacrifices therewith. Then the king inclosing the place, made it holy after he had tried the matter. And the king tooke many gifts, and bestowed thereof, on those whom he would gratifie. And Neemias called this thing Naphthar, which is as much to say as a cleansing: but many men call it Nephi.

CHAPTER II

What Ieremie the Prophet did.

IT is also found in the records, that Ieremie the Prophet, commaunded them that were caried away, to take of the fire as it hath beene signified, and how that the Prophet having given them the law, charged them not to forget the commaundements of the Lord, and that they should not erre in their minds, when they see images of silver, and gold, with their ornaments. And with other such speeches exhorted he them, that the law should not depart from their hearts. It was also contained in the same writing, that the Prophet being warned of God, commanded the Tabernacle, and the Arke to goe with him, as he went forth into

II. MACCABEES

the mountaine, where Moises climed up, and sawe the heritage of God. And when Ieremie came thither, he found an hollow cave wherin he laid the Tabernacle, and the Arke, and the altar of incense, and so stopped the doore. And some of those that followed him, came to marke the way, but they could not find it. Which when Ieremie perceived, hee blamed them, saying, As for that place, it shall be unknowen untill the time that God gather his people againe together, and receive them unto mercy. Then shall the Lord shew them these things, and the glory of the Lord shall appeare, and the cloud also as it was shewed under Moises, and as when Solomon desired that the place might be honourably sanctified. It was also declared that he being wise, offered the sacrifice of dedication, and of the finishing of the Temple. And as when Moises prayed unto the Lord, the fire came down from heaven, and consumed the sacrifices: even so prayed Solomon also, and the fire came downe from heaven, and consumed the burnt offerings. And Moises said, Because the sinne offering was not to be eaten, it was consumed. So Solomon kept those eight dayes. The same things also were reported in the writings, and commentaries of Neemias, and how he founding a librarie, gathered together the acts of the Kings, and the Prophets, and of David, and the Epistles of the Kings concerning the holy gifts. In like maner also, Iudas gathered together all those things that were lost, by reason of the warre we had, and they remaine with us. Wherefore if yee have neede thereof, send some to fetch them unto you. Whereas we then are about to celebrate the purification, we have written unto you, and yee shall doe well if yee keepe the same dayes. We hope also that the God, that delivered all his people, and gave them all an heritage, and the kingdome, and the priesthood, and the Sanctuarie, as he promised in the lawe, will shortly have mercy upon us, and gather us together out of every land under heaven into the holy place: for he hath delivered us out of great troubles, and hath purified the place. Now as concerning Indas Maccabeus, and his brethren, and the purification of the great Temple, and the dedication of the altar, and the warres against Antiochus Epiphanes, and Eupator his sonne, and the manifest signes that came from heaven, unto those that behaved themselves manfully to their honour for Iudaisme: so that being but a few, they overcame the whole country, and chased barbarous multitudes, and recovered againe the Temple renowned all the world over, and freed the citie, and upheld the lawes, which were going downe, the Lord being gracious unto them with al favour: all these things (I say) being declared by Iason of Cyrene in five books, we will assay

CHAPTER II

How he hid the Tabernacle, the Arke, and the Altar.

What Neemias and Iudas wrote.

What Iason wrote in five bookes,

II. MACCABEES

CHAPTER II

And how those were abridged by the author of this booke.

to abridge in one volume. For considering the infinite number, and the difficulty, which they find that desire to looke into the narrations of the story, for the variety of the matter, we have beene carefull, that they that will read might have delight, and that they that are desirous to commit to memorie, might have ease, and that all, into whose hands it comes might have profit. Therefore to us that have taken upon us this painefull labour of abridging, it was not easie, but a matter of sweat, and watching. Even as it is no ease unto him, that prepareth a banquet, and seeketh the benefit of others: yet for the pleasuring of many we will undertake gladly this great paines: leaving to the authour the exact handling of every particular, and labouring to follow the rules of an abridgement. For as the master builder of a new house, must care for the whole building: but hee that undertaketh to set it out, and paint it, must seeke out fit things, for the adorning thereof: even so I thinke it is with us. To stand upon every point, and goe over things at large, and to be curious in particulars, belongeth to the first authour of the storie. But to use brevitie and avoyde much labouring of the worke, is to bee granted to him that will make an abridgement. Here then will we begin the story: onely adding thus much to that which hath bene said, That it is a foolish thing to make a long prologue, and to be short in the story it selfe.

CHAPTER III

Of the honour done to the Temple by the Kings of the Gentiles.

NOW when the holy Citie was inhabited with all peace, and the Lawes were kept very well, because of the godlinesse of Onias the high Priest, and his hatred of wickednesse, it came to passe that even the Kings themselves did honour the place, and magnifie the Temple with their best gifts; insomuch that Seleucus king of Asia, of his owne revenues, bare all the costes belonging to the service of the sacrifices.

Simon uttereth what treasures are in the Temple.

But one Simon of the tribe of Beniamin, who was made governour of the Temple, fell out with the high Priest about disorder in the citie. And when he could not overcome Onias, he gate him to Apollonius the sonne of Thraseas, who then was governour of Coelosyria, and Phenice, and told him that the treasurie in Ierusalem was full of infinite summes of money, so that the multitude of their riches which did not pertaine to the account of the sacrifices, was innumerable, and that it was possible to bring all into the kings hand.

Heliodorus is sent to take them away.

Now when Apollonius came to the king, and had shewed him of the money, whereof he was told, the king chose out Heliodorus his treasurer,

II. MACCABEES

and sent him with a commaundement, to bring him the foresaid money. So foorthwith Heliodorus tooke his iourney under a colour of visiting the cities of Coelosyria, and Phenice, but indeed to fulfill the kings purpose. And when he was come to Ierusalem, and had bene courteously received of the high Priest of the citie, hee told him what intelligence was given of the money, and declared wherefore hee came, and asked if these things were so in deed. Then the high Priest tolde him that there was such money layde up for the reliefe of widowes, and fatherlesse children, and that some of it belonged to Hircanus, sonne of Tobias, a man of great dignitie, and not as that wicked Simon had misinformed: the summe whereof in all was foure hundred talents of silver, and two hundred of gold, and that it was altogether impossible that such wrong should be done unto them, that had committed it to the holinesse of the place, and to the maiestie and inviolable sanctitie of the Temple, honoured over all the world. But Heliodorus because of the kings commandement given him, said, That in any wise it must be brought into the kings treasury. So at the day which hee appointed, hee entred in to order this matter, wherefore, there was no small agonie throughout the whole citie. But the Priests prostrating themselves before the Altar in their Priests Vestments, called unto heaven upon him that made a Lawe concerning things given to bee kept, that they should safely bee preserved for such as had committed them to be kept. Then whoso had looked the hie Priest in the face, it would have wounded his heart: for his countenance, and the changing of his colour, declared the inward agonie of his minde: for the man was so compassed with feare, and horror of the body, that it was manifest to them that looked upon him, what sorrow hee had now in his heart. Others ran flocking out of their houses to the generall Supplication, because the place was like to come into contempt. And the women girt with sackecloth under their breasts, abounded in the streetes; and the virgins that were kept in, ran some to the gates, and some to the walles, and others looked out of the windowes: and all holding their handes towards heaven, made supplication. Then it would have pitied a man to see the falling downe of the multitude of all sorts, and the feare of the hie Priest, being in such an agony. They then called upon the Almightie Lord, to keepe the things committed of trust, safe and sure, for those that had committed them. Neverthelesse Heliodorus executed that which was decreed. Now as hee was there present himselfe with his guard about the treasurie, the Lord of spirits, and the Prince of all power caused a great apparition, so that all

CHAPTER III

He is stricken of God, and healed at the praier of Onias,

II. MACCABEES

CHAPTER III — that presumed to come in with him, were astonished at the power of God, and fainted, and were sore afraid. For there appeared unto them a horse, with a terrible rider upon him, and adorned with a very faire covering, and he ranne fiercely, and smote at Heliodorus with his forefeet, and it seemed that hee that sate upon the horse, had complete harnesse of golde. Moreover two other yong men appeared before him, notable in strength, excellent in beautie, and comely in apparell, who stood by him on either side, and scourged him continually, and gave him many sore stripes. And Heliodorus fell suddenly unto the ground, and was compassed with great darkenesse: but they that were with him, tooke him up, and put him into a litter. Thus him that lately came with a great traine, and with all his guard into the said treasury, they caried out, being unable to helpe himselfe with his weapons: and manifestly they acknowledged the power of God. For hee by the hand of God was cast downe, and lay speechlesse without all hope of life. But they praised the Lord that had miraculously honoured his owne place: for the Temple which a little afore was full of feare and trouble, when the Almightie Lord appeared, was filled with ioy and gladnesse. Then straightwayes certaine of Heliodorus friends, prayed Onias that hee would call upon the most High to graunt him his life, who lay ready to give up the ghost. So the high Priest suspecting lest the king should misconceive that some treachery had beene done to Heliodorus by the Iewes, offered a sacrifice for the health of the man. Now as the high Priest was making an atonement, the same yong men, in the same clothing, appeared and stood beside Heliodorus, saying, Give Onias the high Priest great thankes, insomuch as for his sake the Lord hath granted thee life. And seeing that thou hast beene scourged from heaven, declare unto all men the mightie power of God: and when they had spoken these wordes, they appeared no more. So Heliodorus after he had offered sacrifice unto the Lord, and made great vowes unto him that had saved his life, and saluted Onias, returned with his hoste to the king. Then testified hee to all men, the workes of the great God, which he had seene with his eyes. And when the king asked Heliodorus, who might be a fit man to be sent yet once againe to Ierusalem, he said, If thou hast any enemy or traitor, send him thither, and thou shalt receive him well scourged, if he escape with his life: for in that place, no doubt, there is an especiall power of God. For hee that dwelleth in heaven hath his eye on that place, and defendeth it, and hee beateth and destroyeth them that come to hurt it. And the things concerning Heliodorus, and the keeping of the treasurie, fell out on this sort.

II. MACCABEES

CHAPTER IIII

THIS Simon now (of whom wee spake afore) having bin a *Simon slander-* bewrayer of the money, and of his countrey, slandered *eth Onias.* Onias, as if he had terrified Heliodorus, and bene the worker of these evils. Thus was hee bold to call him a traitour, that had deserved well of the citie, and tendred his owne nation, and was so zealous of the lawes. But when their hatred went so farre, that by one of Simons faction murthers were committed, Onias seeing the danger of this contention, and that Appollonius, as being the governour of Coelosyria and Phenice, did rage, and increase Simons malice, he went to the king, not to be an accuser of his countrey men, but seeking the good of all, both publike, and private. For he saw that it was impossible, that the state should continue quiet, and Simon leave his folly, unlesse the king did looke thereunto. But after the death of Seleucus, when Antiochus *Iason by cor-* called Epiphanes, tooke the kingdom, Iason the brother of Onias, *rupting the* laboured under hand to bee hie Priest, promising unto the king by *the office of* intercession, three hundred and threescore talents of silver, and *the hie priest.* of another revenew, eightie talents: besides this, he promised to assigne an hundred and fiftie more, if he might have licence to set him up a place for exercise, and for the training up of youth in the fashions of the heathen, and to write them of Ierusalem [by the name of] Antiochians. Which when the king had granted, and hee had gotten into his hand the rule, he foorthwith brought his owne nation to the Greekish fashion. And the royal priviledges granted of speciall favour to the Iewes, by the meanes of Iohn, the father of Eupolemus, who went Embassador to Rome, for amitie and aid, he tooke away, and putting down the governments which were according to the law, he brought up new customes against the law. For he built gladly a place of exercise under the towre it selfe, and brought the chiefe yong men under his subiection, and made them weare a hat. Now such was the height of Greek fashions, and increase of heathenish mauers, through the exceeding profanenes of Iason that ungodly wretch, and no high priest: that the priests had no courage to serve any more at the altar, but despising the Temple, and neglecting the sacrifices, hastened to be partakers of the unlawfull allowance in the place of exercise, after the game of Discus called them forth. Not setting by the honours of their fathers, but liking the glory of the Grecians best of all. By reason whereof sore calamity came upon them: for they had them to be their enemies and avengers, whose custome they followed so earnestly, and unto whom they desired to be like in all things.

II. MACCABEES

CHAPTER IIII

For it is not a light thing to doe wickedly against the lawes of God, but the time following shall declare these things. Now when the game that was used every fift yere was kept at Tyrus, the king being present, this ungracious Iason sent speciall messengers from Ierusalem, who were Antiochians, to carie three hundred drachmes of silver to the sacrifice of Hercules, which even the bearers therof thought fit not to bestow upon the sacrifice, because it was not convenient, but to be reserved for other charges. This money then in regard of the sender, was appointed to Hercules sacrifice, but because of the bearers thereof, it was imployed to the making of gallies. Now when Apollonius the sonne of Manastheus was sent unto Egypt, for the coronation of king Ptolomeus Philometor, Antiochus understanding him not to bee well affected to his affaires, provided for his owne safetie: whereupon he came to Ioppe, and from thence to Ierusalem. Where he was honourably received of Iason, and of the citie, and was brought in with torchlight, and with great shoutings: and so afterward went with his hoste unto Phenice. Three yere afterward, Iason sent Menelaus the foresaid Simons brother, to beare the money unto the king, and to put him in minde of certaine necessary matters. But he being brought to the presence of the king, when he had magnified him, for the glorious appearance of his power, got the priesthood to himselfe, offering more then Iason by three hundred talents of silver. So he came with the kings Mandate, bringing nothing worthy the high priesthood, but having the fury of a cruell Tyrant, and the rage of a savage beast. Then Iason, who had undermined his owne brother, being undermined by another, was compelled to flee into the countrey of the Ammonites. So Menelaus got the principalitie: but as for the money that he had promised unto the king, hee tooke no good order for it, albeit Sostratus the ruler of the castle required it. For unto him appertained the gathering of the customes. Wherefore they were both called before the king. Now Menelaus left his brother Lysimachus in his stead in the priesthood, and Sostratus left Crates, who was governour of the Cyprians. While those things were in doing, they of Tharsus and Mallos made insurrection, because they were given to the kings concubine called Antiochis. Then came the king in all haste to appease matters, leaving Andronicus a man in authority, for his deputy. Now Menelaus supposing that he had gotten a convenient time, stole certaine vessels of gold, out of the temple, and gave some of them to Andronicus, and some he sold into Tyrus, and the cities round about. Which when Onias knew of a surety, he reproved him, and withdrew himselfe into a Sanctuarie at Daphne, that lieth

Menelaus getteth the same from Iason by the like corruption.

II. MACCABEES

by Antiochia. Wherefore Menelaus, taking Andronicus apart, prayed him to get Onias into his hands, who being perswaded thereunto, and comming to Onias in deceit, gave him his right hand with othes, and though hee were suspected (by him) yet perswaded he him to come forth of the Sanctuarie: whom forthwith he shut up without regard of Iustice. For the which cause not onely the Iewes, but many also of other nations tooke great indignation, and were much grieved for the uniust murder of the man. And when the king was come againe from the places about Cilicia, the Iewes that were in the citie, and certaine of the Greekes, that abhorred the fact also, complained because Onias was slaine without cause. Therefore Antiochus was heartily sorry, and mooved to pity, and wept, because of the sober and modest behaviour of him that was dead. And being kindled with anger, forthwith he tooke away Andronicus his purple, and rent off his clothes, and leading him through the whole city unto that very place, where he had committed impietie against Onias, there slew he the cursed murtherer. Thus the Lord rewarded him his punishment, as he had deserved. Now when many sacriledges had beene committed in the citie by Lysimachus, with the consent of Menelaus, and the bruit therof was spread abroad, the multitude gathered themselves together against Lysimachus, many vessels of gold being already caried away. Whereupon the common people rising, and being filled with rage, Lysimachus armed about three thousand men, and beganne first to offer violence on Auranus, being the leader, a man farre gone in yeeres, and no lesse in folly. They then seeing the attempt of Lysimachus, some of them caught stones, some clubs, others taking handfuls of dust, that was next at hand, cast them all together upon Lysimachus, and those that set upon them. Thus many of them they wounded, and some they stroke to the ground, and all [of them] they forced to flee: but as for the Churchrobber himselfe, him they killed besides the treasury. Of these matters therefore there was an accusation laide against Menelaus. Now when the king came to Tyrus, three men that were sent from the Senate, pleaded the cause before him: but Menelaus being now convicted, promised Ptolomee the sonne of Dorymenes, to give him much money, if hee would pacifie the King towards him. Whereupon Ptolomee taking the king aside into a certaine gallerie, as it were to take the aire, brought him to be of another minde; insomuch that hee discharged Menelaus from the accusations, who notwithstanding was cause of all the mischiefe: and those poore men, who if they had told their cause, yea, before the Scythians, should have bene iudged innocent, them he condemned to death. Thus

CHAPTER IIII
Andronicus traiterously murdereth Onias.

The King being informed thereof, causeth Andronicus to be put to death.

The wickednes of Lysimachus, by the instigation of Menelaus.

II. MACCABEES

CHAPTER IIII

they that followed the matter for the citie, and for the people, and for the holy vessels, did soone suffer uniust punishment. Wherefore even they of Tyrus mooved with hatred of that wicked deed, caused them to bee honourably buried. And so through the covetousnesse of them that were in power, Menelaus remained still in authority, increasing in malice, and being a great traitour to the citizens.

CHAPTER V

Of the signes and tokens seene in Ierusalem.

ABOUT the same time Antiochus prepared his second voyage into Egypt: and then it happened, that through all the citie, for the space almost of fourtie dayes, there were seene horsemen running in the aire, in cloth of golde, and armed with lances, like a band of souldiers, and troupes of horsemen in aray, incountring, and running one against another with shaking of shieldes, and multitude of pikes, and drawing of swords, and casting of darts, and glittering of golden ornaments, and harnesse of all sorts. Wherefore every man praied that that apparition might turne to good. Now when there was gone forth a false rumour, as though Antiochus had bene dead, Iason tooke at the least a thousand men, and suddenly made an assault upon the citie, and they that were upon the walles, being put backe, and the citie at length taken, Menelaus fled into the castle: but Iason slew his owne citizens without mercy, (not considering that to get the day of them of his owne nation, would be a most unhappy day for him: but thinking they had bene his enemies, and not his countrey men whom he conquered.) Howbeit for all this hee obtained not the principalitie, but at the last received shame for the reward of his treason, and fled againe into the countrey of the Ammonites. In the end therefore hee had an unhappy returne, being accused before Aretas the king of the Arabians, fleeing from city to city, pursued of all men, hated as a forsaker of the Lawes, and being had in abomination, as an open enemie of his countrey, and countreymen, he was cast out into Egypt. Thus hee that had driven many out of their countrey, perished in a strange land, retiring to the Lacedemonians, and thinking there to finde succour by reason of his kindred. And hee that had cast out many unburied, had none to mourne for him, nor any solemne funerals at all, nor sepulchre with his fathers. Now when this that was done came to the kings eare, he thought that Iudea had revolted, whereupon removing out of Egypt in a furious minde, he tooke the citie by force of armes, and commaunded his men of warre not to spare such as they met, and to slay such as went up upon the houses. Thus there was

Of the end and wickednesse of Iason.

The pursuit of Antiochus against the Iewes.

II. MACCABEES

killing of yong and old, making away of men, women and children, slaying of virgins and infants. And there were destroyed within the space of three whole daies, fourescore thousand, whereof fourty thousand were slaine in the conflict; and no fewer sold, then slaine. Yet was he not content with this, but presumed to goe into the most holy Temple of all the world: Menelaus that traitour to the Lawes, and to his owne countrey, being his guide. And taking the holy vessels with polluted handes, and with prophane handes, pulling downe the things that were dedicated by other kings, to the augmentation and glory and honour of the place, he gave them away. And so haughtie was Antiochus in minde, that hee considered not that the Lord was angry for a while for the sinnes of them that dwelt in the citie, and therefore his eye was not upon the place. For had they not beene formerly wrapped in many sinnes, this man as soone as hee had come, had foorthwith beene scourged, and put backe from his presumption, as Heliodorus was, whom Seleucus the king sent to view the treasurie. Neverthelesse God did not choose the people for the places sake, but the place for the peoples sake. And therefore the place it selfe that was partaker with them of the adversities that happened to the nation, did afterward communicate in the benefits sent from the Lord: and as it was forsaken in the wrath of the Almighty, so againe the great Lord being reconciled, it was set up with all glory. So when Antiochus had caried out of the Temple, a thousand and eight hundred talents, hee departed in all haste into Antiochia, weening in his pride to make the land navigable, and the Sea passable by foot: such was the haughtinesse of his minde. And he left governours to vexe the nation: at Ierusalem Philip, for his countrey a Phrygian, and for manners more barbarous then hee that set him there: and at Garizim, Andronicus; and besides, Menelaus, who worse then all the rest, bare an heavie hand over the citizens, having a malicious minde against his countreymen the Iewes. He sent also that detestable ringleader Apollonius, with an armie of two and twentie thousand, commaunding him to slay all those that were in their best age, and to sell the women and the yonger sort: who comming to Ierusalem, and pretending peace, did forbeare till the holy day of the Sabbath, when taking the Iewes keeping holy day, hee commanded his men to arme themselves. And so hee slewe all them that were gone to the celebrating of the Sabbath, and running through the city with weapons, slewe great multitudes. But Iudas Maccabeus, with nine others, or thereabout, withdrew himselfe into the wildernesse, and lived in the mountaines after the maner of beasts.

CHAPTER V

The spoiling of the Temple.

Maccabeus fleeth into the wildernes.

II. MACCABEES

CHAPTER V — the maner of beasts, with his company, who fed on herbs continually, lest they should be partakers of the pollution.

CHAPTER VI

The Iewes are compelled to leave the Law of God.

NOT long after this, the king sent an olde man of Athens, to compell the Iewes to depart from the lawes of their fathers, and not to live after the Lawes of God: and to pollute also the Temple in Ierusalem, and to call it the Temple of Iupiter Olympius: and that in Garazim, of Iupiter the defender of strangers, as they did desire that dwelt in the place. *The Temple is defiled.* The comming in of this mischiefe was sore and grievous to the people: for the Temple was filled with riot and revelling, by the Gentiles, who dallied with harlots, and had to doe with women within the circuit of the holy places, and besides that, brought in things that were not lawfull. The Altar also was filled with profane things, which the Law forbiddeth. Neither was it lawfull for a man to keepe Sabbath dayes, or ancient Feasts, or to professe himselfe at all to be a Iewe. And in the day of the kings birth, every moneth they were brought by bitter constraint to eate of the sacrifices; and when the Feast of Bacchus was kept, the Iewes were compelled to *Crueltie upon the people and the women.* goe in procession to Bacchus, carying Ivie. Moreover there went out a decree to the neighbour cities of the heathen, by the suggestion of Ptolomee, against the Iewes, that they should observe the same fashions, and be partakers of their sacrifices. And whoso would not conforme themselves to the maners of the Gentiles, should be put to death: then might a man have seene the present misery. For there were two women brought, who had circumcised their children, whom when they had openly led round about the citie, the babes hanging at their breasts, they cast them downe headlong from the wall. And others that had run together into caves neere by, to keepe the Sabbath day secretly, being discovered to Philip, were all burnt together, because they made a conscience *An exhortation to beare affliction, by the example of the valiant courage of Eleazarus, cruelly tortured.* to helpe themselves, for the honour of the most sacred day. Now I beseech those that reade this booke, that they be not discouraged for these calamities, but that they iudge those punishments not to be for destruction, but for a chastening of our nation. For it is a token of his great goodnesse, when wicked doers are not suffered any long time, but forthwith punished. For not as with other nations whom the Lord patiently forbeareth to punish, till they be come to the fulnesse of their sinnes, so dealeth he with us, lest that being come to the height of sinne, afterwards hee should take

II. MACCABEES

CHAPTER VI

vengeance of us. And therfore he never withdraweth his mercie from us: and though he punish with adversitie, yet doeth he never forsake his people. But let this that we have spoken be for a warning unto us: And nowe will wee come to the declaring of the matter in few words. Eleazar one of the principall Scribes, an aged man, and of a well favoured countenance, was constrained to open his mouth, and to eate swines flesh. But he chusing rather to die gloriously, then to live stained with such an abomination, spit it forth, and came of his owne accord to the torment, as it behoved them to come, that are resolute to stand out against such things, as are not lawfull for love of life to be tasted. But they that had the charge of that wicked feast, for the olde acquaintance they had with the man, taking him aside, besought him to bring flesh of his owne provision, such as was lawfull for him to use, and make as if he did eate of the flesh, taken from the sacrifice commanded by the king, that in so doing hee might bee delivered from death, and for the olde friendship with them, find favour. But he began to consider discreetly, and as became his age, and the excellencie of his ancient yeeres, and the honour of his gray head, whereunto hee was come, and his most honest education from a child, or rather the holy lawe made, and given by God: therefore hee answered accordingly, and willed them straightwaies to send him to the grave. For it becommeth not our age, said he, in any wise to dissemble, whereby many yong persons might thinke, that Eleazar being fourescore yeres old and ten, were now gone to a strange religion, and so they through mine hypocrisie, and desire to live a litle time, and a moment longer, should bee deceived by me, and I get a staine to mine olde age, and make it abominable. For though for the present time I should be delivered from the punishment of men: yet should I not escape the hand of the Almightie, neither alive nor dead. Wherefore now manfully changing this life, I will shew my selfe such an one, as mine age requireth. And leave a notable example to such as bee yong, to die willingly, and couragiously, for the honourable and holy lawes: and when he had said these words, immediatly he went to the torment, they that led him, changing the good will they bare him a litle before, into hatred, because the foresaid speaches proceeded as they thought, from a desperate minde. But when hee was readie to die with stripes, he groned, and said, It is manifest unto the Lord, that hath the holy knowledge, that wheras I might have bin delivered from death, I [now] endure sore paines in body, by being beaten: but in soule am well content to suffer these things, because I feare him. And thus this man died, leaving his death for an example of a noble

II. MACCABEES

CHAPTER VI

courage, and a memoriall of vertue not only unto yong men, but unto all his nation.

CHAPTER VII

The constancie and cruell death of seven brethren and their mother in one day, because they would not eate swines flesh at the kings commandement.

IT came to passe also that seven brethren with their mother were taken, and compelled by the king against the lawe to taste swines flesh, and were tormented with scourges and whips: but one of them that spake first said thus: What wouldest thou aske, or learne of us? we are ready to die, rather then to transgresse the lawes of our fathers. Then the king being in a rage, commanded pannes, and caldrons to be made whot. Which forthwith being heated, he commanded to cut out the tongue of him that spake first, and to cut off the utmost parts of his body, the rest of his brethren, and his mother looking on. Now when he was thus maimed in all his members, he commanded him being yet alive, to be brought to the fire, and to be fried in the panne: and as the vapour of the panne was for a good space dispersed, they exhorted one another, with the mother, to die manfully, saying thus: The Lord God looketh upon us, and in trueth hath comfort in us, as Moises in his song, which witnessed to their faces declared, saying, And he shall be comforted in his servants. So when the first was dead, after this maner, they brought the second to make him a mocking stocke: and when they had pulled off the skin of his head with the haire, they asked him, Wilt thou eate before thou bee punished throughout every member of thy body? But hee answered in his owne language, and said, No. Wherefore hee also received the next torment in order, as the former did. And when hee was at the last gaspe, hee said, Thou like a fury takest us out of this present life, but the king of the world shall raise us up, who have died for his lawes, unto everlasting life. After him was the third made a mocking stocke, and when he was required, he put out his tongue, and that right soone, holding forth his hands manfully, and said couragiously, These I had from heaven, and for his lawes I despise them, and from him I hope to receive them againe. Insomuch that the king, and they that were with him marveiled at the yong mans courage, for that he nothing regarded the paines. Now when this man was dead also, they tormented and mangled the fourth in like maner. So when he was ready to die, he said thus, It is good, being put to death by men, to looke for hope from God to be raised up againe by him: as for thee thou shalt have no resurrection to life. Afterward they brought the fift also, and mangled him. Then looked hee unto the king and said, Thou

II. MACCABEES

CHAPTER VII

hast power over men, thou art corruptible, thou doest what thou wilt, yet thinke not that our nation is forsaken of God. But abide a while, and behold his great power, how he will torment thee, and thy seed. After him also they brought the sixt, who being ready to die, said, Be not deceived without cause: for we suffer these things for our selves, having sinned against our God. Therefore marveilous things are done (unto us.) But thinke not thou that takest in hand to strive against God, that thou shalt escape unpunished. But the mother was marveilous above all, and worthy of honorable memorie: for when shee sawe her seven sonnes slaine within the space of one day, she bare it with a good courage, because of the hope that she had in the Lord. Yea she exhorted every one of them in her owne language, filled with couragious spirits, and stirring up her womanish thoughts, with a manly stomacke, she said unto them, I cannot tell how you came into my wombe: for I neither gave you breath, nor life, neither was it I that formed the members of every one of you. But doubtlesse the Creator of the world, who formed the generation of man, and found out the beginning of all things, wil also of his owne mercy give you breath, and life againe, as you now regard not your owne selves for his Lawes sake. Now Antiochus thinking himselfe despised, and suspecting it to be a reprochfull speach, whiles the yongest was yet alive, did not onely exhort him by wordes, but also assured him with oathes, that he would make him both a rich, and a happy man, if hee would turne from the Lawes of his fathers, and that also he would take him for his friend, and trust him with affaires. But when the yong man would in no case hearken unto him, the king called his mother, and exhorted her, that she would counsell the yong man to save his life. And when hee had exhorted her with many words, she promised him that she would counsell her sonne. But shee bowing her selfe towards him, laughing the cruell tyrant to scorne, spake in her countrey language on this maner; O my sonne, have pitie upon mee that bare thee nine moneths in my wombe, and gave thee sucke three yeeres, and nourished thee, and brought thee up unto this age, and endured the troubles of education. I beseech thee, my sonne, looke upon the heaven, and the earth, and all that is therein, and consider that God made them of things that were not, and so was mankinde made likewise; feare not this tormentour, but being worthy of thy brethren, take thy death, that I may receive thee againe in mercy, with thy brethren. Whiles she was yet speaking these words, the yong man said, Whom wait ye for? I will not obey the kings commandement: but I will obey the commandement of the Law that was given unto our fathers, by Moses.

II. MACCABEES

CHAPTER VII

And thou that hast bene the authour of all mischiefe against the Hebrewes, shalt not escape the bandes of God. For wee suffer because of our sinnes. And though the living Lord bee angrie with us a little while for our chastening and correction, yet shall hee be at one againe, with his servants. But thou, O godlesse man, and of all other most wicked, be not lifted up without a cause, nor puffed up with uncertaine hopes, lifting up thy hand against the servants of God: for thou hast not yet escaped the iudgement of Almightie God, who seeth all things. For our brethren who now have suffered a short paine, are dead under Gods Covenant of everlasting life: but thou through the iudgement of God, shalt receive iust punishment for thy pride. But I, as my brethren, offer up my body, and life for the Lawes of our fathers, beseeching God that he would speedily bee mercifull unto our nation, and that thou by torments and plagues mayest confesse, that he alone is God; and that in me, and my brethren, the wrath of the Almighty, which is iustly brought upon all our nation, may cease. Then the King being in a rage, handled him worse then all the rest, and took it grievously that he was mocked. So this man died undefiled, and put his whole trust in the Lord. Last of all after the sonnes, the mother died. Let this be ynough now to have spoken concerning the idolatrous feasts, and the extreme tortures.

CHAPTER VIII

Iudas gathereth an hoste.

THEN Iudas Maccabeus and they that were with him, went privily into the townes, and called their kinsefolkes together, and tooke unto them all such as continued in the Iewes religion, and assembled about sixe thousand men. And they called upon the Lord, that hee would looke upon the people that was troden downe of all, and also pitie the Temple, prophaned of ungodly men, and that he would have compassion upon the city sore defaced and ready to be made even with the ground, and heare the blood that cried unto him, and remember the wicked slaughter of harmelesse infants, and the blasphemies committed against his Name, and that hee would shew his hatred against the wicked. Now when Maccabeus had his company about him, hee could not be withstood by the heathen: for the wrath of the Lord was turned into mercy. Therefore he came at unawares, and burnt up townes and cities, and got into his hands the most commodious places, and overcame and put to flight no small number of his enemies. But specially tooke he advantage of the night, for such privie attempts, insomuch that the bruite of his manlinesse was

II. MACCABEES

spread every where. So when Philip sawe that this man encreased by little and little, and that things prospered with him still more and more, hee wrote unto Ptolemeus, the governour of Coelosyria and Phenice, to yeeld more aide to the kings affaires. Then forthwith choosing Nicanor the son of Patroclus, one of his speciall friends, he sent him with no fewer then twentie thousand of all nations under him, to root out the whole generation of the Iewes; and with him he ioyned also Gorgias a captaine, who in matters of warre had great experience. So Nicanor undertooke to make so much money of the captive Iewes, as should defray the tribute of two thousand talents, which the king was to pay to the Romanes. Wherefore immediatly he sent to the cities upon the sea coast, proclaiming a sale of the captive Iewes, and promising that they should have fourescore and ten bodies for one talent, not expecting the vengeance that was to follow upon him from the Almighty God. Now when word was brought unto Iudas of Nicanors comming, and he had imparted unto those that were with him, that the army was at hand, they that were fearefull, and distrusted the iustice of God, fled, and conveyed themselves away. Others sold all that they had left, and withall besought the Lord to deliver them, being solde by the wicked Nicanor before they met together: and if not for their owne sakes, yet for the covenants he had made with their fathers, and for his holy and glorious Names sake, by which they were called. So Maccabeus called his men together unto the number of sixe thousand, and exhorted them not to be stricken with terrour of the enemie, nor to feare the great multitude of the heathen who came wrongfully against them, but to fight manfully, and to set before their eyes, the iniury that they had uniustly done to the holy place, and the cruell handling of the city, whereof they made a mockery, and also the taking away of the government of their forefathers: For they, said he, trust in their weapons and boldnesse, but our confidence is in the Almightie God, who at a becke can cast downe both them that come against us, and also all the world. Moreover, hee recounted unto them what helps their forefathers had found, and how they were delivered, when under Sennacherib an hundred fourescore and five thousand perished. And he told them of the battel that they had in Babylon with the Galatians, how they came but eight thousand in all to the busines, with foure thousand Macedonians, and that the Macedonians being perplexed, the eight thousand destroyed an hundred and twenty thousand, because of the helpe that they had from heaven, and so received a great booty. Thus when hee had made them bold with these words,

CHAPTER VIII

Nicanor is sent against him: who presumeth to make much money of his prisoners.

Iudas encourageth his men, and putteth Nicanor to flight,

II. MACCABEES

CHAPTER VIII

and divideth the spoiles.

Other enemies are also defeated,

And Nicanor fleeth with griefe to Antioch.

and ready to die for the Lawes, and the countrey, he divided his army into foure parts: and ioyned with himselfe his owne brethren, leaders of each band, to wit, Simon, and Ioseph, and Ionathan, giving each one fifteene hundred men. Also (hee appointed) Eleazar to reade the holy booke: and when he had given them this watchword, The help of God; himselfe leading the first band, he ioyned battell with Nicanor: and by the helpe of the Almightie, they slew above nine thousand of their enemies, and wounded and maimed the most part of Nicanors hoste, and so put all to flight: and tooke their money that came to buy them, and pursued them farre: but lacking time, they returned. For it was the day before the Sabbath, and therefore they would no longer pursue them. So when they had gathered their armour[1] together, and spoiled their enemies, they occupied themselves about the Sabbath, yeelding exceeding praise, and thanks to the Lord, who had preserved them unto that day, which was the beginning of mercy, distilling upon them. And after the Sabbath, when they had given part of the spoiles to the maimed, and the widdowes, and Orphanes, the residue they divided among themselves, and their servants. When this was done, and they had made a common supplication, they besought the mercifull Lord to be reconciled with his servants for ever. Moreover of those that were with Timotheus and Bacchides, who fought against them, they slewe above twentie thousand, and very easily got high and strong holds, and divided amongst them selves many spoiles more, and made the maimed, orphanes, widowes, yea, and the aged also, equal in spoiles with themselves. And when they had gathered their armour together, they laid them up all carefully in convenient places, and the remnant of the spoiles they brought to Ierusalem. They slew also Philarches that wicked person who was with Timotheus, and had annoied the Iewes many waies. Furthermore at such time as they kept the feast for the victorie in their country, they burnt Calisthenes that had set fire upon the holy gates, who was fled into a litle house, and so he received a reward meet for his wickednesse. As for that most ungracious Nicanor, who had brought a thousand merchants to buy the Iewes, he was through the helpe of the Lord brought downe by them, of whom he made least account, and putting off his glorious apparell, and discharging his company, he came like a fugitive servant through the mid land unto Antioch, having very great dishonour for that his hoste was destroyed. Thus he that tooke upon him to make good to the Romanes, their tribute by meanes of the captives in Ierusalem, told abroad, that the Iewes

[1] That is, the enemies armour.

II. MACCABEES

had God to fight for them, and therfore they could not be hurt, because they followed the lawes that he gave them.

CHAPTER VIII

CHAPTER IX

ABOUT that time came Antiochus with dishonor out of the countrey of Persia. For he had entred the citie called Persepolis, and went about to rob the Temple, and to hold the citie, whereupon the multitude running to defend themselves with their weapons, put them to flight, and so it happened that Antiochus being put to flight of the inhabitants, returned with shame. Now when he came to Ecbatana, newes was brought him what had happened unto Nicanor and Timotheus. Then swelling with anger, hee thought to avenge upon the Iewes the disgrace done unto him by those that made him flie. Therfore commanded he his chariot man to drive without ceasing, and to dispatch the iourney, the iudgement of God now following him. For he had spoken proudly in this sort, that he would come to Ierusalem, and make it a common burying place of the Iewes. But the Lord almightie, the God of Israel smote him with an incurable and invisible plague: for assoone as hee had spoken these words, a paine of the bowels that was remediles, came upon him, and sore torments of the inner parts. And that most iustly: for hee had tormented other mens bowels with many and strange torments. Howbeit hee nothing at all ceased from his bragging, but still was filled with pride, breathing out fire in his rage against the Iewes, and commanding to haste the iourney: but it came to passe that he fel downe from his chariot, caried violently, so that having a sore fal, al the members of his body were much pained. And thus hee that a little afore thought he might command the waves of the sea (so proud was hee beyond the condition of man) and weigh the high mountaines in a ballance, was now cast on the ground, and carried in an horselitter, shewing foorth unto all, the manifest power of God. So that the wormes rose up out of the body of this wicked man, and whiles hee lived in sorrow and paine, his flesh fell away, and the filthinesse of his smell was noysome to all his army. And the man that thought a little afore he could reach to the starres of heaven, no man could endure to carry for his intollerable stinke. Here therefore being plagued, hee began to leave off his great pride, and to come to the knowledge [of himselfe] by the scourge of God, his paine encreasing every moment. And when hee himselfe could not abide his owne smell, hee saide these wordes: It is meete to bee subiect unto God,

Antiochus is chased from Persepolis.

Hee is striken wit a sore disease,

331

II. MACCABEES

CHAPTER IX

and promiseth to become a Iew.

and that a man that is mortall, should not proudly thinke of himselfe, as if he were God. This wicked person vowed also unto the Lord, (who now no more would have mercy upon him) saying thus: That the holy citie (to the which hee was going in haste to lay it even with the ground, and to make it a common burying place) he would set at liberty. And as touching the Iewes, whom hee had iudged not worthy so much as to be buried, but to be cast out with their children to be devoured of the foules, and wild beasts, he would make them al equals to the citizens of Athens, and the holy Temple, which before he had spoiled, hee would garnish with goodly gifts, and restore all the holy vessels with many more, and out of his owne revenew defray the charges belonging to the sacrifices: yea, and that also hee would become a Iew himselfe, and goe through all the world that was inhabited, and declare the power of God. But for all this his paines would not cease: for the iust iudgement of God was come upon him: therfore despairing of his health, he wrote unto the Iewes the letter underwritten, containing the forme of a supplication, after this maner. Antiochus king and governour, to the good Tewes his Citizens, wisheth much ioy, health, and prosperity. If ye, and your children fare well, and your affaires be to your contentment, I give very great thankes to God, having my hope in heaven. As for mee I was weake, or else I would have remembred kindly your honour, and good will. Returning out of Persia, and being taken with a grievous disease, I thought it necessary to care for the common safety of all: not distrusting mine health, but having great hope to escape this sicknes. But considering that even my father, at what time he led an armie into the hie countries, appointed a successor, to the end, that if any thing fell out contrary to expectation, or if any tidings were brought that were grievous, they of the land knowing to whom the state was left, might not be troubled. Againe considering, how that the princes that are borderers, and neighbors unto my kingdome, waite for opportunities, and expect what shalbe the event, I have appointed my sonne Antiochus king, whom I often committed, and commended unto many of you, when I went up into the high provinces, to whom I have written as followeth. Therefore I pray, and request you to remember the benefits that I have done unto you generally, and in speciall, and that every man will be still faithfull to me, and my sonne. For I am perswaded that hee understanding my minde, will favourably and graciously yeeld to your desires. Thus the murtherer, and blasphemer having suffered most grievously, as he entreated other men, so died he a miserable death in a strange countrey in the

He dieth miserably.

II. MACCABEES

mountaines. And Philip that was brought up with him, caried away his body, who also fearing the son of Antiochus, went into Egypt to Ptolomeus Philometor. CHAPTER IX

CHAPTER X

NOW Maccabeus, and his company, the Lord guiding them, recovered the Temple, and the citie. But the altars, which the heathen had built in the open street, and also the Chappels they pulled downe. And having cleansed the Temple, they made another Altar, and striking stones, they tooke fire out of them, and offered a sacrifice after two yeeres, and set forth incense, and lights, and Shewbread. When that was done, they fell flat downe, and besought the Lord that they might come no more into such troubles: but if they sinned any more against him, that he himselfe would chasten them with mercie, and that they might not bee delivered unto the blasphemous, and barbarous nations. Now upon the same day that the strangers prophaned the Temple, on the very same day it was cleansed againe, even the five and twentieth day of the same moneth, which is Casleu. And they kept eight dayes with gladnes as in the feast of the Tabernacles, remembring that not long afore they had helde the feast of the Tabernacles, when as they wandered in the mountaines and dennes, like beasts. Therefore they bare branches, and faire boughes and palmes also, and sang Psalmes unto him, that had given them good successe in clensing his place. They ordeined also by a common statute, and decree, That every yeere those dayes should be kept of the whole nation of the Iewes. And this was the ende of Antiochus called Epiphanes. Now will wee declare the acts of Antiochus Eupator, who was the sonne of this wicked man, gathering briefly the calamities of the warres. So when he was come to the crowne, he set one Lysias over the affaires of his Realme, and [appointed him] chiefe governour of Coelosyria and Phenice. For Ptolomeus that was called Macron, chosing rather to doe iustice unto the Iewes, for the wrong that had bene done unto them, endevoured to continue peace with them. Whereupon being accused of [the kings] friends, before Eupator, and called traitor at every word, because he had left Cyprus that Philometor had committed unto him, and departed to Antiochus Epiphanes; and seeing that hee was in no honorable place, he was so discouraged, that he poysoned himselfe and died. But when Gorgias was governour of the holds, hee hired souldiers, and nourished warre continually with the Iewes: and therewithall the

Iudas recovereth the Citie, and purifieth the Temple.

Gorgias vexeth the Iewes.

II. MACCABEES

CHAPTER X

Iudas winneth their holds.

Idumeans having gotten into their bandes the most commodious holdes, kept the Iewes occupied, and receiving those that were banished from Ierusalem, they went about to nourish warre. Then they that were with Maccabeus made supplication, and besought God, that he would be their helper, and so they ranne with violence upon the strong holds of the Idumeans, and assaulting them strongly, they wanne the holds, and kept off all that fought upon the wall, and slew all that fell into their hands, and killed no fewer then twentie thousand. And because certaine (who were no lesse then nine thousand) were fled together into two very strong castles, having all maner of things convenient to sustaine the siege, Maccabeus left Simon, and Ioseph, and Zaccheus also, and them that were with him, who were enow to besiege them, and departed himselfe unto those places, which more needed his helpe. Now they that were with Simon, being led with covetousnes, were perswaded for money (through certaine of those that were in the castle) and tooke seventie thousand drachmes, and let some of them escape. But when it was told Maccabeus what was done, hee called the governours of the people together, and accused those men, that they had sold their brethren for money, and set their enemies free to fight against them. So he slew those that were found traitors, and immediatly tooke the two castles. And having good successe with his weapons in all things hee tooke in hand, hee slew in the two holdes, more then twentie thousand. Now Timotheus whom the Iewes had overcome before, when he had gathered a great multitude of forraine forces, and horses out of Asia not a few, came as though hee would take Iewrie by force of armes. But when hee drew neere, they that were with Maccabeus, turned themselves to pray unto God, and sprinckled earth upon their heads, and girded their loynes with sackcloth, and fell downe at the foot of the Altar, and besought him to be mercifull to them, and to be an enemie to their enemies, and an adversarie to their adversaries, as the Law declareth. So after the prayer, they tooke their weapons, and went on further from the city: and when they drew neere to their enemies, they kept by themselves. Now the Sunne being newly risen, they ioyned both together; the one part having, together with their vertue, their refuge also unto the Lord, for a pledge of their successe and victorie: the other

Timotheus and his men are discomfited.

side making their rage leader of their battell. But when the battaile waxed strong, there appeared unto the enemies from heaven, five comely men upon horses, with bridles of golde, and two of them ledde the Iewes, and tooke Maccabeus betwixt them, and covered him on every side with their weapons, and kept him

II. MACCABEES

safe, but shot arrowes and lightenings against the enemies: so that being confounded with blindnesse, and full of trouble, they were killed. And there were slaine [of footemen] twentie thousand and five hundred, and sixe hundred horsemen. As for Timotheus himselfe, hee fled into a very strong holde, called Gazara, where Chereas was governour. But they that were with Maccabeus, laid siege against the fortresse couragiously foure dayes. And they that were within, trusting to the strength of the place, blasphemed exceedingly, and uttered wicked words. Neverthelesse, upon the fifth day early, twentie yong men of Maccabeus company, inflamed with anger because of the blasphemies, assaulted the wall manly, and with a fierce courage killed all that they met withall. Others likewise ascending after them, whiles they were busied with them that were within, burnt the towres, and kindling fires, burnt the blasphemers alive, and others broke open the gates, and having received in the rest of the army, tooke the city, and killed Timotheus that was hidde in a certaine pit, and Chereas his brother, with Apollophanes. When this was done, they praised the Lord with Psalmes and thankesgiving, who had done so great things for Israel, and given them the victory.

CHAPTER X

Gazara is taken, and Timotheus slaine.

CHAPTER XI

NOT long after this, Lysias the kings protectour and cousin, who also managed the affaires, tooke sore displeasure for the things that were done. And when he had gathered about fourescore thousand, with all the horsemen, he came against the Iewes, thinking to make the citie an habitation of the Gentiles, and to make a gaine of the Temple, as of the other Chappels of the heathen, and to set the high Priesthood to sale every yeere: Not at all considering the power of God, but puffed up with his ten thousand footmen, and his thousand horsemen, and his fourescore Elephants. So he came to Iudea, and drew neere to Bethsura, which was a strong town, but distant from Ierusalem about five furlongs, and he laid sore siege unto it. Now when they that were with Maccabeus heard that he besieged the holdes, they and all the people with lamentation and teares besought the Lord, that he would send a good Angel to deliver Israel. Then Maccabeus himselfe first of all tooke weapons, exhorting the other, that they would ieopard themselves together with him, to helpe their brethren: so they went forth together with a willing minde. And as they were at Ierusalem, there appeared before them on horsebacke, one in white clothing, shaking his armour of gold. Then

Lysias thinking to get Ierusalem,

Is put to flight.

II. MACCABEES

CHAPTER XI

they praised the mercifull God altogether, and tooke heart, insomuch that they were ready not onely to fight with men, but with most cruell beasts, and to pierce through wals of yron. Thus they marched forward in their armour, having an helper from heaven: for the Lord was mercifull unto them. And giving a charge upon their enemies like lions, they slew eleven thousand footmen, and sixteene hundred horsemen, and put all the other to flight. Many of them also being wounded, escaped naked, and Lysias himselfe fled away shamefully, and so escaped. Who as hee was a man of understanding, casting with himselfe what losse he had had, and considering that the Hebrewes could not be overcome, because the Almighty God helped them, he sent unto them, and perswaded them to agree to all reasonable conditions, and [promised] that hee would perswade the king, that he must needs be a friend unto them. Then Maccabeus consented to all that Lysias desired, being carefull of the common good; and whatsoever Maccabeus wrote *The letters of Lysias to the Iewes:* unto Lysias concerning the Iewes, the king granted it. For there were letters written unto the Iewes from Lysias, to this effect: Lysias unto the people of the Iewes, sendeth greeting. Iohn and Absalon, who were sent from you, delivered me the petition subscribed, and made request for the performance of the contents thereof. Therefore what things soever were meet to be reported to the king, I have declared them, and he hath granted as much as might be. If then you wil keepe your selves loyall to the state, hereafter also will I endevour to be a meanes of your good. But of the particulars I have given order, both to these, and the other that came from me, to commune with you. Fare ye wel. The hundred and eight and fortie yeere, the foure and twentie day of *Of the king unto Lysias:* the moneth Dioscorinthius. Now the kings letter conteined these words, King Antiochus unto his brother Lysias sendeth greeting. Since our father is translated unto the gods, our will is, that they that are in our realme live quietly, that every one may attend upon his own affaires. Wee understand also that the Iewes would not consent to our father for to bee brought unto the custome of the Gentiles, but had rather keepe their owne manner of living: for the which cause they require of us that we should suffer them to live after their own lawes. Wherefore our mind is, that this nation shall be in rest, and we have determined to restore them their Temple, that they may live according to the customes of their forefathers. Thou shalt doe well therefore to send unto them, and grant them peace, that when they are certified of our *and to the Iewes:* mind, they may be of good comfort, and ever goe cheerefully about their owne affaires. And the letter of the king unto the nation of

II. MACCABEES

the Iewes was after this maner: King Antiochus sendeth greeting unto the counsel, and the rest of the Iewes. If ye fare well, we have our desire, we are also in good health. Menelaus declared unto us, that your desire was to returne home, and to follow your owne businesse. Wherefore they that will depart shall have safe conduct, till the thirtieth day of Xanthicus with securitie. And the Iewes shal use their owne kind of meats, and lawes, as before, and none of them any maner of wayes shal be molested for things ignorantly done. I have sent also Menelaus, that he may comfort you. Fare ye wel. In the hundred, forty and eight yeere, and the fifteenth day of the moneth Xanthicus. The Romanes also sent unto them a letter containing these wordes: Quintus Memmius, and Titus Manlius embassadours of the Romanes, send greeting unto the people of the Iewes. Whatsoever Lysias the kings cousin hath granted, therewith we also are well pleased. But touching such things as hee iudged to be referred to the king: after you have advised therof, send one forthwith, that we may declare as it is convenient for you: for we are now going to Antioch. Therefore send some with speed, that we may know what is your mind. Farewell, this hundred and eight and fortie yeere, the fifteenth day of the moneth Xanthicus.

CHAPTER XI

Of the Romanes to the Iewes.

CHAPTER XII

WHEN these Covenants were made, Lysias went unto the king, and the Iewes were about their husbandrie. But of the governours of several places, Timotheus, and Apollonius the sonne of Genneus, also Hieronymus, and Demophon, and besides them Nicanor the governor of Cyprus would not suffer them to be quiet, and live in peace. The men of Ioppe also did such an ungodly deed: they prayed the Iewes that dwelt among them, to goe with their wives, and children into the boats which they had prepared, as though they had meant them no hurt. Who accepted of it according to the common decree of the citie, as being desirous to live in peace, and suspecting nothing: but when they were gone forth into the deepe, they drowned no lesse then two hundred of them. When Iudas heard of this crueltie done unto his countrey men, he commanded those that were with him [to make them ready.] And calling upon God the righteous iudge, he came against those murtherers of his brethren, and burnt the haven by night, and set the boats on fire, and those that fled thither, he slew. And when the towne was shut up, he went backward, as if he would returne to root out all them of the citie

The Kings lieutenants vexe the Iewes.

They of Ioppe drowne two hundred Iewes.

Iudas is avenged upon them.

II. MACCABEES

CHAPTER XII

Hee maketh peace with the Arabians,

and taketh Caspis.

Timotheus armies overthrowen.

of Ioppe. But when he heard that the Iamnites were minded to doe in like maner unto the Iewes that dwelt among them, he came upon the Iamnites also by night, and set fire on the haven, and the navy, so that the light of the fire was seene at Ierusalem, two hundred and fortic furlongs off. Now when they were gone from thence nine furlongs in their iourney toward Timotheus, no fewer then five thousand men on foote, and five hundred horse men of the Arabians, set upon him. Whereupon there was a very sore battell; but Iudas side by the helpe of God got the victory, so that the Nomades of Arabia being overcome, besought Iudas for peace, promising both to give him cattell, and to pleasure him otherwise. Then Iudas thinking indeede that they would be profitable in many things, granted them peace, wherupon they shooke hands, and so they departed to their tents. Hee went also about to make a bridge to a certaine strong citie, which was fenced about with walles, and inhabited by people of divers countries, and the name of it was Caspis. But they that were within it put such trust in the strength of the walles, and provision of victuals, that they behaved themselves rudely towards them that were with Iudas, railing, and blaspheming, and uttering such words, as were not to be spoken. Wherefore Iudas with his company, calling upon the great Lord of the world (who without any rammes, or engines of warre did cast downe Iericho in the time of Iosua) gave a fierce assault against the walles, and tooke the citie by the will of God, and made unspeakeable slaughters, insomuch that a lake two furlongs broad, neere adioining thereunto, being filled ful, was seen running with blood. Then departed they from thence seven hundred and fifty furlongs, and came to Characa unto the Iewes that are called Tubieni. But as for Timotheus they found him not in the places, for before hee had dispatched any thing, he departed from thence, having left a very strong garrison in a certaine hold: howbeit, Dositheus, and Sosipater, who were of Maccabeus captaines, went forth, and slew those that Timotheus had left in the fortresse, above tenne thousand men. And Maccabeus ranged his armie by bands, and set them over the bands, and went against Timotheus, who had about him an hundred and twentie thousand men of foote, and two thousand, and five hundred horsemen. Nowe when Timotheus had knowledge of Iudas comming, he sent the women and children, and the other baggage unto a fortresse called Carnion (for the towne was hard to besiege and uneasie to come unto, by reason of the straitnesse of all the places.) But when Iudas his first band came in sight, the enemies (being smitten with feare, and terrour through the appearing of him that seeth all things)

II. MACCABEES

fled amaine, one running this way, another that way, so as that they were often hurt of their owne men, and wounded with the points of their owne swords. Iudas also was very earnest in pursuing them, killing those wicked wretches, of whom he slew about thirtie thousand men. Moreover, Timotheus himselfe fell into the hands of Dositheus, and Sosipater, whom he besought with much craft to let him goe with his life, because hee had many of the Iewes parents, and the brethren of some of them, who, if they put him to death, should not be regarded. So when hee had assured them with many words, that hee would restore them without hurt according to the agreement, they let him goe for the saving of their brethren. Then Maccabeus marched forth to Carnion, and to the Temple of Atargatis,[1] and there he slew five and twenty thousand persons. And after he had put to flight, and destroyed them, Iudas remooved the hoste towards Ephron, a strong citie, wherin Lysias abode, and a great multitude of divers nations, and the strong yong men kept the wals, and defended them mightily: wherin also was great provision of engines, and darts. But when Iudas and his company had called upon Almighty God (who with his power breaketh the strength of his enemies) they wanne the citie, and slew twentie and five thousand of them that were within. From thence they departed to Scythopolis, which lieth six hundreth furlongs from Ierusalem. But when the Iewes that dwelt there had testified that the Scythopolitans dealt lovingly with them, and entreated them kindely in the time of their adversitie: they gave them thankes, desiring them to be friendly stil unto them, and so they came to Ierusalem, the feast of the weekes approching. And after the feast called Pentecost, they went foorth against Gorgias the governour of Idumea, who came out with three thousand men of foot, and foure hundred horsemen. And it happened that in their fighting together, a few of the Iewes were slaine. At which time Dositheus one of Bacenors company, who was on horsbacke, and a strong man, was still upon Gorgias, and taking hold of his coate, drew him by force, and when he would have taken that cursed man alive, a horseman of Thracia comming upon him, smote off his shoulder, so that Gorgias fled unto Marisa. Now when they that were with Gorgias had fought long and were wearie, Iudas called upon the Lord that he would shew himselfe to be their helper, and leader of the battell. And with that he beganne in his owne language, and sung Psalmes with a lowd voyce, and rushing unawares upon Gorgias men, he put them to flight. So Iudas gathered his host, and came into the city of Odollam. And

CHAPTER XII

[1] *i.* Venus.

II. MACCABEES

CHAPTER XII

when the seventh day came, they purified themselves (as the custome was) and kept the Sabbath in the same place. And upon the day following as the use had bene, Iudas and his company came to take up the bodies of them that were slaine, and to bury them with their kinsmen, in their fathers graves. Now under the coats of every one that was slaine, they found things consecrated to the idoles of the Iamnites, which is forbidden the Iewes by the Law. Then every man saw that this was the cause wherefore they were slaine. All men therefore praising the Lord the righteous Iudge, who had opened the things that were hid, betooke themselves unto praier, and besought him that the sinne committed, might wholy bee put out of remembrance. Besides, that noble Iudas exhorted the people to keep themselves from sinne, forsomuch as they saw before their eyes the things that came to passe, for the sinne of those that were slaine. And when he had made a gathering throughout the company, to the sum of two thousand drachmes of silver, hee sent it to Ierusalem to offer a sinne offering, doing therein very well, and honestly, in that he was mindfull of the resurrection. (For if he had not hoped that they that were slaine should have risen againe, it had bin superfluous and vaine, to pray for the dead.) And also in that he perceived that there was great favour layed up for those that died godly. (It was an holy, and good thought) wherupon he made a reconciliation for the dead, that they might be delivered from sinne.

CHAPTER XIII

Eupator invadeth Iudea.

IN the hundreth forty and ninth yere it was told Iudas that Antiochus Eupator was comming with a great power into Iudea; and with him Lysias his protector, and ruler of his affaires, having either of them a Grecian power of footemen, an hundred and ten thousand, and horsmen five thousand, and three hundred, and Elephants two and twenty, and three hundred charets armed with hooks. Menelaus also ioyned himself with them, and with great dissimulation encouraged Antiochus, not for the safegard of the countrey, but because hee thought to have bin made governour. But the King of kings mooved Antiochus minde against this wicked wretch, and Lysias enformed the king, that this man was the cause of all mischiefe, so that the king commanded to bring him unto Berea, and to put him to death, as the maner is in that place. Now there was in that place a towre of fifty cubites high full of ashes, and it had a round instrument which on every side hanged down into the ashes. And whosoever was condemned

II. MACCABEES

of sacriledge, or had committed any other grievous crime, there did all men thrust him unto death. Such a death it happened that wicked man to die, not having so much as buriall in the earth, and that most iustly. For inasmuch as he had committed many sinnes about the altar whose fire and ashes were holy, hee received his death in ashes. Now the king came with a barbarous and hautie mind, to do far worse to the Iewes then had beene done in his fathers time. Which things when Iudas perceived, hee commanded the multitude to call upon the Lord night and day, that if ever at any other time, he would now also helpe them, being at the point to be put from their Law, from their country, and from the holy Temple: and that hee would not suffer the people, that had even now been but a little refreshed, to be in subiection to the blasphemous nations. So when they had all done this together, and besought the mercifull Lord with weeping, and fasting, and lying flat upon the ground three daies long, Iudas having exhorted them, commanded they should be in a readinesse. And Iudas being apart with the Elders, determined before the kings host should enter into Iudea and get the city, to goe foorth and try the matter [in fight] by the helpe of the Lord. So when he had committed [all] to the Creator of the world, and exhorted his souldiers to fight manfully, even unto death, for the Lawes, the Temple, the city, the country, and the common-wealth, he camped by Modin. And having given the watchword to them that were about him, Victory is of God; with the most valiant and choice yong men, he went in into the kings tent by night, and slewe in the campe about foure thousand men, and the chiefest of the Elephants, with all that were upon him. And at last they filled the campe with feare and tumult, and departed with good successe. This was done in the breake of the day, because the protection of the Lord did helpe him. Now when the king had taken a taste of the manlinesse of the Iewes, hee went about to take the holds by policie, and marched towards Bethsura, which was a strong hold of the Iews, but he was put to flight, failed, and lost of his men. For Iudas had conveyed unto them that were in it, such things as were necessary. But Rhodocus who was in the Iewes hoste, disclosed the secrets to the enemies, therefore he was sought out, and when they had gotten him, they put him in prison. The king treated with them in Bethsura the second time, gave his hand, tooke theirs, departed, fought with Iudas, was overcome: heard that Philip who was left over the affaires in Antioch was desperately bent, confounded, intreated the Iewes, submitted himselfe, and sware to all equal conditions, agreed with

CHAPTER XIII

Iudas by night slayeth many.

Eupators purpose is defeated.

He maketh peace with Iudas.

II. MACCABEES

CHAPTER XIII — them, and offred sacrifice, honoured the Temple, and dealt kindly with the place, and accepted well of Maccabeus, made him principall governor from Ptolemais unto the Gerrhenians, came to Ptolemais, the people there were grieved for the covenants: for they stormed because they would make their covenants voide. Lysias went up to the iudgement seat, said as much as could be in defence of the cause, perswaded, pacified, made them well affected, returned to Antioch. Thus it went touching the kings comming and departing.

CHAPTER XIIII

AFTER three yeres was Iudas enformed that Demetrius the sonne of Seleucus having entred by the haven of Tripolis with a great power and navie, had taken the countrey, and killed Antiochus, and Lysias his protectour. Now one Alcimus who had beene hie Priest, and had defiled himselfe wilfully in the times of their mingling (with the Gentiles) seeing that by no meanes hee could save himselfe, nor have any more accesse to the holy Altar, came to king Demetrius in the hundreth and one and fiftieth yeere, presenting unto him a crowne of golde, and a palme, and also of the boughes which were used solemnly in the Temple: and so that day he helde his peace. Howbeit having gotten opportunity to further his foolish enterprise, [and] being called into counsel by Demetrius, and asked how the Iewes stood affected, and what they intended, he answered therunto; Those of the Iewes that bee called Asideans (whose captaine is Iudas Maccabeus) nourish warre, and are seditious, and will not let the realme be in peace. Therfore I being deprived of mine ancestors honor (I meane the hie Priesthood) am now come hither. First verily for the unfained care I have of things pertaining to the king, and secondly, even for that I intend the good of mine owne countrey men: for all our nation is in no small misery, through the unadvised dealing of them aforesaid. Wherefore, O king, seeing thou knowest all these things, bee carefull for the countrey, and our nation, which is pressed on every side, according to the clemency that thou readily shewest unto all. For as long as Iudas liveth, it is not possible that the state should be quiet. This was no sooner spoken of him, but others of the kings friends being maliciously set against Iudas, did more incense Demetrius. And foorthwith calling Nicanor, who had bene master of the Elephants, and making him governour over Iudea, he sent him forth, commanding him to slay Iudas, and to scatter them that were with him, and to make Alcimus high priest of the great

Alcimus accuseth Iudas.

II. MACCABEES

Temple. Then the heathen that had fled out of Iudea from Iudas, came to Nicanor by flocks, thinking the harm and calamities of the Iewes, to be their well-fare. Now when the Iewes heard of Nicanors comming, and that the heathen were up against them, they cast earth upon their heads, and made supplication to him that had stablished his people for ever, and who alwayes helpeth his portion with manifestation of his presence. So at the commandement of the captaine, they remooved straightwayes from thence, and came neere unto them, at the towne of Dessaro. Now Simon, Iudas brother, had ioyned battell with Nicanor, but was somewhat discomfited, through the suddaine silence of his enemies. Neverthelesse Nicanor hearing of the manlinesse of them that were with Iudas, and the courageousnes that they had to fight for their countrey, durst not try the matter by the sword. Wherefore he sent Posidonius, and Theodotus, and Mattathias to make peace. So when they had taken long advisement thereupon, and the captaine had made the multitude acquainted therewith, and it appeared that they were all of one minde, they consented to the covenants, and appointed a day to meet in together by themselves, and when the day came, and stooles were set for either of them, Iudas placed armed men ready in convenient places, lest some treachery should bee suddenly practised by the enemies; so they made a peaceable conference. Now Nicanor abode in Ierusalem, and did no hurt, but sent away the people that came flocking unto him. And hee would not willingly have Iudas out of his sight: for hee loved the man from his heart. He praied him also to take a wife, and to beget children: so he maried, was quiet, and tooke part of this life. But Alcimus perceiving the love that was betwixt them, and considering the covenants that were made, came to Demetrius, and tolde him that Nicanor was not well affected towards the state, for that he had ordained Iudas, a traitor to his realme, to be the kings successour. Then the king being in a rage, and provoked with the accusations of the most wicked man, wrote to Nicanor, signifying that he was much displeased with the covenants, and commaunding him that hee should send Maccabeus prisoner in all haste unto Antioch. When this came to Nicanors hearing, he was much confounded in himselfe, and tooke it grievously, that hee should make voyd the articles which were agreed upon, the man being in no fault. But because there was no dealing against the king, hee watched his time to accomplish this thing by pollicie. Notwithstanding when Maccabeus saw that Nicanor began to bee churlish unto him, and that he entreated him more roughly then he was wont, perceiving

CHAPTER XIIII

Nicanor maketh peace with Iudas.

II. MACCABEES

CHAPTER XIIII

that such sowre behaviour came not of good, hee gathered together not a few of his men, and withdrew himselfe from Nicanor. But the other knowing that he was notably prevented by Iudas policie, came into the great and holy Temple, and commanded the Priestes that were offering their usual sacrifices, to deliver him the man. And when they sware that they could not tel where the man was, whom he sought, hee stretched out his right hand toward the Temple, and made an oath in this maner: If you wil not deliver me Iudas as a prisoner, I will lay this Temple of God even with the ground, and I will breake downe the Altar, and erect a notable temple unto Bacchus. After these words he departed; then the Priests lift up their handes towards heaven, and besought him that was ever a defender of their nation, saying in this maner: Thou, O Lord of all things, who hast neede of nothing, wast pleased that the Temple of thine habitation should be among us. Therefore now, O holy Lord of all holinesse, keepe this house ever undefiled, which lately was cleansed, and stop every unrighteous mouth. Now was there accused unto Nicanor, one Razis, one of the Elders of Ierusalem, a lover of his countrey men, and a man of very good report, who for his kindnesse was called a father of the Iewes. For in the former times, when they mingled not themselves with the Gentiles, he had bin accused of Iudaisme, and did boldly ieopard his body and life with al vehemency for the religion

He seeketh to take Rhasis,

of the Iewes. So Nicanor willing to declare the hate that he bare unto the Iewes, sent above five hundred men of war to take him. For he thought by taking him to do [the Iewes] much hurt. Now when the multitude would have taken the towre, and violently broken into the utter doore, and bade that fire should be brought to burne it, he being ready to be taken on every side, fell upon his sword, chusing rather to die manfully, then to come into the hands of the wicked to be abused otherwise then beseemed his noble birth. But missing his stroke through haste, the multitude also rushing within the doores, he ran boldly up to the wall, and cast himselfe downe manfully among the thickest of them. But they quickly giving backe, and a space being made, he fell downe into the midst of the void place. Neverthelesse while there was yet breath within him, being inflamed with anger, he rose up, and though his blood gushed out like spouts of water, and his wounds were grievous, yet hee ranne through the midst of the

who to escape his hands, killeth himselfe.

throng, and standing upon a steepe rocke, when as his blood was now quite gone, hee pluckt out his bowels, and taking them in both his hands, hee cast them upon the throng, and calling upon the Lord of life and spirit to restore him those againe, he thus died.

344

II. MACCABEES

CHAPTER XV

BUT Nicanor hearing that Iudas and his company were in the strong places about Samaria, resolved without any danger to set upon them on the sabbath day. Nevertheles, the Iewes that were compelled to go with him, said, O destroy not so cruelly and barbarously but give honour to that day, which he that seeth all things, hath honoured with holinesse above [other dayes.] Then this most ungracious wretch demanded, if there were a mightie one in heaven that had commanded the Sabbath day to be kept. And when they said, There is in heaven a living Lord, and mightie, who commanded the seventh day to be kept, then said the other, And I also am mightie upon earth, and I command to take armes, and to do the kings busines: yet he obteined not to have his wicked wil done. So Nicanor in exceeding pride and haughtinesse, determined to set up a publike monument of his victorie over Iudas, and them that were with him. But Maccabeus had ever sure confidence that the Lord would help him. Wherfore he exhorted his people not to feare the comming of the heathen against them, but to remember the helpe which in former times they had received from heaven, and now to expect the victory, and aid which should come unto them from the Almightie. And so comforting them out of the law, and the prophets, and withall putting them in mind of the battels that they won afore, he made them more cheerefull. And when he had stirred up their minds, he gave them their charge, shewing them therewithall the falshood of the heathen, and the breach of othes. Thus he armed every one of them not so much with defence of shields and speares, as with comfortable and good words: and besides that, he tolde them a dreame worthy to be beleeved, as if it had bin so indeed, which did not a litle reioyce them. And this was his vision: that Onias, who had bin high Priest, a vertuous, and a good man, reverend in conversation, gentle in condition, well spoken also, and exercised from a child in all points of vertue, holding up his hands, prayed for the whole bodie of the Iewes. This done, in like maner there appeared a man with gray haires, and exceeding glorious, who was of a wonderfull and excellent maiestie. Then Onias answered, saying, This is a lover of the brethren, who prayeth much for the people, and for the holy citie, (to wit) Ieremias the prophet of God. Whereupon Ieremias, holding forth his right hand, gave to Iudas a sword of gold, and in giving it spake thus: Take this holy sword a gift from God, with the which thou shalt wound the adversaries. Thus being well comforted by the words of Iudas,

Nicanors blasphemie,

Iudas incourageth his men by his dreame.

II. MACCABEES

CHAPTER XV

which were very good, and able to stirre them up to valour, and to encourage the hearts of the yong men, they determined not to pitch campe, but couragiously to set upon them, and manfully to trie the matter by conflict, because the citie, and the Sanctuarie, and the Temple were in danger. For the care that they tooke for their wives, and their children, their brethren, and kinsfolkes, was in least account with them: but the greatest, and principall feare, was for the holy Temple. Also they that were in the citie, tooke not the least care, being troubled for the conflict abroad. And now when as all looked what should bee the triall, and the enemies were already come neere, and the army was set in aray, and the beasts conveniently placed, and the horsemen set in wings: Maccabeus seeing the comming of the multitude, and the divers preparations of armour, and the fiercenesse of the beasts, stretched out his hands towards heaven, and called upon the Lord, that worketh wonders, knowing that victorie commeth not by armes, but even as it seemeth good to him, he giveth it to such as are worthy: therefore in his prayer he said after this maner: O Lord, thou diddest send thine Angel in the time of Ezekias king of Iudea, and diddest slay in the host of Sennacherib, an hundred, fourescore, and five thousand. Wherfore now also O Lord of heaven, send a good Angel before us, for a feare, and dread unto them. And through the might of thine arme, let those bee stricken with terror, that come against thy holy people to blaspheme. And he ended thus. Then Nicanor, and they that were with him came forward with trumpets, and songs. But Iudas, and his company encountred the enemies with invocation, and prayer. So that fighting with their hands, and praying unto God with their hearts, they slew no lesse then thirty and five thousand men: for through the appearance of God, they were greatly cheered. Now when the battell was done, returning againe with ioy, they knew that Nicanor lay dead in his harnesse. Then they made a great shout, and a noise, praising the Almighty in their owne language: and Iudas, who was ever the chiefe defender of the citizens both in body, and minde, and who continued his love towards his countrymen all his life, commanded to strike off Nicanors head, and his hand, with his shoulder, and bring them to Ierusalem. So when he was there, and had called them of his nation together, and set the priests before the altar, he sent for them that were of the Towre, and shewed them vile Nicanors head, and the hand of that blasphemer, which with proud brags he had stretched out against the holy Temple of the Almightie. And when he had cut out the tongue of that ungodly

Nicanor is slaine.

II. MACCABEES

Nicanor, he commanded that they should give it by pieces unto the foules, and hang up the reward of his madnesse before the Temple. So every man praised towards the heaven the glorious Lord, saying Blessed be hee that hath kept his owne place undefiled. He hanged also Nicanors head upon the Towre, an evident, and manifest signe unto all, of the helpe of the Lord. And they ordained all with a common decree, in no case to let that day passe without solemnitie: but to celebrate the thirteenth day of the twelfth moneth, which in the Syrian tongue is called Adar, the day before Mardocheus day. Thus went it with Nicanor, and from that time forth, the Hebrewes had the citie in their power: and heere will I make an end. And if I have done well, and as is fitting the story, it is that which I desired: but if slenderly, and meanly, it is that which I could attaine unto. For as it is hurtfull to drinke wine, or water alone; and as wine mingled with water is pleasant, and delighteth the tast: even so speech finely framed, delighteth the eares of them that read the storie. And heere shall be an end.

CHAPTER XV

The end of Apocrypha.

END OF VOLUME V

EDINBURGH
T. & A. CONSTABLE
Printers to His Majesty
1903

CPSIA information can be obtained
at www.ICGtesting.com
Printed in the USA
BVHW03s0233270418
513861BV00005B/120/P

9 781333 846183